HONORABLE ASSASSIN

HONORABLE ASSASSIN

BOOK ONE OF
THE MACMASTER CHRONICLES

a novel by

Jason Lord Case

RED PETAL PRESS

NEW YORK

First edition copyright ©2009 Jason Lord Case

ISBN: 978-0-9825616-2-1

Published by Red Petal Press, New York.

Book and Cover Design, and Cover Photographs by Red Petal Press

This book is a work of fiction. Names, characters, businesses, organizations, places, events, and incidents are the product of the author's imagination or are used fictitiously. Any resemblance to actual persons, living or dead, events, or locales is entirely coincidental.

Printed in the United States of America

For my dear wife Sylvia,
who still believes in me.

I would like to thank my parents,
David and Mary Case, who raised me to read,
and my sister Mardou Case without whom this series
would never have reached the press.

Chapter One
Sydney

Terry woke with needles in his arms and tubes running up his nose and his penis. He was groggy and weak. Sensors were attached to his chest and head, and there were bags of saline and other unknown liquids dripping into his veins. He had difficulty swallowing with the tube running down his throat; it gagged him. His eyelids felt like sandpaper and his skull throbbed with waves of pain and nausea. He did not recognize the room he was in, or the emaciated, corpse-like body in the bed next to his. He was terrified and started to cry, a reasonable reaction for an eight-year-old boy waking from a coma.

His sobbing caused Terry to gag again on the tube in his throat and he reached up, grabbed the tube running up his nose, and pulled. The feeding tube slid up his esophagus and out through his sinuses. He needed to reset his grip twice to pull the entire length out. He almost vomited as he felt it slithering out of his stomach but did not, and was able to take a deep breath once it was clear.

The tears stopped flowing as Terry's memories began to return. He had no idea how he had gotten where he found himself. He remembered the long and boring ride to Sydney Harbor. He remembered his father checking the systems on his yacht before sailing from Berry's Bay. His mother was stowing the supplies for the day and talking to somebody unknown on her huge mobile phone. He remembered how her golden hair shone in the midday sun, how she smiled at him and it lit up his world. There was the memory of his mother pointing out Elton John's Sydney mansion. He did not know who Elton John was and thought she had said the name backward. Then they passed the Prime Minister's house situated right after Neutral Bay.

The beach at Shark Bay had been crowded with beautiful, suntanned bodies and Terry remembered thinking he would rather have been on the beach than on the boat but he had not said so. They had passed the red and white spike of the Hornby Lighthouse. He had always liked seeing the lighthouse, it let him know the day was over on the way back in, and that the land was behind them on the passage out. North Head was less visible on the other side of the harbor's mouth.

About 130 kilometers south was Comerong Bay, where they had sailed in and docked at Greenwell Point where Terry's father had walked into the town to visit what he said was an old friend. Terry and his mother ate some lunch in the park right off the docks.

The sensors on Terry's chest began to itch as he lay in the hospital bed and he reached up and pulled them off. Suddenly, an alarm went off, a single, unwavering tone from the machine next to his bed. Panic began to set into Terry's young mind and he thought about how much trouble he would be in for pulling the sensors off. His first thought was that he needed to get out of there. He pulled the needles out of the inside of his elbow and the back of his hand, throwing them on the floor and then tried to pull the catheter out of his penis. It would not come. He grabbed his penis with his left hand and the tube with his right and pulled as hard as he could but to no avail. The catheter would not budge. His struggles stopped as nurses began to run into the room in a state of disorder. They were all telling him to do, or not do, all sorts of different things. Terry released his hold on the tube and began crying again.

The tests they put the young man through seemed interminable. Two days of CAT scans, PET scans EEGs, EKGs, sonograms, blood tests, urine tests, (Terry was very glad they had removed the catheter while he slept) reaction tests, vision tests, hearing tests and psychological exams. The boy began to get upset that nobody would tell him how he had gotten there, or where his parents were.

"Do you know what year it is, Terry?" The psychologist was a beautiful young woman named Doctor Sherry Cherry who could disarm almost any man, short of a total sociopath. She was warm, friendly and beautiful, inviting confidences not easily shared.

"Yes, it's 1987. October of 1987."

"Close, Dear. It's actually November Third. The hospital staff did not know when you would wake up, that's why we have you on the long term convalescent floor. We are all so happy to have you back." Sherry's lovely smile was genuine. She had not been in the field long enough to become jaded.

"So, I was sleeping for a month?"

"Technically, Dear, you were in a coma. You came to us unconscious and stayed that way for 10 days. Do you remember what happened?"

"I was sailing with Daddy and Mummy, down the coast. We stopped so Daddy could see someone."

"Do you know who you were stopping to see?"

"Oh no. I didn't see him. I ate lunch with mummy in the park. She always liked that park. Me too."

"Do you remember the name of the park?"

"Greenwell, Greenwell Point. I like that park because there is a hollow tree with a big place to hide. At least it used to be big. I couldn't fit in it this time. Mummy said it's because I am getting big."

"Indeed, you are a fine young lad, tall and strong."

Terry blushed at the praise. He was another of a hundred patients at Sydney's Saint Vincent Public Hospital who was on the verge of falling in love with Sherry Cherry.

"Do you remember what you did after lunch?"

"No. That is, I think I took a nap. Daddy was visiting someone. Can I see my Mummy?"

"I'm afraid that will not be possible, Terry."

"They're dead, aren't they?"

"What makes you say that, dear?"

"If they were alive they would be here, with me."

"I'm sure they loved you very much."

"They are dead, aren't they?"

"Oh, Sweetheart, I hope not. We don't know where they are. We found you floating in the ocean near Cunjurong Point."

"Cunjurong Point? That's all the way down by Mollymook. That's a hundred kilometers from Comerong Bay. Greenwell Point is in Comerong Bay at the junction of the Shoalhaven and Crookhaven Rivers."

"My goodness. You certainly know your geography. I'll bet one in a thousand grown men couldn't have told me that."

"Daddy always insisted it is important to know where you are. If you don't know where you are, how do you know where you are going?"

"And do you know where you were going?"

"No. Daddy didn't tell me."

"Do you remember leaving Greenwell?"

"No. I was eating lunch with Mummy and then I woke up. I was here. Can you call my house and see if they are home?" Terry's eyes were beginning to well up with tears.

"Of course I will. I called yesterday. I'll call again today. I think we've talked enough today. We'll have another little talk tomorrow, ok?" Sherry Cherry flashed him a dazzling smile and reached out to squeeze his shoulder. It did not bring a smile to Terry's face but it stopped the tears.

There were two plainclothes policemen in the hallway. A nurse escorted Terry back to his room and Ms. Cherry went to speak with the Inspectors. Within half an hour, Terry was asleep.

4

The following day there was a kindly-looking, older gentleman in the room with Sherry Cherry. He introduced himself as Inspector Barlow. He wore a nice suit and his haircut was perfect. Though his hair was mostly grey, he was not going bald. His face was clean shaven. He asked most of the questions.

"Do you mind if I call you Terry?" he asked.

"No, that's my name."

"All right, Terry. We have hundreds of men looking for your parents, but we have not found them yet. I need to ask you some questions about them so you can help us find them. You do wish to help us find them, don't you?"

"Yes, Sir."

"That's a good boy. I must say you're very mature for your age."

"Thank you, Sir. Daddy always said it's manners that separate the classes."

"A wise man. Tell me more about your father."

"Well, Inspector Barlow, my daddy is two meters tall and blond. He wears glasses for reading and smokes a pipe but only in the evening with his drink. He likes to have a drink of brandy on the veranda at the end of the day, when the sun goes down. He calls it his little vice."

"I see. He doesn't drink a lot then?"

"No, Sir, he says more than one will mean he is a drunk. He doesn't want to be a drunk."

"Very good, then. Tell me about the people who come to visit him. You know, his friends."

"Daddy doesn't have a lot of friends. He plays golf with them, but they don't come to the house much."

"So you don't see many of his friends."

"No. Sometimes his brother will drop over from Molong."

"What is your uncle's name?"

"Uncle Ginger."

"And does Uncle Ginger look like your father?"

"How could he look like my father?"

"What I mean is does he look like he is your father's brother."

"Well, I guess… I mean he is my father's brother so who else could he look like?"

"Could you describe him to us?"

"He is a little shorter than Daddy, but he's wider. He lost his hair on top, but he has a big red beard and his teeth are bad and his breath smells."

"I see. Is Ginger a nickname or is it his given name?"

"I don't know. He's Uncle Ginger."

"Does Uncle Ginger have a nice place?"

"He lives on a farm. He raises chickens and sheep and he has some grape fields. He grows his own feed for the sheep. I stayed with him for a couple of weeks last summer."

"Did you like staying there?"

"No. Uncle Ginger made me work every day and he doesn't have a telly. He doesn't even have a telephone."

"Are there any other relatives?"

"My Mummy had a sister but she's crazy. They wouldn't let her come over any more."

"I see. Terry, do you know what your father does for a living?"

"Insurance."

"And he goes to work every day, does he?"

"Some days. He says he has other people working for him so he doesn't need to go to the office every day."

"Very good, then. I'm still confident we will find your parents alive and well. I want you to keep your chin up. You are very mature for 10 years old, and I must say you handle yourself very well."

"Eight. I'm eight," Terry said, beaming with pride.

"Only eight? Well, bless me. You are quite a little gentleman for eight years old. I'm going to leave now. I'm going to go looking for your father."

"If you find him, will you tell him I love him?"

"Of course I will. Or perhaps we can bring him here and you can tell him yourself. Sherry, take good care of this boy, he is really quite special."

"I will, Inspector, he is one of my very favorite patients." The smile was back on Sherry's face as she began to ask questions about what he could remember.

"I had a dream. I was on the grass in the park in Greenwell Point with Mummy. Daddy wasn't there and then he was there. He was running and there was a monster chasing him."

"What did the monster look like?"

"I couldn't see it. Then I woke up."

"Inspector, were you able to glean any information from the child?"

"Yes, Superintendent, I was. It seems George Kingston has a brother named Ginger in Molong. Child Services can look into that after we have a talk with him. We already knew he doesn't conduct business from his home, but it seems there is a golf course he favors and conducts business there."

"Anything else?"

"Miss Cherry tells us he still has no memory of what happened after the yacht left Greenwell. She seems confident that his memory will return, but that it may take a while. A traumatic event like that can shock the mind and remove the memory."

"Inform her that it is imperative that we find out what happened."

"Yes Sir. I'll call in a few minutes. She was still with him when I left the hospital. Is there any more information I can use?"

"Nothing substantial. Yes, he owns the insurance company in Orange, The Kingston Agency. A subsidiary of the Helping Hands Insurance Corporation. It seems the books are in good order and the Agency makes a good profit but nothing that allows a man to buy a yacht. His home was shut down as if he expected to be gone for some time. The furnace and air conditioning was shut off. The hot water heater was turned way down. What man does that for a day off?"

"So he wasn't planning to come back for a while, and he has an alternate source of income. Have we gone through his personal books, bank records?"

"I have a woman looking into them now. I'll have her report whatever she finds to you. I think he is a very careful individual, but he needed to finance that purchase somewhere. There is a safe in his home and we will be getting authorization to open it soon. I don't think we will find much inside but it is worth a look."

"Very well then. I'll report again as soon as something changes. I think I would very much like to go out to see this Ginger, if you don't mind?"

"Yes, Inspector, I think that it might be a capital idea. Call first."

"I can't call; the man has no phone. I'll leave in an hour or so. Oh, about the wife, Marcia Kingston. She came from a well-to-do family in Canberra. Parents were professors at Copland College. They're both deceased. She did not work outside the home. We are looking into extramarital affairs and the like, but I don't think we'll find anything. She seems to have been deeply devoted to her son and husband. Local officials say she was a religious woman and spent quite a lot of time on volunteer work. We still have feelers out, but I don't think we will dig up anything on her."

Inspector Barlow was on the telephone with Sherry Cherry when the news came in that the Kingston yacht had been located 80 kilometers due south of Ulladulla and 23 kilometers east of Tuross Head. The fuel slick that was released on a calm day allowed the pilot of a small plane to spot the location. He called it in and the police dive team located the wreck. It had been scuttled next to Bass Canyon, the immense underwater rift that shadows the entire southeastern side of Australia. Whoever had sunk the yacht had undoubtedly intended to drop it into the canyon and thereby effectively lose it forever. It was a good plan but they were a couple of kilometers short of the shelf break. As a result, the yacht was resting about 200 meters below the surface, not the 3000 meters it would have been if it had been sunk in the trench itself. Divers had identified the wreck as Agamemnon, George Kingston's vessel, but no bodies were found.

Inspector Barlow ruminated over the information for a while. Insurance was always motivation for sinking a ship but he discounted it in this particular instance. One cannot collect, even from one's own insurance agency, if one is presumed dead. There was no evidence that George had a drinking problem or that he was in debt from gambling or drugs. His one excess seemed to be the yacht and he spent quite a number of weekends sailing. He lived far enough from the ocean that his home was not very expensive and it was modestly furnished.

The real question he wanted answered was where did George go when he visited Greenwell Point? Who did he see and what did he do? Whoever George visited in Greenwell Point might have the answers to the real questions.

Barlow took a deep breath and exhaled through his nose. He was getting nothing done and the case was getting

9

colder and colder. He tossed his jacket over his shoulder, smoothed his thick, graying hair back and went to report to his Superintendent before leaving for Ginger Kingston's farm in Molong.

When Inspector Theodore Barlow pulled his unmarked Holden into Ginger Kingston's driveway he was unpleasantly surprised. The farm was in a state of disrepair that made it look deserted. Some of the outbuildings were sagging and threatening to collapse. The smell of animal waste was to be expected on any farm that dealt in sheep and chickens but here it was overwhelming. The rusty hulks of tractors that had not run in many years adorned the sides of the house though there was newer equipment visible through a broken window in the nearer barn.

When he stepped out of his vehicle, Barlow got his second unpleasant surprise. Standing on the unpainted, sagging side porch was a man in overalls and rubber boots holding a double-barreled shotgun. The man had no shirt on but his chest was covered with a huge red beard. A cigar protruded from the beard like the tail of a squirrel from its nest.

"What business do ye find here?" asked the man.

"Ginger Kingston I presume. Inspector Barlow here. I'm conducting an investigation into the disappearance of your brother George."

"He's missing, eh? What does that have to do with me?"

"I assume it has nothing to do with you, but as his only relative outside the home I thought there may be something to be learned."

"Let me see yer badge."

Barlow produced his badge and edged sideways slowly to move away from the business end of the shotgun. Kingston squinted at the badge and shrugged. The shotgun pointed toward the ceiling and its wielder grunted and motioned with his shaggy head. The top was bald but the sides were in desperate need of a trim.

Inside the house was the same sort of shambles as the rest of the farm. The side porch led to the kitchen where newspapers were piled up all over the place. The dishes in the sink had gone past the point of unwashed and would soon qualify as genuine archeological finds. The kitchen table held a pile of unopened bills, newspapers, dirty glasses and coffee cups, a liter bottle of Bundaberg and a can of Coopers Ale.

"Shot of Bundy, Inspector?"

"Oh, I don't imbibe in the stronger spirits, I..."

"Crack a Cooper, then?"

"Yes, a Coopers would help cut the dust."

Ginger Kinston moved to the refrigerator and opened the door. Inside were what appeared to be examples of genetic experiments along with a dozen cans of ale. He tossed one across the room and Inspector Barlow caught it. When he cracked the top it blew beer all over the unopened bills on the kitchen table.

"Oh, I'm dreadfully sorry. I didn't think it would fly so."

"Cripes. I never intended to pay them anyway." To Barlow's surprise, Kingston swept the bills and newspapers off the table and onto the floor. "Grab a chair. If you want a shot of rum, take one."

"No, no rum. The Coopers is good." The correct protocol for drinking an Australian ale is to guzzle the first half of it immediately and Barlow did just that. His immediate reasoning was that to gain the confidence of an alcoholic, nothing works better than drinking with him.

Ginger poured himself about four ounces of Bundaberg Rum and knocked it back, draining what remained in his can as a chaser.

"So, Inspector, what's this about my brother?"

"Well, Mr. Kingston…"

"Call me Ginger."

"Very well, Ginger, it seems, excuse me," Barlow belched voluminously. "It seems your brother has gone missing about two weeks now. His son was found floating in the water off Cunjurong Point on October 24th. We have just located the wreck of his yacht off Tuross Head."

"October 24? That's almost two weeks ago. You mean to tell me you're just getting around to telling me now?"

"The boy just woke up. He was in a coma all this time and we didn't know who he was until he woke up. We never would have found the yacht if the fuel tank hadn't developed a leak after it hit the bottom." It was a small lie but effective.

"Oh. The boy is still alive?"

"Yes, Terry is awake and seems none the worse for the experience. He misses his parents, of course, but we may still find them."

"Two weeks later?"

"Stranger things have happened." Barlow took another huge drink from his can.

"Better to keep your feet on the earth, anyway."

"That's always been my thought as well. Tell me, Terry says you visited George's house from time to time, what was your business with him?"

"He's my brother. I don't need business to visit my brother."

"No, certainly not, but people don't do things for no reason. I assume you've had reasons for visiting him."

"I need money from time to time. The farm is not as profitable as might be expected and he has plenty of money. Sometimes I stop by for a loan. Just until I can get wool to market, or get paid for eggs and chickens. I pay him back when I can."

"But there is no problem between you? Money problems or the like?"

12

"If you think I killed him and sank his boat, you're out of your mind. He's the only brother I've got. We don't see each other often enough. Don't get me wrong, we fought when we were kids, all boys do, but we never hated each other. We grew up on this farm. If there was ever a problem we settled it the old-fashioned way, but we never shot each other. We started hunting together when we were six and seven, or seven and eight, or so... We never shot at each other. If I was going to kill him I would have done it when we was teeners. I always been a better shot. When I'm sober enough."

"You were never a suspect. Do you know of anyone who would wish to harm them?"

"Nobody I know of. He don't talk of his business. He sells insurance. Sold me insurance on the farm, cheap. He's a good man." Ginger poured himself another glass of rum and held it in salute. "To George. May he live long and... well, may he be alive."

"So you can't think of anyone?"

"I told you, I don' talk business wit' George. Hey, what happens to the boy?"

"That is not my department. Health and Human Services or Orphan Services will determine what to do with him once the doctors say he can leave the infirmary."

"Drop him off. I'll take care of him till his father shows up."

"As I said, Sir, Orphan Services will handle that."

"No worries. Say, did you talk with his representative, Mr... uh... Shwartz or Shvance... uh... Stein... cripes. Streng, that's it, Streng.

"Is this his legal representative, Mr. Streng, and is his office in Orange?"

"So far as I know. He may have something for you."

"We'll contact him. Thank you for the information."

"You think I'm a slosher, don't you?" Ginger went to the refrigerator and got himself another can of Coopers.

"The evidence points in that direction."

"I can stop drinking any time I want."

"It may be a good idea to consider wanting to."

The man with the huge red beard picked up the half burned cigar from the ash tray and fished in his pocket for his Zippo. He lit the stub without setting his beard on fire and spat out a bit of tobacco. "I'll need to if I want to help George's son, won't I?"

"It will make a large difference with Services."

Ginger took a deep breath and shook his head. "The bastards never let a man be a man, do they?"

"They take a dim view of drunkenness."

"Right, then. It's time." Ginger surprised his visitor more than he had when he had greeted him with a shotgun. He picked up the half full bottle of rum and walked to the sink. He uncapped the bottle and poured it into the drain.

"Well, that's the way the old bugger is. It happens at odd times. He lost his wife 10 years ago, to cancer, and got drunk for about two years. Then he sobered up for a while. Look, when he's not drinking he works like a Tasmanian devil and when he is, nothing gets done about the place. It's been six months, right about on time, I'd say. If he poured his bottle down the sink then he'll be alright for a while. Would you like one of us to check up on him?"

"No, I don't think so, Constable. Orphan Services and the Health and Welfare people will be popping in to see him. Thank you for your concern. If Mr. Kingston has any incidents in the next few days, give us a ring, will you? His record shows he thrashes people from time to time."

"Certainly, Inspector. He hasn't been drinking in the taverns for a while but we'll call if there's a problem."

14

"Thank you, we'll be in touch." Inspector Barlow hung up the phone and thought about all the men he had known who had said they could stop drinking anytime they wanted to. He could not count on one hand the heavy drinkers he knew who really could.

Ten o'clock came around and Theodore Barlow went back to Saint Vincent Hospital to see Terry Kingston again. Doctor Cherry was still busy with another patient so the inspector leafed through the Sydney Morning Herald looking for anything relevant that came from a different direction. He had found nothing when Sherry Cherry sauntered down the hall. Her long blonde hair was tied back in a tight bun and secured with ornamented black hair sticks. The style accented her creamy skin, long neck line and smiling cheeks. Inspector Barlow had been married for many years and loved his wife but Doctor Cherry could have brought out the worst in him.

The inspection room seemed close and exceedingly warm, even though the air conditioning kept it at a comfortable level. Barlow and Cherry spoke alone for a while and agreed to let the doctor ask the questions this morning.

"So, Terry, we'll need to be letting you off, soon enough. You seem to be quite healthy despite your ordeal."

"Have you found Mummy?"

"No Dear, I'm afraid we haven't"

"Where am I to go then?"

"That will be determined by Doctor Curlew. He works with Heath and Welfare."

"I don't like him. He's mean."

"Doctor Curlew can be brusque, but he has your best interests at heart. Tell me, do you remember any more of what happened?"

"I had another dream. Daddy was running and yelling, then we were on the boat. The monster was chasing him."

"Was the monster swimming after you?"

15

"No, it had a boat. It was in one of those little, fast ones and it was chasing us. I couldn't move, I couldn't help. I didn't see it, but I knew it was there."

"Did the boat have a name?"

"Daddy's boat was Ag-a-mem-non," he said carefully.

"Not your daddy's boat, Dear, the one that was chasing you."

"I didn't see it, the name. It was sparkly. Blue with sparkles."

"Dark blue or light blue?"

"It was dark blue with twin Evinrude engines."

Inspector Barlow was not paying much attention until this point but he began writing notes now. He found it interesting that a child could remember the color of a dream and the kind of engines it had. It was as if he had been listening to an orchestra but only a few of the instruments were playing. The composer had just added music for a new instrument. While he knew dreams were unreliable bits of evidence, details of this kind were not to be overlooked.

"Was there anything else, Terry?"

"No. Maybe I'll remember more tomorrow."

"I think you're doing just fine. I shouldn't be surprised if you remember the whole affair tomorrow."

"Ok."

"Terry, when you visited your Uncle Ginger, was he drinking a lot of beer?"

"No. He didn't drink any brandy either. Daddy says he drinks a lot but I never saw him drink anything but water. He made me work every day and he doesn't even have a telly, just lots of chickens and sheep."

"I'm sorry that you don't like him, but he may be your last living relative. If we can't place you with him you may need to go to the orphanage instead."

"I've never seen the orphanage."

16

"I don't think you would like it. Thank God they don't have the old system. You'd be sent to the Fairbridge Farm School in Molong instead of going to live with family. You should be glad they shut that one down in the early seventies."

"Uncle Ginger has the farm without the school, so it doesn't matter where I want to go. I have no choices that I like."

"Oh, Dear, I'm so sorry." Doctor Cherry opened her arms and gave him a long hug. Terry was not crying.

The representatives of the Health and Welfare Department were skeptical as to the efficacy of placing a child with Ginger Kingston. He had a record of drinking and fighting in bars. They headed out to the farm to take stock of the area.

When the social workers pulled in the driveway they were surprised to find that Ginger was not only sober but painting the house. He was on a 15-meter ladder, painting the outside of the attic. He greeted them with a huge smile and asked if they were there to help him paint.

His beard was trimmed and his hair had been cut. His clothes were clean except for some paint spatter and his demeanor was friendly and open. He invited the workers into the house where everything was in relative order, though musty and old. The furniture was threadbare but still serviceable, if no longer comfortable. There were no animals in the home.

The two social workers asked Mr. Kingston a few questions about Terry and whether he was willing to take over his custody. Ginger replied in an affable and affirmative way explaining that he had no children of his own and that his wife had passed away from lymphoma 10 years earlier. He explained that Terry was a likeable child and a good worker and he would be happy to adopt him.

The older of the two workers explained that he could not adopt the boy until it was confirmed that George and Marcia were dead. Their bodies had never been found. It made no difference to Ginger.

The government employees left quite satisfied that the stories they had heard about Ginger Kingston were either exaggerations or complete fabrications.

Chapter Two
Bradley and Cooter

"Sure, she's a fine looking sheila, but you can't keep her chained up down there forever." The speaker was tall and well groomed. He had good teeth and was wearing contact lenses. His suit was worth a week's pay for some people, a month's for others.

"Why not? It's got nobody looking for it. Husband and son are dead. I say we just use it for what she's worth. You have the contacts; what do you say we make a snuff film out of it? We can make quite a bit off that." The other man was shorter and needed a hair cut. Dressed in a tee-shirt and blue jeans that looked like they could use a wash, he did not look like a professional man. A scar ran down the left side of his face, making his mouth droop on that side. Somebody had slashed him with a broken bottle, blinded his left eye and scarred him horribly.

"Bloody cracker, what happens when they trace it back to us? There's a lot more here than just some woman. She's not a runaway teenager, that's the Viper's wife. What do you think his friends will do if they find out we got his wife, let alone what happens if they find out we killed him. They don't know now and I don't want them to know."

"Bollux, they'll never know."

"How can you be so sure? You're getting stupid now. If you remember, I wanted to take her out when we did her man. It was you, thinking with the wrong head again, that put us in this situation."

"What situation? We got it secure. It's locked up tight. That sweet little round bottom is mine and I intend to do whatever I want with it."

"You're a dripping idiot. We should have fed her to the sharks and walked away clean."

"The sharks can have that fish, but not 'til I'm done with it." The man rubbed the scar on his face and chuckled.

The tall man grimaced and looked out the window at the fields of wheat. "Why do you live out here anyway? There's no company, no stores, no neighbors except the farmer that owns the land, and I don't suspect he drops by for a game of gin rummy."

"That's it precisely. Nobody comes here. They think I'm some crazy hermit. I cooked up a story about having been left some money and wanting no part of people. So they leave me alone and that's just right by me."

"I couldn't live this way. Away from people an' all."

"Oh, I'm not exactly away from people. I got me a nice fresh one in the basement."

"That's not what I mean and you know it. Well, make sure you dispose of her proper when you're done with her."

"Like I said the sharks can have that fish." The shorter man grabbed his crotch pointedly. "I'll take care of it. Eh, you ever find out why they wanted the Viper done in?"

"No, nobody's talking. I think he must have done the wrong guy or something. Maybe he turned on his contacts and started talking to the bobbies."

"I doubt it. This man was in the business two or three years before I was. I heard of his jobs while I was still in the Academy. That makes it about five years before you. How long you been doing this?"

"About five." The man picked at some imaginary lint on his suit.

"Five years, don't time fly? That means he been at it maybe 10 years. I heard he was responsible for those jobs the papers called the Porno Killer. You know, the lads that were doing the flicks with little boys? I also heard he done a man once in a provincial station. Leastways, that's what they say. Right in the station, in handcuffs, right in front of the

Assistant Commissioner. They didn't even know the bugger was dead for an hour."

"That may be stretching the point. I will admit to his being skilled, however."

"Well, thanks for the delivery. I look forward to working with you again some time, Bradley."

The taller man cocked one eye at him and said, "I have told you I would prefer we did not use our proper names."

"What? Afraid the field mice might hear? Like I said, nobody comes out here and if they did they might just find a home in the fields out there."

"I do see your point. I just can't do it. Too dead out here. I need some excitement from time to time. The kind you don't need to tie up to keep around."

"To each his own."

"Ok, Cooter, I'll be in touch if there is anything that requires your special talents."

"Have a safe trip, Brad-lee."

Cooter waited on the porch as his associate drove off. "Wankah. Thinks he can come around here in his fancy suit and tell me what to do with my property? Day may come I'll have to do him. I might like tossing him off the back of that fancy boat." He turned and went into the house to cook some mutton and mash.

Terry had never felt so isolated. Orange was not a large town but it was large enough that he had some friends and enemies. He knew every girl and boy in town; there was enough diversity he could learn new things about them all the time. On Ginger's farm there was nobody but Ginger.

It took Rough and Ready, the two sheepdogs a little while to get used to his presence. They were all business and could take care of the sheep for days at a time, without direction. They couldn't open the gates and draw the water, but when it came to protecting the flock and herding them

21

back from the pastures they were the best. They were no company, however.

After a week of being on the farm, Ginger contacted Jerry Cuthbert, a neighbor who agreed to take his new charge to school for a fee. The price was reasonable and Terry got to ride with other children, though they were older than he.

Three other boys rode in the Land Rover and either Ruth Cuthbert or Jerry drove them. Terry had little to say to them since they had come from different backgrounds and were different ages.

In school, the boys thought Terry was stupid because he didn't know the things they knew. He got in a lot of fights but was alone against the others so he rarely won the altercations. He did learn how to take advantage of getting an opponent alone.

When he spoke to Ginger about the fights he got very little sympathy. Ginger told him he would need to get stronger and faster and meaner. Then he took Terry out to the pasture and he taught him about the sheep and the dogs. He took pains to impress on his nephew that there were many sheep and only two dogs, but the dogs made the sheep do what the dogs wanted them to do. Then he asked Terry why and would not let him leave the pasture until he had arrived at an answer that satisfied him. This was only the beginning of Ginger's educational process.

Ginger was not an educated man but he was intelligent. He recognized the problems with relocating a child to the country and taught his charge many things. As time went by, he warmed to the task of educating the child he had never fathered and became quite a mentor. The relationship was by no means one-sided. Terry had learned a lot from his parents and reciprocated when he could. The child acted as a great motivator to the man and served to keep him off the sauce and focus his attentions. The farm began to prosper again. The sagging barns were shored up and painted. Some of the old tractors were repaired and some were sold. The interior and exterior of the house were painted and repaired. Terry Kingston learned more that summer than he had in all his previous years. There was much he did not enjoy, but he was never made to do extraneous work and was always served with an explanation for his tasks. He did not dig holes merely to fill them in again but he did dig a lot of holes, and he moved rocks until he grew calluses on his hands.

Terry learned how to split wood for the fire. At eight years old he did not have the necessary size and strength needed for the task but he attacked it with gusto. It seemed his body always ached in the mornings and he went to bed exhausted every night, but he was growing like a weed and being well fed.

The neighbors were impressed by the civilizing effect that having a boy about produced in Ginger Kingston. It was not that there was anyone close enough to really call a neighbor, but the population of Molong was in the hundreds in 1987 so anyone within 20 kilometers was considered a neighbor.

It was on Christmas recess, lasting the entire month of January, that Ginger began to teach Terry about guns and hunting. He started with safety lectures and made his student recite his rules. He taught him how to disassemble and clean pistols, rifles and shotguns. Then came the target practice.

A .22 pistol was easy enough to handle. Terry's sharp blue eyes focused well on the target and he was soon a fine shot with it. The first time he used a 12-gauge shotgun it knocked him down. He could barely carry it as it was, and the recoil was too much for him, so they switched to a .38 pistol. Terry had found his favorite weapon in the Smith and Wesson revolver.

Marcia Kingston had no way to mark the passage of time except her monthly cycle, and as far as she could tell, she had been a prisoner for three months. Her captor had no name she knew except Master. It was the only name he allowed her to use.

She had been chained in his basement for about a month before she allowed herself to act at being "broken." Her hate for him never subsided, but she knew her only chance was to play at submission. She was given no choice but to be subservient, however she did not acquiesce willingly until a sufficient amount of time had gone by. When she felt the time was right, she began to pretend that she was his willing slave instead of a captive. She began to fake orgasms and tell Cooter she loved him. She began to beg to perform oral sex on him and pretended she loved to have him come in her mouth. It took about two months of this before he began to believe her act.

She could not have gotten out of the shackles by herself, even if she had succeeded in pulling the chain from the wall; they were locked around her wrists and ankles with padlocks.

It was in the third month when he finally allowed her to take a shower. She came out of the shower pretending it had made her amorous but Cooter would have no part of it. He took her back to the basement and locked her back up before he abused her. She thanked him for it.

Two days later she asked if she could cook for him. He refused the offer but the seed had been planted. It was a week before he let her shower again but this time he allowed her to go into the kitchen and prepare some food but not before chaining her to the handle of the gas oven.

She cooked him rice with gravy and sausages and while he was eating, she made a show of touching herself. He told her to stop but she claimed that the combination of the shower and standing there, naked and chained while her master ate, had made her sex drip.

24

After he was done eating he told her to get on her knees and he stood in front of her and dropped his pants. It was the best chance she had been afforded to date. She reached down to the end of the chain and actually opened the oven door to allow her to take his pants off. She was cooing and telling him how much she loved to do this for him when she brought both hands up with the shackles on her wrists and smashed him in the scrotum.

Cooter buckled forward as his captive slammed her steel restraints into his testicles. It might have been enough to temporarily incapacitate him, but Marcia was in no mood to go with half measures. She stood and grabbed the circular grate from one of the stovetop burners and proceeded to smash his head in. She did not hit him once, nor a dozen times, she continued screaming and pounding him until she had no more breath to scream. When she finished she was on her knees, covered in his blood, gasping for breath. She had pounded his head into a pulpy jelly, punctured both his eyeballs and smashed out all his teeth. The calm she had displayed while acting the part of Cooter's slave had disappeared; now she was frantic and shaking like a leaf.

The keys to her restraints were in the pocket of his pants as were the keys to his automobile. She was unchained, but still stark naked, and covered in her former master's death fluids but she could not bring herself to wear any of his clothes. The game was over and the last strands of her tortured nerves snapped. She did not know where she was but that was the least of her concerns. Tearing out of the house she jumped into the driver's seat. The automobile started without a problem and she tore away from the farmhouse in a cloud of dust and spray of gravel.

The state of her mind was such that she did not trust any of the neighbors; she had not met them and did not know who they were. As far as she knew they were in collaboration with the man she had just beaten to death.

Once she saw the sign for Hume Highway she knew more closely where she was. Hume Highway passes Goulburn on the south, but the exit to Sloan Street takes you right into town. Quite a few truck drivers noted that there was a mad bloody woman, driving into town at top speed, and stark naked. The first petrol station she saw was a Kangaroo Fuel and she screamed to a stop in the parking lot.

The teenage boy who was running the Kangaroo Fuel station would remember that January 16 for the rest of his life. The reporters and the police were all there, asking questions and taking pictures. They all wanted to know about the naked crazy woman who had charged into station screaming that she needed help and then collapsing on the floor. He told them all he knew, concentrating on her obvious distress and her physical condition. She was emaciated and covered with bruises, most of them old. She had a black eye but most of the visible damaged was eclipsed by the fact that she was covered with drying blood.

The ambulance arrived simultaneously with the police. By the time they got there, the mysterious woman was wrapped in a blanket that had been in the back room. The medical technicians had tried to find the source of the blood but it was quickly obvious that it was not hers. They hustled her into the ambulance and headed for the Goulburn Community Medical Center.

The constables had nothing to say to the news reporters, so the reporters went back to the station and interviewed the young man who had reported the incident. He reveled in his 15 minutes, knowing it would be over before he could capitalize on it.

Though she was not comatose, it was obvious that she was at the end of her faculties so the police did not take a statement that day.

The following day, Marcia woke screaming, "I'll kill you, you bastard," and thrashing about. She had been dreaming about having Cooter chained to the same wall he had enjoyed having her chained to. The orderlies calmed her down and the doctor administered a sedative. It was several hours into the evening before she was in any condition to give a statement. When she did it was a real eye-opener. She told them her name and address and the fact that her husband had been killed. She told them her son had been killed, since the last she had seen of him was when he went over the side while they were being chased by the two men in the speedboat. The Goulburn Police did not know he was still alive. She told them where her husband had been shot, and how the two men had boarded the Agamemnon and taken her prisoner. Then she detailed the story of the dungeon and the man she had killed.

There was little doubt that she had been shackled, the abrasions on her wrists and ankles confirmed that. There was more than enough evidence of abuse, both physical and sexual. She could not have led them to the house, even if she were allowed to leave the hospital. The escape had been in a blind panic. She knew she was on Route 31, Hume Highway, but she did not know what direction she had been traveling in. The police had already run the plates from the car and gotten an address. Marcia's testimony merely filled in some of the blank spots they had encountered when they found the owner dead on his own kitchen floor.

The Police in Orange were alerted and shortly after that, the Sydney office got the news. The reporters in Goulburn did a little research and found the story of the missing couple and their son but the rescue of Terry had never been printed. The Sydney office had kept it as quiet as possible. The news agencies were not excluded from the new story however and ran it everywhere. The tale of a woman, who beat her captor to death and escaped her dungeon, was international news. It did not take Bradley two seconds to ascertain that his fears had come to fruition and a very dangerous witness was at large. He was in Goulburn before the end of the day. The only thing that kept Marcia alive that night was the constables assigned to her protection.

Inspector Barlow called the Molong Police Station personally, and asked that a constable be sent to the Kingston Farm to inform Ginger and Terry that Marcia had been located, alive. The news did not reach them until 8:30 at night and Ginger would not chance driving that far after dark. He promised Terry that they would visit his mother the following day, Monday. Terry quite naturally threw a fit and demanded to be taken immediately. The sun was still up and he wanted to see his mother, but Ginger was adamant. They would leave first thing in the morning.

Terry had another dream that night. This time he could see the faces of the men in the boat that was chasing them. They got closer and closer and then started shooting. Terry dreamed of his mother screaming and the Agamemnon veering sharply to the right. That was when he went overboard. He was about to hit the water when he woke up. The sun was peeking over the horizon; as far as he was concerned it was time to leave.

It was fortuitous that the pair had not left the night before. The old farm truck that Ginger drove was 20 years old and had not seen repairs in some time. The first problem was a flat tire. It was not much of a problem since there was a spare but it cost them a little time. The second problem was when the exhaust fell off at the muffler. This cost them a bit more time but Ginger repaired it with an old fruit juice can and a coat hanger from the bed of the truck. It was noisy but it was no longer dragging. The real problem happened when they stopped for fuel in Blaney. The truck would not even turn over, the battery was dead. A jump got the truck started, but it died again as it went into gear. The alternator was shot and the gas station did not do repairs so Ginger and Terry walked to the nearest parts store and bought an alternator and a couple of wrenches. Terry was worried about his uncle who was complaining all the way back to the truck about not bringing any tools with him. Once the alternator was replaced it was necessary to get another jump to start the engine. They finally hit the road again. The entire trip was about 350 kilometers and should have taken them three-and-a-half hours, it took them most of the day.

It was almost seven o'clock in the evening when they got to the medical center on Goldsmith Street. Visiting hours were definitely over by then but the staff was very understanding about the situation. They let Terry visit with his mother for an hour, then Ginger spoke with her privately for a few minutes. He looked particularly grim when he left the room. Terry complained when they could not take Marcia with them right then and there.

The sun was getting low in the sky and the sheep and chickens needed to be secured. The engine in the old truck fired up and they started putting out of the parking lot when Terry saw the man from his dream. He was walking in the side entrance. The side entrance should have been locked but was not. Terry started yelling, pointing and grabbing his uncle's arm. He was so insistent that Ginger pulled to the side and parked the truck on Faithful Street. Terry was frantic and could barely make himself understood. He kept pounding on Ginger's arm as he told him that the man who had piloted the boat that had chased them just went into the hospital.

Ginger Kingston was skeptical but had not noticed the boy did not lean toward flights of fancy, so he got out of the truck and headed toward the door the youngster had indicated. The door should have locked automatically when it closed but it pulled right open. Somebody had stuffed a matchbook into the lock, blocking the mechanism. Ginger charged into the hallway bristling like a guard dog. None of the elevators were sitting open so he ran to the other end of the hall and up the stairs. On the second floor he turned back down toward Marcia's room. He slowed when he saw the constable sitting on the bench outside the door, and Terry rushed past him. Terry was flinging himself through the door when Ginger realized the constable had a huge wash of blood behind him on the wall. He had been shot through the chest as he sat there. Then there was the sound of the muffled .40 caliber pistol, coincident with Terry's scream. Another shot rang out and a hole exploded in the door. Ginger slid under the hole in the door and pulled the constable's .40 caliber, model 22, Glock from his holster. First he chambered a round, then he grabbed his nephew's ankle where it was lying, just outside the doorway but he could not pull him out of the room. The door was jammed up against him. Standing to his full height, he kicked the door open and tried to get a bead on the intruder.

Bradley was in the room, expecting just what he got. The door flew open and he shot Ginger Kingston in the chest. The constable's sidearm went off almost simultaneously but the shot went wide. Bradley had not seen Terry lying on the floor. When the door had opened the first time, he was facing the other way, shooting Marcia in the head. When he had turned and blew a hole in the door, Terry was already lying flat and covering his head with his hands. The killer finally saw the boy lying on the floor and took aim at him, just to remove any live witnesses, but the boy was too fast. He was already rising and was behind the wall before Bradley could peg him. Once Bradley was in the hall, he took another shot but missed as the boy flung open the door to the stairs and tore down them in a panic. People were beginning to stir and doors were beginning to open. A nurse came out of the nurse's station behind him and demanded to know what was going on. He could dally no longer and sped for the stairs at top speed. He never saw the boy hiding under the stairs on the ground floor as he made his exit as quickly as he could. He left the Medical Center by the same door he had entered, and disappeared.

Upstairs, the nurse let out a protracted scream and then ran back to the nurse's station to call the doctors and the police. It is said that there is no place like a hospital to get sick, but there is also no place like a hospital to get shot. There was no hope for Marcia but Ginger was still alive. He had twisted at the last millisecond so the bullet did not catch him straight on. That is not to say he was not in critical condition; he had been shot at relatively close range with a .40 caliber pistol. Not many men can say they had survived such an encounter.

The nurses and doctors worked feverishly on the injured redhead, getting him into surgery within half an hour and shaving his incredibly hairy chest. The bullet had passed through him so there was nothing to remove, but there was quite a lot of damage nonetheless. If Bradley had been using hollow points, Ginger would be dead.

The doctors patched their gunshot victim up and put him in an oxygen tent, but nobody gave a thought to the boy he had been with until another patient who was sneaking downstairs to the candy machine saw him huddling under the stairs.

The eight-year-old Terry Kingston was in a frightful state. He had just come out of a coma 11 weeks earlier, and his inexpressible joy at finding his mother alive imploded as he witnessed the assassin blow the top of her head off. When they found him under the stairs he was catatonic. He could not speak and only gave the most rudimentary responses. The mental and emotional shock to his formative brain had overloaded his circuits and his conscious mind had retreated behind a wall, hiding from the world. They put him in a hospital bed in the long-term care ward.

The Goulburn Community Health Center did not have a parallel to Sherry Cherry, few places in the world did. Their resident psychologist was reaching retirement age and while she was a kindly woman, she was more used to working with rape victims and wives abused by their husbands. The Health Center had a very reputable rape crisis center, but they could do little for catatonic children.

When Inspector Barlow got the news it literally floored him. That is, he was sitting down in his chair and the casters rolled back. He actually fell on the floor with the telephone in his hand yelling about incompetence and witness protection. Then he got the news about the Constable on guard at the door, and he sobered considerably. He apologized for his demeanor and demanded that they put two men on each of the rooms. He also told them to expect him personally.

Barlow headed for Goulburn first thing the following day, but there was little he could do when he got there. Ginger Kingston was in an oxygen tent and heavily sedated. If his condition worsened he would be put on a breathing apparatus, since his left lung had been damaged badly. The Inspector could get nothing out of Terry; he was still catatonic. The one thing the Inspector found was the matchbook that was still jammed in the lock of the Faithful Street side door. It was an advertisement for a strip club in the Kings Cross area of Sydney. It was not much of a clue but it was something. The killer had left no fingerprints, though he had left the brass casings and the bullets that had ended Marcia's life and almost killed her brother-in-law. The inspector turned over the matchbook to forensics but it had no fingerprints on it except, oddly enough, Ginger Kingston's. Ginger's truck had been towed to the impound lot.

While his uncle could not be moved, Terry Kingston was deemed to be in better hands in the Sydney Hospital. He had been treated there before, in what had to be called 'a related matter'. In what was a serious breach of protocol,

Theodore Barlow offered to transport him personally. He called Doctor Sherry Cherry and told her not to leave work until he got there with his charge. He told the Goulburn office to inform him as soon as Ginger was capable of speaking. He called the Molong office and told them of the shooting and asked if there was anyone who could watch the farm for a short while. He exceeded his authority by telling them that Ginger would pay somebody for the basic services of feeding the chickens and watering the sheep, letting them in and out of the paddock morning and night and feeding the dogs. He did not know if there was anyone who would do that but he felt he needed to try. Then he bundled his young charge into the unmarked police car and drove him back to Sydney.

In the Saint Vincent's Community Hospital, Terry was given a private room with two constables posted at the door. Inspector Barlow impressed upon them that there had already been two members of this family killed and another in critical condition with a gunshot wound. Then he told them a constable had been shot to death guarding their charge's mother and that the boy was an eyewitness. It served to ensure that they were on the job.

Terry did not respond that day, nor the next. It was five o'clock, Thursday morning, January 21st when he erupted from his self-imposed solitude and woke screaming like a banshee. Doctor Cherry was not there yet but she rushed to work as soon as she got the telephone call. One of the interns had been charged with calling her if Terry woke during the night shift. She did not bother showering or putting on her makeup so she was quite a sight when she walked through the door but Terry did not care. She was like a beacon to a drowning sailor. His beloved mother and father were dead and he was sure Uncle Ginger was going to die as well. Doctor Sherry Cherry was the closest thing he had to family except for his mad aunt. When she came through the door unwashed and disheveled he jumped from the bed and threw his arms around her, not wanting to let go.

Sherry left to go home and get a shower and some breakfast about nine o'clock. Terry was sad to see her go but understood she needed to take care of herself. There would never be a replacement for his mother but if anyone could do it, Sherry Cherry could.

There was no need for sedatives. Terry went to sleep after eating lunch but his dreams were horrific. He had nightmares about being chased on land and on the water. At first he could not see the monster that chased him.

He needed to be roused for dinner and ate ravenously. The doctor visited him more as a formality than anything else; there was nothing he could do. Terry's problems were psychological: his blood pressure was high, he was jumpy and he was having nightmares.

Sherry visited with him after the evening meal and he told her of his dreams. She was highly solicitous and quick to tell him that it was not unusual for him to have nightmares after all he had been through. She told him that Theodore Barlow had brought him back to Sydney, which went a long way in helping his relationship with the Inspector. She asked questions about his memories and his dreams and embraced him repeatedly. She was surprised that he did not cry when he was describing his mother's death. She could not have known that he would not shed another tear for 30 years.

Inspector Barlow visited him the following day and asked many of the same questions Doctor Cherry had. He wanted to know everything about the man who had shot Marcia Kingston. He was pleasantly surprised to find that Terry's memory of the day his father had been shot was returning. The only thing Terry could not tell Inspector Barlow was the name of the boat that had chased them.

On Saturday, Inspector Barlow brought another man with him, a police sketch artist, who fabricated a credible likeness of the man Terry had seen in the hospital room. On Monday, February 14th, the police got a very similar sketch from Ginger, in Goulburn. An examination of the slugs from the two weapons exonerated him of any charges in the double homicide. If the killer had been using hollow points, the evidence would still have been there since the constable did not use them, but it would have been a dead issue since Ginger would no longer be there.

The newspapers had already run the story of Marcia Kingston's murder. The reporters were on that like a cane toad on a snail and were spotted for weeks, sneaking around, looking for further tidbits.

As bold as he was, Bradley wanted nothing more to do with the Goulburn Medical Center. His primary objective had been accomplished and while he would have been much happier seeing Ginger's obituary, he was relatively sure that he could not be identified. Truthfully, the boy bothered him more than the adult; he had gotten a better look at his face. He finally made the connection and realized that the boy was the same one that was on the *Agamemnon*. He would have bet good money that the boy had drowned that day. The police would have liked to keep the names out of the news but it was impossible. Bradley knew his enemies' names and knew they could not stay under protection forever.

Bradley was drinking a pint of bitters when he thought the man he had shot knew he was in the room, and knew why he was there. That meant the man had either seen him enter or been in the hospital when he did. He had been cautious when he slipped in and had not seen the pair, so they must have seen him enter and came in behind him. A smile crossed his face as he went to a pay phone and dialed a number. He knew a woman who worked in the Roads and Traffic Authority. She was older and very appreciative of a good meal and a roll in the hay. He would take her out a couple of times first and then ask her to get him the information he needed. Whoever this Ginger Kingston was, he was sure to have a driver's license and a registration. That would give Bradley an address. It was all a cakewalk from there.

Chapter Three
Dead Man Walking

Terry had been forced to spend a couple of weeks in the orphanage while Ginger continued to heal in Goulburn. It was unpleasant but not cripplingly so. He had been depressed and introspective, as could be imagined. He did discover that he was not alone in his tragic world; many children lost their parents. Most of the orphans had lost their parents to auto accidents.

Doctor Cherry visited Terry every third day, trying to keep his spirits up. It worked to some extent. Inspector Barlow also visited him once and asked a lot of questions that the young boy could not answer. The questions were mostly about his father's affairs and protracted periods when George had gone away on business. The elder Kingston had not made any of his additional business known to his son and so the boy had no answers.

The day Ginger was released from the hospital was a Monday, February 22nd. The sun was hot and the residents of Goulburn were trying to get things done before the full midday sun roasted the streets.

The police took their charge to the impound lot to get Ginger's truck, but they were not authorized to provide him with an escort any further than the county line. The Australian Protective Services had only been created three years earlier when 420 constables transferred over from the Australian Federal Police. Nonetheless, when Ginger reached the county line, they were on the job. Protective Services was obviously paramilitary from their uniforms. They did not look like anyone to be taken lightly. Their orders ended with returning Ginger Kingston to his home, however. He was not going to get long-standing protection. They were unhappy about it, but there was nothing they could do when Ginger told them he was unable to drive the entire trip that day. None of them complained loudly, after all, they knew he had taken a .40 caliber slug in the chest and they respected that.

Tuesday came and saw the arrival at the Kingston farm of both residents, delivered separately by Protective Services. Ginger arrived first and was greeted by two of the local constables.

"It's good to see you, mate. We thought maybe you'd picked one too many fights this time." The shorter, brown-haired constable, Billy, had arrested Ginger several times for fighting and public drunkenness.

"Billy, James, I don't mean to be rude but I suffered a serious setback and had to drive a long way. I hope you'll forgive me if I don't offer you a pint."

"Hah, we're on duty, mate, can't be tippin' it now. Anyway, you look like you been dragged halfway here. You should probably get some rest."

"I probably need to check the farm."

"No need for that. Jerry Cuthbert and his boys been seein' to it."

At that point the Protective services team said their goodbyes and headed back toward Orange.

"Dangerous looking blokes, eh?" Ginger asked.

"Not if you're on their side. As I was saying, Jerry and his boys took care of the place while you were gone. Me and Jimmy, here, we'll be stoppin' back from time to time, just to see if you're all right. You know they ran your name in the paper, don't you?"

"Yeah. That was right sharp of 'em."

"So you may be in more danger than you know."

"I can handle myself. Anybody comes around here lookin' for trouble, they'll find it, by God."

"Right, then. If there's anything we can do…"

"There is. I need a dog. I need a dog that hates everybody and everything and will wake up the dead if anyone comes in the driveway. Is there any chance you can get me one? I know there must be something in the pound that fits that description."

James laughed and pulled up his sleeve. There was a pair of small bandages on his forearm. "I got the perfect thing. One of them German dogs, Doberman. This thing eats raw meat and anything else it can. They say they're smart dogs but this thing almost got popped. I was too afraid of blowing me own arm off, so I didn't shoot it, but that's the only reason. We'll check it for you. It's got all its shots but it's just as mean as... Crikey, Ginger, it's as mean as you with a belly full of booze."

"Capital. Bring 'im by soon as you can. You know I got a boy here now. I need to protect him."

"How you plan on keeping the dog from eating the boy?" Billy was laughing.

"I'll chain it to the porch with tow chain."

"I think this thing will tear the porch off the house. You better be careful yourself."

"I can take care of myself. Thank you for stopping by and feel free to come around any time. Ah, here's Jerry and his boys. I'll need to be thanking them."

"Ah, right... We, ah... We told him you'd pay him for his help."

"No worries. Thank you again. Jerry, how are you, mate? Come on over here and fill me in on it all." Ginger was moving toward the porch, he could not stand any longer.

The Protective Services team that brought Terry Kingston home had never seen a little boy as interested in armaments as he was. He also seemed quite knowledgeable, considering his age. He told them that he was allowed to shoot targets and they asked why he was not hunting yet. He explained that he had lived in the city most of his life and just moved to the farm a little while back.

When they dropped Terry off, the team talked with Ginger for a while. Terry went out to check on the chickens and sheep. He found the animals to be well cared for by the neighbors who had even done some fence repairs. When he returned to the house, Ginger was sleeping, knocked out by the pain medication. Terry quietly took his uncle's .32 revolver and a box of shells and headed for the woods on the other side of the meadows. Today would be the first time he shot a living thing. It was far from the last.

Inspector Barlow had not been one to hang out in the red light district of Kings Cross. It was not that Barlow was a prude, or even that he was all that monogamous, but he was there for a different reason now. He had occasion to be there officially from time to time, investigating the occasional biker murder. The biker gangs were divided into two camps; hard core and wannabes. The killings usually involved the hard core bikers taking offense at the wannabes and starting a fight. It would not be long before the wannabes stopped bothering.

The Plucked Rose was a strip club with rooms upstairs for additional income. The beer flowed freely and the ladies were pretty. The matchbook Inspector Barlow had found in the lock of the hospital's side door was from The Plucked Rose.

It would have been a mistake to come on too strong in this area. The police were respected but not loved in the Kings Cross area. They were never assisted without a cash flow back and even then it was likely that the information gathered was old or incorrect. The best information gleaned in that area of town was by keeping your ears open and your mouth shut. If he had flashed the composite drawings and started asking questions, Barlow would have gotten nowhere. As it was, he never spotted his objective. He tried hanging out in some of the other local clubs as well, drinking lightly and remaining unobtrusive, but he got nowhere. They knew he was a cop, the management of these establishments could smell a cop when one walked in the door. They did not know what he wanted, but they knew he was there on business since it was not the women and he was not looking for drugs. One by one they noticed his presence and then noticed his absence.

Bradley had seen the old farm truck in the lockup, and had even entered the office expecting to inquire about recent impoundments, but he had gotten spooked when he saw a man in the office that did not look like he belonged there. Sitting in a chair, reading the newspaper with no obvious function pegged the man as an officer of some sort. The assassin left quickly, without making eye contact.

The hotel room was within surveillance range of the impound lot and the underpaid nurse alerted Bradley when Ginger was released. A sniper rifle was trained on Kingston when he drove his truck from the lot but the two local constables were enough to keep Bradley from taking his shot. He would get a better shot later.

When the Protective Services men took over at the county line, Bradley gave up for a while. He wanted a quick, clean operation; one in the head of the man, one in the head of the boy, and go. He was in no mood for a shoot out with killers. He headed off in a different direction and spent some time in Canberra before heading to Melbourne in Victoria. He felt safe being out of New South Wales and thought he would go back to eliminate the two Kingstons in a while. A while turned into 'some time later' and then to 'when I get around to it.'

The assassin decided he liked Melbourne a lot and rented a small house on the Yarra River with access for watercraft. He took a train back north and piloted his boat down the coast. He spent a good deal of time on the *Ellsinore*. He thought that recent events in Melbourne would

41

serve to keep attention off the less flamboyant members of society. The previous year had seen the Hoddle Street Massacre in August, where 7 died and 19 were injured, and the Queen Street Post Office Massacre in December.

It was not that Bradley intended to stop working; he just moved his operations south for a while. His disguise as a computer systems repair and analyst was vague enough to allow him to tell anyone who asked that they would not understand.

It was August 17, 1991, when the Strathfield Massacre occurred, that Ginger Kingston saw the writing on the wall. The government was already making noises about gun control. It was obvious to anyone who paid attention to the news that they would be registering everyone's firearms before long, so Ginger began to acquire more guns. It was not that he needed them; he was just upset that he might be denied access to them in the future.

Terry Kingston was happy to see the arsenal growing. The more new guns he used, the better he got. He read books about arms training and began to learn how to assemble and disassemble weapons blindfolded. It was quite possible that he was the most knowledgeable munitions expert in the country, at least among 12 year olds.

The woods behind the farm soon had little remaining wildlife. Ginger had told his nephew repeatedly not to shoot something he was not going to eat but that did not always hold. One would not eat a fox, but it was not even a natural member of the Australian ecosystem and shooting a fox was considered mandatory. Rabbits had to be shot on sight and they were, of course, both edible and tasty. Both the foxes and rabbits had been introduced to Australia by Europeans for the purpose of hunting them but they took hold much too successfully and became massively destructive to the country's natural fauna. Terry was happy to assist in their eradication. He also learned to clean and cook all manner of wild game.

He had reached an acceptance level in the school by dint of the fact that he was growing quickly and was in the best of shape. He had learned how to fight and was actually told that he needed to stop thrashing his classmates. His justification was that they had been starting the fights and that he was merely giving them what they were asking for.

On the farm, he learned how to work as Ginger worked, indefatigably. He fixed the fences, split the wood and repaired all manner of mechanical equipment. He sheared sheep and slaughtered them when necessary, killed chickens and hunted all manner of pests.

It was that year when Ginger bought him a car. It was a 1968 Holden, Monaro GTS 327 and, though it ran when they pulled it the barn, it needed a lot of work. The years had not been kind and it had been beaten by a series of young owners.

Terry was nonplussed by the gift. It would be years before he could drive on the roads and a car like the Monaro could not negotiate the fields. He could already drive a standard transmission and was actually quite good at keeping the truck moving in the mud, but this was different.

"Look here, boy. What we have is a truly fine automobile despite its appearance. It has a V-8 Chevrolet engine so parts are reasonable. It still runs so it hasn't ruined the crankshaft. The heads are worn but they can be salvaged or replaced. The body is Australian so we won't need overseas body panels. This is a project that you can finish or not, but you will pay me for the parts as soon as your father's lawyer releases the proceeds from the insurance business. That will be when you turn 17. Imagine what it will feel like to pull up to school in an honest to goodness classic."

"Yes Sir."

43

"All right. The first thing we need to do is disassemble it and determine what needs to be done. We need to mark each piece and keep the bolts and nuts together and mark them. This is the only way we can put it back together, when we know where everything goes."

"Yes Sir."

"You seem a wee bit scared by the prospect."

"Yes Sir."

"Stop saying that and go and get some masking tape and tags from the back. We are about to learn everything there is to know about this car. Tomorrow we go down to town to get a ledger and a manual. I hope you're ready to work."

"Yes Sir."

"Stop saying that and split me some wood."

Terry's trepidation was eclipsed when he heard the awe in the voices of the older boys when they heard he had been given a Monaro 327.

Halfway through September of 1995 Terry Kingston had a life altering experience. He was in school when it happened and it came from a most unlikely source. He was being forced to watch a movie of a Shakespeare play and, like his classmates, thought this was a waste of time. Then he saw the setting for the first act of the play; Ellsinore. He saw that name and the bottom dropped out of his world. Gone was the screen and the classroom and the children. He was back on the Agamemnon, eight years old and being chased by two men in the *Ellsinore*. His reaction was almost like epilepsy; he stiffened up and started shaking though he was not foaming at the mouth. For the first time since he was half his present age he recognized the name of the speedboat. It was the last piece of a puzzle that had been haunting his dreams ever since it happened.

"Uncle Ginger, I remember. I saw it today in school and I remember the name of the boat that was chasing us the day they killed my father. I want to find that boat and I want to kill the bastard who shot you."

"Is that right? Suddenly you are the avenging angel, eh? You think you can just find out where this boat is and go there and shoot this man?"

"Yes, Sir, that is exactly what I think."

"So you're going to go in there without a plan? Without backup? Without a driver's license or a second thought?"

"I know what he looks like and he won't be expecting me. I intend to find him and kill him and you won't stop me."

"Look here, boy, I don't intend to stop you. I don't intend to try to stop you. What I do intend to do is keep you from throwing your whole life away on something because you didn't think it through. When you hunt foxes you go where the rabbits are. You know the fox will be after the rabbits so that's where you look for him. That is not all there is to it though, is it?"

"No. You need to watch the rabbit runs. The fox doesn't set up too close to the hole because he needs some space to get the rabbit before it reaches its burrow."

"Aye, that's one aspect, but there is so much more that you are so used to doing that you don't even think about it any more. You don't walk on their trails, you don't stand upwind, you don't walk through poison ivy, and you don't walk through nettles."

"But there is no parallel to that in the city."

"You don't know he is in the city. You don't alert another fox who will in turn alert your prey. You don't wait 'til you see the fox to load your gun. You don't go shuffling through piles of dead leaves. What I am saying is there is so much more to hunting than pulling a trigger. That is compounded 10 times when you hunt a thinking prey. Especially when you are hunting a professional. How many cars have driven down the road since you got home from school?"

"Two, three if you include Jerry Cuthbert's car."

"That is what I mean. You remember things like that. Now then, boy, was either of those cars a big block?"

"No Sir. I can tell a big block. I might be fooled by another V-8, but both those cars had whiney four cylinders."

"Good. You notice things like that. Now, do think there is a chance that this man will not notice the rumble of a high-compression 327? Do you think you can drive that Monaro around a suburban neighborhood undetected?"

Terry was silent. He resented being spoken to like a child even if he was one.

"Now, what is your source of reference to know where this boat is?"

"I thought I could go to town hall…"

"No. Go to the library in the school and talk to the librarian. She will be able to tell you when and where the records are available, or she can find out. It's probably registered under a phony name anyway, but the library is always a good place to start. Don't tell anyone why you want to find the information, make up a story. Tell them I want to buy the boat. I saw it and just loved it and wanted to find the owner so I could tender an offer to buy it. That way you smooth over the path and people are less likely to remember you. Your interest is in the boat, not the man who owns it, but you need his name and address to find the boat."

"I see."

"You are sure of the name?"

"Yes. Ellsinore."

"Then ask the librarian how to find that. Town hall will only have records for this area so that is worthless. Oy, I got another idea or two as well, but you start with the library."

"All right, Uncle. I'm going to need to get my learners license as soon as I'm 16. So I can get where I need to go. I also need to finish upgrading the brakes on the Monaro. We got her running like a dingo but the old drum brakes stop her like a land train."

"Oy. Order the parts, I'll put it on yer bill."

"Uh, Uncle Ginger? Can't we use the computer at the Insurance Company to access the database at the RTA and find out if the *Ellsinore* is registered in Wales?"

"Now yer thinking. We do that next. Do yer research first. Go to the library. Oy, the new springs came in today. I'll show you how that's done after you clean out the paddock."

"Yes Sir." Terry grabbed a shovel and tossed it into the wheelbarrow.

"I'll be back in an hour. I need to get a tank of acetylene and some brazing rod."

"Ok, Uncle."

Ginger watched Terry's back retreat and realized he was not going to be able to control him for much longer. He was getting too strong, too tall and too smart to restrain. The only thing he was going to be able to do was direct him. He shook his head and started the engine on his old truck.

Ginger had not been much for birthday presents or Christmas presents. He was a firm believer in earning what one received so Terry never got anything much given to him because of a special day. He worked for what he got. On his 16th birthday he got taken to the Road and Traffic Authority to take the first of the tests. He passed the test and left feeling strong. It was 10 weeks since he had remembered the name of the craft that had chased him, and he had not yet been able to locate it. The name of the craft was not so easy to cross-reference as the numbers would have been.

The search would have been easier if Terry had known to look in the VicRoads database instead of the RTA. Ginger was unwilling to help in the search beyond basic advice. He not only wanted his nephew to work through it himself, he did not want the culprit found any too soon. There were things Terry needed to master within himself before he could be considered ready for the odyssey he was considering. For one thing, he could not legally drive by himself for the next year.

It wasn't until May of 1996 that Terry got a break in his search. The Helping Hands Insurance Corporation sold an insurance policy for a dark blue fiberglass Bullet boat with dual Evinrude motors. The policy listed the name of the boat as *Ellsinore*, to be changed to *Ripsaw*. The man buying the policy, Grant Macintosh, had his home and his automobile insured with the Dartmouth Insurance Agency, a Helping Hands Office in Orbost on the Snowy River, well to the south. The new owner of the boat made his living by running several lumber mills.

Ginger got the letter from the Kingston Agency and almost tossed it out, then he considered hiding it in a drawer. His hand snaked over to where the bullet had torn into his chest and he changed his mind.

The trip was 660 kilometers and there was no way Ginger was going to allow Terry to go it alone. He knew that with a teenager's typical brash, he would try to go in like Hitler into Poland and probably get arrested rather than learn anything. Terry could still not drive alone, legally, and would not be able to until he passed the driver's test. He couldn't take that test until December. The trail might well be cold by then, however.

When Terry got home that day, Ginger only told him that they would be taking a trip that weekend. He did not tell him why or where they were going. He did tell Terry that they would be going in the Holden and they changed the oil in it that night.

It was three o'clock in the morning, Saturday morning, when Ginger rousted his nephew from a sound sleep and told him they were leaving. Terry was surprised that Ginger was wearing a suit. He did not know Ginger owned a suit. Terry fell asleep in the passenger's seat half an hour later. The trip took 11 hours with a stop for lunch and something that Ginger promised would be explained.

Terry walked into the Whale Mart and bought a bottle of hair dye at his uncle's request. They went to a public rest room in a deserted park and Ginger dyed his hair and beard blond. It was a sloppy job but relatively effective. Terry was, of course, intensely curious about the whole affair, but he was assured that there was a good reason and it would all be revealed to him.

They had a little trouble finding the house, since it was off the beaten path, but they located it eventually. Ginger was glad the boat was not parked in the driveway. He was not certain they were on the right track and he didn't need Terry going ballistic. Terry had been driving at that point and Ginger had him park so the interior of the car was masked by a tree. Then he left his nephew behind the wheel while he went to the door with a ledger in his hand.

"Good afternoon, Mr. Macintosh."

"G'day Sir."

"Mr. Macintosh, my name is Frederick Samuels. I am an employee of the Helping Hands Insurance Corporation. I have been informed that you purchased the *Ellsinore* about a week ago and I am here to tell you that there may be some irregularities with the registration." Ginger opened the ledger and handed Grant a business card with the Helping Hands logo and the name Frederick Samuels on it.

"They said nothing when I registered it."

"No, they wouldn't have. The irregularity involves the fact that this boat was reported wrecked at one point and should not have been reregistered until it was certified by the insurance company. May I ask where the vessel is being kept?"

"Well, I just... It's on a trailer out back. It didn't look like it had been wrecked."

"I need to look at the vessel and certify that it is the same vessel. Do you have the registration on hand?"

"Yes, just a moment." Grant Macintosh disappeared into the house for a moment and then returned with the document. The two of them walked around the building and sure enough, there was a dark blue fiberglass Bullet with twin Evinrude engines.

Ginger climbed onto the trailer and onto the deck of the boat. "It does not look as though the numbers have been changed," he said as he copied the vehicle identification numbers into his ledger. Then he climbed out and performed a cursory inspection of the hull. His inspection completed, he said, "There may have been some sort of mistake. This vessel does not look as though it was ever wrecked. Now, we do not have the name and address of the former owner, since it was not insured through the Helping Hands Insurance Corporation. The computer system is still relatively new and there may have been a mistake in the information. May I bother you for the name and address of the man you bought the vessel from?"

"Of course. Give me a moment. I'm sure I have that information in the house. Tell me, doesn't VicRoads provide that for you?"

"Yes, they will if we wish to wait for some time. The Corporation will not honor any damage claims until we get the matter sorted out, however. We cannot do that until we speak with the man who claimed the vessel was wrecked. I assure you that you are in no trouble, but if there was a claim

50

filed by the former owner then he may be in a great deal of trouble. We take a dim view of insurance fraud."

"Oh, I see. Well then, wait here a moment and I'll fetch it for you." It only took a moment and Grant returned with a scrap of paper. The name was Percy Darrow and the address was north of Melbourne.

"Thank you, Mr. Macintosh, this will expedite things greatly. Expect a call from our office in a day or two verifying that your policy is again in force."

"Uh, thank you Mr. Samuels. I was planning on taking the boat out tomorrow. May I do so?"

"I'm sure there won't be a problem, but if there is an accident, wait until you hear from us before you file a claim, just to be safe."

"Very well, thank you for your concern."

"Just keeping our end up. Have a safe weekend, Mr. Macintosh." Ginger walked around the side of the building and back to the car. He told Terry to slide over to the passenger seat. He breathed a slow sigh of relief and drove slowly to a petrol station.

"Are you going to tell me what we are doing down here in Victoria?" Terry asked, trying not to make it sound like he was whining.

"Yes, killer, I'm going to tell you, but I need to make sure we are on the right track. There are things you need to know first and I will share those with you as well. It's time you knew, but I know a thing or two about boys and their big mouths. After I tell you these things you are going to need to keep your mouth shut. You have been a good chap and I think you have the capacity but this is so bloody dangerous that if you open your mouth I will shoot you myself."

"Oh hell, Uncle, you need to trust me more than that."

"I'm pulling over here and you're going to fill the tank."

Terry Kingston chewed on his lip as he was filling the petrol tank. What on earth could be so secret and important that this farmer would kill him over? Ginger was not one to threaten folk lightly. If he said he was going to give you a drubbing, you had better expect to defend yourself. If he said he was going to shoot something it had better expect to take a bullet. Terry's father had let his mother issue the discipline most of the time unless the offence was particularly heinous and since Terry was an only child he didn't get in much trouble. He was coddled a bit but not spoiled and he had learned how to use his brain from his father. His uncle had taught him how to use his back. At 16 years old and still growing, he presented a formidable picture but he knew better than to cross Ginger. His uncle had beaten Terry a few times, not to excess or too often, but he had given him a severe knockabout a few times and Terry knew better than to think he could better him. Terry could fight, but there was something about the way Ginger handled himself that used his opponent's strength and weight against him. Terry was taller but not so broad as his uncle and he was just coming out of the truly awkward stage of physical development.

The pump stopped and Terry paid for the petrol, then they left town with Ginger driving. They continued south on the Prince's Highway until the got to the port city of Lakes Entrance and stopped at a nice dark restaurant where they took a private booth in the back, away from the other patrons.

To Terry's surprise, Ginger ordered himself a rum and cola. Terry had not seen Ginger drink in all the time they had lived together. He knew there might be a problem brewing. His uncle had beaten up some of the local fathers and Terry had been informed that this had been one of the reasons he had been forced to fight so much in school.

The food was good and the waiters left them alone but were on hand. Ginger said nothing while they ate and ordered another rum drink after they were done.

"Terry me boy, we are about to do something I have not done in many years. Your father was much better at it than I, much more subtle. He had a way of moving in and moving out so nobody noticed he was there. He could walk through a crowded room and have nobody see him. He was nondescript that way, even though he was tall."

"Two meters is not that tall, I'm almost that now."

"Boy, we are not having a discussion. I am going to tell you some things and you are going to keep your trap shut. There are things you do not know and you will never know if you don't stop talking and start listening."

Terry recognized the tone of voice. He was very curious but there would be no hurrying the explanation. It would come in time. He did hope the information came before Ginger got too drunk. There was no telling what might happen if he did.

"What you know of your father is only half of what he did. He was a calm and considered gentleman and a devoted family man." Ginger took a large sip of his drink as if he needed it to continue. "He was also a world class assassin."

Terry's jaw dropped. He had never gotten the slightest inkling of this part of his father's life. If George had survived, Terry might have suspected something after a while but he had never gotten a clue during his formative years. He was about to stammer some sort of protest but the look in Ginger's eye silenced him.

"This is not something I suspect, boy, this is something I know. He and I did some work together years back. I am a better shot than he was but he was so subtle about it that he always made me look like an amateur. There are rules to this sort of an existence and he followed them scrupulously. Do you want to continue this conversation?"

Terry nodded his head, struck dumb by the revelation.

"I will continue but I have already warned you that if you open your mouth to any of your school chums, or the silly little sheilas you'll be plucking, I will shoot you myself and bury you in the fields in four or five pieces. Am I making myself as clear as I can?"

"Yes Sir."

"Good. This is not a joke or some sort of game. I will not do it willingly, and I will not enjoy it, but if you can't keep your mouth shut, I will dismember you and fertilize the corn with your body. You never leave witnesses alive, that includes family, friends, lovers, and children, if they can't keep their big mouths shut." Ginger called for another drink and ordered Terry a cup of coffee.

"That is the first rule, boy, you never leave witnesses alive."

"I understand, but why are you telling me this now?"

"I created a witness when I went to that man's house and started asking questions about the dark blue boat he had in the back yard."

"Is he the one...?"

"No, but he is now a witness. Tell me what he witnessed."

"He saw a man in a suit, driving a Holden Monaro, who wanted to know about the boat in the back yard."

"Wrong. He saw a blond man in a suit and hat, from Helping Hands. He may or may not have seen you, depending on how curious he got. He saw a confused claims examiner."

The waiter brought the drinks and Ginger said nothing until he had left them alone again. Then he said, "Do you want to continue this conversation?"

"Yes Sir."

"Then you had best be aware of all the rules involved. You never leave fingerprints. You never allow yourself to be fingerprinted. You never call attention to yourself. You never accept a woman or child as your primary target. You never agree to work with the police unless you can eliminate the entire station force and destroy all evidence. You never talk. The men who hire and distribute jobs in this part of the world are limited in number, but they are ruthless. I have been expecting the man who shot me in the hospital to appear at the farm for the past eight years. I do not know why he has not. It has been a mistake on his part, boy. He knew where we lived, there is no doubt about that. We did not know where he was until today and we still cannot be sure it is him. What are the rules?"

"You, uh, I never, uh, I... I never talk. I never go after women and children. I never leave a witness. I never work with the constables. I never leave fingerprints or let them fingerprint me."

"Not bad. You never call attention to yourself. I'll be asking you again so don't forget. There is one more lesson that does not constitute a rule, just a guideline. If they don't find a body they can't be sure the victim has been eliminated."

"Yes Sir. I never..."

"Shut up and listen. I don't know who this man is. I have an address and it might be false. I have a name and it is sure to be false. Men in this game change their names and if you address them by a name they used for a specific purpose, it could get you killed and you will never see it coming. Telephones are very dangerous. You cannot see who you are talking to. You don't know who is listening. When you pick up a phone it pinpoints your location. They can also be very useful but they must be used with the greatest of caution."

Terry looked at his uncle in a new light. He knew, now, what it was that had bothered him all these years. Ginger had always spoken too correctly for what he was, an old farmer with a bad reputation. He had always known too much about too many things. There had always been an air about him that bespoke something more than his history justified. Now Terry knew what it was. He was in the middle of a life-changing event. He was about to taste something that he had wanted for years but never really expected to happen.

"We need to rent a van. Preferably a work truck type, not too many windows."

"Will we rent that here?"

"Yes. The farther from the target the better. Your best tool is going to be misdirection. I have been remiss in your education. There are things you need to master, things you need to understand, but there was no time and I could not tell you why I was having you learn these things." The rum was making the man's face florid and he looked uncomfortable in the suit.

"There will be lots of time to learn, later. I need to know where we are going next," Terry said cautiously.

"We are going to a hotel and establish a titular alibi. We also need to think of a good reason for being here."

"Fishing. We could say we were here to fish."

"It doesn't hold water by itself but with a little embellishment it may. Remember the first rule? Don't leave witnesses. Unless they have witnessed only what you want them to see. Then you make sure they remember it the way you want them to."

"That's why you went blond, why you didn't want him to see me."

"That's a given, but not all. I do not believe that when I left that man's house, he said to himself 'something is fishy.' If called to testify against me in a courtroom, could he recognize me? I don't know, probably. But if asked for a description he will say I am a blond man. Remember, always buy supplies at the larger stores. If you stop in an apothecary and buy hair dye, whoever is behind the counter will remember you."

"I'll remember that."

"If the new owner of the boat were a danger, we would be required to return to Orbost and eliminate him. Can you do that?"

"I don't know, Uncle, I wouldn't be required to eat him too, would I?" Terry said with a grin.

"This is no joke, boy. Would you be able to walk up to that man who never did nothing to you and put one between his eyes?"

"Yes Sir, I would. I mean I could."

"Assassins have gotten a bad rap in Western Culture. Nobody respected what they were capable of doing, or what was required to perform the vital and necessary role they held. I am too old for this; it's a job for the young."

"What does your…"

"Shut up and listen, boy. At your age you know nothing of age, you haven't stopped growing yet, but if you don't learn to shut up you will finish growing. Now, as I was saying, the Japanese knew and understood what it took to be a quiet and effective killer. They would not need to hide and scurry about like mice in the dark. They would be addressed with respect. People would say "Good day Honorable Assassin."

Chapter Four
Melbourne

"Jerry, I'm sorry about this. Terry and I went to the coast to do some fishing and we've lost a ball joint on the Holden. It won't take more than a day or two. Do you think your boys could take care of the animals for us? Yes, that's right. The Doberman is chained to the block we poured on the side of the house. The feed is in the shed behind the house. Tell your boys to be careful feeding him. No, the sheepdogs are all right but the Doberman will probably try to take a chunk out of them if he gets a chance and he's sneaky. Tell them to fill a bowl and push it to him with a stick. I'll take care of them when I return. Yes, a couple of days. If you could let them out on the way to school on Monday and then let them back in at night, the dogs will take care of the rest. Proper. Thank you again.

"Alibi, boy. Always have an alibi. Now, we're here to do some fishing so we need to rent a boat, but we need to rent our own boat. We don't need someone taking us to the best fishing spots; we just need a boat."

As it turned out they could rent a small fishing boat for a week. It was just a 15-foot aluminum shore cruiser, nothing to take out of sight of land.

The moving van was just as easy. Ginger rented it under an assumed name; Horace Paylee. He had a driver's license under that name as well. Apparently he had possessed the license for a very long time because the picture looked 25 years younger than his present age. The picture also showed him with blond hair.

The boat and the hotel room were rented in Ginger's real name. They were going to be here for a couple of days. As far as anyone else was concerned, they would never visit Melbourne. The last prop for the play was the ball joint. To complete the subterfuge they bought a set of manual spring compressors, a pickle fork and a small tub of grease, necessary tools to replace a ball joint. The owner of the parts shop had to order a ball joint from one of his sister stores. He swore it would be there the next day.

At the end of Lagoon Road off Jacaranda drive in the town of Metung, Ginger found the perfect opportunity. A series of lakes joined Metung with Lakes Entrance and nobody lived at the end of Lagoon Road. The drop off was too sharp to launch from and there was no evidence that there were many parties held there. After scoping out the area, Ginger drove the rented van back to a break in the trees a half a kilometer off and hid it as best he could. Then they drove the Holden back to Lakes Entrance and parked it at the dock.

Dock was a generous term for the rotten pilings and rotted boards but that was not the point. The point was they had rented a small fishing boat and gear. They bought some live bait and took an extra can with gasoline. It was very late in the day to be heading out and the proprietor pointed this out. Ginger assured him that they were not going out to sea but up the channel to the lakes. This assuaged the man's fears. One couldn't get in much trouble in that direction.

The engine started easily and purred away without a hiccup. It ran better than they would have expected and took them the 12 miles to Lagoon Road's dead-end without incident. The drop off was too sharp to run a trailer down and there was a locked gate at the end of the road preventing anyone from trying. This did not even slow the pair down. A length of nylon rope and a little elbow grease hauled the boat off the water and into the trees. A length of chain served to fasten the bow to a tree. They took some branches and leaves and covered it as best as could be expected then went down the road to the van. The van was unmolested. They started her up and went on their way. As far as anyone was concerned they were fishing on the lakes.

They drove onto Jacaranda Drive and down Broadlands Road. One of the last streets before the river was Kookaburra Street and Terry started humming to himself. Ginger heard him humming and joined him, singing the words on the second time through.

"Kookaburra sits in the old gum tree
Merry, merry king of the bush is he
Laugh kookaburra, laugh kookaburra
Gay your life must be."

Terry fell silent, withdrawing into himself and remembering why they were here. After about an hour Ginger started asking him questions. He asked him about the rules of assassination and the reasons for them. He asked about why he had done this and that and when it is appropriate and inappropriate to use a disguise. He asked him when it was appropriate to make a spectacle of one's self and when it was best to hide. He presented his nephew with a wide range of scenarios and queried him about the best way to handle the situation. The lessons did more than pass the time as the sun went down; they were important in calming Terry's nerves.

Ginger knew Terry was a good shot with almost any weapon. He had attempted to instill in him the necessity for walking quietly in the forest. He had told him about sneaking up on a fox and that the best hunters were those who could sneak up on a fox. He knew Terry was not that good, and considered it almost impossible any way, but he had done what he thought appropriate for the situation.

"Why do you suppose he never came for us, Uncle?"

"I can't say, boy."

"Oh. When are you going to stop calling me boy?"

"Soon."

"What do we do if it is not him?"

"I can't say, boy."

"What do we do if it is?"

60

"We'll know when we get there. I haven't done this sort of work in a long time and I won't know what needs to be done until I assess the situation. It may be that we have the wrong man but the boat fit your description and it was called *Ellsinore*. Years back I had the resources and contacts to discover and determine this sort of thing. I dropped those contacts years ago and would not dare contact them now."

"Why not?"

"As I said, the number of men doing this sort of work is limited in this part of the world. If I were to begin making noises, the word would reach the target. I could not be sure that he is not working for the same people I used to do work for."

"Can I do it?"

"I don't know, boy. Can you?"

"Yes."

Before morning the two Kingstons were sitting within sight of their destination, wearing coveralls. It was a modest, well kept home with river access from the back. A new Cadillac sat in the driveway, a very unusual sight in Australia. Luxury cars were rare in themselves; American luxury cars were even scarcer.

"This is a point where we make a decision, boy. We can shoot this man from a distance, this side of the river. We can set up on the other side of the Yarra and shoot him from there when he comes out to the back, a much more difficult shot but safer. Remember that this man is a professional. Professional enough to kill your father, God rest his soul. He will not be expecting us but he may well be expecting somebody. A man who does this for a living can always expect there to be hard feelings on somebody's part."

"Is that why he killed my father?"

"I can't say, boy. That is the last option we have and the reason I mentioned his possible vigilance. We can go in the house, tie him to a chair and force him to tell us the details of the operation and the reasons behind it."

Terry's young mind was still trying to grasp all that had been thrown at him in the past two days. The facts were like separate blades of grass and he was trying to pluck them and bind them together like a bowerbird building his nest. "You mean torture him?" he asked.

"Has he not tortured us?"

Bradley had not forgotten about Ginger Kingston and his young charge. He had simply become complacent. His contacts had pinpointed the farm and the fact that Ginger had worked it for many years. His contact at Motor Vehicles had given him the name and number and he had simply followed the information. Yes, he was George Kingston's brother, but there was no information linking him to any of the actions attributed to George. Yes, he was a witness, but he lived a very long way off and the likelihood of their ever meeting was extremely remote. The police had ceased looking for Bradley in connection with George and Marcia's death years before and Ginger had no history of working with or for the police. It would not have been a difficult job but any damage they could have caused had been done, and they were not pursuing it with the police or the media so Bradley simply let sleeping dogs lie.

There had been other jobs along the way. A mayor, who would not stop needling a police captain to take care of certain problems, was never found after he left for work one morning. The police chief was no longer in charge and the problems had only gotten worse. A contractor who refused to allow the union into his business ended up falling into the dig for a foundation and breaking his neck. A minister who was constantly up in arms about prostitution was found drowned in his own baptismal pool. Bradley became more and more subtle as he matured in his profession.

He thought about George Kingston from time to time. He had admired 'The Viper' and had wanted to learn more about the techniques and style his victim had employed. The history of his jobs was muddled and Bradley did not dare seek out anyone who might have known him so he was confined to researching the newspapers. It was a poor source of information and did nothing to enlighten him. When internet access became the norm, Bradley threw himself into that and found so much more than he could have expected. A search for keyword 'Viper' brought up lots of stuff about crocodile hunters and snake wranglers but it also brought up a site devoted to 'The Viper' and the jobs attributed to him. Being closer to the source than some of the people contributing to the site, Bradley knew that some of the jobs were erroneously credited. His pride swelled enormously when he saw that a job he had done when he was considerably younger was attributed to 'The Viper.' George's exploits had grown into the stuff of urban legend and his fame had grown exponentially. People started inventing jobs that had never been done and slapping the 'Viper' name on them. Bradley itched to straighten them out but, as a professional, he could not say the slightest thing.

Bradley had been in the business longer than most. He had been assassinating people for about 13 years and had contacts in all the organizations in Melbourne and Sydney. If he had wanted, he could have had Ginger and Terry eliminated at any time. It may have been out of respect for George that he did not. He wasn't actually sure. By the beginning of 1996 Bradley had amassed all the money he was ever going to need. He had not been fingered or described since the Kingston case eight years earlier. He had stopped taking simple, little jobs. His reputation commanded a high rate of return and he even commanded a consulting fee. He had never taken on an apprentice, though there was one young man who had been so insistent that he had pretended to take the boy under his wing and fed him to the crocodiles instead.

One of the things Bradley had learned from his study of George Kingston was that stability deflects suspicion. The authorities had never suspected George Kingston of anything. He had a position and a means of income. He did not spend extravagantly: his vehicles were not top of the line, his house was enough for his family but no more than they needed, he dressed professionally but not in silk, and he went to work in the morning. Bradley truly admired his choice of professions. An insurance agency allows the staff to take care of the business while the boss is out doing other things. Bradley had emulated this theme by starting up several convenience stores and petrol stations. The staff took care of the business when he had prior commitments. The business gave him the air of respectability and something to occupy his time between his less socially acceptable assignments.

Any job Bradley accepted now was a matter of choice. He would assassinate someone if he wanted to. Two years earlier a member of the organized crime network had tried to extort a job out of him, threatening to expose him to the authorities if he did not comply. That man had been found at the bottom of a ravine, in the charred remains of his own car with the bodies of his wife and two children.

"Uncle, I want to know."

"Boy, I need you to realize where we are and what we are doing. You will address me as Horace, or better yet, Mr. Paylee. If they take us, do not reveal even your name as long as I am alive. I will arrange the solicitor and we will work from there. If I am killed, deny all knowledge of my activities and tell them that I wouldn't tell you what we were doing here. Deny everything and call Mr. Streng. He will get you out and provide representation.

"Yes Sir, Mr. Paylee."

"Now what is it you want to do?"

"I want to know why he killed my father and mother. I want to know if it was a paid job and if so, who paid and why."

"I hope you understand what you are asking me for. That turns this into a complicated procedure instead of a simple killing."

"Yes Sir, I understand that."

"And what will you do with the information you have, once you have it?"

"Then I intend to kill him as well."

"The man that paid the job?"

"Yes Sir. Whoever made this happen will pay."

"I don't think you understand the ramifications of what you intend to do. The men who pay for other men's lives are protected well and avenged if they come to a difficult end."

"What are you saying?"

"In short, you are going after the sort of tree that sprouts dozens of branches when you cut off the top. You can prune the top, this bloke in this case, but if you wish to kill the tree you need to go very deep and kill the roots. The roots are protected by the branches. Do you see what I am saying?"

"I think so. You mean that to get to the man who ordered it done I will need to get past all manner of protection. I'll need to kill all the killers first, before I can get to the real objective."

"That's right. I would advocate a simple head shot from a distance and leave it at that. We have our alibi and no one will be the wiser. You will be vindicated and I can go back to being a rancher and farmer. There is a lot to be said for a quiet uneventful life."

"How many men have you killed, Mr. Paylee?"

"Only a few, but this is not about me. This is about you. I know your father did not want this sort of thing for you. He wanted you to go to university and study to become a doctor or some such."

"I'm sorry, but the time for that is passed. If you don't wish to assist me in this, I will do it alone."

"Not bloody likely. I refuse to have your blood on my hands. If you try this thing alone, you end up dead. That is not a possibility. That is a certainty. I will not have you go off half-cocked. We do this one and then set up the next one. You've been waiting half your life but you have much to learn before you can go any further."

"The door opened. Our man is coming out."

"Keep your cool, boy. This man will know we are here if he sees too much of this van. Get in the back so he can't see you.

Both of them were in the back watching with scopes when the Bradley exited the house and got in the Cadillac. There was no doubt that he noticed the van parked down the street, he looked right at it for a second more than another man might have.

"That's him, isn't it," Ginger said.

"Should we follow him?"

"No, boy, to follow him would be to cement his suspicions. He is a professional killer and like all professionals he is paranoid. You remember asking me why we had no television? I'll tell you now, that a television will fill your head with all sorts of false impressions about what a man can and cannot do. If this man sees this van elsewhere, he will know we are watching him. He has already marked us once. We will need to move quickly, but we know nothing about what the man is doing and I no longer have the contacts that allow research. We need to be in his house when he returns and I am willing to bet he has an alarm system we will need to bypass. I'll take the torches, you grab the toolbox and follow me."

Dressed in grey coveralls, they could have been plumbers or electricians, contractors of some kind. They both had engineers' caps covering their blond hair. Once they were behind the building they opened the tool box and put on driving gloves. The back of the house was out of view from the neighbors. The alarm system was in place but it was the sort that activated when the door opened, not when the glass broke. It would have been deemed sufficient since there were bars set into the door. Your average thief would have been stymied by this arrangement but a well prepared man would not. It was a matter of minutes to cut through the bars with the small oxy-acetylene torch, then they broke the glass. Terry was inside immediately but Ginger waited a while, to make sure none of the nosy neighbors were investigating, and then he climbed inside as well.

The front door had a peephole instead of a window so there was no way one could see inside until the door opened. The only thing the invaders were concerned with now was that one of the neighbors had heard the glass break and called the constables. This did not happen.

The living room window had sheer curtains that allowed the occupant to see out through them but did not allow anyone to look in. Terry set himself up on the couch and watched the road and the driveway while Ginger scouted the rest of the house. He did not expect there to be any women in the house and he was correct. Their target was a bachelor. After ensuring they were alone, Ginger set up breakfast. They had both napped in the van and were quite keyed up so they were not in danger of falling asleep.

The Cadillac pulled in the driveway about four hours later. The man got out and looked down the street at the van. There was no doubt that he was suspicious now. After opening the door and keying in the alarm code, he turned around with a pistol in his hand. He wasn't sure what had alerted him but he knew something was wrong. He could smell it.

"I know you're in here, step out with your hands up or I'll kill you right there," he said.

Terry was terrified. He and Ginger had been careful not to disturb the living room but Bradley had known anyway. Between the living room and the kitchen was a counter, with stools, that served as a dining room table. Terry stuck his hands up, above the counter but did not reveal the rest of his body. He was waiting.

"All right, you little wallaby, step out where I can… Unggg." The crackle of the stun gun cut his sentence short but it also tightened his finger on the trigger. The shot went wide but the report was loud. More than one such shot and the neighbors would surely report it as gunfire.

The invaders wasted no time in binding their victim's hands, feet and mouth with duct tape. They would have taped him to a chair but there was no appropriate kitchen chair to use so they stood him against one of the pillars that connected the kitchen counter with the ceiling and taped him to it.

"How did you know he would know?" Terry asked.

"It's a function of the business. While most men would stand there thinking something is wrong but doing nothing about it, this man suspected something and pulled his gun. He has probably worked up more enemies than us and knew somebody would come for him some day. Check the front; I'll check the back. He might have company."

"I came pretty close to getting shot." Terry's hands were still trembling.

"Actually, I was in more danger than you. I expected him to take off his jacket and put it in the closet, that's why I was in there. I couldn't see him when he turned around. If he'd seen me coming out of that closet door, I'd have caught that round. He would probably have shot you too."

"So we got lucky?"

"Luckier than we deserved. It was a sloppy setup and I didn't even know it until it went down."

"What's next?"

"That's up to you, boy. You have the man. You wanted some answers. Get them." Ginger lit a cigar and sat down on the couch.

Terry was shaking worse, now. He was shaking with rage and fear and anticipation. He walked into the kitchen and picked the cutting torch out of the cabinet where it had been stashed, but he was shaking too badly to light it. He sat down on the couch, next to his uncle, trying to calm down.

"The first time is the hardest. The first time you kill a man, the first time you torture a man, it gets better as you get practice," Ginger told him. "This man has killed enough that he doesn't have a conscience any more. He would kill you as easily as slapping a mosquito. Go look in his eyes and see if he still has a soul."

Terry did not move. He had slaughtered chickens and sheep but this was different. He was paralyzed by the prospect. All the way here from the coast he had been anticipating the moment, but now that it was here, he found himself unable to act.

"Allow me to demonstrate. There is no need for subtlety in this. The subtlety was all in the preliminaries, the action itself is brutal and messy." He stood from the couch with the cigar in his teeth and walked across the living room. When he reached the man taped to the post he punched him in the face. "See, no subtlety, no planning, no remorse. This thing shot me and your mother and your father and he would have shot you if he could have. I believe he tried. So, do what you wanted to do all these years."

Terry rose, walked across the floor and reached into the man's back pocket, pulling out his wallet. Then he went through the rest of his pockets finding his keys, a cigarette lighter, a pack of cigarettes, a money clip with a wad of bills, a pocket knife and a full clip for the man's pistol. The money went into Terry's pocket. He shook out a cigarette and lit it clumsily with the driving gloves still on.

Ginger said nothing to his nephew. He returned to the couch and smoked his cigar quietly, savoring the smoke and watching surreptitiously.

Terry smoked about half the cigarette and then put it out on the bound man's forehead. The man thrashed about but could get nowhere. He was held securely.

When the tape was ripped off his face, Bradley knew better than to raise a fuss. He already counted himself among the dead unless he could pull off something miraculous.

"Peter Dingham," Terry said, holding open the man's wallet. "That's not your name."

"What is this all about? I've done nothing to you. I've never seen you before in my life. Take the money, the television, anything you want. Just take it and leave." Bradley was trying his best to sound convincing.

"Oh, you're wrong there. You killed a man on a boat, eight years ago. Some time later you shot my mother in front of me. I have been seeing that in my dreams for years. You murderer!" Terry punched him in the eye. "That was just the preliminary. That was as easy as you'll ever see from me. I want to know why."

"You're insane. I've killed no one. I am a businessman. I own petrol stations, for the love of God. I don't know you."

"No, you wouldn't recognize me, would you. I was only eight years old when you chased me down the stairs in Goulburn Hospital. You should have stayed. You should have made sure I was dead. You should have killed us when we slept. You didn't and now your past has come back to haunt you." Terry punched him again.

70

"Look, lad, I never saw you in my life. Please, I have money in a safe in the floor. You can take that as well, just let me go. I won't call the coppers, I promise."

"LIAR!" Terry's voice broke as he yelled and he punched his captive again. "This pistol is a Glock 22, the same .40 caliber pistol you shot my mother with."

"This is coincidence. Please, let's be reasonable. I never even fired that gun."

"You've ruined my life and killed my family. I would recognize you in the dark. If you're a religious man, now would be the time to pray." Terry grabbed the spark tool and lit up the acetylene and then added the oxygen slowly until he had a nice blue point inside the flame.

"Ok, ok, it was me. You don't need that. I'll tell you anything you want to know but you don't need that." Bradley knew he could not talk his way out of his predicament by denying all knowledge.

"Why did you do it?"

"If it's any consolation, it wasn't personal. I had nothing against your father; in fact I admired him greatly. It was simply a job and I don't know why the job was set. I was paid to kill your father. I had to kill your mother because she was a witness. You must know your father did the same thing to many men and women. We were the same. If he had been paid, he would have killed me and anyone around me. He was very good. I never found out why they wanted him dead, just that they did."

"You are not the same as he was. He was a good man…"

"He was a good assassin. They never caught him because he killed every man, woman and child that could identify him. I can help you. I can help you get to the men who ordered him killed."

Terry glanced at Ginger who shook his head. Terry then took the man's pocket knife and tried to use it left handed but could not. He put the live torch on the counter top with the flame blowing downward toward the floor. Then he cut the suit off the man in a few places where the tape allowed it to show.

"Oh, for the love of God, no! Please. I'll tell you. Don't use that bloody thing on me. I got my directions from Sparky Robinson."

"Who does Sparky work for?"

"I don't knooooooo." The flame got closer and Bradley panicked. "Ok, Ok he works for the Troy Brothers."

Terry glanced at his uncle again, who nodded his head this time.

"Why?"

"I don't know. Your father was the best. I didn't want to kill him but it was the job. If I didn't do the job, somebody would have killed me."

"Well, somebody is going to kill you now, but you are going to suffer first."

Terry pasted the tape back over Bradley's mouth and touched the flame to his belly. Bradley could not scream but he did thrash about wildly. The smell of his own flesh burning filled his nostrils.

Terry backed off, revolted by the smell and the cruelty of his own actions. He pulled the tape off once more and asked, "Who did my father work for?"

Bradley spit on the floor. "Boy, you know I fucked your mother in the ass?"

"What?"

"That's right. I fucked her in the ass and she loved it. She kept begging me for more. Every time she saw me she got down on her knees and sucked on my cock and begged me to fuck her in the ass."

"You..."

"I'd fuck her in the ass and make her suck the shit off my..." Those were the last words Bradley ever spoke. Terry

72

grabbed the Glock off the counter and pumped five rounds into his bound body. Then he took the knife and began to slash and stab at the corpse, swearing incoherently.

"Oh, shit," said Ginger. "Stop that, boy. Put your cap on. Grab the torch. No, shut the bloody thing off. Leave the gun. And the knife. I got the tool box. Come on, boy. They'll be on us now. You've had your revenge. Let's go."

"There's money in the floor safe."

"Forget about it. Leave your gloves on, boy. Take his keys. You drive his car, slowly, a couple of kilometers south. Then you get in the van. Go, go, go."

The two tried to keep their faces covered as they exited the front door. The silent alarm went off, one minute later, at the security company. The telephone rang but there was no answer. The police were notified and some local constables dispatched. False alarms were common, but this one came in conjunction with a shots fired call.

Terry tried to keep the speed down but the Cadillac was quite powerful and handled much differently from what he was used to. Ginger walked calmly to the van, opened the rear doors and put the tool box in. Then he calmly reached in and grabbed a handful of intentionally dirty axle grease and wiped it on the license plate. He removed his gloves and entered the vehicle. It started quickly and he pulled out at a reasonable speed. He did nothing to generate additional interest in himself. The Cadillac was out of sight before he entered the main road, but he saw it parked in the entrance of a park. Most of the 250 kilometers of the Yarra River is dedicated to parkland. Bradley had gotten a really prime piece of property.

Ginger pulled in behind the car and Terry jumped out with the cutting torch in his hand. He threw open the van door and all but flew inside. Ginger pulled into the park, rolling his window down and listening. There was enough vegetation to keep them hidden from sight. It was not long before the sirens came screaming down the road. As soon as they had passed, Ginger pulled out of the park and headed back the way the police had come from.

The boat and tackle had been returned. They even caught a couple of fish on the way back. The coveralls had been sunk in the dark water of the river. The van was wiped clean and returned. The Holden was jacked up and the spring compressed when the patrol car pulled up behind it. Ginger explained that they had come down for some fishing and told the constable what they had caught. He apologized for doing the work on public land and explained that they had lost a ball joint and needed to replace it. The constable knew a little about the workings of the car's steering and watched as they popped the ball joint off with the pickle fork and a hammer. He had a short conversation with them about the car itself, told them to work and drive safely and left them to draw the new ball joint into place. They got the work done and left town, stopping for a front-end alignment along the way. The receipts for the parts and the alignment as well as the return of the boat and tackle were kept as proof of where they had been and what they had done. They had no proof for the previous day but if the question ever came up, they were fishing. The receipt for the van was destroyed.

"You know he played you, right?"

"He played me? Yeah, he did, he played me. I let that son-of-a-bitch get under my skin. He popped me off so bad I shot him."

"That's what he wanted. He didn't want to get tortured to death. He knew we were on him hard and there was no way we could let him live. Wouldn't have, even if we could have. His last hope left him and he knew. So he played you."

"I... I don't care. He told me what I wanted to know. And I finally got some of what I wanted."

"How does it make you feel?"

"I don't know."

"The first time is always hard. It's good you had reason or you probably couldn't have done it."

"It feels kind of hollow. Like... like I did it, but it wasn't really me and it didn't really happen. I shot him with his own gun and he just sort of exploded. I was so pumped up. He sort of just exploded. You know what, Uncle, it feels good. That piece of rat shit. It feels good."

"Don't get too attached to that feeling. That path leads to madness."

"It didn't feel good that I had him. It scared me. I almost threw up when I burned him. But after I shot him. That's when it felt good, I guess."

"Now, tell me, what are the rules?"

"Never leave fingerprints. Never talk about it. Never work with the constabulary. Never attract attention to yourself. Never leave witnesses."

"Now, what rules did we break?"

"We left a witness. The new owner of the boat."

"What should we do about it?"

"Kill him?"

"Do you want to?"

"No, not really. I don't think we need to."

"Good. I'll phone him and tell him that the registration has been straightened out. Tell him that there is no more trouble with the insurance and he'll be happy and hopefully nobody ever asks him about it. I doubt anyone will. But that's the trade-off. The connection is there, but it's so much less dangerous to let it lie than to kill another man that we'll just let it lie. We're stopping in Sydney on the way home."

"Sydney? That's well out of our way."

"A man needs to indulge himself sometimes."

"I think I already did."

"This is a different sort of indulgence."

Before they reached Sydney, Ginger had dyed his hair red again. It did not look right because he was actually beginning to go grey but it made him look younger. He also shaved off his beard.

In Sydney they went to the Kings Cross area and, as Ginger had said, they indulged themselves. Terry had never had a woman before but his paid partner complimented him repeatedly and it made him feel wonderful. When they drove off, Ginger said, "A man needs that from time to time, eh, mate?"

Terry looked at him intently. His uncle had never called him "mate" before. He had the feeling he was no longer a boy in Ginger's eyes. In fact he no longer felt like a boy.

Chapter Five
Inheritance

Terry Kingston was no longer the same after his little adventure. He said almost nothing to anyone his first day back at school. He had a nightmare that night about being bound to a wall and seeing Bradley abusing his mother. He could not help her and Bradley leered at him when he pulled out his gun and shot her. He woke up shaking like an impact hammer.

The dreams where he was chained up were over in a couple of days and replaced by nighttime visions of medieval battles. Sometimes he was watching from a hilltop like a conquering hero and sometimes he was in the thick of it with his sword arm slick with blood and his shield absorbing hammer blows.

After a week, Terry threw himself into his work. He began to study late into the night, after his chores were done. He still hunted but his primary focus was no longer shooting the animals, it was sneaking up on them. He split cord after cord of wood, until they had enough extra that they began selling it to the neighbors.

Terry stopped fighting in school. He had plenty of opportunity, mostly from the older class, but he no longer felt it worth his while. He studied the upper class and decided that there was one lad in particular that no one else wanted to fight. He was not much of a fighter really, but he was very big. Terry decided that this was the one that he would make an example of and one day he challenged him to a fight. The upperclassman would not fight him even though Terry called him some rather vile names and impugned the honor of his family. Terry had learned not to turn his back on an enemy but in this case he did it deliberately. The lad charged at him as soon as his back was turned.

Terry wheeled around and then sidestepped the oaf. His opponent was on the ground without his ever throwing a punch. He was told that the ground was the best place for him to stay, but the big lad was angry now so there was no stopping him. Terry played him like a matador playing a bull, presenting a target for the charge and then moving aside. After doing this four times he knew his opponent would not fall for it again, so he stood his ground, braced himself, and caught the charging fool by the waist. He used the bull's momentum to pick him up and dropped him on his head. That was the last fight Terry Kingston ever had to get in, all the while he went to that school.

Research was easier into the affairs of the Troy Brothers than it had been into Bradley's. They were somewhat notorious, well protected, and deeply feared individuals. They were the accepted heads of a crime syndicate that spanned all but the southernmost part of New South Wales. Their reputations were such that anyone reaching mid-level criminal status was required to pay a tribute to them. They administered the large shipments of drugs and other forms of contraband. They had their fingers in the legal businesses as well. Protection was afforded to those who contributed to their coffers and accidents occurred when one did not. The Australian businessmen were a hard-bitten lot but the Troy Brother's methods were savage enough to convince even the most hard core individualist to come around. All the houses of manly pleasure paid for their protection, and the protection of their ladies. Any drug dealers above street level needed permission to operate. It was almost as if they bought a license and renewed it monthly.

There were things the research did not uncover. Much of the constabulary was making extra money by ignoring some things, and acting on others that may have been ignored otherwise. Many of the judges and politicians were on the

Troy payroll. Rumor had it that even Colby Carmichael, the Commissioner of Australia's Taxation Office, was a recipient of the brothers' largesse.

It would be extremely difficult and dangerous to even ask too many questions about the brothers' affairs. To get close enough to ask them the kinds of questions Terry Kingston wanted answered would be suicide for most men. Ginger made sure Terry understood that completely.

Time went by, and Rough and Ready got old. They were the finest of dogs and fantastic with the sheep but they were reaching the age where they would need to be replaced. Ginger bought their replacements as puppies, from the same man he had bought his current canine assistants from. The puppies were naturals. They needed little training, most of what they learned was taught to them by their predecessors. Terry was aware that he was going to need to put the older pair out of their misery soon. Arthritis had set into the dogs' hips and they were in constant pain.

When the day came, Terry took them out into the fields one at a time and shot them in the heads with his own .38 revolver. He dug a separate grave for each of them, said a prayer over each of them and went home to clean his gun. It was much more difficult for him to dispatch Pincher, the Doberman. Pincher had been his from the first day they spent together. Pincher also hated every other man on Earth. He was not so unfriendly to women, but Terry was the only man the creature loved. It abided Ginger, but did not like him. It never bit Ginger, but Ginger never turned his back on Pincher. When the day came for Terry to pull his best friend out into the field and put one in his brain he took it very personally. He moped about for days afterward, but he never cried. He had not cried since he was eight years old.

Terry's grades had improved substantially by the time he graduated, but he never aspired to a university education. He had effectively distanced himself from the rest of the graduating class. The farmers' daughters were amenable to his affections, but he could not see being with one of them for long. Romance was not a large component of his personality. He enjoyed sex at any opportunity but traditional love was something that eluded him.

The one thing that drove Terry was revenge. The question of why his parents had been killed was always there, but it was secondary now. He had not developed a taste for killing; it was not something he enjoyed. He just saw it as a necessity. Everything dies in its time, he reasoned, hastening that demise is sometimes a critical function of a small segment of society.

1997 was an eventful year, at least the end of that year was. Terry turned 17 December 1st and it was like a Christmas present. The proceeds of The Kingston Agency were turned over to him as well as ownership of said subsidiary. Most 17-year-old boys would have gone mad with a sudden influx of money such as that but Terry was not that sort. He invested much of the money in rock solid stocks and certificates of deposit. He paid Ginger for the bills he had incurred in restoring his vehicle and gave him a handsome present as well. He set up a trust fund that gave Ginger a monthly stipend. Said fund would revert to Terry when Ginger passed away.

In 1998, after he graduated from high school, Terry took over the operation of the insurance agency, at least in name. The business had done well while in the hands of those his father had entrusted and so the young man saw no reason for changes. The staff was pleased that he had no plans for major changes and delighted that they were allowed to keep their jobs. Terry's number one requirement was that the staff teach him how to use the new computer system and search the internet. He kept a close eye on the finances and did some research into the past practices of the office. He had suspected that there would be some misappropriation of funds over the years but he could find nothing out of the ordinary. The building itself was looking a bit shabby by that time and he made a few repairs and painted the place inside and out by himself, at his own expense.

The computer systems were extensive, for the time, and as he learned how to use them, they became his primary research tool. The insurance network, which had originally been only for the Helping Hands Corporation was expanded to enable him to worm his way into the files of other companies as well. This was not legal, of course, but there was so little protection against hackers in those days that it was easy and relatively cheap. He had a university student who was in need of money and amorously involved with a woman that was outside of his price range. The student was happy to install some private programs for a fee.

Terry took a room in the town of Orange. His father's house had been sold years before and the proceeds were part of his "coming of age" money. That money had been handled well over the past few years. Terry Kingston could have bought a seaside house if he had wanted one and a Rolls Royce to park in the driveway. He continued to drive the Holden and lived in a room with a kitchen.

One of his expenses was a subscription to a gym. He made sure there were a large percentage of women at this particular gym. He was not looking for a long-term woman but his chiseled body and inexhaustible energy commanded the interest of many. Short-term women were always available and he took the advice of enjoying himself while he was young.

The Troy Brothers were in their late forties. They had been in charge of criminal operations since their mid twenties. Their meteoric rise in clandestine operations was due to their complete disregard for moral guidelines. In the last two and a half decades they had directed so many operations that they could barely remember some of the men they had caused to die. They cared nothing for the lives they ruined.

Adam Troy lived on Unwin Street off Bayview Avenue in the Earlwood area of Sydney. He owned the entire block of land on the south side of Unwin St. that borders Wolli Creek. The house was magnificent and the land itself was very valuable. The fence around the property was patrolled by ruthless men during the day and hungry dogs at night.

Abel Troy preferred a more central location and was less inclined toward luxury. He owned a hotel on Castlereagh Street in the business district. He kept the top floor of the hotel for himself; the penthouse suite was nowhere near the size of his brother's estate but it made him feel safer. The elevator no longer made it to the top floor and the two stairwells were locked and guarded. The floor below his residence was filled with offices staffed by employees of their own businesses. There was one other way out. The helicopter pad on the roof housed their favorite mode of transport.

The brothers conducted business from various locations, many the offices of shell companies that did no actual business but were incorporated nonetheless. Much of their business was legitimate and they were working toward divesting themselves of some of the less savory enterprises. The problem was that they had eliminated any competition at their level and they were loathe to simply set the businesses adrift.

Adam would leave his mansion in a bulletproof limousine to meet his brother. Abel took the private elevator from the business floor and joined his brother in the rolling fortress when they were going to a different location. They varied their routes and their destinations randomly to prevent being set up. Often enough they conducted business from the upper floor of the hotel. Only legitimate businesses operated there.

"What's your plan, mate?" Ginger asked. He had been sober for a while now. He had gone on a drinking jag for a couple of months after the "little job" he had helped Terry with, but that had not lasted.

"I can't truly say, Uncle. These men are not the sort of blokes you can walk up to and shoot. I've done some reconnaissance but I don't see any easy mark. I've got some contacts in Sydney now, but not anyone of influence. It's almost impossible to get close to them. They have their men and they're not looking for new recruits. I can't just walk up and ask for a job application.

"I thought I could shoot them from a distance, but they are so well protected that I can't get a vantage point. I thought about going into the older one's mansion in Earlwood but the place is like a fortress."

"It's good to see you're not so bold in your youth, that you think you can do that. You'd never even get in the house." Ginger relit his cigar. "This one cannot be done physically. You'd need an army of good men and many would die. You need to get inside their minds. The real meaning of strategy is to know what your enemy is going to do, to prepare for it when they do it, and then to make them do it when you want them to. The best con men in the world are those who leave their mark with a good feeling until the payoff does not show up. The best is when they don't know they have been conned until it is too late to do anything about it. If you let them know you are watching you will end up dead, so stop. If you let them know they are under attack, they will be prepared for it. That is not always bad, but you must know what they are going to do and make them do it when you want them to do it. Tell me what you know about them."

Terry described what he had learned of their habits and routine. One of the worst problems he faced is that when they were not engaged in business, they did not stay together. They acted as if they knew they were targets and wanted to make sure one of them survived if there was an assault. They went to restaurants occasionally, never together, and it was never predictable where they would go. The outside of the eatery was always well guarded while one of them was inside.

"You're still thinking of walking up to them and shooting them. These men cannot be taken that way. They have good protection. The only place they are vulnerable is in their information flow. They must be fed information that causes them to believe something that is not true and then capitalize on that misinformation. The only way you can do that is to hit them in the wallet. That means you need information that only members of their organization can give you or perhaps God himself."

"There may be someone else… I can't tip my hand too soon, though. I'm going to need identification that reads something other than Kingston. I cannot chance them remembering they had my father killed and putting two and two together."

"The agency is your best source for the information. A good laminator and a small picture will fix it up. Use a legal name, register a vehicle in that name, insure it through a different agency of Helping Hands. This is all possible. Within a couple of weeks we can get you an ID, but investigate the history of the name. If you are going in, you'll want a criminal from the other side of the country. If you're working with clean, then make the man clean. Prison time is dangerous because gangsters know men in prison. Are you getting all of this?"

"Should I use a dead man?"

"Be careful with dead men, they show up as dead when a search is run on their names. I personally like taking the name and enrolling it in university. Doing that brings all manner of applications from credit card companies. Then you can work up a history, a portfolio so to speak. Enrolling in university, in Sydney, would give you a proper history and reason for being there. Never use credit for anything you don't want people to know you have. Your history can include books but not bullets. You see?"

"Gosh, Uncle, why did you teach me none of this before?"

"I don't want you doing this thing. In my opinion the action in Melbourne was the end of it, but if you are set on doing it then I will provide you with everything I can to help."

"Thank you. I'll consider everything you say carefully, but I think I will be killing these men one way or another."

"Are you hungry?"

"I thought I'd stop in the diner in town. Would you like to come?"

"No. I have work that needs doing. Say, I've had some trouble with foxes since you left. At first they were just taking rabbits, but they started in on the chickens last week. Would you like to take a stab at them?"

"I can do that. It's been a while."

"Stay the night. I've got some interesting things to show you."

"Interesting? In what way?"

"First, I picked those up a couple days back." Ginger indicated a crate in the corner of the kitchen. Inside was a couple dozen sticks of dynamite. "We'll be popping some stumps tomorrow. There are a few things about dynamite I'd like to show you. I also got one of these."

"Blimey. A night scope."

"That should make it easier to take a fox, eh?"

"Easier to take a lot of things."

The night scope was ungainly but it had a terrific range. It was clearly not designed for close work. Terry got one of the foxes that night; he took another in the morning light along with four rabbits. He took the tails from the foxes, cleaned and skinned the rabbits and slept the morning away while Ginger cooked.

"I'll tell you, Uncle," Terry said over a cup of coffee. That scope was not designed to work with that little rabbit gun. It's much too long range for that. You should send it back."

"Finish your chow, mate, I got another surprise for you."

After breakfast, Ginger told Terry to grab a shovel. They went into the barn and Ginger moved a tractor out. He instructed Terry to dig under where the tractor had sat. Terry did not question, he just dug until he hit cement. He dug around the extent of the square block which had a large ring set into one side.

Ginger ran out the cable on the hoist they had used to pull the Holden's engine. It was chained to the main beam of the barn. He hooked the loop and drew the concrete block back. It was hinged on one side. Underneath the block was a set of stairs that led down to a security door. Inside the door was a dark room that smelled, not musty as you would expect, but clean and slightly oily. When his uncle turned on the fluorescent lights the sight floored Terry. It was a climate-controlled, subterranean arsenal.

Terry's words were disjointed and slurred. It was as though he was drunk or had taken a beating.

In the room were shotguns, pistols, automatics and sniper rifles along with sealed boxes of ammunition. It was not new equipment, some of it was quite old. There was a .45 caliber Thompson submachine gun like the ones used in the old Cagney movies. There was a 7.63mm Tokarev from the 1940s. There was a Stoner 63A Commando from 1967.

86

There was an entire rack of M16s and another of AK47s. There was a box of hand grenades from WWII, rocket launchers from Israel and a wide variety of pistols. There was also a 1986 Mauser SP66; a German made .308 sniper rifle. The crown jewel for Terry was the .50 caliber Barrett. Someone had written on the cover of the box "One shot, one kill, death from afar!"

"Gawd awmighty! Where did all this come from? When did you dig this pit? Why didn't you tell me about it? Do they all fire? Have you got rounds for this monster? Oh, there we go. How on earth did I miss all this? Gawd! This is like a dream come true. When did you get this?"

Ginger stood there with a face as expressionless as the concrete slab. He exhaled a cloud of smoke and the silent system sucked it up.

"Uncle, say something."

He could maintain the stone visage no longer and smiled broadly. "Mate, many of these weapons were used by your father and myself in the early years. The more recent ones were shipped to me. That big killer came from the Gulf War, actually, I think it was the Iran-Iraq war. It was bound for Iran and got diverted here. We dug this thing out and poured the concrete before you were born. We sealed it tight and installed the air and electric systems ourselves. I never wanted to show it to you." His smile disappeared. "If you hadn't been so determined, I never would have. You got yourself set on hunting the biggest game in the country and I told you I was going to give you all the support I could. I still don't like it, but I can't let you go off and get yourself killed."

Terry was like a half disciplined child in a candy store. He wanted everything and felt awkward touching anything. Finally he settled on the Thompson. He picked it from its handmade oak cradle and took one of the three drum cartridges as well. "I can't believe it. This gun is older than you. They were never supposed to be sold to anyone outside of the bobbies. Gawd, it's beautiful."

"I don't know how well that still works," Ginger replied. "I haven't fired that monster since… well, for years now."

"Let's take it out."

"Clean it first."

"It's clean."

"How do you know a cockroach didn't crawl into the breech and die? I taught you better than that. Disassemble it and clean it. Emotions and firearms have no place in the same room. I told you about going off half-cocked. You can't use a tool until you know how to use it, and by God this one is no different."

"It's lighter than I would have expected. How did you get it?"

"It's four kilos with a 27mm barrel. The drums weigh about a kilo apiece. We got it from a man who knocked off an armored car, in America, then moved down under. He mailed it to himself in pieces. He's not alive any more."

"Did you…"

"No. I didn't do that many jobs with your dad. No, this man was old and had no more need to kill a room full of people."

"Well, that was nice of him."

"I should say. This is one of the finest short range weapons ever made. This one was made in the mid twenties so it has the Cutts Compensator on the barrel. It uses the .45 caliber automatic round. The jacket on those shells is slightly longer than the pistol round and uses a 230-grain load. The shells are reloadable so pick them up after you're done. That gun is too old to use in a modern action. It's too unique and identifiable. I'll let you use it around here but take my advice and leave it here. Remember never call attention to yourself."

88

"All right. I understand. I would like to try it out though."

"Go hook up the trailer to the tractor and we'll go back and have some fun at the tree line."

Ginger's insistence that each gun be disassembled, cleaned and oiled before use shortened the time and number of weapons they took to the tree line with them. The .50 caliber sniper rifle was indeed a marvel of destruction. The armor piercing rounds blew through tree trunks like butter. The incendiary rounds lit them up. Nobody was close enough to hear the automatic fire so there was no curiosity from the neighbors.

The dynamite instruction was almost as interesting as the old guns. Of course there were no bridges or buildings to demolish, but Terry picked up the idea of directed energy easily. He never knew how much there was to be learned or how many types of explosives could be made. Though he never reached a level of real proficiency, he did learn enough to hold his own in a conversation.

Terry stayed at the farm for a week instead of the one day he had planned. He disassembled every weapon in the bunker, oiled and reassembled them. He shot every weapon in the arsenal, broke them down and cleaned them afterward. It was quite an education for someone who thought he knew guns. He learned the inherent flaws and strengths of some of the different, older designs. He also found a cache of cold hard cash.

The crate was on the bottom of a stack of crates full of ammunition. Terry was looking for shotgun shells when he found it. They were small bills but there were enough of them to fill a rocket crate. It caused Terry to think.

After a week, Terry could hit a beer can at half a mile in a crosswind, with the Barrett. He was no Commando, only because he had not gotten the training. His physical condition was extraordinary, his eyes were clear and strong and his hands were rock steady. He could run for an hour without breathing hard. He may not have been able to beat an Army Ranger in hand-to-hand combat, but his upbringing had taught him so much more than military training would have. He could rebuild an automobile from the ground up. He could weld with an arc welder, a MIG welder and an oxy-acetylene torch. He had little experience with a TIG welder, but he could hold his own with it. He could throw any good knife accurately at 30 feet, a hatchet at 40 feet and a cut down woodsman's axe at 60 feet. He was a prime specimen of manhood and had no issues with his self awareness. He could do whatever needed to be done whenever it was required. He felt like a superman.

Ginger Kingston was about 50 at this point. While he was not an old man, he was no longer what he had once been either. A life of working hard and playing hard had left their marks. He had a bit of bursitis, a bit of arthritis and his knees were showing signs of wear. Years of cigars and alcohol had no good effect on him either. He could no longer run the way the younger Kingston could, so Terry was surprised when his uncle said it was time for some training. Ginger had not meant that Terry would be training, he was training himself. Terry had left for Orange and Ginger trained every three days, taking one day off after three, and then starting over again. He would never be in the shape he had been when he was young, but the excess flesh melted from his bones and he began packing on muscle again. It made him feel so good he had no desire to pick up a drink. After three months, he did not look like the man he had been. It was as though he was reversing his age.

Terry spent his days in research and training as well. Some of the bodybuilders at the gym had tried to get him to enroll in the competitions but he simply told them he was not interested. He said he couldn't stand the thought of shaving his whole body. In truth he simply wanted nothing to do with the spotlight. He couldn't attract attention to himself.

Every other week he would visit the farm and practice with the firearms, mostly the armor piercing sniper rifle. He joined his uncle in training while he was there and was amazed at the transformation. It was not long before they began to train in hand-to-hand combat and Terry had a rude awakening coming. He no longer felt like such a superman as the man who was twice his age trounced him regularly.

Ginger still had no telephone or television, but there was no longer any question why. The only question was how George and Ginger had communicated. It seems that George had simply sent a letter on Kingston Agency letterhead in a company envelope. They used a simple code to indicate what was required and Ginger would show up in a couple of days with the required munitions. He returned to the farm with cash and stashed it away. They had been using a steel plate covered with straw in the barn, but when George had been killed, Ginger filled the spot over the concrete barrier with soil. George's body had never been found so Ginger had left the currency in the bunker with the munitions against his possible return.

It was a lesson for Terry in honor and integrity. They had never had any excess of money in the past few years and Ginger Kingston could easily have plundered the secret stash but had not. Ginger chewed on his cigar for a while and told Terry, when he asked, that the money was part of his inheritance and that he could have it if he wanted it. Terry thought about it for a while and filled his wallet but left the majority of it in where it was. He told him it was good to have a little stashed away for a rainy day.

Chapter Six
What Price Revenge?

"Shit, bo... mate, anyone can kill anyone. If you don't get it right what's the use. Can you take a moving target at a mile?" Ginger was talking while he and Terry were sparring.

"If I'm planted and the wind's not too bad."

"But, you take out one, ubgh," Ginger grunted as Terry got a quick shot in. "Take one out and the other will know you're coming."

"That's why I gotta..." Terry did not finish the sentence he waded in with a flurry of shots, the sixth or seventh too wide. He left himself open for a second and Ginger bloodied his nose. They didn't have gloves or helmets on, they were just bare knuckle punching. It didn't take long to get tired of that. They didn't often practice using the Marquis of Queensbury rules but it made a nice change since Terry could actually win these fights. There were no hard feelings when they were done.

"I'll tell you what..." Ginger sidestepped a roundhouse, grabbed Terry's elbow and wrist and jacked his arm around behind his back. Terry spun the other way and dropped to one knee. The fight was over and he had Ginger's balls in his hand. Ginger was impressed, slapped Terry on the back and they headed back to the kitchen. "I'll tell you what. If you want we can give them the old one-two. It'll take some planning and the coordination needs to be perfect."

"What's the old one-two," Terry wanted to know.

"That's when one is the set up and two is the kill. Or, we can be subtle about it, find out who the main players are and work on them instead. A quick kill is one thing, like the mercy you showed the old dogs. I prefer a more circuitous route to the target."

"I'm listening."

92

Only a few people had access to the Troy brothers. In their role as corporate industrialists they entertained wealthy businessmen and politicians. In their role as criminal executives they spoke only with the world's most powerful men, though usually through their representatives. They were becoming more and more legitimate as the years went by and giving the direct control of the unsavory operations to their underlings. There were five men directly under them who issued the orders and directions seldom came from the true powers any more. As long as the money kept flowing there was no problem, but when there was a hiccup in the torrent of illegal liquid assets, there was real trouble. Incompetence was met with direct and often irrevocable response.

Jimmy Cognac was in charge of the Melbourne area including Tasmania.

Tony Samfier was much more politically motivated and had control from Canberra to the Victoria border.

Randy Arganmajc was in charge of the most profitable region, Sydney proper.

Roy Tap covered the coast from Newcastle to Brisbane. Most of the cocaine that came in from South America was entrusted to his charge.

Rudy Christian had the dubious honor of controlling the northern Queensland coast. He also negotiated with the heroin suppliers north of Australia. Many of the ships stopped in New Guinea on their way down from South-East Asia. Rudy had a private estate on Badu Island where much of the Asian heroin was stored temporarily. It was sealed in transport containers, and protected by a group of paramilitary killers. Rudy ensured a slow and steady supply of the powerful drug to the cities of the south, keeping the price high and occasionally withholding supply to increase the cost.

The problems began as small incidents that would ordinarily be handled at the street level. Small-time dealers being robbed at gunpoint by masked men driving cars stolen from other small-time dealers was barely enough to open eyes. It was certainly nothing to bother the mid-level executives with. The events began happening in Sydney in 1999.

Organized crime among the street-level drug addicts and small-time dealers is anything but organized. There is no loyalty, no consistent and regular supply, no honor among thieves. The street gangs try to keep things regulated but the business is so inconsistent that one man can supply a group for a while and then he gets frozen out and another source appears. Suppliers cut their powders into oblivion as they become more and more dependant on the drug itself and then a new source is necessary. One pipeline gets busted, or gets out of the business before it happens, and another source must be found. Marijuana suppliers harvest at different times and there are times when there is none available. And people talk.

When one is looking for a score, an addict won't refer him to his connection, but connections can be made easily in pubs and clubs. Some people are more open with their products so dropping names happens as well.

Developing a list of victims was easy for Terry Kingston. He would drink lightly and share in whatever the drug was but always with the objective in mind. His primary thought was not to become a junkie like those he was carousing with. He had been warned and watched carefully, himself. It was an insidious slide down a slippery slope, especially for a brash young man eager to prove he could hold his own in the party scene. Before such a man knew it had happened, the drugs were all that mattered.

Heroin and opium were much more available than cocaine in New South Wales. The trade routes from Asia were old and well established. While it was less available, cocaine was more desirable because it allowed a person to still

94

function, drink and dance, while high. It also took longer to destroy a person's life.

Amphetamines were not a huge problem in Sydney at that time, though they were growing in popularity. One snort of crystal methadrine and one could party all night and all the next day. The long-term consequences of the drug were, as of yet, unknown.

Threats of incarceration almost always turned addicts into snitches, sometimes turned dealers into snitches, but the chances of the police finding an informer decreased dramatically as they went up the ladder. A classic failure of the witness protection program reminded the middle and upper echelon of the criminal enterprises what happened to men who were willing to talk to the establishment.

Wally Brochade had been mid-level management when he was caught with a shipment of heroin. He was looking at life in prison and decided that it would be best if he rolled over on his employers and took the chance. The case never made it to trial. Wally was kidnapped from a transport van by four armed men and was found a day later tied to a tree, upside down, his tongue was cut out and had been replaced with his manly parts. He had died suffocating on his own balls. His family had been similarly tortured and murdered. His wife's head was found in the toilet of the family home, her body was never found. Even his children were tortured and mutilated, dismembered and spread about the blood soaked house. The family dog was cut in half with a machete.

Most of the street-level dealers didn't know anybody with the kind of power and authority necessary to order them tortured and mutilated. There was no formal organization at that level. The addicts would give up their suppliers and most of the low level dealers were addicts themselves, selling drugs so they could get their own supply. This was where the police began their investigations but they were constrained by the laws. Terry Kingston had no such constraints.

"Have you ever seen what happens to a man when this kind of power is run through his body?" Terry asked his partner, casually.

"Aye, the flesh curls up like paper in a fire and his muscles spasm like a speared fish. The eyeballs pop out and start to bleed, the tongue swells up and the man often bites it off. Sometimes they can't talk afterward so we just kill him and leave him there."

Terry and Ginger were both dressed in white painters' suits with butchers' aprons. Their heads were covered with grotesque leather masks that covered their features. They both wore gloves, though Ginger's were driving gloves and Terry had welding gloves on. The man taped to the chair was obviously terrified, though he couldn't speak through the tape over his mouth.

"It makes a horrible stink too, as the flesh burns." Terry concluded as he fit the welding rod into the clamp. "An arc welder is not the greatest of devices to extract information but it is as effective as anything else. The real trouble is it turns the subject into a gimp."

"Aye. The muscles never work quite right afterward. The damage makes them limp and stumble. They have the shakes forever and tend to piss themselves. No matter, this one doesn't deserve considerations."

"Soak him down."

Ginger poured a pitcher of water over the addict's head at Terry's request, and Terry affixed the ground clamp of the arc welder to the man's left foot. Walking behind the victim Terry pulled out a battery-powered stun gun and gave the bound man a shot to the back of the neck. After squirming about for a while, the man slumped unconscious. When he revived he was more than willing to tell the men anything he knew about everybody he knew. There was only one name that held any significance, Demetrius Marlowe. Demetrius dealt in cocaine and moved it in ounces. He had been in business for quite some time but had never been caught because he kept it in a different location from his residence. The victim did not know where that was but he did know Demetrius' home address and phone number.

"Should we kill him?" Terry asked.

"I'm not sure. Do we need to kill you?"

The victim answered emphatically that they did not, that he would never tell anyone what had happened.

"Bear in mind, you little shit, that if we ever find out you told anyone about this we will release the information that you are a stool pigeon working with the police, and then we will kill your mother. I believe she lives on Cooper Street."

The man could say nothing more. He had been broken. He began mumbling promises as his torturers packed up.

As a final assurance, Terry returned to cut the dealer loose and stuck the barrel of a shotgun in his mouth. "You will never know who is watching and who is one of ours. If you speak to the police we will know. If you speak to your friends we will know. If you speak to your sainted mother we will know and our vengeance will be swift and brutal. You will watch what is left of your pathetic family die before we kill you and your death will be so much worse than death itself."

Demetrius Marlowe was not as easy a mark to apprehend. He was the owner of a small stamping plant in the Rosebery area and he made sure his businesses never overlapped. He never walked anywhere and spent little time in the pubs. On the surface, he was a very respectable man in a respectable part of town and he never involved his family in either of his business ventures.

Ginger was quick to tell Terry that to involve the man's family in their little operation was to court disaster. "Women always want to go to the police. Especially in this case, she would run screaming to the constabulary proclaiming her husband's innocence and demanding justice. We must be more careful than that, or the notoriety might end up killing us."

"We could kidnap her and make demands on her husband." Terry opined.

"No, too complicated. We need to keep it as simple as we can. The more people involved, the more people who know, the more likely that the affair gets exposed prematurely. What we want to do is to get in and get out with the information. We can threaten his family, but I do not want them to ever see us. Pictures of the family should be all we need to facilitate the flow, along with some of the cruder and messier methods. Any time you can convince somebody of something, without having to actually do it, that is the way to go. Convince somebody of a consequence, and you get his undivided attention. He may roll over easily, or he may require more convincing, but if he is the only one who knows we were there, the chances are he will be silent after we are gone."

"I see what you mean. So we should do it right away, before our junkie friend loses his fear and opens his mouth?"

"Agreed," Ginger said as he relit his cigar.

"His home, in Summer Hill, is undefended. I do not feel good about abducting him there, however. They call it The Village because everybody is looking out for everybody else's business." Terry pulled out a cigarette and lit it. "I think there are too many busybodies and that we should grab him in the industrial district."

"Agreed, Rosebery is more appropriate. At the end of second shift would be best, but his manager locks the place up. He doesn't show up at that time of night."

"He would if there was an emergency."

Demetrius Marlowe got the call that night. Someone had driven the forks of the fork lift through the oil tank on one of the Bliss presses. It was an above ground tank unlike most, which were under the floor. He rushed to the factory to take care of the situation.

Nobody would admit to the accident, even when he promised no repercussions would be issued. He spent a couple of hours trying to determine what had happened and then he left. He did not get far, however, because his car overheated. He pulled over to the side of the road and a van pulled up next to him. He thought they were there to help an unfortunate citizen but such was not the truth. Two men in executioner masks grabbed him, shocked him unconscious, and stuffed him, bound, into the van.

"We are going to make this as painless and simple as possible as long as you cooperate with us. Currently, we have two men outside your home on Carrington Street. These men are not civilized in the traditional sense of the word. They will, upon instruction, invade your home and murder your children with your wife watching. Then they will repeatedly rape her, torture her, and then disembowel her while she is still alive. I'm sure this is nothing you had planned for her this morning but unless you cooperate, this is precisely what will happen." The speaker was the shorter of the two men. The location was a motel room, looking like any other motel room.

"Who are you?" was all Marlowe was able to say at this point.

"We are the men who have everything you are and everything you own in the palms of our sweaty little hands. We can do whatever we wish to you, right now, without repercussions. My partner is of the opinion we should pop out one of your eyes and skull fuck you but I told him otherwise. I informed him that you are a gentleman and will be able to grasp the desperation of the situation and the

99

dedication of your captors. I'm afraid he is a bit bloodthirsty, however. He would like nothing more than to begin carving you up."

Terry brought out a straight razor and began sharpening it on a leather strop fastened to the back of the chair. The aspect was terrifying. The executioners' masks lent a surreal aspect to the proceeding.

"Why are you doing this to me?"

"Because, my dear Demetrius, we know you are a drug dealer hiding under the disguise of a legitimate businessman. You are a blood cell in the artery of the Sydney drug trade and you have information that will save your life. You will give us this information or we will be forced to use methods that have been banned in all civilized countries for centuries."

"What do you want… want to know?"

"Who supplies you with your cocaine? We know you sell it by the ounce. That means you acquire it by the pound or kilo. We want to know where you get it and who gets it to you." Ginger's voice was as refined and erudite as he could make it. It sounded incongruous coming from the mouth hole of the torturer's mask.

Terry on the other hand was growling like an animal. It was the most extreme example of good cop/bad cop that had ever been portrayed.

"Now, are you going to tell us what we want to know or shall I tell my associates to begin doing what they do best?"

"Oh, God! You don't understand. What you are threatening me with is the same thing they will do to me when they find out I talked."

"I'm afraid you do not understand, sir. You have the opportunity to go on with your boring, pedantic life, unchanged and unscarred, or you have the opportunity to be mangled and see your family's mutilated bodies lying in pools of their own blood. The decision is yours and yours alone."

Demetrius Marlowe was an entrepreneur. He had seen an opportunity to make some clandestine capital and then regretted it, but could not escape the spiral he was caught in. He had looked for a way to escape the situation but was unable to find a way out. His underworld connections had pictures of him hidden away somewhere, pictures of him in compromising positions. He was also pragmatic. He could see what was going on. It was obvious to him that a rival faction was muscling in on the cocaine trade and that they had their own suppliers or they would have been demanding he take them to his hoard. He chewed on his lower lip for a second, trying to get an angle that would leave him and his family in the clear and yet eliminate his culpability.

"I'm not who you are after. I'm only the middle man, a little fish." He didn't try to deny what he had done or who he was. It was obvious to him that the time for denial was yet to come. He did not break down and cry as a lesser man might have.

"My dear sir, you are precisely who we are after. My associate wants to taste your blood and the only thing keeping his barbaric appetite in check is myself. Now, tell me who it is that supplies the cocaine and you will ensure your continued survival and that of your family. The alternative has already been laid before you and, I assure you, without your cooperation it will be forthcoming."

"All right, I'll tell you everything I know but I need some modicum of certainty that I will be left in the clear."

"As you have iterated you are a little fish, of no real concern to me. Your life hangs by a thread that I will cut without the slightest compunction if I suspect that you are not being completely forthcoming and utterly truthful. On the other hand, if your information is deemed to be worthy, you will be released to go your own way. I do not feel it necessary to remind you that speaking of this to your connections within the organization that supplies you will be absolutely disastrous. They will at that point do what I will not. Are we in agreement?"

"We are."

"Good, then spin me a tale of supply and demand. When I am done you will be released to your lovely family.

"I got contacted first by Bruno. I don't know Bruno's last name but he is an idiot. I never would have done business with him but the follow up was Mark Valentine. Mark works for a man called Randy. I don't know Randy's last name either. When it is time to make a payment or to get a delivery, I call a receptionist who sets up an appointment for me. It is set up in deserted offices or public places like restaurants. I show up and either Mark or Bruno or both is there to meet me. I don't know where their houses are, I don't know where the offices, you know, the real offices are. I'm just a middleman."

"Yes, a very efficient operation. So, how often do you call him?"

"I can't call him now. They will know it was me if I set him up and then he will do the same thing you will. I told you, I'm not the one you want."

"Tell us where you have met these men."

"They won't be in these places. I can't even recall some of the spots."

"Associate, kindly refresh the gentleman's memory. No scars."

Terry made a noise like a disappointed dog and slipped his razor back into his smock. Then he punched Demetrius six times, four in the belly and two in the face.

When Mr. Marlowe was again able to speak it seems that his memory had improved. His attitude was also improved somewhat. He stopped asking for things that could not be bargained for and he continued supplying names of streets and locations of buildings, restaurants and nightclubs.

Terry was behind him so he could not see the younger man plotting the locations on the map.

"Well, Mr. Marlowe, you have given us something that amounts to nothing," Ginger said as he reached over and picked up the receiver of the telephone. He dialed a number and waited an appropriate time. "Associate Number Two, you and Number Three may proceed..."

"Wait. Wait, please. I can give you more. I can give you what you want."

"Hold on for a few minutes, Number Two. If I do not call you within 15 minutes, make sure there are no witnesses. Yes, you may have your way with the woman." He hung up the phone. "As you were saying, Mr. Marlowe?"

"Mark Valentine hangs out at Victor's on Saint George Crescent on Drummoyne Bay. He is there every weekend. He has a tattoo on his shoulder of a heart and a bunch of roses. You know, a play on his name. He is 178 or 180 centimeters, sandy blond hair, wears sunglasses a lot, even inside."

"That is a start. Associate."

Terry hit Bartholomew in the stomach three times, causing him to vomit spittle and bile upon himself.

"That, Mr. Marlowe was for being less than forthcoming. Your children have 13 minutes to live unless you give me something more. Your wife will live longer but she will wish she had been killed with the children. Now give me something real or I may let you live knowing that you could have saved them and did not."

"But I don't know... Wait. He drives a BMW, a gold one. He smokes American cigarettes, Camels. He has a titanium ring with a diamond in it on his right hand. Uh... He wears tailored suits and prefers a grey or black suit. He wears Armani shoes. He, uhh... Shit, that's all I know."

103

"Nine minutes. I don't believe you. You're going to let my associates rip your children limb from limb to protect this vile creature?"

"But, God help me I don't know anything else. I…"

"Calm down and think of every conversation you ever had with him. Think of everything he said, every offhanded comment. Does he have family in Queensland? Does he like sport fishing? Does he hunt foxes?"

"Sport fishing! Maybe not fishing but he has a boat. It's… uhh… oh, furtheluva God. Uh…"

"Five minutes Mr. Marlowe."

"I'm trying. It's a 42 foot… *Bacchus*. That's it, that's the name. Please, call off your men. Please!"

"A 42- foot yacht named *Bacchus*. We may be able to use that. Where does he dock it?"

"I don't know."

"Three minutes, Mr. Marlowe."

"I don't know. He hangs out at Victor's on Drummoyne Bay. There is a dock there, right under the Gladesville Bridge, you know, across the, uhh, Parramatta River. I bet he berths it there. I'm sure of it. Please!" Demetrius Marlowe was becoming desperate now and grasping at straws. He had told them all he knew.

Ginger picked up the phone and dialed a number. He told his imaginary associates on the other end of the line that they were to stand down and let the Marlowe family sleep. He repeated it again, forcefully, as if he got some resistance from the man at the other end of the line.

In a matter of minutes they had bundled their captive back into the van, making sure he was blindfolded, to prevent his knowing where he had been held. They dropped him off at a restaurant that would be opening in an hour, with a strong admonition against saying anything and a pack of cigarettes to keep him company.

"What are the chances?"

104

"Terry, one of the things you will need to learn is that it is almost impossible for people to keep secrets except from themselves. If a man does not want to know something then he will deny it to himself or simply refuse to think about it and thereby deny all evidence."

"Ok. But I…"

"Trust me, this is going somewhere. Did you plant the tracker?"

"Aye. The tracker is under the back seat and I took the clamp off the radiator hose. It left a bit of a mark, like you could tell it had been clamped off if you knew what you were looking for. All in all, it was a brilliant method of stopping him in the middle of the industrial area."

"Thank you. I do have my moments. Have a look-see. What's he doing?"

Terry got out of the van with a scope and slipped around the side of the abandoned church to determine that Demetrius Marlowe was walking back to the steps of the restaurant. He had used the pay phone next to the road and was now waiting for someone. He smoked as he waited.

As Terry watched a taxi stopped and picked Marlowe up. The sun was coming up. Terry got back in the van. "I think he's just going home. He called a cab."

"Good. As I was saying, people seldom keep secrets, but I think this one has enough sense to know what will happen if he opens his mouth. We have about a week to make a move. Give it a couple of hours and we have some telephone calls to make."

Between Five Dock Bay and Drummoyne Bay there were lots of boats. The *Bacchus* was not berthed at the docks under the Gladesville Bridge, but it was found, a couple of kilometers south, at the docks on Birkenhead Point. It was a handsome vessel, well cared for. The identification numbers were all that was needed to determine the name and address of the owner, using the insurance companies' program. Terry took care of it from a laptop computer hooked to the telephone line in the motel room. Ginger was amazed at the system. He had fallen behind the times so drastically that he didn't even know it was possible. Terry jibed at him about not even having a telephone line. Ginger replied that he was certain to never have one now for fear that people would be spying on him through the computers.

"Yep. Mark Valentine has a policy against this boat with the Ranchers Insurance Company. He opened the policy through the Wallton Agency on Underwood Road in Homebush. He also has a homeowner policy through them for a residence on Cornwall Road in Regents Park. There is no one else on the policies so he is not married, currently. His beneficiary in the event of his death is… Well, well, Randy Arganmajc."

"Capital. Will this thing tell me his shoe size as well?"

"No, Uncle, but it will tell us he drives a 1998 BMW, gold colored and he has not reported an accident with it. He did, however report some damage to the Mercedes he was driving two years ago. It looks like he hit a tree with it. No charges were filed."

"License plate number?"

"PKY 449."

"Capital. That's all we're going to need. Where is Marlowe's car?"

"It looks like it's been towed to a garage on Youngswood, north end of Rosebery."

"Amazing. Things sure have changed."

"I'm thinking, Uncle, that we've seen nothing yet. The advancements being made are increasing so fast that one man cannot keep up with the progress."

Demetrius Marlowe had counted himself very lucky to escape his captors, though he was still not sure what it was they had intended. He had no love for his underworld

106

contacts and only continued with the operations because they had insisted and had too much on him. Privately, he knew they would never turn him in to the police. He was much more likely to be killed and buried in the outskirts of the city or fed to the sharks. He continued making his sales as if nothing had ever happened and after a week he stopped considering every stranger as a potential executioner. He accepted his next shipment and tried not to look too nervous. His problems began at that point. The day after he accepted the shipment of cocaine he was alerted to a break in. The office he stored the drugs in was a small-time retail outlet in a strip mall. It had a security system, which had been tripped by the burglars, but the safe box was nothing more than a fire safe and it had been wheeled out the door and stolen in its entirety, with half a million Australian dollars worth of cocaine inside.

Bruno Ziegel was the first person to contact Demetrius about the break in who was not a policeman. He got there before the insurance investigator.

Marlowe had never considered insuring the contents of the store and the safe for the actual cost of replacement. He would have been hard pressed to explain how he could have anything worth that much money in so small a safe.

Bruno was not interested in the insurance payoff. He was interested in how he was going to get paid the money Marlowe owed him and he was not shy about asking.

At first, Demetrius offered to give him the deeds to two businesses, legitimate, profitable businesses. Bruno was not interested. His was a cash only business and that was all there was to it. Marlowe assured him that he would pay the money but that he needed some time to amass the capital. He would need to sell some properties and take out some loans. Bruno gave him two weeks to get the money. That was the time frame he would have had the return on the cocaine in. There was no mention of men in executioners' masks but there was a definite hint of a forthcoming execution if the money was not delivered on time.

"What's your take on it, Bruno?" Mark Valentine asked tossing out a half finished Camel.

"I don't think he's trying to fuck us, Mr. Valentine. I think he was stupid enough to let somebody know where his product was and that somebody stole it."

"Ok, look, I want everybody on the lookout for somebody trying to unload a little weight or somebody with a big stash that has no reason to have it. Cocaine makes people stupid and whoever stole this from us is exceptionally stupid. When we find our idiot we need to make an example of him. We may need to make an example of Marlowe as well. I'd like you to visit him on the agreed upon date and regardless of what he pays you, break one, no, break both his legs. Do not deliver to him again, ever. He is out of favor. I do expect my return on investment from you or there will be the same sort of repercussions in your bullpen. Have I expressed myself sufficiently?"

"Yes, Sir, Mr. Valentine. I'll make sure it happens."

"Call me in a couple of weeks. We'll go sailing."

"Oy, Uncle, they really shove this shit up their noses?"

"They can stick it anywhere they want, I don't care. What matters is what we do with it."

"It's worth a lot of money, eh?"

"Can it. We are not drug dealers. This shit is responsible for destroying men's minds. It makes you happy for a little while and then it sucks your brain out and turns it into chum. The only thing a man is good for after a while is drawing in sharks."

"I'd like to try some. So I know what I'm dealing with." The truth was that Terry had done cocaine a couple of times, and heroin once, but he did not know how Ginger would react.

108

"You're a man, I can't tell you what to do. I can tell you, if you start doing that shit, we're done working together." Terry could not have known it was a hollow threat. The truth was that Ginger was really enjoying the action. He wouldn't stop frivolously.

"It's not worth that."

"That's what I've been trying to tell you. Stick to beer. The worst it will do is make you fat and stupid."

"So who are we going to stick with it?"

"I can't say, yet. I think we got away clean. I'll wake you about two in the morning. I think we need to get another big dog to protect the place but until we do, we need to keep on the alert. If we made any mistakes, they'll be coming for us."

"Right-o. I'll get some tucker and sleep early. Oh, when are we going to get the tracker back?" Terry asked opening the refrigerator.

"I think we need another one. I don't want to go anywhere near Mr. Marlowe for a while. He may well be found in the trunk of that fancy German car."

"No worries, I took the identifying numbers off the tracker."

"I don't know if they can track it back by the signal."

"Not if I don't access it. Hey, what about this cheap safe?"

"Oh, we can use that as well. We just make sure the proper people find it."

"Right. Beer?"

"No, and I would appreciate it if you don't drink while on watch. If we are going to do this, we do it right, or we die."

"Well, I'll have one with supper and then turn in."

"Two days."

"Eh?"

"Two days and we go to the suburbs and find a willing victim. Someone who deserves what he gets."

Two days later they contacted the eldest son of Beth and Jerry Cuthbert and told him to take care of the place for a couple of days. Jerry Junior was more than happy to since the pay was good and the work was easy.

With all the factories in Blacktown, there was a good smattering of taverns but the clientele were all of the older, stodgier variety. Their first choice was a poor one. They had more luck near the airport, in the Quakers Hill area. They found a club that catered to the younger crowd and observed it for a while, after dark. It wasn't the sort of place where a line formed at the door and you only got in if you were pretty enough or cool enough. It was a coke den. The windows were covered well enough that one could not see in from a car. One of them would need to go in and Ginger was too old. His appearance would send up red flags. It had to be Terry and he would need to certify himself as one of the crowd. In most places buying people drinks qualified you, but not here. Here you needed to be passing around the cocaine and snorting it yourself. Terry looked the part but his experience was almost nonexistent and with Ginger watching he did not want to slip up.

Sitting on a bar stool with a draught, Terry watched and listened. The music was loud and the crowd was lively. They were drinking and dancing and passing around cylinders that dispensed a little snort or they used little spoons. Many of the men had grown the fingernail on one little finger long and used them as a spoon for snorting. Everybody in the place was doing it and it did not take long before someone offered Terry some. He refused and told the man he was sticking to beer. It got him a funny look and then more funny looks. It was obvious that he was in the right place but unless he joined in their brand of celebration he would be marked as a narcotics agent. The funny looks became more obvious and a dead zone formed around him. He finished his second beer and left.

"Look, I felt like those blokes were going to lynch me. I can't stay in a place like that without blending better and without doing what they are doing I can't blend," he told his uncle.

"We've had this conversation."

"Well then, we need to look some other way. It's not worth a row with you, and I need you for this. Let's drive off."

"All right. We're being watched now. They marked us. We need to try a different club. Let's try something off a ways."

They knew Liverpool would be a wash as soon as they saw Cowpasture Road. They got a laugh from it and headed downtown to the Annandale area instead. This was a hotbed of activity. Scantily clad women and well-dressed men partook of a variety of illegal substances openly. The clubs were hopping.

The ruse was simple. Terry pretended to be very drunk. He saw the man with the diamond rings, the one people deferred to. He stumbled into the man on the way to the bathroom and dropped a very large bag of cocaine on the floor as he did. The man said nothing, just pocketed his incredible good fortune. It worked smoothly and Terry stumbled out the door unidentified and unnoticed. There was no need to make friends and no reason to blend.

The heavily stoned victim did not notice that he was followed when he left the club 20 minutes later. He went home to secure his prize. When he woke in the morning, he did not see the fire safe, which had been cut through the back, sitting in his back yard.

Mark Valentine had been at Victor's the night before. He found a message on his answering machine when he arrived home. It told him that "the Irishman" had stolen

111

Demetrius' "item" and sold it to the man at this address. Mark made some calls and arranged to have a crew meet him in the morning.

Four men got out of the 1987 Lincoln Town Car in front of the house on Denman Avenue. It was very early in the morning and three of the four men were hung over to some degree. The fourth man did not drink; he got his pleasure from less socially acceptable means.

Two men went to the front door and two moved to the back. The doorbell worked and was quite loud, bringing to owner of the house to the front door. The two men in front pushed their way in and knocked the owner to the floor. The back door was opened and the two men from the back yard pointed out, as they entered, that there was a safe in the back yard with a hole cut in the back.

The man who was not hung over was then employed in his favorite form of recreation: torture and mutilation.

Two blocks down the street Terry Kingston wiped the sweat from his forehead. It was not the temperature that caused him to perspire. He had seen the men enter the house and he had developed a pain in his stomach. He had not considered that there might be innocent victims in the house that would suffer the wrath of Mark Valentine. The intended victim had been alone in the club. It was not until after he returned to his home that the question of collateral damage had reared its ugly head. He might well have a wife and children in there that would not survive the interrogation.

It was too late to change the plan now, and it was too late to walk away. The dice had been rolled.

Inside, the victim was already in horrible shape. Valentine had instructed his mechanic to "soften him up" and that man had gone to work ruthlessly. The other three were in the kitchen having breakfast. There was nobody else in the house. They could not have known but their target's wife had taken the children and left three months earlier because of domestic violence issues.

Mark Valentine pulled his gloves back on after breakfast, and instructed a man to clean all the prints up. The owner of the house looked like he had been softened up the way a cube steak is softened up. He was babbling uncontrollably, pleading for his life. The story that he stuck to until the bitter end, was that he had picked up what someone else had dropped. He had not known the man and did not know where the safe came from. He disavowed all knowledge of "The Irishman." Of course, his breakfast guests did not believe him. Once they determined they could not get the correct information from him, he became a liability and his throat was cut. He bled to death in his own living room, secured to a chair with baling wire.

Terry's hands were sweating as he saw the door begin to open. He was sitting on a wooden box between the front seats of the van. It gave him the correct height to rest the barrel of the Mauser on the lip of the window. The SP66 fired a .308 round, held one in the chamber and three in the magazine. The scope had already been sighted in. The van was parked close to the corner with clear access right across the front lawn of the corner house.

Terry wiped his right hand on his denim work pants. There was a ringing in his ears and he worked his jaw to equalize the pressure. Unbidden the old tune came into his head. "Kookaburra sits in the old gum tree." The men had reached the street. "Merry, merry king of the bush is he." The Mauser barked and one man dropped. "Rack, rack, sight. Laugh." The Mauser barked again and second man dropped as those remaining headed for cover behind the Lincoln. "Laugh kookaburra, laugh kookaburra, gay your life must be." The third shell smashed through the Lincoln's radiator, destroyed the cooling fan and cracked the water pump.

113

Terry set the rifle in the back of the van and started the engine. The two remaining gangsters had opened fire with their pistols but they did not know what they were shooting at so the neighbor's automobiles suffered some broken glass and bullet holes, but the van was not struck. Looking over the rim of the window, Terry saw his uncle coming up behind the two men, with a shotgun. One of them turned around but never got off a shot. Ginger tore him in half with buckshot and then shot Mark Valentine. He had tried to shoot Valentine in the arm and leave the man alive but the buckshot was too efficient at that range. The man was dead before he hit the ground.

As Terry drove up to the carnage he saw his uncle pull a .32 revolver and systematically shoot each corpse in the head. It was a vision he never forgot. It was not so much the fact that he did it; it was the cold and machinelike efficiency with which he did it.

Ginger got in the van and the two drove off without a word. Ginger was reloading his pistol and Terry was humming the kookaburra song. The petrol tank was full and the pair did not need to stop until they got to Orange where they swapped out the van for the Holden and went to breakfast at a local diner. In the diner they acted as normal as could be possible. After breakfast they sat on a railing by the road and smoked. Terry was curious how his uncle could be so calm.

"It's not that I'm calm. I just look calm. Most of what you see is what you want to see. You look calm as a clam and that's what you want everyone else to see."

"I'm shaking inside, like I had an electric wire running through my chest and somebody is turning on the power from time to time."

"You'll be fine. I'll be fine. What do you say we get a dog? You know, a guard dog? Today."

"Yep. That's a good idea. A puppy, so we can train it?"

"No. We go to the pound and get the meanest, nastiest, snarling piece of junkyard monster in the place. Muzzle him and take him home with us. I don't care if he hates me, as long as he hates everybody else as well."

Terry stopped in at the office for a few minutes, just to check on things and access the news. The police were counting the slaughter on Denman Avenue as a drug deal gone wrong. They had no suspects.

The pound at Orange did not have what they were looking for, and Clergate did not have a pound but they found what they needed in Mullion Creek. Mullion Creek had a lot of horses, and dogs that chased horses were usually shot on sight. This dog actually liked horses, however, it hated people. It had been dropped off by someone, or had escaped and migrated to this area. When Ginger asked about a dog pound he was told there was none, but if he could capture the mastiff running around with the horses, he could have it. They would have shot the dog if it chased the horses but it did not. It actually seemed to think its job was to guard the horses. It was half the size of a horse anyway. The rancher would have kept it but for the fact that it wouldn't allow anyone near the herd.

The capture was not difficult but restraining the animal was. It weighed almost two hundred pounds and when roped it hauled two grown men around as if it was trained to pull a trailer. It took half the day and five pounds of beef to calm the animal down. Terry immediately named the dog Hercules and spent a couple of hours bonding with it. He needed to punch it in the head half a dozen times to get its attention and half a dozen more to get its respect. Later he complained that he had almost broken his hand bonding with the creature.

Hercules turned out to be not only massive but intelligent as well. After a couple of days he became the guardian of the farm. He accepted Jerry Cuthbert Junior without question since the younger man spent so much time on the farm. He was not fond of Jerry Senior, but begrudgingly allowed him access. Anyone else pulling in the driveway would be best advised to remain in their vehicle until they had been cleared. He was no sheep dog in that he would not herd them. He did, however, protect them. Ginger took a shine to the massive beast and it fell in love with him the way Pincher never had.

Chapter Seven
Twist the Knife

Demetrius Marlowe had managed to come up with the money he owed his underworld associates by selling stock holdings and some property he owned. The fact that his immediate contacts had been killed did not relieve him of the debt. He was left out of the business after that and was immensely relieved. It was not long after that he hired a manager to run his businesses and he moved to New Zealand.

The Troy Brothers offered a very large bounty on the head of "The Irishman." It yielded no verifiable results since no one had heard of this phantom gangster.

The Kingston Agency continued to be run efficiently and effectively. Its owner would appear from time to time to use the computers and check the books but he seldom had any issues with the staff. His employees had been in their positions so long that some of them were nearing retirement age.

In the year 2000, just after the entire world breathed a collective sigh of relief that the "Y2K" problem had not created global anarchy, the Irishman problem emerged again.

Terry kept his room in Orange as his primary residence. He also rented an apartment on Henley Road in the Homebush area of Sydney under the name Thompson Barber. He paid six months in advance so there was no question or contact from the landlord. The Homebush area is just south of the railroad tracks and Henley road is only two and a half blocks from Centenary Drive, which crosses the tracks. Just over the tracks, Centenary Drive merges with Route 4 giving quick and easy access to the outer loop of expressways. Homebush is home to the workers in the industrial area on the other side of the tracks as well; middle class factory workers, hard drinking but honest and dependable. Most of all, they minded their own business. For anyone who asked, Terry worked a third shift job in Auburn: just far enough away so nobody would expect to recognize him, just near enough to allay suspicions about the commute, night shift so he could go about his business during underworld business hours.

Under the nickname Tommy, Terry infiltrated the lower echelon of the drug world. He bought drugs and used drugs and sold occasionally. He transported drugs up and down the coast and got a good reputation as a wheelman and a cool head under fire. And he waited.

Once the drug addicts trusted him, as much as a drug addict can trust anyone in the seedy world of rip-offs and judicial sting operations, Terry began to make small moves. He already understood the motivations but was shocked at the amount of money there was to be made. He was not in it for the money, although he did make some along the way, he was there for real opportunity. It was not long in coming.

One of the things Terry learned from the first "Irishman" incident was that killing mob members did little, but upset the hornet's nest. Within a day Mark Valentine and Bruno had been replaced. Valentine's spot was taken by Henry Cuthbert and Bruno was replaced by Victor Wellington. The only way to really upset the apple cart was to hit them in the pocket.

The 1968 Holden Monaro was a great way to start conversations. It could hold its own against the newer vehicles and was an endless source of conversation. Terry drove it when and where it would be seen but he did not rely on it for business. It was, after all, over 30 years old and garnered too much notice on the street. Terry kept it in a rented garage space and drove a Land Rover for business. It had more cargo space and, while it was not generally an urban vehicle, there were a sufficient number of them around that his did not evoke comment.

In June of 2000 Terry Kingston managed to wrangle an introduction to Victor Wellington. Victor was a bit of an odd duck. He dealt drugs but did not partake in them. He drank to excess but only on Saturdays. He visited the ladies of the night but only liked oriental women. He was short for an enforcer but nobody to underestimate. He carried an expandable baton with a lead ball on the end and was highly proficient with it. He also carried a pistol but was not known to pull it out except in the most dire of circumstances; he preferred the baton.

Victor agreed to meet "Tommy" because he had heard good things about his driving abilities and he was in need of several good wheelmen. The job was not drugs, this time, but guns. Terry told Victor he had no problem with that and Victor said they might be in touch.

Terry kept a cell phone with him at all times but Ginger still refused to have anything to do with them so the only options open were to drive to Molong or to write a letter. Terry opted to write Ginger a letter which was delivered a couple of days later. The following day, the cell phone rang and Ginger Kingston was the caller. They had a short conversation about the situation, without any specifics. Terry pleaded with Ginger to get a phone but Ginger refused. The following day the phone rang again. This time Ginger was calling from Terry's room in Orange. He called to say he had laid in supplies and was merely awaiting the specifics of the operation.

Five men were in the mini-van. It was not uncomfortable; there was air conditioning and the tinted windows kept the glare and inquiring eyes out. The trip north was boring until the four passengers started talking and telling tales of heroism and derring-do. Terry was sure that most of them were lies and he fabricated some of his own, being careful not to name names or provide any sort of location or time frame.

There was some trouble on the Pacific Coast Highway at the bridge over the Karuah Estuary. Apparently a man had gone missing and his boat had been found empty so there was quite a search and rescue operation going on. The mini-van was not stopped for long and it was not searched, but it did make the drivers nervous for a short while.

The munitions had been offloaded from a ship at Port Macquerie somewhat over 300 kilometers north of Sydney. What the drivers did not know was that they were expected to transfer the crates from the intermodal truck trailer to the four smaller trucks they would be driving. This caused a bit of friction and a fight almost broke out.

Terry grabbed one of the other drivers, the one least upset by the situation and made a pact with him. Together they loaded the first two trucks with half of what was in the trailer and headed out. There was no doubt in Terry's mind that the remaining guns and ammo would be loaded somehow.

Once Ginger got the call, he headed out from Orange. The only good way to the Pacific coast Highway from there was to get to the outskirts of Sydney and head north to Route 15 and east. It was a 350 kilometer trip and took almost four hours. Terry got the call when his uncle was on Adelaide Street in Irrawang, north of Newcastle. Terry and his associate had already passed Irrawang and he did not know the location of the other two trucks. All he knew was they had "Fresh Fish" printed on the sides and the picture of a dancing fish.

Ginger set up a watch on the overpass of Mount Hall Road. He had field glasses, a camera, several cigars and a thermos of coffee. His van was out of sight. He did evoke some comments standing there and the local constables noted his presence but did not question him, as he was not causing any trouble. He only had to wait for an hour before the first of the trucks passed under the bridge. He did not

120

wait for the next one, just quickly packed his gear and headed for the van. He could not have caught the first one but he waited just off the entrance ramp for the second one. It passed his location five minutes later.

"What do you mean torpedoed?" asked Henry Cuthbert, trying his best to control his voice.

"The last truck didn't show up and the driver didn't answer so we went looking for it. You'll see it on the morning news. They evacuated two square miles around it and we couldn't get anywhere near. It shut down both sides of the bloody SN Freeway. Nothing was moving between Asquith and Brooklyn. I got the news on the CB radio. Somebody took a rocket and torpedoed the last truck. The fire hit the bullets in the back and all hell broke loose. Jimmy was driving. I suppose he's dead." Victor had lost all pretense of calm and was shaking in fear. He had been promoted prematurely after Bruno was shot and had not developed the nerves needed for this sort of position. He made an adequate thug but he was no manager. Henry was charged with the management operations.

"Fuck, who knew about the operation that could have done this. Are you sure there was a body? I mean, are you sure Jimmy's dead?"

"I can't be sure of anything. I couldn't get anywhere near the fire. They didn't even let the fire department near the fire. From what I understand they just let it burn. I told you, they shut down the freeway. The truckers said there were bullets flying everywhere. What a mess."

"Shit. The other trucks are safe?"

"Yeah. Bonner brought the first one in and then Tommy. Jimmy and Joe were arguing about loading theirs so they were an hour late on the road. Joe got here but Jimmy was 10 minutes behind him, like you said to. He was last in line."

"Good God, this is going to be a mess." Henry picked up the telephone. "Ralph, the three trucks that came in today, I want that stuff transferred to a semi. Lock it up. I want those trucks washed and fueled and ready to go. I want the semi out of there and in a truck stop until further notice. Get a driver to stay with the load. Label it "Hazardous Material" and give the driver layover pay from the time he hits the stop. I want the bill of lading to say he's carrying bleach and I want that truck locked up tight. No, don't worry about it. Send it to Melbourne, give it week, no two weeks to get there but I want it to stay right outside of town. And tell the driver if he leaves it alone I'll feed him his youngest son. Now get it done."

"You forgot the run they were on. What happens when the coppers come around asking why the bloody truck was full of guns instead of fish?"

"Those trucks haul fish every day. That is what they do. If one of our drivers decides to try something outside our purview, we are only responsible for the liability incurred, not for his bloody actions. We knew nothing about any guns."

"Of course not, Henry. I know nothing about it."

"Now go away, I have some damage control to implement. Go down to the Randy Penguin and get a drink, if they're still open. I'll call you there."

Henry picked the phone back up and dialed the number for Abel Troy. The phone was busy. He could not have known the reason. Abel Troy was at that moment getting the news "Compliments of the Irishman."

The Sydney area held well over three million people in the year 2000. By the end of June there was also a huge influx of foreign interest, due to the Olympics. There were so many new faces, it completely disrupted the underworld information system. The tavern owners were ecstatic since their business increased impressively. The demand for drugs, particularly marijuana and cocaine, went through the roof. Several shipments of cocaine from Peru had been arranged months earlier and arrived at Brisbane in the beginning of July.

Terry got wind of the big shipment through keeping his mouth shut and his ears open. He was not scheduled to meet the delivery.

Bonner had gotten the honor of hauling this one down. He was set to drive up the coast in a deadhead semi and swap the empty trailer out for one full of blankets, Indian artifacts, uncut jewels and $3,000,000 worth of pure cocaine. Bonner trusted Terry to some extent. They had done a lot of drinking together. Bonner mentioned offhandedly that he was scheduled to go to Brisbane. There was no discussion of what the load was or of the fact that Bonner was not a real truck driver. Yes, he had a Commercial Drivers License, but he did not drive tractor-trailers often. Terry decided he needed to get a CDL as well, though he never did. It was not that he could not drive a tractor, he simply never got around to the formal training.

When Bonner headed north, Terry had the specs on the tractor. He also got a look at the two men who were with Bonner. He did not recognize either of them but they looked very dangerous. This did not bother Terry. If he had his way, these men would never get a chance to be dangerous. They had not seen him but he had not been able to get the tracker on the tractor, either.

It is difficult to follow a professional truck driver in anything but another truck and impossible to do so unseen. The drivers in the cabs of the big rigs that so many commuters love to hate are charged with the task of not killing anyone. When there is nothing but truckers on the road this is not a difficult proposition. It is a different matter when the roads are clogged with hundreds of cars, each driver intent on his own agenda and destination. A lemming run of humanity flowing around the trucks like stones in a river, but the stones are moving too. Truck drivers' eyes are in their mirrors constantly. They need to be. Each full-sized tractor and trailer combination has at least six blind spots where the hapless pedestrian commuter, self important and aggravated, can hide. If the driver does not keep watching his mirrors, he does not see the smaller vehicles approach. He may not know they are there. That is a formula for disaster. On top of the fact that they are always looking behind themselves, any large hill will slow a loaded truck down and any automobile that does not pass a truck that is creeping up the hill, in a low gear, is immediately suspect.

This was the first operation Terry had attempted without Ginger. He had no time on this one and cursed his uncle's refusal to have a telephone installed. He also cursed his own lack of foresight in not keeping an RPG launcher on hand.

Sydney to Brisbane takes a full day and full day back, on a good day of hard running. Bonner would not be pulling back through Newcastle until late the following day, at the earliest. Terry took his time and found his spot. There were thousands of spots to choose from but Terry wanted one close enough to the road that he could get right back on without having to waste time. Just south of Haxham and north of Minmi, there were a number of dirt roads used by people from Newcastle to run their ATVs about. The east side of the road was off limits since it was a farmers' cooperative, but the west side was free and there were several stands of trees to choose from.

Terry hid his Land Rover as best he could behind the tree line and took up a position inside the trees. He broke off some fresh branches and gathered some dead ones to make himself a bower under the bole of a fallen gum tree. Then he lay down in the back of his vehicle and smoked for a while. Then he took a nap.

The sun had not quite set when Terry's target drove into view. He had calculated the time and mileage carefully but had almost missed it. If the sun had set before the truck reached him, his preparations would have been in vain.

Diesel engines run on heat and pressure so they need massive radiators. When the three .22 caliber bullets punctured the truck's radiator, a huge cloud of steam and coolant enveloped the cab. Bonner jammed on the brakes and pulled to the side of the road.

Terry grinned and swapped the smaller rifle for his Mauser. The grin disappeared when he saw the car behind the truck pull over as well. Initially he thought it was some well-meaning travelers stopping to help, but he soon realized that it was an escort. Two men got out of the car with automatic weapons. Terry's grin returned as he adjusted the distance on his scope.

Three men got out of the cab of the truck, one of them pulling the cowl forward to expose the engine. The two men Terry had marked the day before moved to the back of the truck to join their escort.

"Four shells, four shots," Terry said, as he squeezed the trigger the first time. "One," he said as the first man collapsed. "Two," indicated the second man's demise. There was no immediate three as the remaining two gunmen ducked behind the idling car.

"Kookaburra sits under the old gum tree. Merry, merry king of the bush is he." Terry sang softly as he waited. His enemies had no targets and wasted no bullets firing blindly. They had seen the direction the shots had come from but they could not see Terry. Both men were holding automatics and they had enough range to reach him but they did not take a shot without a target.

One of the men scampered around the road-ward side of the truck before his assailant could get off a shot but when the last man tried to he was cut down. Time was of the essence now; Terry could not afford to let this standoff become protracted. He swapped his short magazine but he had no shot, now. The truck could have moved for a short while but not for long. The car was idling in expectation. Terry shot one of its tires, which exploded with a bang, but he still had no live target.

There was no more time left to wait. Terry slid out of his cover and headed for the Rover. The light was failing quickly. He started the engine and drove down the tree line until he was confident he had passed the truck. He pulled his twin .38 revolvers as he slid through the woods. He slipped within sight of the truck but could not see the two remaining men. He hazarded that they may be hiding in the cab. That suited his purposes well. He holstered his guns and pulled a pair of fragmentation grenades off his fishing vest. After tossing them, Terry made sure there was a tree between the truck and himself. The grenades bounced under the cab and exploded. Terry could hear the bark of his tree shredding from the shrapnel. He could not risk exposing himself so he wrapped a rag around his face and pulled a fishing cap adorned with flies over his head.

"Never leave a witness," he muttered as he yanked open the passenger door. Inside the cab were the ruined remains of Bonner and the remaining gunman. "Sorry, mate," he said and shot each of them once in what had been their heads. Then he moved to the back of the truck and shot each of the three men lying there, in the head. He left that gun at the scene.

He ran back through the trees in the semi-darkness and jumped back into the Land Rover. A kilometer down the road he found access and sailed back toward Brisbane and then west from there. He spent the last few hours of the night in his room, in Orange, cleaning his guns and smoking too much.

The constables had a wonderful time with the scene. Homicide detectives from Brisbane were there all night. The bodies were identified, tagged, bagged and shipped. The reporters were not invited to the party but they were there anyway. The morning edition read "Vigilante Sniper Kills Five North of Brisbane".

The truck was hauled away once the crime scene investigators were done with it and it was unloaded at the impound yard. The cases of uncut stones were valuable but not worth a sniper attack. The blankets were still in good shape but the Indian artifacts had suffered a bit from the shrapnel and the cocaine that was hidden inside them was spilling out.

The news reported that there was a drug war going on. They tried to downplay it and made sure they specified that it was not in Sydney. The City Council and Lord Mayor of Sydney were foaming at the mouths. There was no possible way they could have a drug war erupting just as the Summer Olympics were about to start. Everyone from the Superintendent to the Commissioner would be released from service if they did not squash this "foolishness." They had one month to track down the perpetrators and either capture or kill them. There would be no excuses and no reprieve.

The police force went on a rampage. They raided the coke bars, they arrested everybody who was even suspected of dealing drugs. They rounded up every heroin addict on the streets and threw them in jail. They arrested the homeless, the drunken, the pot smokers and the unlicensed pimps. In short, it became dangerous for an Australian citizen to walk the streets after dark. The tourists were left alone if they could prove they had entered the country recently but the residents of the city were put on alert. If they were disruptive in the slightest way they would suffer ninety days in jail. Nothing was going to spoil Sydney's shining moment. The jails were bursting with inmates and the city began to ship them out to work farms, wholesale.

The visions the Troy Brothers had of vast revenues pouring in from the drug trade at the games disappeared. It was not so much the monetary damage that the affair caused as it was the long-term damage. Supply routes were disrupted and older, respected employees were being imprisoned. The police that had looked the other way so often were now forced to exercise their judicial authority. The customer base was drastically decreased as it was increasingly arrested. The owners of the coke bars were indicted and the extremely lucrative outlets were shut down. Marijuana growing facilities that had been overlooked were raided and the crops burned.

It was not just the lower level distribution chain that suffered either. Drug sniffing dogs were brought in to truck stops and distribution terminals. The sensitive noses of these dogs cost the Troys more than any Irishman could have alone. It got so bad that the truck drivers who had been smuggling illicit loads for years started refusing the jobs. Some of them insisted on taking vacations and some of them quit. Even legal commodities were becoming harder and harder to get transport for.

Terry spent the next couple of weeks between Orange and Molong, never heading toward Sydney. He had never given a thought to the carnage he would cause within the underworld network until it began to happen. Once the dragnet began, he sat back and laughed. He and Ginger had many good conversations about how to cause something to happen without doing it yourself.

Terry refused to answer his cell phone when Victor Wellington called and did not return his calls. He made the mistake of answering it when Henry Cuthbert called.

"Tommy, where have you been?"

"Uh, Henry. I, uh, I left the city for a little while. Things are so bloody hot in Sydney I thought I'd just lay low for a while."

"No laying low. I've got a job for you."

"But, Christ Almighty, there's somebody out there killing drivers. The Road Patrol is on us like ticks on a dingo and I think it's a bad move."

"Look here, you little shit! What you think is of no concern to me. If you don't get your ass down to Melbourne to pick up this load, I'll make sure you never work again. I'll get five big wogs to exercise your asshole 'til you can never walk again. Am I making myself clear?"

"Uh, yes, uh I guess that's clear."

"You call me when you get to Melbourne. I'll make this one worth your while but if you ever try to buck me again, I'll have you killed or worse. Get going, now, and call me when you get there."

"This looks promising, Chief Inspector Rahim."

"What is it, Sergeant?"

"The ballistics on the rifle shells we pulled from two of those men match the rifle used in the Denman Massacre."

"Sergeant Farrel, I wish you wouldn't call it that. It sounds like we have wholesale slaughters here on a regular basis."

"Sorry, Inspector. The Denman case is in a Sydney suburb, Annandale, I think. Same sort of MO. Shot the drug dealers from a distance. None of them left alive. Finished them off with a bullet to the head. Now in Sydney, that was done with a .32. Up here that was done with a .22 caliber pistol, the pistol was left on the scene. The killer used hollow points, so we don't get a lot of ballistic evidence, but we don't need it. He left the gun there."

"What else did it tell us?"

"Nothing much. Serial number is gone, ground off. No prints on the gun. No unexplained prints in what is left of the truck. Get this, this guy is prepared. Like a mechanic, a tool for every job. He shot the radiator with .22 long rifle slugs. That stopped the truck. He shot the men we found behind the truck with military grade .308 slugs. He blew up the cab of the truck with World War Two ordnance, American pineapples. Then he went in the truck and shot each of the men in the head with hollow point .22 shells, walks behind the truck and does the same for the three men in the back, and leaves that gun there."

"Did he need to do that?"

"They were all dead before that point."

"So, he's thorough and efficient as well as being a dead shot. Did he take any other guns with him?"

"I don't think so. Each of the men was found with a weapon, even the driver."

"Then that gun is supposed to tell us something. I want it examined with a fine-toothed comb. Now, what about the vehicle?"

"We got plaster casts of the tire marks, Goodyears, aftermarket. They sell them anywhere. The wheelbase indicates it's probably a Land Rover. We got a couple of good casts of the killer's boots. He was wearing rubber boots. Oh, I got an aerial view of this." Sergeant Farrel pulled out a one meter by half meter overhead shot of the area. "Here is the truck, with the car right behind it. This wooded area is where we found the foxhole. There was no brass left at the scene, no gum wrappers, no cigarette butts, no piss stains on the trees. He gave us nothing."

"Wrong. He gave us everything, we just don't know how to look at it to see what it really is. I want every tire store in the State questioned. I want to find out who is driving a Land Rover with this kind of Goodyears on it. Get me a list."

130

"Inspector?"

"Yes?"

"Do you think this is the same bloke who blew up that fish truck full of guns?"

"I'm going to reserve my judgment until all the evidence is in."

Two days later a witness came forth. She was a college student who was understandably nervous about the whole affair. She had been driving up to the truck as it exploded. She hit her brakes and slid to a stop by the side of the road. She had seen a tall man with a rag tied around his face, a fishing vest and a fly fisherman's cap on, come around the back of the truck and shoot three times. Then he had gone into the woods. At that point the young lady gave her car all it had and got the hell out of there.

The police grilled their witness for a couple of hours but she could give them no more than she had. The police concentrated on finding anyone who had been seen wearing fly fisherman's gear that day but there were no leads. Nobody had seen such a man. The witness insisted that there was no way she could identify the man. She had not seen his face and did not know the color of his eyes or hair.

The police were looking for a fisherman. The Troy Brothers were looking for an Irishman.

The newspapers released the composite sketch that their witness had pulled from her memory. It could have been a picture of Jack the Ripper for all the good it did. The vest and hat had come from an earlier time and there was no tracing them. The mistake the police had made was mentioning the rubber boots. Terry burned them in the wood stove, making sure there was nothing left. He swapped the Land Rover for the van and stashed the Rover away in a barn. He left it on jack stands and swapped the Goodyears out for a set of Coopers on new Cragar steel rims.

When he got cajoled into making a run from Melbourne he stayed on the straight and narrow: no drinking, no drugs, no women, no speeding. He took the back roads and drove carefully. Starting out at three in the morning let him arrive about three in the afternoon. He was surprised by the bonus he received and did not even know what he was carrying. He didn't care. If he was to continue doing what he was doing he would need to be in Henry Cuthbert's good graces. Victor Wellington was aggravated at him for not calling in, but he put it off by telling him he got no service outside the city. Victor had trouble like that as well so he let it slide but there was something in his eyes that Terry did not like. He also did not like the fact that his associates had seen the van. It would be useless after that day. The van mysteriously caught on fire that night and Terry authorized the compensation check for Thompson Barber a week later. Needless to say his insurance rates didn't go up.

Chapter Eight
The Specialist

"Good morning, Brother."

"Good morning, Abel. Are we still going to the warehouse this morning?"

"Unless there is a change in plan."

"No, no change in plan. The flight will arrive at 9:14. That means we will be waiting for about an hour before the specialist gets there."

"Abel, I know I agreed to this yesterday but I'm still unsure about it. Bringing in new people is always a risk and this one isn't even from the country. How is he supposed to find what we can't, if he doesn't even know the lay of the land?"

"Relax, Adam. You know the procedure and this one comes very highly recommended. Royal Scots Dragoons, action in the Middle East, ruthless and deadly. They say he's worth every penny. If he does not produce, we do not pay. The down payment is negligible. Let's face it, if he can get rid of the Irishman, he'll be worth every penny and more and if he can't, then we don't pay. He goes by different names but I have it on good authority that his given name is Gordon MacMaster."

The limousine crawled through town and out to a warehouse on Elizabeth Street in the Lakemba district. An inside loading dock served as a parking spot for the limo and the office was bulletproof. The phone lines were swept for bugs on a regular basis and a log kept of the activity. There was a computer with internet access in the office but neither of the brothers had bothered learning how to use it. They paid subordinates to do that sort of thing.

Inside, the warehouse was relatively secure. The employees went through a different kind of pre-employment screening than most companies. It was important they were able to forget things very easily.

Abel laid out the figures the accountant had cooked up for him. The numbers inflated the sales and revenue of a number of concerns to account for the influx of dirty money. Of course, with the increase in revenue, one must have an increase in output as well. To increase sales one must increase expenditure and delivery. That was where things could get treacherous in the laundry chain.

If a company wants to do business it needs to make sure the books look right. Raw materials in, must equal finished goods out, to a certain extent. The warehouse on Elizabeth Street held a lot of finished goods that had been purchased, paid for, and reported as sold. Much of this material could not have been sold: squirt guns with no cap for the fill hole, glow in the dark hula hoops, action figures from movies that bombed at the box office, plastic cactuses and stuffed two-headed sheep. They sold a truckload of singing plastic fish to themselves at least once a year. The cost for these things was negligible though they paid full price on the books.

Adam often groused about what he thought was an overly complicated system but Abel was in charge of the figures and insisted that it had worked thus far, why would it require a change? Buying their own merchandise from themselves with drug money had made them very rich and respectable in the legitimate businesses arena. From time to time the goods were shipped overseas and sold again under a new set of production numbers and the companies recouped most of their investment cleanly. At least on the books. The raw materials were sold to themselves again and their partners in crime got their cut. All their partners had to do was inflate their production and shipping numbers to match the repeat deliveries and make sure they pay taxes on it. The taxes were,

134

after all, what the government was really concerned about and with this system, they got their cut too.

Adam and Abel finished their business with the accountant and shooed him out the door. The next order of business was waiting in the employee lounge, drinking machine coffee out of a paper cup. The warehouse manager pointed out the door to the office and the specialist filled the doorway entering it.

Some men can walk into a room unnoticed. They can walk through a crowd without being seen. The specialist was no such man. He was about 194 centimeters tall with flaming red hair and beard. He had shoulders like an ox and hands like sledgehammers. His thick brogue gave him away as a Scotsman, though Adam and Abel couldn't have told Scot from Irishman.

"Call me Glasgow," rumbled from his chest.

"So, mate, where you from?" Terry asked casually. He already knew where the man was from and he had a good idea why he was here.

"Glasgow."

"Glasgow. Is that in Queensland?"

"No. Scotland."

"Oh. You're in town for the Olympics, then?"

"Something like that. I'm a photographer."

"It'll be a while before there's anything to photograph."

"Oh, there's always something to photograph in a city like Sydney."

It was still early for the drinking crowd so the place was relatively empty. Terry had taken a stool at the bar and was nursing a beer. He had seen this big Scotsman informally interviewing another wheelman, in a different tavern but had not been seen, himself. The photographer disguise was a handy one, considering that the Olympic Games would be bringing in trainloads of them from overseas. It gave the newcomer a good excuse to be carrying around telephoto lenses and long distance viewing equipment. It did not explain the bulge under the man's jacket however. Photographers seldom carried guns.

"Are you planning on doing any wildlife photos while yer here?"

"I hadn't planned on it. There's plenty of photos of kangaroos and koala bears out there. No money in it, unless the Smithsonian or Geographic contracts you for it."

"I could show you some spots outside the city where you could get some shots of native life but we'd need to take a plane out there. It's too far to drive."

"No, I don't think so. Like I said, that's not in my contract. I'm looking for shots of Sydney night life right now. I need to get a feel for what goes on in the city."

"Well, enjoy yourself. This area is not so slanted toward young women and dancing. We do more billiards and head knocking around here."

"That can make for a good study as well."

Terry finished his beer and said his goodbyes. He might be wrong about the photographer but he saw no reason to be too accessible. On the street he walked to a different bar, watching carefully to see if anyone was following him. Nobody did. The bar he walked to was more of a lower class establishment, where men were engaged in proving that they were tough. The air was heavy with macho.

After Kingston had sat for a couple more beers, he saw four large and outwardly pugnacious men enter the bar. He had seen a couple of them before but did not remember where. It was not long before the hackles on his neck rose. There was going to be trouble with these men.

While his instincts had worked in predicting the fight, Terry was too late to avoid it because it was clear they had targeted him for their abuse. Whenever possible, Terry avoided confrontation because he did not want to call

136

attention to himself but in this case it was not an option. They had him surrounded and he was alone. He had no mates with him. The situation called for him to strike first or take a beating. His only other option was to pull a pistol and that was to be avoided at all costs. He almost never took out a gun unless he intended to shoot something.

If Terry had more experience and savvy, he would have known he was being set up. Three men surrounded him and one stood by the door. As it was, he only knew he needed to diffuse the situation or suffer the consequences.

"Gentlemen, let me call a shout and we'll all get pissed," Terry said in an attempt to avoid what he saw coming.

"I won't be schooling with a poofter the likes of you," one man replied.

"Oh, well then, perhaps I can…" The sentence was never finished verbally. A large, round, glass ashtray sat on the counter and Terry butted his cigarette in it before smashing that man in the face with it. The man went down and did not get back up.

The man on his left managed to punch Terry in the face and spin him off his bar stool, but it was a glancing blow because he was already turning in that direction. He dropped to his knee and punched the second man in the crotch. As the unfortunate buckled forward, his nose met Terry's rising head. The man who had punched Terry from the left would have been well advised to watch his own flank as well. A foundry worker who had been playing pool had seen the situation developing and was not one to see a man bullied. That assailant went down, struck in the head with a pool cue.

Terry and the foundry worker looked at each other for just a second and then both headed for the door. The bartender was already calling the police department. The fourth man, the one who had a post by the door, ran for cover. Terry headed south and his new friend headed north but Terry was not satisfied that the incident was as innocent as it had appeared. He stopped a block away and stepped into the shadows of a doorway. He saw a couple of men exit the pub and head the other way. He also saw the reflection of the lights on the lens of a camera, in the front seat of a car across the street. There was not enough light to photograph anything outside the bar but maybe enough to see inside.

The automobile started up and headed, slowly, out of the neighborhood. The police showed up a couple of minutes later, but there was nothing to report except that there had been a scuffle. The fighters had all left the premises and the damage had been minimal; one broken pool cue and a smashed ashtray. Fortunately the fight had not spread this time.

"Victor, I think we have a problem," Terry told his immediate contact. It was late morning and Terry had walked to the pawn shop where Wellington conducted business.

"Come in the office and we'll talk about it." Victor said, signaling to the counter man that he would be stepping off. "What's the trouble?" he asked when he had closed the door behind them.

"I think we have an inspector of some sort looking into our business. He's a big man, red hair and beard, maybe 25 or 30. He's been asking questions, nothing suspicious, just talking to the crew. Says he's a photographer from Scotland. I think I saw him photographing me last night."

"Well that's what photographers do, isn't it?"

"Right, but not the way he did it. I can't say for sure, but I think I saw him hiding in a car outside the pub I was having a drink in. I think he's dangerous. I think he's a copper of some kind."

"I'm sure it's nothing, but I'll look into it."

"Right then. Well, I know it's not cricket to target the man but I think this one…"

"I said I'd look into it."

"Right then. That's all I had."

"No, that's not all. I've got a run for you."

"I'm not sure that would be the best idea. If this man is…"

"Are you telling me how to run this business?"

"No, Victor, not at all. I'm merely saying that if this man is…"

"If he's got a bead on you then the best thing you could do is shut up, take this run and get out of town. I… Will… Investigate. You… Will… Drive. Are we clear?"

"Yes, Sir." Terry could barely stand the condescending tone in Victor's voice. It took everything he had to control himself and not bash the man's skull in at that point. Later he realized that he would have enjoyed that way too much. He had been warned that to enjoy killing is the path to madness.

"The truck is already loaded. It is at this address." He handed him a slip of paper. "They will inform you of the destination upon arrival. Your payment, on delivery, includes a bonus if you get it there on time. Now get moving."

Terry thought it strange that he had been given a time-sensitive run in that manner. He had not been called in, it had been handed to him as if he happened to be there so he got it. The address was the warehouse end of a PVC piping factory. The truck was loaded and locked. The destination was on the manifest. He was going to a concern off Hindmarsh Drive in Phillip, just across the Tuggeranong Parkway from Canberra.

The truck ran smoothly and the day was mild; summer was over. There was no indication that he was being followed, but that did not mean he was not. There was something else that bothered him about this run, but he could not put his finger on it. It seemed legitimate enough and the paperwork was all in order. A light load, in a short truck, so there was almost no chance of getting rousted by the road patrol. There was plenty of time to get there so he was sure to get the on-time bonus. It was too easy. That was what was wrong. It was too easy.

The run went smoothly and the unloading was uneventful. Terry got his bonus in cash, which was very unusual but not unheard of. Then the real job was explained to him. He would be taking a crate full of something to the next destination, in Melbourne. None of this had been explained to him before he left Sydney, but they made it clear in Phillip that he had no choice. He would be delivering this load.

There was no sleeper on the truck and it was eight hours farther to his next destination. He had three hours under his belt already but with some judicious adjustments to the log he could still pull it off, legally, if he hurried. So he logged the loading and unloading times as an hour longer than they were and got on the road. Regardless of whether he went north or south, Terry had to skirt the Australian Alps to get to Melbourne. He chose the southern route as being less hilly, though more populated. He kept the truck at close to the speed limit and was not surprised when he was passed by several full-sized trucks. He increased his speed to match them but was careful not to go so fast as to catch them. The road was not busy as he headed south on the Monaro Highway. He had intended to turn west onto Princes Highway at Cann River but he never made it. As he passed the heavily forested area south of Noorinbee, he heard the bullets strike his radiator.

"Fuck. Some bastard is using my own tricks against me. Thank God they didn't do it in some mountain pass or I'd be boxed in."

Terry floored the truck and held his finger on the windshield washer, trying in vain to keep the coolant from obstructing his view. He would not make it far but he knew

140

if he didn't get past the trap he would never get out of there at all.

It was not far down the road when he heard the first rattle in the engine. It would seize up soon, so he pulled it off the road, jumped out the passenger side and ran into the trees. He heard a vehicle grinding to a halt behind him and men yelling as the doors slammed.

When he felt he was far enough off the road, Terry peeled off his driving gloves and turned back in a sweeping arc, trying to get behind whoever was hijacking his load. He heard two men blundering through the forest behind him and soon enough saw two more men at his truck. They had cut the lock, thrown up the roller door and were moving his load into the back of a panel van. It was seconds later when a Ford Explorer pulled up behind them and one man got out.

"He is undoubtedly the bugger who shot my truck," thought Terry. *"I'll need to deal with these two first, however."*

The two men pursuing him were city-bred thugs. There was no doubt they knew their jobs and were probably quite efficient in the city, but they were no match for Terry in the woods. At another time he would have taken pleasure in sneaking up on them, but he was pressed for time. As he waited for the pair, who were not smart enough to distance themselves from each other, he heard a scream behind him, from the road. He did not have the option to check it out, the two men were too close. He would much have preferred to take them quietly, with a knife or an axe, but once again he did not have time for the hunt. They came around the bole of a large tree and he shot each of them in the side of the head, simultaneously, one round from each revolver. They dropped like stones.

Hoping the men at the road had assumed that his pursuers had shot him, Terry slipped up on the three vehicles parked at the edge of the trees. What confronted him was not what he expected. The Explorer and the van were idling but the three men were not in them. They were lying by the side of the road with bullet holes in them. He did not recognize any of these men, or the two dead in the woods.

"What in the name of God is this?"

Terry froze, just within sight of the incident, behind the vehicles. He saw a car pull up and then take off in a hurry, its owner obviously deciding not to help after all. The crate from the back of the truck had been transferred to the back of the van. With no scope or binoculars, Terry could only rely on his natural sight, but that did not tell him where the shots had come from.

"Bloody hell, I got two, no… I got three choices. I can scamper like a rabbit, into the woods. I can get in that Explorer and leave the load here. Or… I can jump in the back of that van." With Terry, the decision was the action. He ran full tilt out of the woods, cutting in close to the Ford and diving into the back of the van. He pulled the doors closed behind him as quickly as he could and was relieved that no bullets came pounding through them. He leaped into the driver's seat, slammed the shift lever into drive and floored the accelerator. No bullets pierced the van as he drove off.

Cann River was only five kilometers away but there was no place to hide the van there. It was a service town and the only reason for its existence was that it marked the confluence of the Monaro Highway and Princes Highway. Instead of turning west on Princes Highway as he had intended, Terry took Tamboon Road south and pulled off into an orchard. He backed the van around so he could see the road but could not be approached unseen from the road, took a deep breath and shut off the van.

"Christ, I'm in it now. At least one witness drove off. He saw the van. My pistols are hot now but I got no other weapons. The paperwork said PVC but those men were not stealing piping. It's got to be drugs of some kind and if I get caught with them I'm done for. If I don't deliver, they'll think I stole it and I'm done for. Shit. Is there a

map in there?" It turned out there was a map in the glove compartment but there was nothing but farm roads south of Cann River and none of them led anywhere. *"Shit. The manifest in the truck will lead them right to the destination. Oh, hell. I left that in my pocket, good. I can't go to Melbourne or I'll be in it with the constables. North then. Find a spot. Make a call."* Once again, to decide was to implement and Terry headed back to Princes Highway and north from there. About 30 kilometers away he pulled off onto a dirt track in the Alfred National Park and pulled back as far as he could, about four kilometers. Then he tried to make the call but there was no service.

Terry got out of the van and slipped into the woods. He did not think he had been followed, but there may have been a tracker in the van. It was only a matter of minutes before he heard another vehicle making its way down the dirt track road. From the condition of the road, it could not have seen more than a dozen vehicles a year, and most passenger cars would have gotten stuck in the mud if they went any further. The sound of the engine stopped and Terry knew he was right. He reached in his pocket and pulled out two shells to replace the ones he had used, slipping the empty brass into a hole in a log.

It did not take long to determine that his current target was not the same class of clumsy buffoons as he had shot earlier. He had slipped out of the Land Rover and had not closed the door, let alone slammed it. He had slipped into the woods on the far side of the trail from Terry and was undoubtedly making his way toward the van.

If Terry disabled the Land Rover he would not be able to get around it to get out. He was not sure he could go much further down the road in the van as the track degraded badly further on. Also, he wanted the Rover. The van had been marked but he did not think the Rover had. It was a perfect swap, all he had to do was kill the man who had driven it and that should not be a problem.

The track was not easy to follow initially. The man had some skills for forest work. As it got closer to the van and the ground got damper, the footprints were easier to pick out. Terry was stepping over a fallen log when he heard the voice behind him.

"Ye'll be stopping right there. If you make one untoward move I shall kill you where you stand." The voice had a heavy brogue that Terry had heard before.

"You must be the Scotsman who's been taking pictures." Terry said without turning around.

"Aye, and you'll be the Aussie who almost got hijacked. Now drop your weapons. Do not think for a minute I will hesitate to kill you."

Terry dropped his pistols in front of him thinking the log would make good cover but his captor was having none of it.

"Back yourself off that log and move toward me slowly, backward. I want to see your hands at all times. You may be driving but yer no driver. Good. Now take off your vest. Turn around."

Terry turned around and looked right into the barrel of a 9mm automatic. "You're very good in the woods," he said. "Not many men can sneak up on me."

"You still have a lot to learn. I didn't sneak up on you, I merely let you slink past me and there I was, behind you."

"Who are you, really?"

"That's not important. Let's just say I'm your guardian angel."

"You shot the men back there at the truck?"

"Aye, that is to say I shot three of them. You shot once that I heard, but you were the only man that came out of those woods. No, you're no driver."

"And you're no photographer so let's come clean. You didn't shoot me when you had the chance, then, and you didn't shoot me now, so I think you won't be shooting me."

144

"I'm thinking you were planning on shooting me," the Scotsman said with a crooked grin.

"I was. I didn't know but that you were just another member of whatever team it was that tried to kill me and take my load."

"If I find it necessary I will kill you, but I don't see it now. Your pistols are dirty, now, right? Both of them?"

"Yes. If I had another I would have tossed them into a river."

"Pick them up, one at a time, two fingers. Crack them and empty the shells into your hand. Now put the shells in your pocket. Give it to me. Now the other one. Keep the pistols in your holsters and put your vest back on. We need to get rid of them where they won't be found. They'll be searching the rivers around the bridges. An area like this has nothing happen for 10 years and when it does they get onto it like a terrier with a rat. We need to move and we need to move now. We leave the van here, but first, I want to know what is in the crate. Walk in front of me and don't even consider putting your hand in your pocket."

"You never told me who you are."

"And you don't need to know. Call me Glasgow."

Back at the van Terry found an old-fashioned jack handle that could be used as a crowbar and he opened the crate. Inside was a load of heroin.

"You didn't think it was plumbing, did you?" asked the Australian.

"No. I knew she wasn't plumbing."

"Would you have taken the job if you knew you were hired by drug dealers?" Terry cocked an eye at Gordon, attempting to gauge his reaction as well as his words.

"A job's a job. I always see the job through, regardless of what it is. I was told that someone using the name Irishman was playing hob with the legitimate concerns of the

Brothers Troy. I suspected something was foul but a job's a job."

"What now?"

"Well, lad…"

"I'm nobody's boy."

"No, and that you're not. Mate, then. What we do now is deliver the load, mate. The van stays here. We'll set them on it later. We need to put the load in the Land Rover and deliver it. You see, my job is not done. I contracted to find the Irishman and I have not yet done that. We did manage to remove some fools from the scene, but unless I miss my guess, none of them was the man I'm after."

"What makes you think so?"

"The man I'm after destroys the product or leaves it for the bobbies. Those men were stealing it. They were after the load for their own ends, not to hurt the business but to profit from it. No, those fools had nothing to do with the Irishman."

Halfway back to the road, the Scotsman had Terry stop the Rover and bury the revolvers off the trail after wiping them clean of prints. The rest of the trip was uneventful. The men at the destination were suspicious but that was cleared up with a phone call.

Terry spent the first part of the trip looking for a way to get the drop on his new accomplice. That proved to be impossible, or at least too dangerous to attempt, especially with a crate of heroin in the back of the vehicle. It was not too long before the Scotsman's wit and casual manner impressed Terry a great deal. He was already impressed by the man's hunting skills. He decided that he could have done worse for a partner. He also decided that he would kill this Glasgow soon. It is always beneficial to know who is hunting you, it evens up the playing field.

After the delivery, the day was done. The two checked into a motel for the night, planning on driving back to Sydney the following day. The telephone call was placed from Terry's room and a message was left. The number went straight to a message pager. The phone rang with the return call about a beer and a half later.

"Glasgow here. Yes, Sir, we have thwarted an attempt to highjack the load. The truck was disabled and had to be left on the scene, unfortunately. No, Sir, I do not wish to have this conversation on the telephone. Yes, Sir, Mr. Barber acquitted himself with style. It would be my pleasure. We will see you tomorrow evening then. Thank you very much, Sir." The Scot hung up the phone and turned to Terry, "Mr. Troy says you are to get a bonus for actions above and beyond the call of duty."

"Which one?"

"Which what?"

"Which Troy did you speak with?"

"Well, it wasn't actually one of them at all, it was a subordinate. I'm sure he has sufficient swing to authorize a bonus, however."

"I'm sure he does, I just like to know who I'm dealing with."

"You'll meet him tomorrow evening. He wants to meet you personally. In the mean time, we need to get something to eat or we'll get drunk.

It seemed to be in each man's interest to get the other drunk, as well as it was in each man's interest to keep himself sober. Terry wanted to know everything he could about this new card in the deck and the Scot wanted to know where Terry had learned to track and fight. Neither of them wanted to tell the other anything and the night turned onto a cat and mouse game of lying and telling more lies to cover up the lies that had already been told. Before long, they had told so many lies they had forgotten half of what they said and more of what they heard.

Morning came and the men rolled out of their beds. The motel had a pot of coffee brewing in the office and breakfast was a short way off.

"When are you planning to go to the police with your story?" the redhead wanted to know over eggs and sausage.

"Shit. I hate dealing with them but I suppose I'm going to need to. I'll need a barrister on hand if I'm to be interrogated."

"Let me make another call. It may not be necessary. Did the paperwork list you as the driver of record?"

"Well, yes, but I have that in my pocket."

"Then that load got hijacked, plain and simple. Let me make that call."

Gordon called from a pay phone instead of the motel phone, but he was clearly unsure about the sanctity of the phone at the other end of the line. He made some inquiries about the dead men on the Monaro Highway. Who did they work for? What was their capacity? He finished up with the questions, "Oh, then he was the man driving the truck? And he was killed in the hijacking? And the load was never delivered? "He hung up the phone and said, "All right, Mr. Barber, you are cleared. It seems one of the unfortunate victims of the robbery was the driver in question and the load of polyvinylchloride is now on the black market."

"Brilliant."

"Not so. Did you sign anything in Canberra where you picked up the load?"

"I think so."

"Mmm. We need to stop there on the way north to adjust the paperwork."

Once they were on the road, there was nothing to do but talk so they did a lot of it. Terry was full of questions about what his new associate did for a living. It was not a security guard job that caused people to shoot each other with high-powered rifles.

"You are an assassin, right?"

"That is a term I have heard applied to my class of gentleman adventurer before, though it is not one I prefer."

"Mercenary, then?"

"That is also appropriate."

"How is it you came to this profession?"

"I was in the Military. Royal Scots Dragoons, as was my father. He made a career of it until it killed him, I decided on money over honor and became a freelance."

"You've seen action then?"

"Aye…" It looked as though he would not say more and then started speaking anyway. "I stopped counting the number of men I'd killed. It's not the men though. It's when you need to kill women and children that makes it so bad."

"You've killed children?"

"Aye. When I had to. We all did what we had to, or we never came home. Many of us never did. I'd like not to talk about it."

"Very well. What you do now, I have some familiarity with it."

"I know you drive a truck but there is something else, something driving you that is not money or laziness or drugs. Not one of the usual motivations for blackguards."

"Is that what you think I am? A blackguard?"

"You transport loads for a living. You suspect what they are, but you do nothing about it, so you are a blackguard."

"And what if I had a different agenda?"

"Then you would not… Is there something here I am supposed to know?"

"No. I am just a blackguard truck driver."

The two men fell silent. Something had just happened and neither knew exactly what. A curtain had fallen between them. They knew each other a very short time. They had developed respect for each other but not trust. Each recognized that they had said too much and there was no way to take it back.

When they reached the warehouse in Canberra the dock clerk fished out the paperwork in question. The only thing that really saved Terry was that he had not left his copy in the truck. The paperwork was officially changed to read Byron Burger instead of Thompson Barber. Byron Burger had been found dead on the side of the road the day before. Terry and Glasgow had a short conference with the plant manager. The manager was understanding and compliant. An emergency load of PVC had been sent south the previous day. Byron Burger had driven it. It had been hijacked and Byron was killed.

The manager had already seen the morning news. He was waiting for the constables to contact him. Glasgow reminded him that it would be best if he showed up on their door first. Then the pair headed north again. The plant was closed when they arrived in Sydney so they vowed to come back in the morning to adjust the original manifest so it read that Byron Burger originally drove the truck out of Sydney.

They stopped for some dinner and drinks and, at 10 at night, they appeared at the Riggers Club, inquiring after Mr. Randy Arganmajc. They were admitted as far as the coat closet and asked to wait. Truthfully, they were not dressed for the Riggers Club and should have changed clothes before presenting themselves.

The concierge returned and as tactfully as he was able he asked them if they could use the servants' entrance in the back of the building. They acquiesced and went back out. Terry should have known they would not make it in the door dressed as they were. He knew the long and honored history of the Riggers Club. The Scotsman could have been forgiven for not knowing.

They waited for a short time, in the pantry, before Randy Arganmajc joined them. Randy was wearing an Italian

150

silk suit. His palms were soft and limp when he shook hands. Glasgow apologized for not knowing that the club required a jacket and he introduced Terry as Thompson Barber.

"Ah, yes, I have heard some good things about you," Randy lied.

"Well, you are about to hear some more. It may be good news but I think not."

"You are about to tell me about the affair in Victoria. You are going to tell me that the men involved were in the employ of one Tony Samfier. What more is there?"

"Due to the quick thinking and sharp wits of your driver, that load was delivered. I know your interest in that particular load ended when it was delivered in Canberra, but if you contact your men in Melbourne, you'll see that the load was delivered intact, despite the fact that the truck was disabled. I was in contact with the top of your food chain yesterday and he authorized a bonus, in cash. I thought it best we spoke to you about it personally."

"I'll have it delivered tomorrow. I need a couple of questions answered, however. Who sent you on this trip, who knew where you were and who knew what you were carrying?"

"Honestly, Mr. Arganmajc the only one I can say for sure is Victor Wellington. He handed me a slip of paper when I stopped in to tell him about a suspicious character I caught sight of."

"What suspicious character?"

"This one." Terry pointed at the Scot. All three of them chuckled.

"Oh. So you went into the office and he handed you a job."

"That's right, the pawn shop office. He said the truck is loaded and locked and I'm to take it to Canberra and right away. Time sensitive and I got a bonus for delivering on time. In cash, no less. Then when I was unloaded, that's when they stuck the crate in the back and told me I was taking it to Melbourne and I wasn't going to stop till it got there."

"That was the crew in the warehouse in Canberra?"

"Right. Now I don't think they had anything to do with the ambush. They didn't seem nervous or surprised to see me when I showed up this morning to change the manifest."

"You changed the manifest?"

"Just the name. It wasn't my idea but we changed it to one of the dead guys. The load was never officially delivered, since we didn't have the truck, it was stolen but you can make the call. You'll find that the load has been delivered."

"I think that is all I need to know. Remember to wear a suit and bathe next time you come here. This club is not for the public."

The men that hit the truck were indeed all in the employ of the organization headed by Tony Samfier, in Canberra. They were lower level men, not the sort to plan out an operation of this magnitude. It may well have been either of the intervening layers of management that had set it up. This did not matter to the Troy brothers. In their less pristine affairs, it was the responsibility of the managers to ensure that their subordinates are behaving themselves. Tony disappeared. Tony's family disappeared. Tony's first assistant disappeared and several of that man's associates. The operation was done silently, with precision and finesse. The bodies were never found and the positions were filled a week later.

Chapter Nine
The Verdict

"So, Specialist, in your opinion have we found and eliminated the Irishman?" asked Adam Troy over a snifter of very old brandy.

"No, Sir. I believe the men who performed this operation were riding on the coattails of the notoriety. They wanted you to believe it was the Irishman who pulled off the operation but they were merely thugs, following orders. I cannot be sure who hatched the plan but it was one of theft, not spite. They would have killed the driver but not out of malice. They were doing a job as instructed."

"Your reputation is secured by this very statement. A lesser man would have taken credit for the operation, taken the payment and disappeared."

The Scotsman smoothed his bushy red beard and cracked an uneven grin. He took a draw from the fine Cuban cigar he was enjoying and filtered the smoke through the hairs. "If I had done that, you would have known. What kind of specialist would I then be? Perhaps a deceased one."

"You are a good judge of men. How did you know that particular load was going to be attacked?"

"I didn't. I was watching the driver of that load, not the load itself. He is a very capable man, not given to panic and is working toward your best interests. A lesser man would have died in that incident but not this one. Thompson Barber not only took the bull by the horns, he delivered the load. He never asked for the bonus, that was my idea. I told him about it and he hasn't mentioned it since. He's a good man and on your side."

"But you were watching him. Why were you watching him?"

"He's not been with you that long, right? He's young and sometimes the young are ambitious, their ambition not yet tempered by good judgment. I tested his spunk the night before and found him not wanting in spine. He saw me watching him, not something I would have expected of a fool. His first move the following day was to report that he was being watched. It was Victor I suspected, not Tommy. I realize in these troubled times that a little bit of discretion is advisable but to send a lone man on a mission of such importance seemed either foolishness or cunning. It turned out to be the latter."

Abel Troy set his snifter down on the luxurious hardwood table and said, "There may well be a long-term job for you here when you have completed your current assignment. We can always use a man with a canny eye for this sort of thing."

"Thank you, gentlemen. I'll consider that a vote of confidence and return to my assessment of the crew and the situation. I'll assume Victor Wellington will not hamper my investigation?"

"You may safely assume that he will no longer be working for any of our concerns."

"Then I thank you for your time and your attention. And I thank you for this marvelous brandy. In my opinion, it would be best if Thompson were given a month off and supplied with a vacation of sorts. I'm sure you have a travel office somewhere that would find it possible to work in a complimentary cruise or something. Most of the attacks are done north of the city so I will be concentrating my efforts northward after I eliminate some of the suspects. Yes, I am still convinced that the information is coming from the Sydney area."

"Very well. I shall make arrangements," Adam Troy seemed very pleased with himself.

The redheaded Scotsman did not precisely follow the game plan he had outlined. It had been his observation that most men of wealth did not reveal all they might and certainly

154

no more than they had to. He had already determined that though they owned many legitimate businesses, they had financed their empire with drugs and guns. He had nothing against guns, they were an integral part of his life, but he was not in favor of the growing drug trade. He also wanted to find out what sort of men he was really dealing with. Their money was good but their ethics were suspect.

Two days later, at the end of the working day, Henry Cuthbert showed up at the warehouse with four men in trench coats and a hooded, bound figure. Gordon MacMaster knew then that Victor's time was limited. From an adjoining rooftop, through the high-powered scope of a rifle, he saw Victor Wellington tortured to death in despicable and unmentionable ways. He was no stranger to torture and the extraction of information but there was no information asked for. The man was made an example of in front of his associates as a warning. The message was clear and brutal.

Gordon MacMaster set down his rifle and pulled on his beard for a moment. His senses were alert for anyone on the roof with him but his mind was working in a different mode. Gordon had killed many men in many different ways. He had shot them from afar and he had felt their life's blood gush over his face. He had poisoned, though not often and he had thrown men off buildings and cliffs. He thought back to a time when he was not as practiced as now, a time when he still had the principles and patriotism of the Royal Scots Dragoons.

As part of the United Nations force in Iraq, MacMaster had been tasked with a specialized job. Despite being called "The Mother of all Conflicts" by Saddam Hussein, Desert Storm was more of a flash in the pan. Unfortunately, several men were trapped in Iraq when hostilities ceased. They had been inserted in pairs, as sniper teams; they were called Desert Rats. MacMaster was one of them and while his attention was taken by a target, he and his spotter were captured from behind.

The rules set forth by the Geneva Convention have no sway in the Middle East. The treatment of prisoners by any of the former Ottomans is as it always has been. Torture is as accepted a tool now as in the dark ages and almost looked upon as necessary. Psychological warfare is as important, or more so, than physical slaughter. They consider an enemy who is terrified into inaction to be better than a dead one. And so, Gordon MacMaster was forced to watch the torture of his partner, spotter and friend. They cut off his eyelids, they clamped a battery to his testicles, they shattered his hands and broke his legs. Then they told Gordon that the only way he would get out of the mud hut they were sequestered in was if Gordon beheaded his partner and fellow Scotsman himself. By this time his spotter was praying for death.

They presented the battered but unbeaten MacMaster with a shamshir, a curved Persian sword, and instructed him he was to decapitate his partner on film or he would get the same treatment. He looked into the eyes of his partner and saw the pleading, the desire for death, the will to die. Four men covered him with automatic weapons as he raised the sword high. He screamed "For Scotland" cut the man's head from his body, following through with a whistling arc into his nearest tormentor's crotch. The man screamed and lurched forward. Two of the Iraqis didn't even see what he had done, they were concentrating on the man's head rolling on the floor.

Even with his wrists tied together, Gordon MacMaster managed to wrest the automatic weapon from the hands of his injured opponent. The lead began to fly and two men were down before the other two understood what had happened. Then they went down. Gordon cut his bonds on the bloody edge that he had dispatched his Brother-in-Arms with and secured the remaining weapons.

The incident never made the news because it was so far behind enemy lines. There were no authorized missions that far inside Iraq and no foreign soldiers were captured. There would have been a media storm from both sides if word had reached the networks. MacMaster had never learned the name of the town he was held in, but when the following day arrived, there was nothing left living in that little desert town. In a cancerous and all consuming rage, he had killed every man woman and child living there and he had not stopped there. He killed the sheep and goats and chickens. The sole survivor was a dog that ran from the carnage when it began.

That was the day the Scotsman had compromised his principles. That was the day he learned there is no glory in war, only in surviving. That was the day he decided that there would be no more killing for queen and country. A piece of Gordon MacMaster had died that day but another was born. Gone was the bright-eyed patriotic soldier and born was the slayer. Gone was 'My country right or wrong' and born was The Honorable Assassin.

Sitting on the roof and witnessing the torture of Victor Wellington was enough. His pervasive guilt over the slaughter of innocents was blamed on the torturers in that little Iraqi village. He transferred that guilt and a portion of the rage that still lived inside him like a parasite, waiting to burst through to the surface, to the men in the warehouse. He reserved a portion of it for the men pulling the strings.

"Well, mate, did they do you right?"

"I'll say. A bloody European cruise," Terry grinned. "I've never been to Europe. It says a Mediterranean playground. It stops in Spain, France, Monaco, Italy, Greece, Turkey and then back. Ah, I think it goes to Gibraltar, wherever that is."

"Enjoy it, mate. There's nothing like a little international influence to round out a man. 'Now is the winter of your discontent made summer by this glorious son of Troy.'"

"What's that supposed to mean?" Terry cast a suspicious eye on his drinking partner. He had noticed that the Scot was given to quoting the masters when in his cups, but he seldom understood the quotes and seldom yet recognized them.

"Never mind. It's not even appropriate."

"Well, I'm leaving in a couple of days so I got no jobs coming up. I'm going to drink beer and chase women here, and then I'm going to drink beer and chase women there."

"Capital. Sounds like a plan, mate."

"Oy, we'll have you sounding like a backwoods Aussie yet."

Ginger got the letter with the address of the PVC factory and its adjoining warehouse a couple of days later. Terry explained in his missive that he did not really think it was necessary, but that he had been given the cruise by direct order of the top men and that to refuse would be a faux pas with long-reaching consequences. A simple explosion would be sufficient and something indicating it was the Irishman behind it would remove all suspicion from Terry's head if any remained. He wrote that if nothing happened while he was gone then he would be unable to continue his present path. He felt sure the cruise was the Scotsman's idea. His respect for this "specialist" was growing. This was becoming a dangerous game. At the same time, his reputation was growing and his position was becoming less tenuous.

Terry had been gone a week when the Irishman put a bundle of dynamite under a propane tank outside the warehouse, blowing half the building off in the middle of the night.

Terry had the time of his life on his Mediterranean cruise and flew back after two weeks, departing from Gibraltar. He was surprised to be met at the Sydney airport by the large Scotsman. He was taken to a tavern where they had a couple of beers and the specialist told him he wanted an assistant. Thompson Barber was the assistant he wanted and that was what he had gotten. Terry's acceptance of the position was all that was wanting. Terry ran his fingers through his blond hair and asked what the job consisted of, knowing he was going to accept it anyway.

Ginger got a surprisingly well written letter from his nephew a few days later.

Uncle,

I wish to thank you for the details of the endeavor you undertook on my behalf while I was on holiday. It made for a wonderful surprise upon my return. I have been selected to be an assistant to a specialist, who is charged with the pursuit and apprehension of the Irishman.

I am particularly pleased with this turn of events as it allows me to refrain from delivering loads of a questionable nature. While I was sailing, I had serious misgivings about my chosen path. I had visions of myself acting as that which I have detested for so long. It is fortuitous that I have been chosen for a calling more near what I would care to pursue.

I will be in touch but I feel it imperative that you maintain your current anonymity for the present. My new mentor is a man of exceptional ability and fortitude who has much to teach me. I will visit when I feel comfortable doing so. Give my best to the dogs.

Sincerely,
Thompson Barber

Ginger laughed uproariously when he read the letter, then he read it again and burned it.

159

Terry Kingston was in high spirits. He loved the cruise and was delighted to have been chosen to find himself. His good humor was not to last long however. He began to wonder what he was about to embark upon. He went to the library and began to look through the newspapers from the past couple of years. It was tremendously time consuming but they had not begun scanning them into a database yet so the only way to find anything was by hand.

The Olympics began and the city was overrun with tourists. There were crowds on the streets all day and night, most of them with mistaken preconceived notions of the nature of Australian life. The police forces were kept on overtime just controlling the crowds. The tavern owners were overjoyed. The beer flowed freely and the influx of foreign money was a welcome boost to the economy.

Terry was in constant contact with his mentor by phone. It was almost the only number he dialed. They ate dinner together nightly, in different restaurants, and coordinated what they had learned. Terry was fascinated by the man's methods which combined a sort of amateur forensic science, study of human nature and interrogation. His own research was revealing a few things as well.

When the pair walked into The Roo in the downtown business district, they had not been expecting anything but dinner. Terry was thinking about the gym and his mentor was thinking about dinner.

"God bless me, Gordon MacMaster!" came from a man seated in a booth with a tall attractive blonde woman. The woman started chattering in German.

"Seien Sie ruhiger Dummkopf. Kennen sie nicht meine Name hier," came from the Scotsman's mouth.

The man in the booth slowly and carefully put both his hands on the table on either side of his meal. "I am not here looking for you and I do not seek trouble. I am here for the games. I'm sorry I thought you were somebody else. I

160

apologize." His accent was thick but his diction was good. He turned his eyes from the Scot and told his woman, in German, that they would be leaving now and there were to be no questions.

Terry watched them closely as he took his own seat. They waited only until the Scot turned his back on them and then they headed for the door.

The rack of lamb was good in The Roo and they drank it down with beer. Terry did not know how to broach the subject discreetly so he waded in. "Where did you learn to speak German, Gordon?"

Gordon MacMaster tossed a rib bone onto his plate and said, "That fool was mistaken. He thought I was someone else."

"No worries, mate. I've got no secret agenda. That man knew you from somewhere, though. He was terrified. He thought you were here to kill him."

"He was mistaken. I never saw him before in my life."

"Let's cut the crap, Gordon MacMaster. You might not have known him but he knew you. He knew who you are and what you do." The look on his face told it all. If Satan himself had sprung up out of his dinner plate, he would have gotten the same look.

"Call me Glasgow. Do not use my proper name again or Satan himself will spring out of your rack of lamb."

Terry grinned but Gordon did not; it was clear he had issues with his given name. The two sat looking at each other for a few seconds and Terry's grin faltered. He dropped his eyes to his plate and addressed himself to the remains of his dinner. He did not know how far Gordon would go to protect his identity and did not want to find out the hard way. He felt he had won a round but there could be repercussions. His uncle's words rang in his ears, "Never leave a witness." It was a standard of the industry.

The next day, in the library, Terry did a search for "Gordon MacMaster" on the computer. There was nothing appropriate. He looked up the "Royal Scottish Dragoons" and found a long and illustrious history of combat and honor leading back to the seventeenth century. He studied the history of the "Royal Scots Greys" and paid particular attention to their recent exploits. No names were listed but the regiment was honored for their work in the deserts of southwest Asia. There was no mention of assassinations, but they would not have been acknowledged if there were any. Assassination was against the rules.

After a bit more research, Terry found his mark, his Irishman.

Indicted twice but never convicted, Lee Pierce had been drummed out of the police department. His crimes, it seems, were a manic desire to enforce the law by whatever means necessary. He had beaten suspects to a pulp on a number of occasions and even shot one to death. It was the one he shot but didn't kill that had finished his career. As is usual, the powers that be had supported or at least turned a blind eye to his methods as long as they could. He was apparently as honest as could be desired but much too brutal to maintain his position. He seemed the perfect candidate. This was compounded by his recent retreat into a sort of seclusion. He had managed to get a pension of sorts from the government and was living on it, as well as arms sales, in a trailer north of Sydney.

When Terry suggested Lee Pierce as a potential candidate, Gordon went to Henry Cuthbert to ask Henry to get registration and purchase records for the ex-constable. The records were obtained but not really necessary. Henry knew Lee and had purchased weapons from him in the past. It was determined that he owned not only the trailer but the land it resided on. It was determined that Lee's wife had left him during his legal troubles and that no others claimed the

162

trailer as a residence. It was further determined that Lee was a legal arms dealer of sorts who sold weapons out of his home and possessed an arsenal. The license was current and his client list, though unavailable officially, was rumored to include customers from both sides of the judicial divide.

Terry made a convincing case for his choice of suspect and Gordon was in agreement. The man's history of moral indignation backed up by force and brutality played well. The only thing missing was proof. Terry tried to convince his mentor that there was no need for proof. They did not need to catch the man in the act to know it was him and they were not tied by the government's rules of engagement. The proof would be in the pudding. They would take out Lee Pierce and the attacks would stop. Gordon was not so easily convinced, however.

"Assassination is an art," he told his protégé. "If he is the Irishman, then, yes, the job is done but I need to be sure. If the Irishman gets his weapons from this man, and we decommission this man, then the attacks will stop for a time due to the supply lines being cut." He took a huge guzzle of beer, belched and then continued. "If the Irishman knows this man in a different capacity and the man has some sort of unfortunate accident, it may spook him and send him underground, temporarily. This would lead us to believe we had gotten our man, when in reality all it would do is make us his next target. Or you, possibly, since I will have been gone for other venues. Assuming he is good enough to know who caused the accident. The profile is undeniable, but I would like some further indications."

Terry popped the last of his chips into his mouth and chewed on them slowly. His mind was racing a mile a minute. He was learning so much about what he was up to that his head hurt getting around it all. He did not dare take direct action without Gordon's approval. To do so would be a fatal error in judgment. The fact remained however that

Terry was assisting with finding the Irishman and the sooner a scapegoat was found, the sooner the specialist, Gordon MacMaster would leave for parts unknown and stop complicating Terry's life. It was not that he did not appreciate the education, but the Scotsman scared him as well.

Lee's business had no posted advertisement except on the trailer itself. There was no need for him to accept new customers from unknown regions. He had implemented a private policy whereby he expected anyone buying from him to have been referred by a prior customer. The laws regarding firearms had been tightened up as a result of recent actions, some of which the Irishman had taken credit for, but that had not diminished Lee's customer base; it had actually enhanced it.

When Terry and Gordon showed up at the door with a reference from Henry Cuthbert, they were escorted in without question. A call was made and the reference confirmed. Since it was the first time they had done business together, it was inadvisable to ask too many questions about unusual munitions such as hand grenades.

Lee asked a few questions about criminal records. He could not legally sell weapons to Gordon MacMaster under any name since Gordon was not a legal resident, but he was not asked to. The customer was Thompson Barber and Thompson had a clean record. He purchased two .38 caliber Smith and Wesson revolvers, some ammunition for them, and promised to return in a week or so. As a stringer, he did mention that there may be some custom orders in the future. Lee's response was that he was in the business of making his customers happy and that custom orders were just part of the job.

On the trip back to the city Gordon asked, "What did you see?"

"Well, the man had the large bedroom on the end set up with all the racks of guns. One of the small bedrooms on the side had the ammunition. The walls... the walls had some steel plate on them, except for the outer wall. I'm assuming to keep the bullets blowing out if there's a fire, not chopping through the trailer."

"It was stainless. Fewer sparks and tougher than regular plate. A bit costly but not unheard of. What else?"

"Well, he had a fire control system set up, sprinklers. I know they don't make trailers with sprinklers. There were a couple of closets I couldn't see in. No telling what he had in the closets. He had air conditioning set up in the trailer but he also had it set up for the shed in the back. He probably does gunsmith work and reloading back there. Too much heat would cause problems."

"He might do work back there but that was not what the air conditioning was there for. You didn't see the dogs?"

"No, I didn't see any dogs."

"Neither did I, but I did see a couple of large piles of dog shit out back. He does keep the area clean and raked, but he had not cleaned these up. There is at least one big dog in that shed to prevent sticky fingers."

"I thought the place smelled a bit but the smell of machine oil covered the dog stink mostly."

"Always remember that the best defense against unwanted intrusions is a big noisy dog. Anyone willing to shoot the dog would shoot you on the way in too."

A grin lit Terry's face as he thought of Hercules, Ginger's new mastiff.

Once they were back in Sydney, they went to the hall of records. Gordon looked up everything about Lee; Terry researched Linda Pierce. It seemed that Lee had been indicted twice by Internal Affairs for brutality. Both times he had managed to walk when the witnesses refused to testify when scheduled. The third time, he actually shot someone and didn't kill them. With a willing witness and a third charge pending that would most certainly stick, Lee was forced to retire. That was about four years earlier. Linda had left him for good about the same time.

Linda was the daughter of a farm family, good if simple stock. Long-time owners of grazing land and livestock, they had managed to buy up the properties on both sides of them when the land came on the market and so owned a substantial spread. The court orders were sealed, but it looked likely that she had returned to the family farm.

When Gordon mentioned he would like to pay them a visit, Terry insisted that he had more knowledge and experience and he should be the one to go. Gordon did not argue but it led him to ask where Thompson Barber had been raised. Terry told him Tarrytown.

A few kilometers north of Orange, Terry pulled his Holden to the side of the road and opened the petcock on his radiator. He was careful not to drain off too much of the coolant. He didn't want to damage the engine, just make a convincing show of it.

The Pettigrew farmhouse was warm and inviting, the farm well maintained and modern. The family was friendly and more than willing to give him some water for his radiator. He explained that he was a representative of the Kingston Insurance Agency and he was going out to examine some claimed damage when his temperature gauge indicated he was low on coolant, so he pulled in. Having lived in the general area since he was eight years old and on a similar farm, it was not difficult to strike up a conversation about weather and pests and crops and yield and then he got around to insurance. He told them he was certain that he could give them a better rate for insurance than they currently paid if he could just get their names and the particulars on the equipment.

The head of the household was quite old and set in his ways but, while he still ran the farm, his sons and daughters did the work. He had three sons and two daughters. Two of the sons were married and lived in the refurbished farm houses on the properties to each side. The youngest son, Paul Pettigrew, was unmarried and though a large and beefy man, Terry suspected he was a homosexual. The two daughters both lived in the family home. Linda and her sister Lisa were almost the same age. Lisa was a school teacher in nearby Euchareena and Linda worked on the farm, having been recently divorced.

It was not difficult for Terry to catch Linda's eye. She was by far the oldest woman he had ever made a pass at but that diminished neither her looks nor her personality. After he had the particulars recorded for an insurance quote, he was reluctant to leave. He spent some time talking about farm work and noted that he was fond of hunting foxes and rabbits. It worked perfectly. Lisa was still at school and Paul, the youngest son, could not stand the sight of blood, but Linda was more than happy to lend him a rifle and take him out to the woods for a little shooting.

If Terry had thought it would require some work to seduce Linda Pierce he was mistaken. She took him to a secluded glade, set her rifle down and grabbed him. He was more than willing and she was a wildcat. The lack of male companionship on the farm had left her ravenous and when presented with a handsome and well-formed man such as Terry Kingston she was quick to take advantage.

Linda was in phenomenal shape for a woman of her age and had never had any children. Terry was bulging with muscles from his regular trips to the gym and particularly well endowed. The two of them copulated in the woods like wild animals until they collapsed, completely drained. Twenty minutes and a cigarette later they were at it again.

167

Later that day, Terry insisted that he still needed to inspect the damage he had been on his way to see, but promised he would be back the following day to deliver a quote for a policy on the farm.

The following day he did return, much to Linda's delight, and though it was a bit old fashioned, he asked if he could escort Linda to dinner in town. Linda's parents were charmed, and so she and Terry went to dinner, eschewed the movie and rented a motel room for the night.

In the soft romantic glow of the night, Terry pressed her delicately for information on her past. She was reluctant to talk about her previous marriage. She would only say that he had been a bastard and that she would gladly give up the pittance of alimony he paid her to see him in the ground. She refused to tell him how she had gotten the scars on her bottom. This worked well for Terry and he pressed her no further for information. As soon as he was able, he reached for her again and found her ready.

The romance blossomed over the next couple of weeks. Terry did some work on the farm, showing Paul how to replace the head gasket on a tractor, and walking the fence lines. He took Linda to see some of the Olympic Games in Sydney, took her to a movie and generally wined and dined her. He was careful not to respond to the looks Lisa gave him. Lisa was clearly jealous and would have given Terry a ride if he had wanted, but that was not on his agenda. Besides, Linda was all he could handle at present. It was like she was making up for years of lost time.

After a couple of weeks, Linda finally told Terry how she had gotten the scars on her backside.

"He was finally caught," she said. "His viciousness caught up to him when he shot a man. You knew he was a constable, right?"

"No, you never said."

"Well, he was. He came home pissed and angry and put the handcuffs on me and whipped me with his belt. That was when I left him. If I'd had a gun I would have shot him. I hear tell he's got lots of guns now. Of course, he tried to tell me how sorry he was and that it would never happen again, but I knew if I let it go once, it would never stop."

"That's it then. I'm going to kill him."

"No! You'll never get close to him. Lee is a terribly dangerous man. He might shoot you if he knew we were engaged."

"Are we engaged?"

"Well," she said coyly, "in what we are engaged in."

"What you don't know is that I am a terribly dangerous man as well."

"Oh, you certainly are." She reached out her hand and found what she wanted, already primed.

"How bad do you want this done?"

"Oh, I want it."

"No, I mean how bad do you want him punished?"

"What on earth are you asking and why do we need to talk about him?"

"He chained you and whipped you. He left scars on your beautiful bottom and for that he needs to be punished."

She let go of his manhood and looked him in the eye. "You're serious. You really want to kill him?"

"Yes, I really want to kill him."

"Oh, how romantic." There was no more conversation for some time.

In the sweaty afterglow Terry asked her, "What would you be willing to do to see him get his just rewards?"

Lee Pierce was astonished to see his ex-wife at his trailer door. He had not wanted the divorce and had beaten himself up emotionally for a long time over it. He had tried several times to reestablish their acquaintance but it had been

169

in vain. His letters had gone unanswered and she would not talk to him on the telephone. Now, here she was, looking wonderful to him and talking about getting back together. It was too good to be true.

Lee and Linda went on a few dates together and talked about the good times, but she would not sleep with him. At the end of the day she got back in her car and drove off. After a week, it was driving him mad.

It was the beginning of November, the middle of spring, when Linda showed up at Lee's trailer door looking like she had been run through a blender. She would not allow Lee to touch her but asked if she could use his bathroom to clean up. There was blood on her torn clothing and both her eyes were swollen and bruised. While she was trying to get the blood off her shirt she told her ex-husband about the truck driver who had raped and beaten her. She didn't know his name but he was driving an International and heading south from Brisbane. He had raped her after forcing her into his truck at Newcastle and had left her in there, tied up. The abrasions on her wrists were all the proof she needed of that. She had written his license plate number on her shirt. It was all that was necessary to send Lee Pierce into a murderous rage.

As soon as Lee was gone, Linda Pierce opened her trunk and took out a package wrapped in a blanket. After leaving the package in the trailer, she got back in her car and headed for the nearest police station. She walked in and announced in a loud voice that she had just been assaulted by her ex-husband. He had beaten her for refusing him sex and then threatened her with a gun. She claimed he had gone into a rage and left her at the trailer. Her statement contained the quote *"If I stay here I'm going to kill you."*

The man driving the International South from Brisbane was completely innocent. There was nothing in his truck but sundries, imported from South America. He had no idea why

170

the man in front of him kept jamming on his brakes but would not let him pass either. It was obvious that there was going to be a problem so he fished his tire thumper out from behind the seat and prepared to defend himself.

It was not the Irishman's usual *modus operandi* to send a message claiming the destruction, before the destruction had been accomplished, but in this instance he did. The message he left spoke of the job in the past tense as if he had already done it, but the truck indicated as having destroyed was pumping down the road in fine order. Gordon followed the identified truck south after spotting it from the northbound lane and making a quick u-turn. He had spoken to his intern, as he had taken to calling Terry, who had promised he would be waiting at an entrance and would be behind him before he knew it.

When the Jeep passed him at high speed and pulled in front of the truck, Gordon got ready. The man in the Jeep was clearly trying to stop the truck.

The truck stopped and an angry driver got out with a two-foot length of pipe. He was large and would have been able to thump most unarmed men. The man that jumped out of the jeep was far from unarmed, however. The man held a Smith and Wesson 1911 in each hand and as the driver turned to get back into his truck, Lee Pierce shot him through the back. He walked up to the prone truck driver and was obviously about to shoot him in the head when Gordon opened fire with a Glock 22. The .40 caliber rounds from the Glock blew large holes in their target but did not prevent Lee from putting a round in the innocent driver's head as he died. Gordon paused only to put one in Lee's head and then leaped back into his vehicle and drove off at high speed.

"Yes, it was a damn sloppy operation on both our parts," Gordon said. "Both the primaries are dead but I cannot be sure I did not get seen. I would hate for some well meaning citizen to come out and say I was the one they saw shoot a man on the road. I'll be in hiding for a while, at least until the police decide they don't know what the fuck is going on."

"You are sure this was the Irishman then?" Abel was as gracious as always, regardless of the fact that he was discussing a double murder. He smoothed his tie and examined his nails.

"Yes, sir. This was our man. He sent a premature message this time but the voice was the same. I have ended the Irishman's reign of terror. I expect payment will now be forthcoming."

"Of course. A job well done. You will need to go to the warehouse on Barclay Street, after five. You will be paid there."

"I had assumed I was to be paid here."

"I'm sorry, Adam and I never handle cash. It's so dirty. Do you know where the Barclay Street warehouse is?"

"Yes, of course."

Abel saw the cloud cover his specialist's face and asked if there was something wrong. The man said no and left quickly.

The Barclay Street warehouse was the one where Gordon had seen Victor Wellington tortured to death. He wondered what he might be expecting when he got there. He considered calling Terry for backup but, while he trusted the young man as much as an assassin can trust anyone, he did not have enough faith in his judgment. He also wanted not to be the cause of his death.

After five o'clock the warehouse area was empty of traffic but well patrolled by the police. They were bored with their uneventful but necessary routine and usually gathered at the coffee shop about midnight.

Gordon waited for the patrol to pass the area a bit after eight and climbed the fire escape to the roof across the road.

Through the scope he could see men sitting around a desk in an office, playing cards. He took out his cell phone and made a call. Half an hour later a car pulled up and a man carrying a pizza got out and banged on the employee's entrance. The men inside pulled out their pistols, went to the door, and absolutely terrified the young man trying to bring them the pizza they had not ordered.

Gordon was disappointed that he was unable to see the full interaction but he trusted his instincts. It would not be the first time a powerful man had retained his services and expected to be able to get away without paying him. He pulled his cell phone back out and dialed Abel Troy's number.

"Mr. Troy," he began when the secretary had put him through, "there are four armed men at the warehouse you directed me to. As far as I can see they are waiting to eliminate me from the game. You have two options here. Either we take care of this amicably, in a public place tomorrow, or I kill all four of these men and then you and your brother. What do you say?"

"I assure you, sir, there was no such operation planned. I will adjust the meeting place and contact you with the details tomorrow."

"Do not mistake satisfaction for complacency. If I feel my life is being threatened, there is not a volcano in New Zealand you could hide in that I could not find you."

"Threatening me on my continent is a very bad idea, Mr. Glasgow or should I say Mr. MacMaster? I do not suffer threats gladly, nor do I forget easily."

"I do not bother threatening anyone. Why would I? It is a waste of breath. I state the facts as I see them and follow through when necessary."

"There will be no need for follow through. Everything will go as planned and you can go back to Europe with your rewards."

The following day, outside the stadium, in the heart of a weekend soccer crowd, Henry Cuthbert personally handed Gordon an aluminum briefcase full of money. The crowd was moving into the arena, through the metal detectors. It made for a tightly packed crowd on the outside, not the kind of crowd one can move through easily. By the same token, not the kind of crowd that a man can open a briefcase full of liquid funds in.

Gordon MacMaster swam against the tide like a spawning Atlantic salmon and emerged into the road. The automobile traffic was not moving as well as the pedestrians were.

From the third floor balcony of the hotel across the street, a business suited Terry Kingston watched the transaction through the scope of a Remington. He did not keep the weapon trained on his erstwhile mentor, but on the head of his superior within the organization. If Henry had made a misstep, it would have been his last.

Terry did not like the possibility of taking a target in a crowd this size. Even if it had been available in the time needed, the .50 caliber Barrett was out of the question. It was too unique and would have left too much collateral damage.

The plan had been for MacMaster to join Kingston in the hotel room. Terry saw the man enter the hotel and relaxed. He lit a cigarette and sat back, away from the door. The door should have opened before he finished the cigarette, but it did not. Another 10 minutes went by and the door remained closed. Gordon had promised Terry a bonus but it was not this that motivated him. He had learned a lot from the Scotsman and wanted to contact him outside of the country. He suspected that the day would come when he would need to flee the country and it is always good to have friends in new places.

Terry broke down his rifle and stored it in its suitcase. He took off his rubber gloves, put on driving gloves, made

174

sure he had his key card for the room and slipped very quietly and carefully through the portal. The door closed quietly behind him and he moved to the end of the hall, feeling a little foolish and at the same time knowing he might never get out of the hotel if he wasn't careful.

The stairs were deserted, as hotel stairs usually are, and the lobby held only the staff. Gordon MacMaster had disappeared like a puff of smoke.

Terry pulled his driving gloves tighter and considered his next move. The traffic was starting to move a bit freer now, as the crowd filtered into the stadium. There was a public rest room on the ground floor he realized, and entered it. There was no one else there. He went back into the lobby and out the front doors, making a show of lighting a cigarette while looking both ways down the street. There was no evidence of a large assassin or, indeed, of anything untoward. He stood there and smoked his cigarette, knowing he had been deserted and double-crossed and not caring much. What caused him the grief was not the money; it was the trust. He knew, or should have known, that there is no honor among thieves. He should have expected his mentor to disappear like this. There was one other course of action he could have taken but Terry did not think it was in the plan.

By the time Terry finished his cigarette, he was thoroughly convinced that Gordon had headed for the airport or the docks. He shrugged his shoulders and walked back inside, taking the elevator to the third floor. Inside the room, there was a stack of money sitting on his suitcase. He could not believe he had been duped so easily. He actually laughed when he discovered how he had been misled.

"God bless you, Gordon MacMaster. May you live a thousand years and breed a thousand sons."

175

Chapter Ten
Misgivings

Uncle,

It has been an intriguing and exciting few months. I was instrumental in the capture of the Irishman. He was captured post-mortem. I met and said goodbye to an extraordinary man with worldly acumen and microscopic insight. I was sorry to see him go and while I was unable to give him a proper send-off, he has my best wishes.

I have been having some misgivings about my current activities. My resolve has not so much flagged as taken a back seat. I have come to understand the lure of the illicit lifestyle. I do not sympathize with the strata of society with which I have associated myself but I have come to understand them. I have found myself becoming more and more drawn to what I am doing. In short, I am becoming what I pledged to fight against. This realization has caused me incalculable grief and will require a catharsis of some sort, an exorcism.

I have advanced my position due to my recent activities and expect to be engaged in more appropriate actions in the immediate future. I have nothing outlined regarding our previous plan. While it caused some damage, there was always another load right behind it, always another driver, always another gangster. Our activities were nothing but a bump in the road; an expensive bump but nothing more than annoying.

I fear there is nothing I can truly do to stem the tide of corruption that invades this great land. I will continue to work behind the scenes at present but in the long run I may simply retire from this business and perhaps from society as well.

Sincerely,
Terry

Ginger read the letter, amazed at the clarity and presentation. He could not help but wonder where Terry had gotten the style that the letter displayed. He could not take credit for it. The tone of the letter was something entirely different, however. A loss of faith in the innate goodness of man is the top of a long and painful slippery slope, the bottom of which is the loss of faith in one's own goodness, and that is so often self-destructive. Many good men have fallen into the abyss while brooding on the shortcomings of mankind.

Ginger wanted a drink very badly at this point. He actually wanted to get stinking blackout drunk. If he had a bottle of rum on hand, he would have downed it in short order and damn the consequences. Instead, he braced himself and fired up the truck, leaving the letter smoldering in the wood stove.

The nearest pay phone was a good way off and Ginger never used that one. When he finally got through to his nephew, he asked if it was clear to talk. Once he was alone, Terry told his uncle about using a woman for his own purposes and discarding her. It stuck to him like nothing he had ever done before. He had no guilt over delivering drugs. That was part of his cover. There were very few men he regretted killing; they had needed what they got for the most part. He did not even feel bad about misleading his last mentor. He had great respect for Gordon but had still manipulated circumstances to fit his own needs. What was really bothering him, and he had not known it until he spoke with his uncle, was the fact that he would never be able to have an honest relationship with a woman. He did not know how his father had pulled it off in the exact circumstances he found himself in. He had a loving wife and son, blind to his shadowed second life.

Terry got furious when Ginger started laughing on the other end of the line. What kind of cold-blooded warrior gets all oatmeal mushy over a woman he pleased and pushed away? The line went dead quiet when Terry reminded Ginger that he had almost killed himself after his wife had passed away. A few moments of silence went by and then Ginger told his nephew to come home or get laid or jump into the damn river, but to stop pissing about like a schoolboy. Then he hung up. Terry began to wonder if he'd fallen in love with Linda Pierce and didn't know it. He shook his head and went to the pub to get pissed.

When Terry woke the following day, he could not remember how he had gotten back to his apartment or who he had spoken with. This bothered him in the extreme. He could have told anybody anything while he was completely blacked out. He could have done God knows what.

He stood in front of his toilet with a tongue that tasted like fish guts in an ashtray and a headache that flared beyond the boundaries of his skull. He was trying to remember what had happened. He recalled being angry at Ginger and walking to the pub. He could see himself sitting at the bar and drinking some vile liquid of some sort and not caring what it tasted like. He checked his face in the mirror to see if he had been in a fight but there was no physical damage to his face. His knuckles were skinned and bruised but it looked more like he had fallen on concrete or punched a wall than hit anyone. He recited a drunkard's prayer, *"God, forgive me for whatever I did last night, I promise not to do it again."*

He knew the only cure for a hangover was to get drunk again but his stomach felt like he had been drinking battery acid so he dismissed the idea and went back to bed.

The phrase "In Vino Veritas" had never been brought to Terry's attention but he had heard "Loose lips sink ships," and he knew the best way to learn something short of torture was to get drunk with the holder of the secret. When he awoke, still feeling like he had been kicked in the stomach he decided that he had better curb his appetite for strong drink or he would end up dead. As drunk as he had been, he could have said anything to anyone. This led him to a further examination of his situation.

The truck driver that Lee Pierce had shot, just before succumbing to the Scotsman's bullets, was an innocent man as far as Terry knew. He might have a wife and a brood of children left to fend for themselves. He might be supporting his aged mother in a nursing home somewhere or paying for the treatments of his Downs Syndrome brother. He might have… Terry brushed his teeth again and spit in the sink. He might have raped his little sister when he was young or tortured cats in the barn too. Nobody is completely innocent. Nobody is pure as the driven snow. He might have been cheating on his wife and not acknowledged a half a dozen illegitimate children. He might have been a serial killer himself.

Terry lit a cigarette and cleared his throat noisily. He was getting sick of playing the game. It was time he took a more direct action. He had come to realize that nothing he did made any difference in the long run. It was just a short-term scarcity of supply and replaced in no time. He was doing the same work as the police. He also came to realize he was striking at the wrong end of the supply chain. The supply did not stop. He burned a truck load and another comes in right behind it. If he kills, or sets up a gangster for someone else to kill, there is another right behind him with his hand out and a hungry wallet.

Terry was wasting his time attacking the drugs, he might as well try to stop the river. What he should be doing is going after the money. He had tried to hurt the Troy Brothers by destroying their shipments and then delivered more for them the next day. Somehow that didn't make much sense to him any more. He was close enough now, or almost close enough, to inflict some real damage but as an insurance man himself, he didn't want to do the wrong people any favors. He could not see torching a warehouse full of goods that had already been bought and sold once. That would allow the Troy Brothers a free ride to a massive insurance settlement. Plus, the Irishman was dead.

The syrup in Terry's head allowed him to think through all this but slowly, one piece at a time. The drugs had been an easy target once he knew where they were, but aside from a sense of moral righteousness that disappeared quickly, there was no payoff. But he hadn't expected a payoff. He was not doing this to help himself to anything; he was doing it to hurt someone. But it was awfully tempting to take care of himself. After all there was cash in abundance and it was flowing to those he wanted to hurt. Why should he not take advantage of it?

Action was always close behind decision with him, but without information he was swimming blindly. He needed to get closer to his target. He had complained to his uncle that he was becoming that which he detested but this did not seem so to him. Money has a way of blinding people.

It took a few weeks after he broached the idea with Henry Cuthbert before he got a chance for a guard position. He had requested to be assigned to the clandestine cash delivery portion of the business. He had been told it did not exist. He was told it was all done with wire transfers and checks. He knew that was a lie. Drug dealing was always a cash business and always would be.

Terry only got the position because one of the long-term employees on the cash run got prostate problems. He needed to piss every 10 minutes and it became a problem on the long runs between cities. That man was given a less restrictive position and his job was given to a younger man with a good record. Terry took the job as Thompson Barber.

180

The van was not exactly armored in the traditional sense but it was reinforced. Steel plates and sand bags protected the passengers and there was a barrier between the driver and the back of the van. Terry would have expected to get the driver's position but he got lucky. There was little protection for the driver and he would surely die in an attack. The main security of the run was in its anonymity. The labels on the van said "Proteus Armed Security" and for all intents and purposes it was a transport van for security guards. The runs were unpredictable as was the amount of cash transferred and it was not always in cash. The crew always knew what day to be ready but not always what time. One of the benefits of this position was that they never transported contraband of any sort.

There were three other men in the van aside from himself; that included the driver. Sometimes one of the men from the back rode in the passenger seat and talked to the driver, sometimes all three of them sat in the back. They wore their Proteus Security uniforms to complete the disguise and the locked money bags were placed in a locked steel box welded to the inside of the van. It was a hefty affair but nothing that couldn't be opened. Removing it would be more difficult.

The position did not pay as well as some of the more dangerous driving jobs, but it did pay better than a regular security job. It was not exciting or challenging but it was right in the heart of the operation. The transport crew was not allowed to know how much they transported. The bag was locked when it went into the box and they never saw inside the bag. The only indication they had of change was the size of the bag itself and that could be very deceiving. The bag was always bigger the first week of the month and got smaller toward the end.

It should be mentioned that Terry would by no means be the first to consider slipping the money from the van.

181

There had been attempts from inside the organization before. Some of them involved others, outsiders, and some were just mavericks, cowboys. There had only been one such operation that had achieved any success and that was fleeting. A group of men had been rounded up and information was extracted from them. The trail led back to one of the guards and he was found, horribly mutilated, in a dumpster behind a restaurant. The trash was not picked up often, there, and the rats had made a mess of him by the time they found him. They also found his brother, killed but not mutilated, and his sister, raped and murdered. This had happened some years back and nobody had tried anything like it since. Being told about the incident was supposed to remind Terry what happens to those who cross the organization, it served to turn him in the opposite direction. Reminding him that the Troys would go after family, women and children, reinforced his commitment. It didn't matter who replaced them as long as they were removed.

The new position had more access to Randy Arganmajc. Although they had met once, Terry never spoke to him directly, for three reasons.

Randy Arganmajc drove around in new luxury automobiles and wore expensive tailored suits. He was a member of at least two exclusive gentleman's clubs and went sailing on the weekend. He rubbed elbows with the upper crust of society. Randy took those who worked for him for granted; they were invisible to him. Terry Kingston wanted to keep it that way.

Randy was a sharp individual with a head for business. He calculated the angles of offers that crossed his desk and deals that approached him in the smoke-filled rooms of the clubs. If there was a possible benefit for him, he turned his attention toward it, regardless of who was making the offer. This was the one exception he made for his faceless

182

subordinates. Terry had no offers for him and no deals to negotiate.

Despite the fact that Randy was an arrogant child of privilege and a snob, he had quite a magnetic personality. Women were drawn to him and men sought his company. Randy was seldom alone and Terry did not like to be seen by people who might remember him. Moreover, he did not want to like Randy Arganmajc.

When Randy had been forced to replace Mark Valentine and Bruno it had not taken long, but it had cost much in terms of revenue and connections. When he had the decision made for him that he would remove Victor Wellington from service, it had not been as costly. The man who replaced Victor Wellington, Gregory Spencer, was understandably nervous about making a decision. He wanted to check with Randy about everything and was desperate to display his loyalty. At first Randy had found it endearing but it got stale quickly. He knew Gregory was not real management material but his available workforce was diminished. The raids the police had done before the Olympics and the predations of the Irishman had left the younger candidates leery of a career in crime. There would always be men willing to join the organization, but real talent was scarce.

Once Terry had been working within the organization for a time, he began to ask about some of the legendary figures that had preceded him. The only one he was really interested in was The Viper. There was an aura of mystery about him and he had different people tell him different theories about who The Viper really was, but no one had any solid evidence of where he had gone or what had happened. He had simply disappeared. The more intelligent of the crowd knew he had been killed simply because "There's no such thing as an old assassin."

There were no records of when men took positions of power in the underworld. Men's memories were unclear and distorted but it seemed the consensus of opinion was that Randy had taken his present position in 1987. His predecessor, Felix Ribbaldi, had been in power for a long time but had gotten sloppy. He was lured into the cocaine trap and had been addicted to it badly. It was not difficult to look up the records on Felix. Felix had been indicted for trafficking in cocaine and had been offered a deal if he testified against his superiors and suppliers. Felix Ribbaldi had never made it to trial. He had been killed by a .50 caliber round while in custody. The case was still open since the killer had never been found.

Terry's eyes opened wide as he read the old news stories. He had no doubt about who had killed Felix Ribbaldi. The Viper had killed him. Pieces began to fall into place. The information had been there all along, he had simply not known what he was looking for. The answer to the question that had been plaguing him since he was eight years old was right in front of him. All his moral reservations and uncertainty were washed away in a white hot flash of rage and he saw, once again, his mother's brains being blown all over the hospital wall.

It took all he had not to make a mistake at this point. He wanted a drink but refused to go down that path. He wanted to barge into the Riggers Club and blow Randy Arganmajc's brains all over the velvet upholstery but he maintained his seat. He had not done any drugs in a while, it was frowned on in his position, and he did not even consider that outlet. He sat and considered his options carefully. The library would be closing soon and the wrinkled old crone of a librarian was gently reminding the remaining customers of that.

Terry's head spun as he drove back to his apartment. He had been driving the Holden for months now and parking it a couple of blocks away in a rented garage. The walk to the apartment let him check to see if he was being followed. While some might have considered that paranoia, others would have seen it as a reasonable precaution.

While the computer was a wonderful tool, Terry always wrote his letters by hand and mailed them at the post office.

Uncle,

I have discovered that which I sought. The problem came from Iran and was diverted here somehow. I would like very much to talk to this Iranian. If you could make that happen I would appreciate it. I will enlighten you as to the true nature of this business when we share a cup of tea.

Sincerely,
Terry Kingston

The dreams that punctuated his sleep that night were horrific and violent. When he awoke the next day it was as if he had never slept. His co-workers commented on his condition but he told them he was hung over again. Being young and prone to tipping a few, his excuse was accepted out of hand.

When Ginger got the letter, he became somewhat concerned. The Iranian diverted to Australia was obviously the .50 caliber Barrett. That rifle had not been employed in many years. The last time it had been used in an operation was when George had taken it for a job shortly before he had been killed and the only thing Ginger could think of was the assault on the Troy's armored limousine. He hoped his nephew was not planning on doing something stupid. The cup of tea was a pre-arranged signal indicating the room in Orange.

Summer was over and it had been a hot one. The sky was overcast and all the farmers were hoping it would rain once or twice before harvest time. The trip to Orange seemed to take forever and it was dark when Ginger carried the crate containing the rifle into the room. At the last second he hesitated and then he took the ammunition back to the truck. He was very concerned and wanted to talk to Terry before allowing him to use such a unique weapon. "*Do not call attention to yourself,*" was his thought. Death from afar would call attention to the job.

Terry did not make it to Orange until Saturday. He noted that Ginger had left the weapon and not the ammunition. He knew he had to visit the farm but felt he needed to clear his head a bit first. He called Linda Pierce and got a cool reception. They had not been in contact much after the scheme that had ended her ex-husband's life. It had been a necessity that they stay apart for a while.

By the time they saw each other in person, however, Linda had gotten over being angry. They enjoyed each other's company the rest of the day and Terry left in the morning to visit his Uncle. Linda went back home knowing subconsciously that she had been used and not caring much.

Sunday was rainy, though not rainy enough for the crops. Ginger was welding some equipment back together when his nephew pulled in the driveway. Hercules went mad until he realized it was Terry. After a few minutes, the two men went inside and had some lemonade. They made small talk for a while, talking about the crops and the dogs and the sheep. Then Terry asked why there had been no ammunition with the sniper rifle.

"I know you're a grown man and capable of making your own decisions," Ginger said slowly, "but I'm afraid you're about to go into an operation of a personal nature. That rifle has not been used on anything but trees for a long time."

"It works perfectly. There is nothing wrong with it."

186

"I am not so concerned about the gun, as the man. Nobody uses a weapon like that outside of combat. Your father only used it once and I'm afraid the police will make the connection instantly. More than that, I'm sure the men you are currently consorting with will know. Whatever your father did with that rifle probably caused his death."

"I know that. That's why I wanted it. I want them to know."

"You're not using your head. They knew who your father was. They knew his real name. If his weapon suddenly surfaces, they will make the connection instantly and will come looking for me. And you. It's going to take more than a big dog to stop them. I'm not telling you not to do this thing, I'm suggesting that you use a different tool."

"I thought it would only be right if I used the Barrett."

"I won't forbid you from using it, I'm only saying it is too risky. If you do this thing, you'll be signing my death warrant and yours as well."

"You may be right. What would you suggest?"

"What happened to the SP66?"

"I left it in the Irishman's trailer, well, Linda did, actually. It was the final bit of evidence proving his identity as the Irishman."

"Oh... Good move."

"Right. Even the coppers were happy with that one."

"Well then, the Irishman's been retired. He was useful while he existed and now he's dead. I suggest we use a new approach. Tell me, is it the Troy Brothers this time?"

"No. I think it was their number one contact in Sydney that gave the order to have my father killed. Randy Arganmajc took control right after Felix Ribbaldi was shot through the chest with a .50 caliber round."

"Now I understand. Your father did the man and they had him killed for it. Did you find out why your father was contracted to kill the man?"

"He was turning state's evidence. He had been caught and was squealing like a pig."

"There is still something missing. I don't know what but there is something missing."

"I thought so too, but I can't find it."

"Stay the night and we'll formulate something."

"I can't, I have a job of sorts. It involves guarding and transporting money rather than contraband and it gives me a proper in, as well as an alibi."

"All right then. I urge you not to use the Barrett."

"I guess you're right. I will take a few of those sticks of dynamite, then, and a detonator."

"Oh, a detonator. A fuse is not good enough for you any more?"

"Come off it, Uncle. You're teasing me now."

Before he left, Terry got a canvas bag full of explosives and .50 caliber shells.

When he had first taken command of the Sydney underground, Randy Arganmajc had been a very cautious man. A security team had covered him constantly. He not only used them for protection against assassination, he used them for proof that he was not in contact with any one from the other side of the line. He felt, back then, that a little bit of suspicion would get him the same fate Felix Ribbaldi had earned. Over the years, the need for the constant protection had waned but then the Irishman problem had cropped up and he had been forced to replace his subordinates repeatedly. He wanted to reinstitute the protection squad but now he was too short on men. Sydney had been hit hardest by the recent events. The courts had released some of the men rounded up before the Olympics but there were others that had been sentenced to long terms in prison. Many of the new men came from outside of the Sydney area and, while some of them had skills, they did not have contacts and they did not inspire faith.

In the 14 or so years that Randy Arganmajc had been in charge of the Sydney area, he had never been arrested or assassinated. His secret was simple; he distanced himself from the business and ran it from afar. He did not do the street drugs that brought in so much money. He did not gamble ostentatiously, though sometimes he needed to show some excess to out of town clients. He had certain women that he consorted with and he kept them in fine style as long as they were available to him when he desired them and did not bother him when he did not.

Randy spent many of his evenings in the Riggers Club. That august establishment had the finest of spirits and tobacco available but women were not permitted and common drugs were forbidden. The Riggers Club was a gentleman's club and gentlemen did not soil themselves with drugs. The club was not a casino, though games could be played, often for high stakes. The club had good security, better in that it was unobtrusive. The front and back doors had security cameras but never the members' areas. The thick velvet drapes were seldom held open and there were complimentary beds upstairs for those members who could not go home for one reason or another.

Randy was also a member of Bacchanalia, the charter of which said it was a gentleman's club. He did not visit Bacchanalia often and he always went alone. It would not do to let any of the men around him know he had interests in that arena. The club was hidden underground with no sign on the door. The owner was very careful to pay off the men who would have been in charge of investigating him. Multiple locked doors needed to be opened before a member could get into the entertainment area. The entertainment area was a series of rooms where teenage boys were held captive, prostituted, tortured and murdered. None of the boys came from the Sydney area, most of them were from Indonesia. Occasionally a runaway was brought in from another city but mostly it was foreigners. They were promised a new and exciting life in Australia and found torture and death.

Randy paid a great deal of money to be a member of Bacchanalia. In turn, the owner paid protection to both sides of the law. About twice a year Randy would go down to Bacchanalia, all alone, and work out some of his sadistic tendencies on the captive body of some poor immigrant. It cost more if you wanted to torture and kill the boy but that service was available as well. Nobody ever found the bodies because the manager of the club also owned a crematorium.

Randy had been very careful not to let anyone know he visited the underground perversion that called itself a gentleman's club, but it is hard to keep such a secret for long. He had been marked a couple of years earlier and noted after that. All Terry had needed to do to get this information was to bring up Randy's name then sit back and let the crew talk. The Bacchanalia was not common knowledge so nobody was surprised when the young man who had recently joined them didn't know about it. It was half legend and that half had grown to encompass whatever the sordid minds of the age could envision. Many people brushed it off as imaginary.

The Hall of Records had a charter for Bacchanalia. The "gentleman's club" was listed as being 4747 Oedipus Avenue. There was no Oedipus Avenue in the city, of course. It took some asking around to determine that it was actually on Euripides Avenue. Once he had the address, Terry paid a visit to the neighborhood. It was seedy and run down. The buildings were close together and some of them were deserted. As far as he could tell, the club used a warehouse across the street as a parking garage for its clientele. It would have been smart for the owner to dig an underground passage to the warehouse but he never had. When compared to the wide expanses of lawn, cameras and security around the Riggers Club, this was a much more desirable location to plan a shooting.

The apartment that Randy called home had been discarded as a viable spot early in the game. It was a busy building with armed security and hallway cameras. His apartment was higher than the roofs of many of the nearby buildings so a shot from afar was not really available.

Terry took his time planning this job. He did not want to hurry it. He was actually enjoying watching, plotting from the shadows. He had discarded most of the rumors about the club as being fanciful fabrications, but as he observed the building his curiosity was piqued. As was common with a gentleman's club, there were never any women entering the front door. There were never any supplies delivered either. That meant the delivery door was somewhere in the back, but a reconnaissance of the area revealed no loading dock, just a pedestrian door. Surveillance on the back alley had to be done from afar and it was difficult to get a good look, but it became apparent that the supplies were delivered next door after hours and that there must be a connection below ground.

The real nature and horror of the club revealed itself after a couple of weeks of observation. The crate from Thailand was too large to go through the door and so, needed to be broken down outside. When the side was pried off the crate, there were three young boys, bound and gagged inside. The boys were quickly carried inside and the door was closed.

Terry had heard of such perversions but had never been able to believe that men really did these things. With all the women in the world, what made a man want to fuck a little boy? He was sickened by the prospect and quickly made it his mission not to just to kill Randy Arganmajc but to clean out this little piece of Hell in the process.

Bacchanalia had lots of security, most of which did not speak much English. They had been recruited from the

Middle East and would just as soon shoot an Infidel as look at him. The owner of record was a Greek corporation. It was plain that they did not care or investigate the nature of the club. It was purely a business deal for them. The real vermin were the men who managed the day-to-day operations.

Having Randy Arganmajc in the building when the assault was initiated was of importance to the young assassin. But there was no backup on hand. Uncle Ginger could not desert the farm and wait for months. Terry began to time things out. He was figuring out how long each part of the plan took. He was having trouble working it out so he could be on both sides of the building at the same time. He needed backup and did not have it. He was about to give up on trapping Randy inside the building. It was simply too complicated, time sensitive, and impractical.

The last thing Terry Kingston expected was to get a phone call from Gordon MacMaster. He had written the Scotsman off as having left the country months earlier, never to be seen again. Gordon wanted to meet with Terry outside of Sydney. Terry suggested Richmond but Gordon preferred the Leura Railway Station next to Katoomba on the Blue Mountain Railway Line. They would meet there on Saturday. Gordon insisted that they bring no one else to the meet.

It was less than two hours on the train to Leura Station. Terry had never been there before and quite enjoyed the trip. The flora and fauna were a fine change from the flat, dry lands and the concrete of the city. He was displeased to find that his manners were suffering from being trapped in the city. People were more gracious outside the city limits.

The station was actually perfect for a sniper to take out a target. It was an island with tracks going each way around it and a tree-covered cliff on the other side of one track. If MacMaster had wanted to eliminate his witness, Terry would have been a dead man. He started asking himself what he

192

thought he was doing while he hustled to the stairs that would take him over the tracks and into town. The stairs were even more exposed but, he reasoned, if he had been targeted he would have already been dead.

Leura was a charming and picturesque town. In another month there could well be snow on the mountains around it, but it was clear and cold that day.

Terry's phone rang and he got directions to a restaurant, which turned out to be a charming old establishment that had been a post office at one time. Inside he found Gordon MacMaster having a cup of coffee.

"G'day mate, mind if I join you?"

"Mr. Kingston, please be seated."

Terry froze. He had never revealed his identity to anyone in the city. He was certain that he had not been targeted or he would already be dead but he could not help the shock that gripped him. It was not that he was surprised that the secret was out or that a man such as MacMaster could have divined it, it was simply the naked feeling that comes with such a declaration. He felt, and was in fact, exposed.

"Don't worry, I'm not here to throw your secret to the wind. In fact, I'm here to congratulate you on your powers of manipulation. Please, be seated." The Scotsman was smiling and doing his best to put Terry at ease.

"When did you find out?" Terry asked after he took a chair.

"Oh, not until afterward. You see, you managed to fool everyone to some extent. I was relatively sure I was looking in the right direction until the actual moment the truck was stopped. I had studied the prior attacks and while they had been different from each other, they all displayed a level of finesse that Lee Pierce did not possess."

The waitress came to the table and Terry ordered coffee and a pastry. He was charmed by his associate's choice of locations and by his associate as well.

"I should have been put on guard by some of the things you said and some of the questions you asked, but I was focused externally and did not pick it up until I had divorced myself from the situation. I wanted to make sure you got your bonus, but I could not take the chance that you were planning to kill me as well." There was a smile on the Scotsman's lips that did not extend to his eyes.

The waitress came back around with the coffee and pastry. When she had left, Terry replied earnestly, "I had no intention of killing you. What would have given you that impression?"

"Oh, nothing did, I was just being cautious."

"You fooled me completely in the hotel. I was waiting for you and you were already in the room and gone."

"That was simple. What you did with Lee and his ex-wife was better. In fact, it was brilliant. That, by the way, is how I found out what you were up to. If you had been able to cut the woman off clean or eliminate her, I would never have discovered you."

"I think you would have. Once your suspicions were raised you followed through. You would have kept going until you were satisfied. That's the sort of man you are."

"True. You fooled me, if only for a moment. That doesn't happen often and it most often leads to a body bag. Oh, by the way, leaving the Mauser in the trailer was not the best idea. With all the guns Lee had, he would have chosen a more modern weapon. It seemed to work for the police, but not for me."

"So why are you here? What I mean is, why am I here?"

"I recognize talent when I see it and while I think you need a lot of work, I also think you are a natural."

"And that means what?"

"There is a lot of work out there that needs to be done and a limited number of men who can do it. There are plenty who are willing, but the secret is to get out alive. You are a survivor and I have friends that employ survivors. I would like to take you away from here and introduce you to the world. The world will, of course, never be introduced to you."

"Can't do it, mate. I have things I need to do here."

"Let's go for a walk and we can continue this conversation outside."

The town of Leura has many vistas and beautiful outlooks. The two men walked until the reached a secluded area.

"I know you have a business in Orange," Gordon continued. "That business will eventually lead anyone seeking you right to your doorstep."

Terry was floored, now. His respect for the Scotsman was continually increasing. His stomach was also starting to tighten up. "How did you determine all this?" he asked, trying not to give anything away.

"It was not that difficult once I knew where you went on the odd weekend. This is the point, however, if I can do it, anyone can. You have played a game with dreadful consequences and it will come back to bite you eventually. If you cut and run now, nobody will be the wiser, but if you stay, you seal your doom. Not all of the thugs you are associating with are complete morons. Eventually they will ask the same questions I did and they will not be happy when they discover your secret second life."

"What do you intend to do?"

"Me? Nothing. I will simply disappear. As far as they know I have gone back to Scotland and I'm fishing in Loch Ness."

"I must say your proposal is intriguing. I enjoyed that little cruise you arranged for me."

"I thought you would. I must say, bombing the plastics factory while you were in Europe was a stroke of genius. It threw suspicion off yourself masterfully. I suggested the cruise because I had my suspicions of you, but you handled that very well."

"Thank you, but there are a couple of things I really feel I must do before I leave. If I did not know about them I would probably be able to take you up on the offer. But I do know and I must fix them or suffer for it."

"Are they actions or personal items?"

"Personal."

"You do know the danger of pursuing personal items; the danger involved with vendettas?"

"Yes, I'm aware of the rules but my whole life has been vendetta. That is why I am where I am. That is why I have done what I have done."

"Outline it for me and I will see what qualifies."

"How do I know who you are working for?"

"I already told you. I'm working for no one. If I wished you any ill will, I would have exposed you as soon as I knew you were the Irishman. You're working both sides and not as a copper. You think you're some kind of comic book super hero, fighting for truth and justice. You have more honor than all those blighters you work with and still manage to cover it up. That takes natural skill and talent. I suspect that is why you want to stay now. Honor. Tell me what it is you want to do and perhaps I'll throw in a free hand."

Terry stood on the edge of the cliff, revealed and exposed. His fear was not for himself but for those few he had become fond of. Gordon had pushed him so gently he had not seen the edge of the precipice. Now there was no choice but to take the offer of assistance or go over the edge. He could not refuse the free hand.

196

Chapter Eleven
The Free Hand

The roles of the two men were somewhat reversed, but only partially so. Gordon MacMaster acknowledged that the operation was Terry's and Terry admitted he was only partially ready to pull it off. The Aussie had done the reconnaissance and the Scot had the experience. If there had been any chest puffing or leadership challenges as there so often are among young men, then the operation was doomed to failure from the beginning. Gordon was Terry's senior by about 10 years, and he would have walked off in a New York minute.

This is not to say that either man was all that comfortable with the arrangement. To date, the only man Terry trusted was Uncle Ginger, and he even began to question his loyalty at times. MacMaster had not mentioned Ginger so Terry felt sure that he did not know of his existence. Terry intended to keep it that way.

It was difficult not to like Gordon MacMaster. The Scot would teach, not preach. He had a zest for life that extended well past his assignments, but he was never reckless. He and Terry reveled, drank and danced with the ladies but he refused to go out in Sydney. It was Gordon's insistence that he would work better from behind the curtains. If he were identified, the contract would be out on him.

Regardless of the Scotsman's assertion that he was going after Randy Arganmajc as a cathartic balm for his conscience, Terry wanted to make sure there was no doubt in his mind. He observed his former mentor and new partner very closely when he described the Bacchanalia and the red head's reaction went quite a way toward soothing his fears. Planning began immediately and much to Terry's dismay, he found that he was still learning at the feet of a master. There was no question that the operation should be undertaken. It was Gordon's contention, however, that they should be paid for a job of this size and Terry did not see how.

The children chained in the basement were from poor families. Sometimes they were sold into slavery; sometimes they were kidnapped. There was no reward offered for their return. Once freed, they would have nowhere to go but nowhere was better than where they were. There would be no financial gain from that side of the equation.

For MacMaster's part, he had watched Terry carefully before approaching him. In the time they had worked together in the service of their erstwhile employers, Terry had impressed him as being focused and efficient. He listened well and learned quickly. It was not that Gordon had been looking for a protégé, he was simply after the reward he would get for bringing in new talent. What he did know was that personal revenge was a very messy business and he needed to be sure that Terry could display the necessary detachment when the chips were down. The young Australian would need a lot of coaching and direction but he already had the motivation and drive, and he had that other thing, that natural talent that came from nobody knows where. MacMaster would leave himself an avenue of escape if things got too messy and he needed to allow Kingston to be sacrificed. He hoped it would not come to that but was steeled against its possibility.

Terry was against using the authorities on the job. He had never worked much with the police and was not about to start. He was willing to listen, however.

The call went in June 21, 2001 as a fire in the basement of 4747 Euripides. While the street patrol had been paid off, the fire department had not. There was a big row between the guards, the police and the firemen. There would be repercussions along the chain of command.

The second call to 4747 Euripides came in two days later but it was a different scene this time. The front door of

198

the building had been blown in by some sort of explosion and the front rooms were on fire. The guard who had been standing outside the front door was unconscious but alive. Again there was discord between the guards and the firemen. This time the police did not try to stop the fire department from accessing the scene. The guards would not let anyone in the basement but the station chief had the run of the house other than that.

The third call came in the following day. This time there was an acrid smoke pouring from the basement. There was no question but that the fire crew was needed but the guards were refusing to let them in. The compromised police were standing like gelded roosters, not knowing what to do, until the argument escalated and one of the guards opened fire.

Without knowing enough English to understand why the fire trucks were there, and with specific orders to never allow non-members into the basement, Hassim was immovable. One of the smoke-eaters grabbed a fire axe and headed for the basement door with all the intentions of smashing it down and stopping the argument. Hassim shot him. That was all the nerves of the crew could take, and it was as far as the police were willing to go. They turned their weapons on Hassim and dropped him where he stood. They tried to stop the fire fighters from smashing down the new door, but it was too late. They were addressing the second door by then. The third door opened by itself and two Yemeni nationals ran out as the fire department ran in. They did not see the five other men who rode the freight elevator up to run out the back. The smoke was thick and caustic, but it was not deadly, not that any of the men in the dungeon could have known that. What was deadly was the confrontation they ran into when they charged, fully armed, out the back door of the building. The alley was full of police and fire fighters trying to get through the back door. The lack of a common language hindered any communication between them as the guards exited. Then the bullets started flying. It was never determined who had shot first, just that there was a bloodbath in the alley. The Investigators did their best to piece together what had happened but never really got that good a handle on it. Two constables, one fireman and all five guards were killed. Three other firemen and a constable were injured in the rain of fire and lead.

The real story was the inside of the basement: the 15 live boys and the 3 dead ones. It turned out the smoke came from some kind of improvised smoke bomb with a timer. The bomb had been delivered in a crate of noodles.

The two Yemeni men who had exited the front door were the only adults who had escaped the simulated fire. Oddly enough, the police report said they had tried to overpower the officers on the way to the regional station. The police had no option but to shoot them. The city launched a full investigation but there was no one to prosecute. The owner of record was a Greek corporation who had rented the buildings to an Arabian man and had no more business with it. They were not liable for what the man did with the buildings.

Once Bacchanalia was exposed for what it was, the pictures of Randy Arganmajc entering the building became valuable. It didn't really matter that the photographs were fakes. They were delivered to the Riggers Club in his name in a sealed envelope along with a note demanding a large sum of money. The money was to be delivered personally to a location on the docks where it would be exchanged for the negatives and the remaining copies.

The location was chosen carefully. The docks were fronted with little shops and pubs. It was a very trendy neighborhood with a church at each end of the boardwalk.

There had never been any intention, on Randy's part, of paying for the pictures. He did not work that way and

200

never had. The man who showed up with the briefcase had been made up to look like Randy Arganmajc but was not. The two men who followed him were dressed as though they wanted to look like Mafia hit men. They even wore hats and trench coats.

There had never been any intention on Terry's part of trading pictures for money. He knew it was not going to happen. When the man dressed as Randy Arganmajc reached the wrought iron bench painted so gaily red, the telephone in the booth next to him rang. He was clearly unsure about picking it up, the reason for which was obvious once he did finally talk into the receiver. He did not sound like Randy Arganmajc in the least.

The clearly American voice on the other end of the line told him to set the case on the bench and open it. The case was supposed to be full of money but Gordon would have been shocked if it had been. The man's refusal to open the case proved it was empty or perhaps filled with explosives.

It was not a long shot from the church steeple to the two men conspicuously smoking on the boardwalk, but it did require finesse. Terry had decided that leaving one of the three men alive was an acceptable plan. The two Hollywood rejects were in his sights and they went down, one after another. The .223 slugs were chosen carefully for the job since they would not have enough velocity to exit. It was not a guaranteed kill shot but that didn't matter.

The man at the telephone was looking in the wrong direction. He did not see his two bodyguards drop to the deck. His wakeup call was when a slug slammed into his leg. He howled in pain. The other two had not even had that option; they had gotten a clean head shot each and were dead on arrival. The crowd milled around the victims, they were concerned and wanted to help. Everybody wanted to get a look at what had happened. Nobody saw the men leave the churches at each end of the boardwalk.

Of course the newspapers were all over the story. "Sniper On The Loose" capped the stories of the day. There were plenty of witnesses to interview and the police could not put a lid on this one.

The Troy brothers were furious, but not as angry as their main man, Randy. They had been hit so many times in the past year that it was having a real effect on business. Abel Troy suggested to his brother that they needed to replace Randy, but Adam vetoed the suggestion. He was convinced, as was Randy, that the recent incident was some punk emboldened by the success of the Irishman. The survivor was certain that the man on the telephone had an American accent and the MO was different. The weapon was different and the target was different. The Irishman had been eliminated and now they faced a new problem.

The Irishman had never attempted to extort money from the mob, which was what made him so dangerous. He had not wanted anything but destruction. This new threat wanted to make himself rich, and that would be his undoing.

Randy had not explained to his superiors what the photographs were, simply that they were compromising. When the copies of the photos reached their desks, it gave them pause. They did not want to be associated with the scandal that surrounded the Bacchanalia Club, that was a given, but more than that they began to question the character of Randy Arganmajc. Of course, Randy insisted that the photographs were faked, as they were in fact, but that did not clear his reputation.

Those at the top of a corporation seldom know what is happening on the floor. They hire others to manage that section of the business. The top managers never hear about the little things; they hear about the disasters. A good top manager will be in touch with key elements at the lower level of the pyramid, in the trenches so to speak, but this sort of relationship needs time to grow. The lower-level employees

202

need to know they can trust their well-heeled colleagues. If this level of trust has not been gained, the manager will only get what the middle managers want him to get. Very often they get, "everything is fine. We will take care of it. Do not worry about us." And the numbers from the accountants punctuate the statements.

The Troy Brothers had not been in the trenches for a long time and they did not want to be. Their legitimate businesses were overshadowing their seedy pasts and they liked it that way. When they got the photographs of Randy Arganmajc entering the Bacchanalia Club, it proved more than his lack of character; it showed that the photographer had some knowledge of the connection between the men. That could be more dangerous in the long run than whatever sordid perversions Randy engaged in.

The next letter Randy received at the Riggers Club was less cordial.

Mr. Arganmajc,

You have double-crossed me and your men have paid the price. You must have thought I was a joker or someone to dismiss out of hand. I assure you I am neither. The cost for the photographs has doubled and there will be no further contacts between us until this money has been paid. I assure you that if there is a replay of our previous encounter the next to die will certainly be you.

Take an aluminum briefcase with the money inside and meet me at the clubhouse of the Bardwell Park Golf Course on Saturday at noon. If I smell a rat, I will deliver the photos to the newspapers.

Find enclosed a new photograph.

The letter was not signed. The new photograph was of one of Randy's kept women walking from her car to her door.

Randy Arganmajc knew the game way too well to think one payment would fix the problem. Extortionists never stopped until they were stopped by any number of methods. Randy had not dealt with an extortionist in many years. The last man who had tried to extort money out of him ended up stuffed into a sewer pipe. Randy had not paid him money, nor would he pay this man money.

The parking lot of the Bardwell Park Country Club was out of sight of the clubhouse, out of sight of the road and surrounded by trees. The guard shack was by the road. The mobster made note of the fact that the man he was here to see knew he was a member. He exited his car and took the briefcase to the clubhouse with him. He felt much less exposed once inside.

The scotch was good, but the time dragged. By four o'clock he was about to leave when the bartender handed him the phone saying it was for him.

"You have been a very bad boy, Randy." The speaker had an American accent.

"Who is this and why am I talking to you?"

"I am the man who just shot two thugs outside the clubhouse." The cell phone in his pocket rang. He held it to one ear while he held the house phone to the other. Both lines said the same thing though there was a bit of a lag on one. "Do you have the money?"

"No, I was unable to raise it on such short notice."

"Then what is in the briefcase?"

Randy swore under his breath. "All right, you have me. The money is in the briefcase."

"You're lying to me. What's really in the briefcase? A bomb? A gun? Have you got a midget with a knife stuffed in there?"

Randy said nothing. He had known the American was shrewd, but he was starting to feel like a stupid little boy.

"Walk out on the first green with the briefcase. You had better be alone out there as well."

"There's no possibility of my walking out into that field."

"Perhaps you had better reconsider your position. If your death was what I wanted, then you would already be as dead as these two shvances."

"Why can't you just meet me in here?"

"You really don't get it, do you? I have the upper hand. I can reach out and crush you like a bug. You're nothing to me, a spider under my heel. The photographs are merely the icing on the cake. What you are paying me for is your life. You are paying me not to kill you. Now walk out on the first green with the briefcase, open it, and show the money."

The line went dead. Nobody exited the clubhouse. Randy was making phone calls. He had brought four men with him and it seemed at least one of them was dead already. Ten minutes later a Rover with two men in it pulled in the parking lot, hopped the curb and drove to the front of the clubhouse. The door opened and two men exited the clubhouse with their heads low and dove into the vehicle which tore out of the area. Neither of them carried a briefcase. Gordon and Terry were already gone by that time. The two men hiding in the trees waited for anyone coming out of the woods but they saw nobody. An hour later the bomb squad showed up to investigate the briefcase that had been left inside. The briefcase was empty. The newspapers ran the story.

The last thing Randy Arganmajc wanted to see was the police or anyone else finding dead men with a link to him in the woods at the country club. He went to a safe house and sent every man he could spare and contact to search for the two men he had been told were dead. Those two men were found handcuffed around a tree in a drug-induced stupor. The tree had a printed note stuck to it.

Mr. Arganmajc

I did not kill these men. I will not be so generous again. I have been extremely patient with you but my patience has now run out. Your treachery has again doubled the price. This is the last chance I will be giving you to save your life. If you attempt to play with me again I will kill you, every man with you, and both of your mistresses, your sister in Brisbane and your half-brother in Walla Walla. Then I will go after Abel and Adam Troy, your employers, and I will kill both of them. I believe I have demonstrated my willingness and capability sufficiently. You will pay me or I will let you watch and save you for last.

The note was unsigned but the fact that it was printed out on a computer printer before anyone had gone to the clubhouse came as a revelation to some of the men. Almost half of the enforcers and wheel men disappeared that night. Some of them came back later and others moved to different towns and found alternate employment. Some even got real jobs.

When Terry reported to work the following day, the remaining men in the warehouse were frantic. Some of the older members of the crew had mentioned that they planned to take a hiatus. Some of the others did not. There were shipments they could not move and money they could not collect. The network was breaking down.

Randy was seriously rattled by now. He could have paid the extortion fee in the beginning, but the current price tag was more than he could raise by himself. He could not go to Adam and Abel with this or they would see him as weak and ineffective and he would be ruined. He stopped trusting those around him, suspecting that there was an informant in his dwindling number of employees. He got drunk and slapped his women around and threatened his managers. He was still conducting business but his return was dropping slightly and his remaining faithful were doing double duty. Every time the phone rang he jumped. The thing that hurt him the most was that the extortionist seemed to know what he was going to do before he did it.

For the right price, there will always be men willing to put their lives on the line. The three ex-Mossad agents that had formed a bodyguard service did not come cheap but they were extremely effective. They formed a living wall around him during the times he still dared to leave his apartment. They assured him that the next time the American tried to make the trade, they would eliminate the threat. Arganmajc trusted them because they had not been part of the team when the trouble started.

Terry Kingston was working himself ragged. In addition to his regular runs he was driving additional loads, some legitimate. The word was spreading and as leather-tough and immovable as Australian truckers can be, there was always another job for them if they decided to transfer employers. The remaining members of Randy's team were making money hand over fist, a powerful incentive at any time.

The other thing that changed was that people were watching each other more. Keith Harrison, the man who had replaced Victor Wellington after the latter's unfortunate demise, had actually approached every member of the team with the same sort of confidential request. He asked that they not say anything to the others. He told each of them that he only trusted them and that they needed to watch someone else. Some of them kept their mouths shut, others did not.

Then came the September 11th attacks on the World Trade Center in New York City and the whole world sat up

207

and took notice. Then they went back to business as usual with a little more trepidation and heartache than before.

Gordon MacMaster had not made contact for what seemed like a terribly long time. He had been fishing and hiking and generally enjoying the countryside as only a man who has no schedule can do. He had also been thinking. He spoke to Terry about once a week and was pleased at the reaction from the lower class members of the organization. Together the two assassins tried to map out a plan of attack.

It had not happened immediately but what had been a trickle was growing to a stream. East Germans and Russians were arriving in increasing numbers and while most of them were honest hard-working men, there were also those elements that would not have been so welcome. They were the former Soviet Bloc citizens who had managed to wax successful in the hungry economy that existed before the collapse of their Communist system. Attila the Hun and Vlad the Impaler had spawned men such as these. They had slowly been eating into the pie of the Australian black market. At first they had been ignored as inconsequential, then they had been marked as minor competition, skilled but unpopular. The current events made their association seem more desirable, though still distasteful and untrustworthy.

When Randy approached the Eastern European expatriates, he was still dealing from a position of power, but as an Australian he did not have a feel for the history. He should have brought some of his local talent with him instead of the Israelis. The German contingent was insulting and refused to conduct business with Jews, even though they were only present as a security force. The Russians involved were less abrasive about the religious differences, but the services they offered were at more than twice the going rate and Randy was not that desperate. He could see in their eyes that they were waiting for their power to grow to the point where they could make a move. They intended to take over some portion of the illicit trade. He realized that if he did not address this, he would end up with another financial leak that needed to be plugged.

Then the call came in. The exchange was demanded to be made the following day, on the flat floor of a disused rock quarry south of the city. Every thug, brigand and self-styled wise guy in Randy's employ was immediately dispatched to the quarry. It was a failed operation where about four acres of limestone had been excavated. There was a deep pool of water in the middle of the floor and trees ringing the top of the hill to about 270 degrees. The dirt road they used to reach the quarry was the only one available and it ended at the excavation site.

When the gangsters arrived on the scene, there was a large chest sitting next to the drainage pit with a sign on it reading "Put the money in the chest." The men scoured the woods around the excavation but found nobody.

Henry Cuthbert remained in his car while his subordinates searched the area. He had been given no money to deliver; he was given instructions to kill anybody that was in the immediate area of the quarry. There were no farms or homes near the area so unless there were teenagers swimming in the pit, nobody was expected to be there.

Once the men reported that they had found nothing, Henry picked out a victim to open the chest. He chose a young drug addict, a violent and stupid young man who had disgraced himself before. If he were killed, few would miss him. The man approached the box as if it were a dangerous beast and opened the lid from a practically prone position. The only thing inside the chest was an envelope marked Randy Arganmajc.

Cuthbert tore open the envelope, inside was a printed letter that read, "You have failed again and your life is forfeit." He swore and ordered three men to remain on the scene and shoot anyone who came near the chest. They were provided with scoped rifles. Someone had the foresight to bring sandwiches and they were left with the men.

The road the quarry was on was forested on both sides with gullies and streams, requiring bridges. The gangsters heard the explosion that took out the bridge but did not know what it was until the convoy reached the shattered structure. Between the trees and the depth of the gully there was no way around. They were stuck.

Telephone calls were made. Randy Arganmajc was on the verge of panic. His new bodyguards were with him but the majority of his team was trapped in the wilds. The road was not large enough to accommodate a semi as there was no place to turn one around, so Randy tried to dispatch his short trucks to the area. Unfortunately, in the middle of the day, his trucks were all loaded with merchandise or well out of the area.

"G-man?"

"Tarrytown."

"The cash truck has been dispatched to the quarry to pick up the men stranded there."

"Perfect. Is the load secure?"

"Yes. Are you in position?"

"Aye," MacMaster's voice reflected his satisfaction.

"There are two men in the truck. I'm not in it. I'll see you on the way back."

"Perfect."

It was three hours before the cash truck hit the half-buried razor strip and blew the two front tires. They were supposed to be able to drive the truck with a puncture, but the damage to the rubber was too extensive. First the driver called in, then he got out to inspect the damage. Terry was not in the van. He and one of the men who usually rode with the shipment had been dropped off in Hill Top, a small town about 20 kilometers away. It changed the operation, but did

210

not cancel it. There was still not enough room for everybody they had to pick up, but it was decided that a guard and a driver should be left with the load. It was against protocol for the guard in the back of the van to exit the vehicle during a breakdown. Any possible repairs were to be done by the driver and the guards were to stay inside.

The driver never saw it coming. The twin taser leads punctured his shirt and the skin of his back. The voltage seized up his muscles and dropped him to the ground, shaking. Before he could regain the use of his hands they were in handcuffs and his mouth and eyes were covered with duct tape. He never saw his attacker.

The guard in the bed of the van was on alert but he could not see what was happening outside. He did not know what was happening but he had no problem discerning that the van was filling with smoke. He had no choice but to open the back door and he did so, with his weapon at the ready. He called for the driver but there was no response. He could not stay in the van, the smoke was choking him, even with the door open. His natural reaction was to turn toward the driver's door when he jumped out. His eyes were burning and he was choking on the smoke, but that did not prevent him from hearing the hammer of a pistol being pulled back. He should have frozen in his tracks but instead, spun around firing his weapon blindly. It cost him his life as Gordon MacMaster was forced to shoot him.

Gordon stood for a moment looking at the prone form of the guard. He had not wanted to kill him and would not have, given the choice, but the man insisted. The bolt cutters made quick work of the padlock and the cables locking the money bags. Working quickly, MacMaster transferred the cash to a small duffel bag. The securities, checks and bearer bonds were left behind.

The Jeep Gordon had driven in was two kilometers away. He ran the distance retaining his hat and gloves as he ran. When he reached the vehicle, he was thoroughly soaked with sweat. He had encountered no one on the road.

The driver had called road services and Dispatch. He had not called Randy Arganmajc or Henry Cuthbert. He didn't know it was anything but a flat tire. Henry and his crew did not know about the delay until he called Dispatch to find out when they were to be rescued. Dispatch told Henry about the delay and that the tow truck had been sent. The realization that he had been set up twice in one day crashed into his skull like a sledgehammer. He told Dispatch to call the truck and then call back. He called Randy Arganmajc with his suspicions and Randy went wild. Except for some office workers and his bodyguards, his entire crew had been lured into the wilds and neutralized. He began screaming that they should start walking. They needed to get to the truck and secure it. There was no doubt in his mind what had occurred. There was also no doubt as to what the Troy brothers would do to him if he lost the funds being transferred to Sydney.

Dispatch could not reach the truck and called Henry. When Randy spoke with the dispatcher and found out that two men had been dropped off in Hill Top, he all but reached down the phone line to strangle the man. Then he thought better about it. He called John directly and told him that there had been a robbery and whoever came down the road was the thief. John was a senior guard, sitting in a Hill Top pub with Terry Kingston, having a beer.

John and Terry ran to the road that led to the quarry. They were both armed and ready for whoever came down the road. Randy had assured them that two professionals would join them with a vehicle. They did not have long to wait before they saw a cloud of dust heading their way. They tried to stop the vehicle, an older jeep, but it would not stop. At the last second it swerved and hit John, tossing him into the brush at the side of the road. Terry let off a couple of rounds

212

to make it look like he had tried to shoot the driver and then he went to minister to John.

When the Israelis arrived, the ambulance had been there and gone. The police had Thompson Barber in custody as a material witness. He was not charged with a crime so he was not fingerprinted or photographed. He gave his statement, outlining what had happened but he had not seen who was driving the jeep or gotten the license plate number. He explained how they had been diverted from their regular run to pick up some men who had been stranded out in the wilderness, and how he and John had been left in Hill Top to make room for the men. They had been told of a robbery and had taken appropriate action. No, he did not know why the men were down the old quarry road or how they had gotten stranded there. He was careful not to know anything about the money, only that it was picked up regularly in the Capital.

A pair of constables was sent up the road to look for the security van that should have returned from the quarry. When they reached the van they found it jacked up on the back of a wrecker. The wrecker driver was not the crusty old gentleman that regularly drove that vehicle, and the van was filled with armed men. There was quite a scene, with much noise and invective filling the air. The officers were badly outnumbered but there were no shots fired. They called for backup, all available units and there was a terrible mess to be sorted out. This was complicated by the discovery of the tow truck driver further down the road. He had refused to pick up the van until the police got there because there was a dead body lying behind it. All the men found on the road were arrested with the exception of Terry and John who had been nowhere near the incident. The bodyguards had wisely hung back after calling Henry and finding out what he was doing.

Randy never knew who it was that called the Troy brothers and alerted them to the situation. It became irrelevant. Randy was summoned to the home of Adam to answer for the mess. While there, he and his remaining bodyguard were given brandy and cigars, sat in comfortable chairs in the library and made to feel at ease. Randy was not able to be at ease, however, he sat on the edge of his chair fearing for his life.

Adam entered the library with four other men. Each of the men had shoulder holsters filled with pistols.

Randy glanced at his bodyguard who did not smoke but was sitting back with his brandy in a large snifter. The bodyguard did not seem to be concerned.

"Mr. Arganmajc, how long have we worked together?"

"About 15 years now, Mr. Troy."

"Fifteen years," Adam said thoughtfully and then chewed on his lower lip. "And in 15 years we have made some money together, have we not?"

"Yes, Sir. We certainly have."

"Do you think this is sufficient reason for me to overlook your recent foolishness?"

"Mr. Troy, we are under attack, by somebody who is very good at what he does. He has…"

"Enough! You were hired because you were supposed to be good. Now you tell me that there is someone out there who is better?"

"No, Sir. He is simply good, not better. I will get him and I will strangle the life out of him with my bare hands. You'll see, there is no place he can hide."

"Ah, I see. Then you know who you are looking for?"

"I will. I have a witness who saw him. I will get him. I had a plan to have him shot but he turned the tables on me. But I have a witness. I will get him. He can't get away now."

"I will give you one more chance to eliminate this man. One more. I have dispatched lawyers to that know-nothing mountain town to secure the release of your men. I expect results and I expect them fast. You have already lost much

214

respect. If I need to talk to you again, your career will be over."

Randy left the mansion with his bodyguard driving. He was in a state of aggravation he had not felt since he was a teenager. He knew there was no way he could find the American unless he got more information. He repeatedly asked his driver to check to see if they were being followed and made him drive around several blocks to double check. Then he had him drive to his apartment building. He parked outside with the engine running while Randy went inside. It was not long before Arganmajc reappeared with a suitcase and demanded he be driven to the airport.

Two hours later, the Israeli bodyguard appeared at the gates of Abel Troy's mansion with the suitcase in the front seat. Randy was in the trunk.

Chapter Twelve
The Cost of Survival

Terry was not comfortable. He was sitting in the passenger seat of a brand new Holden. The two bodyguards had picked him up in Hill Top to transport him back to Sydney. The two men looked as hard as nails and twice as sharp. They said nothing, even when Terry tried to engage them in conversation. They would not tell him their names. A feeling of dread settled over him and he stopped talking. They did not get near the city until after dark and Terry tried to get them to drop him off at a pub but they would not. He knew he was deep in it when they took his pistols and cell phone from him at gunpoint. He had called Gordon when he first knew he was being picked up but the Scot was too far away to help and Terry had not thought he needed it.

The three men entered the Adam Troy compound. There was a stark contrast between the men charged with protecting the real power and the men conducting business on the streets. Inside the compound were the professionals. They had the same dispassionate look as the Israelis. All three men were escorted to the library where they were joined by both Abel and Adam Troy. The ex-Mossad men spoke familiarly with the heads of the Australian crime syndicate as if they had known each other for many years. This did nothing to allay Terry's fears. The only thing that did make him feel any better was when he heard them say no, he could not have had anything to do with the hijacking. He was in Hill Top at the dispatcher's insistence.

Until this point, Terry had not been placed in restraints. He was not exactly free, however. They had some sort of plan for him that did not involve his free will. Their intentions became more and more plain as time went by. From the library he was led, at gunpoint, into the basement. If there had been a second when he was not under scrutiny

216

he would have bolted, but there was not. The bodyguards watched him like hawks. Through a steel door in the basement was a tiled room lit with fluorescent tubes. The drain in the middle of the floor told the tale. The third of the bodyguards was in this room standing watch over Randy Arganmajc who was strapped to a steel chair. There was no second exit from this room.

When he asked the question, "What is going to happen to me now?" he did his best to sound terrified. It was not a difficult thing to do given the circumstances.

"Do not worry, Mr. Barber, your task is simple." Adam Troy's words were far from soothing.

"Look. I had nothing to do with this affair. I wasn't even in the truck. Dispatch told me and John to get out in Hill Top to leave room for more men from down that road. I don't know why he did that. I heard about the robbery and tried to stop the thief. If he swerved left instead of right I'd be in the hospital or dead and John would be... uh, here."

"Then John would have the opportunity of reporting what is done here. You must understand, Mr. Barber," Adam continued, "There are certain principles which must be followed in all businesses. Have you gone to college?"

"No." Terry's throat was dry to the point of cracking and his voice reflected it.

"Please, give our guest some water. He is dry." Abel Troy seemed no more affected by the situation than his brother. It was as if they were playing a scene in a play and the curtain was going to close so they could go home. Neither of them seemed to feel there was anything out of the ordinary here. It was just another day to them. Their nonchalance made the scene all the more horrible.

Adam started up again after Terry had cleared his palate. "All men should go to college. It is where learning begins."

"I could..." Terry stumbled, not knowing where the conversation was leading.

"No, say nothing. Is it better to be loved or feared?"

Terry said nothing as he had been instructed.

"I'll tell you we decided years ago that it is better to be feared. But, we are not here for philosophical discussions, are we? Fasten our young friend to this chair so he has a good view of the show. You must understand, Mr. Barber, that without witnesses, an event can only be speculated on. With a witness it can be elaborated on. We have found it quite effective to allow members of our organization to experience the effects of desertion and betrayal in a vicarious fashion so they may communicate the nature of it to their friends. It served to keep our attrition rate to a minimum in the past. Very few love us, though."

Terry was strapped to a matching metal chair and the surgical table between Randy Arganmajc and himself was wheeled out of the way so he had a clear view. He heard the door open behind him but could not see who had entered until the man came around him. The small man wore a surgical mask and cap on his head but the rubber apron and gloves were more telling. He said nothing, just pointed to both Terry and Randy. The bodyguards set him straight, telling him that the subject was the older man.

The sharp, glittering eyes of the torturer would haunt Terry's dreams for weeks. What Terry had done to Bradley was nothing compared to what he saw done that day, in the basement operating room. The man in the rubber apron went to work gleefully and with flair. Terry was reminded of Ginger's words, "Don't get too attached to that feeling. That path leads to madness." It was obvious that madness had taken this one.

The bodyguards left the room when the torturer went to work. Terry supposed that the Troys had already left. Terry could close his eyes and turn his head but did not.

Here he was, being forced to watch the torture and mutilation of the man he had vowed to destroy, at the hands of two more men he had vowed to destroy. The only rain on this parade was the fact that he was strapped to a chair and might be next.

The small torturer made wide, sweeping gestures, playing to his audience as if he were on stage in a musical. His tools were kept in a leather roll and he removed them theatrically, sharpening some of them, reverently, before he used them. And no stage was ever more blood soaked. The victim screamed and pleaded to no avail.

If Randy Arganmajc had survived his ordeal he would have been unable to live with the visage left to him. He had been a dashing, man-about-town, a role one could not fill when one's facial features were missing. The torturer had cut off his ears, his nose, his lips and one of his eyes. Randy began pleading for death, knowing it was coming and wanting it more than he wanted to live. Apparently there was nothing more he could say because his tongue was next.

Despite the supposition that Randy had ordered his father killed, Terry could only enjoy so much of this. It was not designed to kill the man being tortured; it was designed to terrify the man watching. It had been a long-standing policy for the Troy brothers that if a man is to be tortured, there must be witnesses who can disseminate the methods and madness to the rest of the crowd. It had worked well for many years but there was a limit. Before long, Terry began to ask that the man simply be killed. He should have kept his mouth shut. The torturer reveled in the attention and began to dance as he dissected his victim. The glee in his eyes was more revolting than the mutilated body of his victim. Terry would have killed this psychopath gladly, had he been allowed to. He would have killed Randy just to end the man's pain. He actually began to feel sorry for the man he had been plotting to destroy.

When his victim passed out from pain and loss of blood, the torturer whimpered in his throat, the only sound he had made during the entire operation. He threw a pitcher of water on him but could not revive him. He stepped back and cast his glittering eye on Terry. It was that look that haunted Terry's dreams, that feral blood lust. He took a step toward the younger man and stopped when a speaker in the ceiling crackled and a man's voice told him to keep his distance. Somebody was watching from a remote location, a guardian angel in a pit of Hell.

Terry was removed from the room and taken to a shower before the torturer was finished with Randy. He had been covered with sweat and the dust of the road and it was cathartic to stand in the hot deluge. His thoughts were spinning madly. Torture was something he accepted as a necessary evil, but he had never actually seen anything like tonight's performance. He was horrified and fascinated, revolted and terrified. His resolve began to waver until he realized that it was the will of the brothers that he be broken by the sight. It was their desire that he become so concerned with what might happen to him that he remain loyal forever.

Dressed in a robe and some shorts, Terry was taken to a dining room where a fine meal had been laid out. He could not eat. There was beer and wine to go with dinner and liquor and coffee for afterwards. Terry drank sparingly. His stomach was not up to the alcohol.

"You may wonder why we have invited you into our home to watch this little ordeal." Adam Troy was dressed in his usual silk suit. "Pardon me, would you like a cigar?"

"A cigarette if you have one," Terry replied, still feeling a little ill at ease.

"Of course." Adam clapped his hands and a butler appeared with a tray of cigars and cigarettes. Terry took a pack, opened it and took one out. There was an ornate lighter on the table in front of him. It was a dragon and the flame came out its mouth, but it was no cheap piece. It was hand crafted silver.

"You have a strong stomach." Adam commented.

"Not that strong. I cannot eat and if I drink any wine I'll probably throw up."

"The fact that you did not throw up tells me that you have a strong stomach."

Terry smoked his cigarette and watched his host. He had no idea what was coming next. He was certain he was being watched remotely but could not pinpoint the camera. He was not tied or cuffed but he was also unarmed.

"We need men with strong stomachs, Mr. Barber. We need men who can maintain a good front. We need men who are not afraid to do what is necessary, whatever that may be. Are you such a man, Mr. Barber?"

"You know I am."

"That is why you are here. You have no family, no woman?"

"No. I find it best to be alone."

"That is good. Too many men say things to women. Women are weak. They cannot be trusted to keep their mouths shut."

"I agree." Terry butted out his cigarette, considered lighting another but refrained.

"Mr. Arganmajc was weak as well."

In his mind's eye, Terry saw Randy Arganmajc pleading for his life even after his lips had been cut off. The vision was nothing he wanted to remember but one difficult to forget. "It may have been difficult to be strong under the circumstances."

"We speak of different circumstances. He had all the benefits and privileges of wealth and power but he turned his back on us. He tried to slither out of the country like a snake when things got tough. He did not have the stomach for it."

"Let's assume I have the stomach. What is it you are suggesting?"

"Most of the men employed outside these grounds are lazy or stupid. You have proven to be neither. You comport yourself well under stress. You keep your body in good shape and practice regularly with your chosen weapons. Why did you choose to walk the path you have?"

"I was looking for a job. A man does what he must."

"Ah, yes. But there are many jobs out there that do not involve personal risk. You could have done any number of things, yet you chose a more dangerous route."

"I was looking for a job."

"Are you a leader or a follower?"

"We all follow someone or something. It is not the sort of question one can ask without qualifying."

"You are a follower then?"

"No, I... Once again, that is a question for posterity. I can lead those I have the authority to lead. When something needs to be done, I can do it or I can order it done. Are you offering me Randy's job?"

"Oh, heavens no. You are nowhere near ready to accept the responsibility of such a position. I do see in you something, however. I feel you may be able to do a better job than some of the men who are now in power. I do question your ambition, though. You do not seem to care for authority. Could you have ordered what was done to Randy?"

"Ordered it, yes. Done it myself, no. I would have killed him long before."

"Yes, the outsider that eliminated the Irishman told us you had no scruples when it came to killing. You do have scruples though."

Terry reached out and pulled another cigarette from the pack. He needed a second to decide how to answer the question. Adam Troy was after something and Terry did not

222

know precisely what it was. It was a cat and mouse game and if the younger man jumped he would become the mouse. He had seen too many dead mice.

"Mr. Troy, I am capable of giving, as well as following, orders. I have no foolish notions about the sanctity of human life. You asked whether I am a leader or a follower, what you are really asking is am I a predator, or prey. The answer is not simple. A crocodile or shark is predator to all around it, even man in the right circumstances. Yet baby crocodiles are eaten by fish and birds. After they get bigger, they eat the same fish and birds that would have eaten them as babies."

"You have a good mind as well as a strong stomach. I think we can safely say there is a place for you in the organization. Now, is it better to be loved or feared?"

"I have seen women love men they feared."

"Because?"

"Because they are weak."

"But…"

"But love is an unnecessary component. They are not mutually exclusive, but fear is more powerful. I have seen men betray the women they love. It follows that fear is better."

Adam Troy seemed satisfied by the answer, though it was not cut and dried. He seemed to have found what he was looking for.

When his cell phone rang, Gordon saw it was Terry's number. He hit the connection but said nothing for a second. There was no sound from the other end so he said, "Roberts Pistol Range." The connection went dead. He closed his eyes and took a deep breath. If they had Terry's cell phone, they had him. There was nothing the Scotsman could do.

The operation had been a success up until this point. They had secured a huge pile of cash. Nobody had seen Gordon's face. He had left no fingerprints and the only fatality had been the guard, who had been shot with the driver's gun. He might have killed the guard he ran down as well. There was no evidence linking Terry to the operation except that telephone number.

Sometimes a man needs to cut and run, Gordon MacMaster felt this may be just such a time. There is no place in the world for a white man to disappear quite like the Australian Outback. Of course, everybody there knows the man is there, but nobody else does. It causes a very localized stir when someone shows up but the ripples go no further than the town. There are no cell phone towers and very few telephone lines. A man could disappear in the Outback forever.

Terry had never met Jimmy Cognac before. Jimmy had been brought north to take over the Sydney area after the unfortunate demise of Randy Arganmajc. Jimmy never commented on his predecessor's demise.

Henry Cuthbert kept his position probably due to the fact that the ranks had been so badly thinned. It took days for the group to be released from custody. The driver was still under indictment since it had been his pistol that killed the guard.

Terry took the spot vacated by the late, unlamented, Victor Wellington. Upon accepting this position he was informed of the manner of Victor's passing. He felt certain that the slightest slip would cause his passing to be every bit as horrible. Eric Tronquilla, the man who had inherited the position temporarily seemed relieved to hand it to someone else and it was soon clear why.

Randy had not communicated the extent to which recent events had decimated his work force. Between the pre-Olympic sweeps and the recent desertions, the Sydney underworld was in shambles. The only groups thriving were those with a customer base separate from the regular Australians and no ties to them. The Asians and the Russians had been hit by the police actions but had been unscathed by the vigilante operations. They had increased their power base and had begun supplying to their competition. Their customer base was growing rapidly, especially among the drug users.

Terry found he was under such scrutiny that he could not escape for the weekend any more. He could not simply slip away and head for Orange or Molong as had been his habit. The Russians and Chinese were eating his lunch, so to speak, and he was expected to do something about it. But his hands were tied as well by the fact that the Russians were supposed to be working with the Australians. The last thing either of them needed at this point was a turf war. The Troys had hoped to assimilate the Eastern Bloc immigrants, but the process was slow. The only choice of a target he had was the Orientals, and they were a very close-knit group. There was no chance at infiltration because of the cultural, language and physical appearance barriers. They operated their own gambling operations, transported their own drugs and worked in a different sort of world.

Terry's new position was as an enforcer in charge of other enforcers. He was expected to be brutal and uncompromising. There had been so many men holding the position lately that many of the men paying for protection or dealing contraband no longer knew who they were supposed to be paying. Terry was also supposed to locate the American who had caused so much trouble lately. This was the second time he was charged with finding himself, but he was only one of several at his level of management charged with the same tasks.

Terry was on his way to talk to a "client" when his phone rang. Gretta, the secretary for the Kingston Agency wanted to retire and wondered when Terry was going to make an appearance in Orange. There were no problems, but they had not seen the owner for months. Terry gave Gretta the number for Linda Pierce and told her to tell Linda that she had been chosen from a limited pool of potential employees. Gretta was skeptical since it was acknowledged that she was the glue that held the office together and not everybody could do the same sort of job she did. She did however acquiesce to the suggestion and promised to make the call.

Ginger got the letter a few days later.

Uncle,

I find it no less than amazing that I have advanced to the point I have when I have nothing but animosity for the organization. This cannot continue. I have painted myself into a corner and cannot wait for the floor to dry. I am now doing things I would never have expected for people I wish to see dead. I have no idea how it got this far.

I'm afraid I need to leave. There is no possibility of staying in Sydney, or indeed in Australia, once I fulfill my destiny. I will be turning the Agency over to a friend of mine. You will be mailed a percentage of the profits. If it looks safe, we will resume communication once I am established elsewhere.

The letter was unsigned.

If it had been difficult to get to Abel and Adam Troy in the past, it was considerably more so now. They had gone into a defensive mode. More and more people were taking swipes at the business, from within and without. They were planning on keeping a low profile until their tracking services had located the most recent danger.

It would have seemed simple to find an American who had been in the country since before June 1st 2001, there are records of such things. There were, however crowds of people moving through the country's airports because of the Olympics. They came from anywhere and everywhere and while most of them went back to their lives and their families, many did not. At least not on paper. It was not difficult to access the records, but more difficult at that point to decipher them and since their basic premise was flawed, their trackers floundered.

The police were having no better luck. There were those who had been paid to find this new threat to the underworld and there were those who simply tried to do their jobs. The new Superintendent, Theodore Barlow, had taken an unusual stand on the assaults to the underworld shipping lanes. Publicly and officially he had denounced the vigilante nature of the attacks. Less publicly he had applauded them. He was actually sorry to see the case closed with the death of Lee Pierce, but he was also unconvinced. He had some research done on Mr. Pierce and concluded that there was little likelihood of his having real access to knowledge of the shipping schedules. There was something that did not add up, despite the evidence. The fact that the assaults on the shipping lanes ended with his death seemed proof positive of Lee's culpability but it did not convince him. He was certain there had been a setup. Pierce was a scapegoat, set up and eliminated with evidence planted.

In his new position, Barlow had a great number of political duties and not nearly as much investigative work. He should probably have retired, but the reduction of crime during his reign as Chief Inspector had made him a celebrity. With a few notable exceptions, he had kept the public safe and truncated the drug supply in Sydney. Now he was forced to smile at government functions and represent the police force to the public without any real investigative function. He only enjoyed his celebrity for a little while before it began to gall him. He did not like his role but found that it allowed him to push through funding that he had always lacked when he was on the streets. He was instrumental in getting a $120,000,000 allocated for battling the drug trade in 2001. Another $ 80,000,000 was allocated for compulsory drug education for children but he had not been involved in that portion of the program.

The New South Wales Police were not indicated in the corruption scandal that rocked the Victoria Police for the past year, though there were some questions about evidence being reintroduced to the streets. The individual cases and questions never made it to Theodore Barlow's level. He had entered the rarified air of the elite governmental employee and was no longer to be bothered with such minor matters. The affair at Hill Top piqued his interest, however. He had never lost his love of the investigation.

According to the police reports, there was a reinforced security van modified to carry liquid funds but the box and the bags were tampered with and no report of loss was filed. There was a guard, allegedly shot by the driver. There were a lot of armed gangland figures that had no business in the small town, and there was a half buried razor strip down the road. Further down the road there was a bridge that had been demolished and a number of stranded vehicles that had no business being there. There was a displaced tow truck driver, a guard who had almost been killed when he was run over, and another who claimed to have been dispatched to a tavern for a beer. The local police had held them as long as they could and released most of them two days after the lawyers showed up.

Superintendent Barlow suspected the Russians. They had been coming into the country in increasing numbers and setting up businesses, many of which were suspect.

Chief Inspector Andrew Slaughter was called in for a conference. Slaughter knew that Theodore Barlow had a habit of looking the other way when the criminals hit each others' operations as long as normal citizens were not affected. There had been a number of such operations in the past few years where the police could not have been nearly as effective as the other members of the underworld. He also knew that the influx of Eastern Europeans and Russians in the past decade had been a cause for concern. They were ruthless and flaunted their savage methods. Moreover, they exported cash back to their home countries, a most unacceptable practice. It was bad enough they didn't pay taxes on it but to send it overseas for laundering was hurting the economy. Barlow often likened it to the Cuban boat people crisis in America where Fidel Castro had emptied his jails into the streets of Miami.

Chief Inspector Andrew Slaughter was promised additional funding, taken from the new anti-drug fund, to investigate the incident and those involved. He was also given the nod to go after the emerging power centers in Sydney: the Orientals and the Soviets.

Jimmy Cognac and Henry Cuthbert were together the entire day. They were going over the same thing Andrew Slaughter and Theodore Barlow were discussing and the questions were much the same. Why was everybody there, who knew they were there, and how had they been manipulated so easily? Jimmy did not want to end up in the same condition as his predecessor. Jimmy had been living the high life in Victoria mostly due to the fact that his people had a lot of constables on the payroll. A lot of things were ignored, a lot of competition was killed or run out of the area,

229

a lot of the competition's merchandise wound up under Jimmy's control. Things were different in Sydney.

The New South Wales Police Force is divided into 80 different jurisdictions. Coordination had been understandably difficult in the past given the distances involved. The dawning of the computer age was changing all that. Files could be sent instantly and in their entirety. Inventories of the evidence lockers could be brought up and updated constantly as well as who checked out what evidence and more importantly, when the evidence was returned. The Sydney area got the computers first and an initiative was on to supply the entire province with them. Many of the older, provincial police felt there was no need for them and that they would continue doing their jobs as they had for the past number of decades without the damn things. This was more outside the city. The younger members of the force were proficient and eager to use the networked system to their advantage.

Part of the advantage of the new system was in cataloguing photographs. The database could eliminate anyone not fitting the description, saving hours of pouring over the old piles of mug shot books. It also pulled up a photo with an ID number.

The system pulled up Jimmy Cognac's face in no time. He had dark hair and dark brown eyes with gypsy features. A gap between his front teeth and a scar across his lip, right above the gap made him quickly identifiable.

The system held Henry Cuthbert's smiling face. He was tall and blond with heavy features and a florid complexion that mixed poorly with the light hair. His eyes were a dark blue and his lips were thick.

The system had no photograph for Thompson Barber. He had never been arrested. He was questioned after the Hill Top affair, but he was never arrested or fingerprinted. Every other man on that job with the exception of John who was still in the hospital was arrested and photographed.

Thompson Barber came up as a non-entity. The population records were incomplete, much of it never got input into any system, records got lost, systems crashed and wiped out years of work. There were many reasons Thompson Barber might have been dropped from the records so there was no red flag flying. Thompson might have been the only man to reach the level he had without having been arrested. He had, after all, gone through the ranks in meteoric fashion and been stuffed into his position out of necessity. He was attracting attention now though. Chief Inspector Andrew Slaughter had instructed his inspectors to find out who the man was and where he had come from. They turned the judicial eye upon him and lit up the spotlight.

The Australian Provincial Police have never been known for subtlety. They are the brutal product of a brutal land. The city police departments are a bit more restrained but still need to deal with a country full of drunks, immigrants and a rising tide of drugs. When called on to act, they do so with all the necessary force.

Terry was giving a pimp a little talking to when the two constables approached him. It was not the money the man owed, that had been forthcoming, it was the way he treated his girls. It was personal. Terry should have known better but he was still way too young to be in the position he held and his past successes had made him cocky.

The pimp knew better than to press charges on the man who had just tuned him up. That would have ended badly for him. The constables would probably charge him with disorderly conduct, but they had no idea how disorderly he could be. They ran up on the scene expecting to restrain him and take him in and got a little more than they had bargained for.

The alley was dark and Terry was done giving his subject instruction. The two constables could not run silently but did manage to get to within a few feet of Terry before he saw them. The billy club was swinging toward his head but that was as close as it got. Terry ducked under the swing and launched himself head first at the constable's midsection. If the man had been ready for it he might have tightened up but it would not have prevented the two cracked ribs he got. Needless to say he dropped like a stone. The second policeman caught Terry across the back with his club, but it was an awkward swing and did not have the requisite force behind it. Terry caught him with a backhand, also with little force behind it, but when the constable raised his club for another swing, he left himself open. Too fast for the man, Terry dropped to one knee and brought his fist up between the man's legs. There was a sickening slapping sound and all the air went out of the constable's lungs. The only sound in the alley, now, was the groaning and wheezing of two downed men and the retreating footsteps of a thoroughly chastened gentleman of leisure. Terry caught himself just in time to prevent putting a bullet into each of the downed officer's brains. He shoved his revolvers back into their holsters and started moving. The first officer reached out for his ankle. Terry kicked him in the face and ran.

"That was stupid," said Henry. "First of all, it's not your job to protect the stupid, drug addict whores from their pimps. If they had seen you slapping him around they probably would have jumped you themselves. Whores need to be kept in line that way and they love their men for it."

"They can't do their jobs from a hospital bed. Besides, how can a woman give a blow job with a broken nose?"

"Tommy, it doesn't matter. You are not in that business. Your business is to make sure they pay on time. I

232

don't care how they get the money or who they get it from. It doesn't matter to me and it shouldn't matter to you either."

"Ok. I just don't like to see men hurt women."

"Get used to it and get over it. Now, the real problem is the patrol you hit. They will be looking all over the city for you. I assume they got a good enough look at you to identify you?"

"Probably. It was dark and I hit them pretty fast. I didn't recognize them so I don't think they knew me. They didn't see what I was driving."

"I wouldn't be so sure."

"I'm not. What do you think? I could turn myself in."

"No, that would be stupid. I'll send out some feelers. Stay out of that area for a while. We'll see."

"Ok. Has that manager of Coley's paid up this week?"

"Don't worry about him. Send Ralph over there at closing time with a cricket bat. He'll pay."

"I'd pay if Ralph showed up with a cricket bat," Terry smiled.

"Somehow I don't think so. Anyway, lay low for a while. I'm trying to get Jimmy to transfer a couple of men from Melbourne to give you a hand. You're getting too well known on the street so you need to lay low. If they show up here, at the warehouse, I'll tell them to fuck off but you'll need to be more careful. You're not in the bloody schoolyard any more. They put the tag on you and who knows what might happen."

Terry pulled out a cigarette, thoughtfully tapping it on the desktop. He had seen what happened to men who fell out of favor. The fact that it had been his fault did not bother him and the thought almost made him smile, but he needed to hold a stern visage and did so. He had recounted what had happened to Randy Arganmajc in gory detail. The shock had worn off but he had felt the helplessness of being strapped to a chair in the mansion's basement and he never wanted to feel that way again. He lit his cigarette and promised to take a less physical role and a more administrative one.

The money that was collected in Sydney never got pooled for long. It went into bank accounts on a daily basis. It did represent a lot of money but it was never in one place at one time. It could not be targeted. The monies that could be hit were the payments for drug shipments and the daily or weekly transports from the other areas. These were large enough to make it worthwhile, but there were too many people watching Terry for him to make a move. Gordon was incommunicado and Ginger required a week's notice. Terry seldom got a week's notice. The multiple losses that the organization had suffered within the past year had tightened up the communication chain a great deal. Nobody knew when a large load was coming in until it was almost there.

So Terry played his game and settled into his role as leader of enforcers. He never showed his feelings about it but he was becoming more and more uncomfortable. He saw the methods employed by his associates and also those used by the newcomers. The Russians were even more brutal and the Orientals, while more subtle, were terrible. The truth was that if the Australian underworld was destroyed it would stop nothing. The replacements were going to be worse.

Sitting in his apartment, half drunk on cheap gin, Terry made a decision.

Chapter Thirteen
Longing for Home

Superintendent Theodore Barlow was not expected to be in his office on Saturdays. He blessed his long-suffering wife as he turned the key in the office lock. The truth was he missed the investigations and some of the grime of the streets had never washed off his skin. He wore a better grade of suit these days and drank a better grade of scotch, but he had always been fond of the physical process, not the political wrangling. The fact that he had made it up the ladder was much due to that long-suffering wife who had forced him to go to fund raisers he had no desire to attend, and dinners he had no appetite for.

There was an emptiness to the Town Hall on Saturdays that Barlow particularly enjoyed. There may have been some interns and clerks finishing up the week's load but for the most part the building was deserted except for the new annex where the main police station was housed. The deserted corridors echoed and rang with his footsteps and gave him an almost nostalgic feeling. The air conditioning had been shut down in the main body of the building but Barlow's office had its own unit.

Saturdays gave Superintendent Barlow a chance to reflect, to work on some of the high profile cases that were no longer really a part of his daily duties and to plan. He had ordered some files delivered to his desk the day before and was pleased to find that they had been delivered. The first file he cracked open on the morning of December 15 was labeled Henry Cuthbert.

Henry was suspected to be just what he was, a middle management mob figure. He had been arrested a couple of times and had spent time in prison for assault in the late eighties. He had never cooperated with the police and had gone back to his shady dealings after being released. There was a mug shot included in the file. It looked like just another mug shot to Barlow; just another scumbag looking sorry to have been caught. There were also some surveillance pictures in the file, black and white, grainy and worthless. His home town was listed as Molong. He had two brothers, one of them deceased, the other still living there. He drove a working man's car and lived in a middle class neighborhood. He had been noticed a couple of times lately. He had been accused of leaving a bomb at the clubhouse of a golf course but there had been no bomb in the case. He had been one of the group of men involved in the debacle south of the city. Once again he had refused to cooperate and the constables were forced to release him.

The Inspectors were convinced that Henry Cuthbert was in charge of what would equate to gangster supervisors. He was seldom seen rubbing elbows with the street-level thugs but often observed meeting with those who did. These lower level wise guys were not interesting to Barlow. He wanted to pick off those at the top. One of these men was Jimmy Cognac. He had come on the scene very recently, reportedly taking the place of Randy Arganmajc, who had disappeared. Jimmy Cognac came from the Melbourne Area where there had been a huge scandal recently. The constables in Melbourne had been raiding the evidence lockers and returning the evidence to the streets instead of getting it destroyed. Jimmy had been exempt from suspicion in this matter only because he never soiled his hands with such matters.

The Superintendent decided that Henry Cuthbert was to be the target and to get him, he would need to turn one of the man's subordinates. There was a small pile of files for these men and he turned his attention to them now.

After examining some of the hard copy files, the superintendent went to his secretary's desk and booted up her computer. It contained a duty roster for the weekend. He

236

determined that Senior Sergeant Randolph Black was on duty both days. Henry did not know Randolph well but he certainly had time to get acquainted. At first he thought he would call the man to his office, but then he realized that it would be more comfortable if he went to the Sergeant's office.

"Sergeant. No, please, sit down. I'm not here for anything serious."

Sergeant Black was unconvinced but he sat back down. "Yes, Sir, Mr. Superintendent. Uh, what can I do for you?"

"You can relax and call me Ted."

"Ok, Ted, what seems to be the trouble?"

"It is almost noon and I have a bottle of 12-year-old scotch that is not planning to get a day older."

"But, I'm on duty, Sir."

"Then this is going to be a part of your duties today. Lock the door. You are in conference with the new Superintendent and cannot be disturbed."

"Yes, Sir!" Randolph Black was not used to this sort of treatment from his superiors and it was clear that this man had not started drinking yet. He only hoped he was not setting himself up for an enormous fall.

"Sergeant Black," Barlow said after a bit of small talk and some scotch. "I have a need to get something on Henry Cuthbert. I need to get a witness against him. A credible witness."

"We have been trying for years. I don't think we are much closer now than before. See, Superintendent, they have created a culture of fear that keeps 'em all clammed up. I'd have an easier time getting a red blenny to turn over."

"Yes, I know, I've heard the stories. The torture... That's it! The torturer. They've got some sick fuck who does the tortures for them, right?"

"Uh, yes, I suppose so."

"Then he is the one we need to get a hold of. The bastards who do the really dirty work are often the easiest to turn. Find out who this bastard is. Give it a try. I'll bet the very thing they use to scare others is a real pudding. I don't care how you do it, I'm covering you on this one. As long as nobody ends up dead, you can use whatever means necessary."

"Oy, there might be expenses involved in this."

That was the sort of reaction Theodore Barlow wanted to hear. He knew he could trust this man to get the job done. He might very well break the back of the mob in Sydney if he went about it the right way.

Barlow took another drink and thought about the Prime Minister's robes.

Evan (Saxon) McCormick was by no means sophisticated. As the president of the largest motorcycle gang in Australia, he was not expected to be sophisticated. He was, however, diplomatic. He had no formal education but he was well read in practical application and leadership theory.

It was almost as difficult to get a conference with Evan McCormick as with the Troy brothers or the Prime Minister and for similar reasons. There were a lot of men who would have liked to see Evan dead. Most of the rival gangs would have been glad to see him expire because he was the glue that held the Dark Knights together.

The makeup of the Dark Knights Motorcycle Club loosely followed military tradition, with a president, a general, majors, a Sergeant-at-Arms and recruits. They were all elected positions, however, so nobody had lifetime rights to any title.

The Sydney headquarters was behind the bar. The whole complex was labeled "Choppers" including the tavern, meeting hall, repair barn. The Motorcycle Supermarket was a

238

couple of miles down the road. Evan owned that as well. A bikie could get anything from boots and a belt to a crank for a pan head. That was just the legal side of the business. Sex and drugs were epidemic and guns were ubiquitous. The whiskey flowed like wine and the bandages were in ready supply. Evan made a show of joining the party from time to time but more often he watched the crowd. He knew with a certainty that the bikies were kept in line with bread and circuses. As long as the party lasted, they were on his side.

The money that flowed through his hands was used well. He had no need for drugs but used them if they were free. He drank but did not need the drink. He used women when they wanted him but turned down as much as he accepted. Moderation was not a subject that bikies considered but it made him a leader among them. And it made him a very powerful man who paid his tribute to the Troy brothers regularly. He knew who could shut them down with a phone call. He knew there were judges that would look one way or another depending on the brothers' direction. He knew the police would let him be, or come crashing down around his ears like a falling tree, depending on what the brothers said.

The bike club and the organized crime syndicate were separate entities entirely except when interests crossed path. The bikies manufactured and sold crank, a powerful and heavily addictive form of amphetamine. They also used it heavily. A little bit of good crank would keep you up for two or three days. You could travel cross country non-stop like the legendary truck drivers, or drink all night and still walk a straight line in the morning. The down side was that the lack of sleep unbalanced a man's mind and he would be irrational in no time.

The Troy brothers did not want much to do with the bikies and their wild life. Once in a while they would sacrifice one of the gangs to the court system so the police could say they had scored a major bust and were winning. They had never sacrificed the Dark Knights and never would as long as Evan McCormick was in charge. He paid his tribute and he kept order. He even kept order among the 'one percenters,' that rare breed of man capable of anything at any time. He did not bind them too tightly, however, men such as that could not be restrained except by armed guards and steel bars.

Despite their reputation, the Dark Knights, under McCormick's rule, was pretty low-key. They made good money from some of their operations but many of them squandered it. Living for the day has always been bikie philosophy; eat, drink and be merry for tomorrow we die. They needed to cut loose from time to time but they did so at the bike rallies outside the city. The rallies were huge events, open to anyone with the spine to attend. Booze, broads and bands kept the parties hopping. The events were held in a neutral zone where no guns were allowed. It was common to have a man or two stabbed during the rally, but nobody had yet been shot.

A rally was the one place a man could get a conference with the president of the Dark Knights. One needed to come in disarmed or be disarmed by the bikies, but it was a small concession to be made.

Initially, McCormick refused to speak with Terry Kingston alone. Terry, in turn, refused to speak with so many people listening in. McCormick told him there was nothing to discuss in that event, but that he was free to hang out and party as long as he wanted. Terry did wait for a while, drinking beer and smoking. He listened to the men around him but said little. While Terry waited, the President of the Dark Knights was getting some research done on Thompson Barber, as Terry was known to everyone in the Sydney area. Laptop computers and wireless signals were not what would have been expected, stumbling upon this group, but they had both. Evan McCormick may not have been sophisticated but he was sharp and cautious.

"Well then, Mr. Barber, what is it that is so important that you must speak to me without my generals?" The tent they sat in was not soundproof but the band was loud and the two were sitting close.

"Mr. McCor…"

"Tsst. Call me Saxon. That is my name."

"Saxon then. What I am seeing is a man who knows how to run men giving tribute to men who know nothing about it."

"Make your pitch."

"I think it would be mutually beneficial for us to form an alliance. Together we could create a dynasty that would incorporate all the various vices man is so eager to pay for. You and I could thrive like foxes if we played our cards right."

"What the fuck are you talking about and why? I already thrive like a fox and have no idea what you are selling. I'll call you if I need a vacuum cleaner."

Terry was unscathed by Saxon's comment. "I am somewhat reticent about speaking in this venue. I don't know who is listening. I don't know the men around you. I only deal with men who possess a certain quality and quantity of honor. Are you indeed such a man or have I misread you?"

Evan McCormick was not used to speaking with men who used such measured words and reasonable tone. His research had authenticated this man but his senses told him that anyone pretending to be a crook and talking like a lawyer is definitely an undercover cop. Trust was not something easily given to anyone outside the club and only a few inside the club.

"Who the fuck are you to talk to me about honor?" Evan asked. "You work for the Troys. I can't think of men with less honor."

"There are many things about me you do not know. Yes, I am currently associated with the aforementioned association, but that is not a permanent situation. I foresee a change in the wind and I will be there when the storm is over. I want to know if you will stand with me. Will you?"

"You're right. This is not the place to carry on this conversation. I don't trust you and I don't think there is anything you can do to make me trust you. I will say you have balls, coming in here and talking shit, but I don't think I like you."

"There is no need for us to like each other, but there is a need for us to trust each other. I need to know if you are the sort of man I can trust."

"Get the fuck out of here before I kick the shit out of you. I still don't know what you're selling."

"All right. I'm going to leave, but we will speak again. I am giving you the opportunity to become more than you are. You have the ability to rise above the crowd, but you limit yourself through your associations. I am suggesting that you advance to the next level of authority. You may be the President of this group but you still pay tribute to others. I am suggesting we step beyond that." Terry rose and nodded to Evan, who did not move.

Kingston had shown up at the rally with half a dozen men but he had not told them why he was there. As far as they were concerned they were going to carouse and get wild. They hung together nervously, however. They did not feel accepted among the bikies. They were dressed wrong and looked out of place.

The one thing that concerned Terry was that Evan might talk to someone else. He had been deliberately vague about what he was up to, however. He had said nothing

242

definitive but that did not matter. It had not gone as well as he had hoped. It looked as though he would need to find a different candidate. Or maybe not.

It had been a month since Superintendent Barlow had first spoken with Sergeant Black and though there had been a real push, there had been no positive results in the search for the torturer. It seemed that it had been a pipe dream.

Evidence against Henry Cuthbert was also difficult to find. Henry conducted business carefully enough to keep himself out of prison. They could probably have gotten him on some minor charges but he would be provided with good lawyers and the city would probably end up sued for harassment. They needed something positive, something big and worthwhile.

"I'm sorry Superintendent, I have been flogging my men to get something for you. I put money on the street, but no one will take it for a good lead. This man has them scared to death or they really don't know. I found nothing on a torturer."

"Well Senior Sergeant Black, at least we have made the attempt." Barlow was relaxed by dint of several glasses of scotch. It was late in the afternoon on a Saturday.

"The Henry Cuthbert thing is not that productive either. He seems to have moved up in the organization when his predecessor, or more than one, was killed. You remember, that was the Lee Pierce thing where he went renegade and started blowing up trucks and the like. Somebody finally shot him." Sergeant Black looked at the scotch bottle but Barlow did not offer him any.

"Yes. Forensics determined that it was not the driver that shot Pierce, right?"

"Uh, I was not on that case. It actually happened north of the city and outside our, that is my, jurisdiction. I can get you a copy of the files on Monday, but we don't have that case here."

"No, thank you. I think I will take a trip up there on Monday if my schedule is clear. I remember there was something about that whole case that did not strike me as clean. I'll be going home now, Sergeant. Are you on the roster for next Saturday?"

"I'm not certain yet, Sir. I can make it happen if you think it would help."

"Yes. If they give you a problem, tell them to see me."

It was actually never a problem for Senior Sergeant Randolph Black to be assigned to boring office duty Saturdays. Nobody else wanted it, and even for overtime pay it was the least desirable assignment to be had on a summer day in Sydney. Black had his own ideas about it however. Meeting with the Superintendent and hashing out big plans without Inspectors or the Chief Inspector made him feel special, important, and destined to succeed. Not finding anything of significant value made him look like a failure. It was imperative that something be found, fixed or fabricated to indict Henry Cuthbert.

Sergeant Black saw the opportunity when one of the constables brought in a runner from the street. He was in possession of a little under an ounce of cocaine in separate little bottles. Half the bottles mysteriously disappeared and nobody ever said anything about it.

A half ounce of cocaine was enough to imprison anyone, especially when it was already packaged for sale.

Terry was looking for another candidate worthy of consideration but the field was bleak. He was in the gym, pumping iron and running, when the bearded man covered with tattoos stopped by for a workout. It put Terry on his guard when that same man joined him in the steam room after the exercise. There was nothing to worry about, however. Saxon wanted a conference and his messenger was being simply being discreet. Messages were often sent this way.

The meeting was not held in any of the usual haunts of either the Dark Knights of the wise guys. It was held in a family restaurant. It was after the lunch crowd was gone but before the dinner patrons started to fill the place. Terry was there before Evan but he was not the first in. There were already several seedy looking characters eating or just drinking coffee. Saxon arrived by himself but he was not alone.

"What are you?" the club president wanted to know. "You have never been arrested. You have never been implicated in any sting operations. You are not a regular customer and you're not a wannabe."

"That's a question that only my eulogy could answer." Terry addressed himself to his ham steak.

"And a mysterious fucker as well."

Terry said nothing. It was plain that Evan McCormick was interested in what he was proposing or he would not be here.

"So why are we talking?"

"Look, Mr. President, our interests coincide but we must barter on a level of trust that we do not currently have."

"Do not call me Mr. President."

"I shall call you…?"

"Call me Saxon."

"Ok, Saxon. Before we are able to have a proper relationship, we are going to need a heightened level of trust as I said. I know I can trust you to work in your own best interests, but that is not a problem since our interests coincide."

"In what way?"

"You want power and control of the illicit trade in Sydney and I want to give it to you."

"Why? What possible reason do you have for wanting to enhance my position?"

"As you have stated, my current employers are men with no honor. I wish to upgrade the man in that position with one of a certain morality that they do not possess, but I feel you do."

"And the benefit to you?"

"I shall obviously advance my own position to one of more authority and influence. I am not looking to be in charge of the operation. I leave that to men with more ambition. I wish to work behind the scenes making things right for my friends and associates."

"But you already have friends and associates. Why would you come to me, a stranger and offer to do anything for me? I suspect your motivation and mistrust you."

"Saxon. You are obviously an educated man. You do not speak like the leaders of, say the Rebels. Yes, I have spoken with him. He is a boor and a lout."

"A boor and a lout? You sound like you come from a hundred years ago."

"This is my point. You understand what I said; they would not have. You have what it takes to lead men who are not a drunken rabble. You have potential. Tell me, who are your biggest competition, your enemies?"

"We need to get back to my first question, what are you? A king maker?"

"Once again, your competition would not even recognize that phrase. You have what it takes to be in charge. Now who is your biggest competition?"

"We don't have much competition but the Berserkers cause us the most trouble. A bunch of one percenters. Why?"

"Honor and trust. If you are going to trust me I need to prove to you that you can. Look for a package in a couple of days. I'm assuming the Berserkers will fall apart without their leader, right?"

"I don't know. I do know I don't want to go to war because someone did something stupid. You planning on doing something stupid?"

"Only my eulogy can say that." Terry rose and said goodbye. He paid the check on the way out.

Saxon sat, still rubbing his chin. He still had no idea what the man was all about but he was certain he would have been successful as a businessman. He would look for a package in a couple of days, but he had no idea what was to be in the package. He was not used to working with such mystery and he did not like it.

Three days later he got the package. It was delivered to the clubhouse in a locked, insulated box. Evan took it into an office and cut the padlock off. Inside, packed in dry ice, was the former head of the Berserkers motorcycle club. That is to say the head of the former head was in the box.

Saxon prepared himself for war but the Berserkers went after a club from Brisbane instead. There was something left with the headless body of their president that indicated The Damned had been responsible.

When the Berserkers hit The Damned, it was like something from an old Western without the Indians. They moved in on the clubhouse, slaughtered everyone in the place and set it on fire. The Damned were not geared up for it and never saw it coming, but their response was not timid either. When the smoke cleared, both gangs had been decimated and the remaining members were searching for new homes. The Dark Knights refused to consider members of either club.

Terry was contacted at the gym that week.

"So you got my fuckin' attention now." Evan McCormick did not look as happy as one might expect after having two of his major rivals dealt with.

Terry hoisted his pint of ale and took a long deliberate drink. They were alone but the back room of this bar had been chosen carefully. There was one small barred window. There was no exit save the door and the bar was full of Dark Knight colors. Not only had he gotten their attention, he had gotten their respect. There was never a question among the bikies whether it was better to be loved or feared. Fear was the only way.

"Saxon, what are you willing to do to consolidate your power?" Terry knew the time for subtlety had passed. He needed to hit him with the plan and suck him in like a jet engine.

"I don't know that I need to consolidate anything. I'm in power now. One word and my brothers will cut you up in little pieces. Nobody will ever hear from you again."

"You misunderstand the situation. I am not threatening you and I have no power of my own, nor do I want it. I'm no leader but you… You are a natural leader of men and heir to the throne of the underworld if you can take it. With the proper direction, the Dark Knights could easily take over the entire city's drug supply; the tarts, the cards, all of it. No disrespect mate, but you'll be sitting in the ivory tower instead of that shitty little compound."

"Watch it."

"I told you, no disrespect. You built that up from nothing but you should be gaining momentum, not clutchin'. There are half a dozen men in this entire country that have the power to make things happen behind the scenes. The only reason they have this power is they have guards around them. Take them out and set your own men in place. Supply the guards and boom, you are in power. You pay tribute to no man, they all pay tribute to you like a Roman Emperor."

"How do I know you're not setting me up like the Berserkers? How do I know there isn't a box waiting for my head?"

248

"Again, no disrespect, but you'd never see it coming if I were."

"Again, no disrespect, but what the fuck are you?"

"I'm nothing but a man who knows what he wants and knows how to make friends. My friends are very happy to be my friends, and my enemies…" Terry knew this was the critical juncture. This was the moment where the pendulum would either swing for or against him. He kept his right hand on his beer, but his left hand was below the lip of the table. He reached the fingers of his left hand under his belt. He took a drink of his beer to cover the movement and slipped his middle finger into the loop of a length of wire he had sown into his belt.

Evan McCormick sat looking into the eyes of the man across the table. The man was young and despite his assertions, ambitious, but he was no stupid little boy running away from home to join the circus. Evan had seen enough strikers with that look to them. Striker is what they called the recruits who did not yet qualify for colors. The man who was calmly drinking ale, and talking about taking over the drug trade for the entire country, was different.

"I'm going to need some more specific information to make a decision," Evan said, slowly.

The moment had passed and Terry slowly pulled his left hand out of the waistband of his pants. The wire stayed where it was. Both men knew he had been sold on the idea, now all that was to be presented was the plan.

"Come now, I'll shout a round." Evan knew that men spoke out of hand when drunk and he very much wanted to get this man to speak out of hand.

Chapter Fourteen
The Berserkers and The Damned

"What do you make of this, Sergeant?"

"That the file on the bike war?"

"Yes, the Berserkers headed up to Brisbane and went all hairy on The Damned. Between the two of them, about 10 percent are left alive from what I gather. Most of 'em went to ground somewhere. We got three of the Damned in jail in Brisbane; weapons charges. They don't appear to be willing to talk."

"Well, Super, I won't be crying over it."

"No, nor will I but what I want to know is, were there hard feeling between these men before? I don't remember any but I have been off the streets for a long time now and things change."

"I don't recall any problems between the two. The Damned stay in the Brisbane area. They've been spotted down here at the bike rallies but never caused a problem. They ran a bit to the darker side of things if I recall. Brought a couple in for heroin some time back. They wouldn't turn over though.

"The Berserkers are crankers. They got a lab or two set up somewhere making the shit and that's what they do. They don't compete with each other I don't think. There is one thing that's strange though. The leader, president if you like, was dead before they went north. He was probably killed by someone in his own club. Cut his head right off, they did. Never found the head, either."

Superintendent Barlow poured them each another glass of scotch. The disappointment at not having found the torturer had passed and they were on to bigger and better things. Sergeant Black was certain of a promotion and the superintendent was certain that things would get done without question.

"I see you had Henry Cuthbert's car impounded. Did you find anything in it?"

"No, not this time. He should be more careful where he parks that thing. There's no telling what might happen."

"So, you think something might happen?"

"Oh, I'm pretty sure something is going to happen."

Something did happen. The Provincial Police pulled Henry Cuthbert over on the expressway and the entire incident was recorded on the dashboard camera of the officers' vehicle. Everything was relatively standard for a traffic stop. The lead constable took the license and registration and brought it back to check for wants and warrants. The German Shepherd in the back was getting very jumpy, so the constable riding shotgun put a leash on him and took him out of the vehicle. The dog went directly to the trunk of Henry's car and sniffed and whined, with his tail going in circles. Naturally the constables wanted to look in the trunk. It was a death sentence.

Henry popped the trunk from inside the car. As far as he knew there was nothing in the trunk, but he also knew without reserve that if the dog smelled something, there was something there. He took what was, in his mind, appropriate action. He pulled his pistol and when the two constables looked into the trunk to find the vials of cocaine the dog had smelled, he popped the door and came out shooting.

The first constable hit was the dog handler. The .45 caliber bullet blew a huge hole beneath his ribs and above his hips. He spun around and went down in a spray of blood. Cuthbert could not see the second constable through the trunk of the car but he fired two rounds through the trunk lid, then he came around to the back. The police dog was restrained by the leash initially; the handler had the thong on his wrist. As Henry came around the back of the car, the handler slipped the loop off his wrist and released the dog.

251

Like a bolt of teeth and fury, the dog leaped straight at his target and as Henry instinctively raised his left hand the dog clamped down on it. The lead constable fired one shot that would have taken Henry in the chest if the dog had not made him stumble backward.

The .45 Smith and Wesson vomited fire and lead. The German Shepherd yelped once as the bullet destroyed its hips. It released Henry's hand as it collapsed and Henry shot it again. The lead constable got off another shot from his Glock and this time the .40 caliber round creased Henry's right arm deeply, near the shoulder. The impact jerked his arm back and the .45 went off involuntarily. It blew a hole in the constable's chest a man could put his fist though. Then the most damning of the recovered footage was recorded. Henry Cuthbert methodically shot each constable and the dog once each, in the head. He closed the trunk and got back into his car. Then he drove away leaving a recording of his black deed still running on the dashboard camera and three victims behind.

Henry was not feeling his best. His left hand was chewed and torn by the dog. His right shoulder was bleeding badly where the constable's bullet had passed through it. He was driving a car that was already called in and had two bullet holes in the trunk lid. It was not till he was a couple of kilometers from the scene when he realized that he had left his driver's license and registration in the police vehicle.

"This is kind of a cozy setup. I like the idea and it practically guarantees privacy." Gordon MacMaster was chewing on a cigar but did not light it.

"All you need is two rooms. I can trust the tart to keep her mouth shut for a while, but if the questions get asked she'll fold like the wilted rose she is." Terry was smoking a cigarette, listening to the water running in the shower.

"So you've approached the Dark Knight President and proposed that he take over the Sydney Mafia?"

"I wouldn't call it Mafia. That's an Italian… Sicilian term. It doesn't really apply."

"Let us not mince words here. We are playing a game that has too many consequences to be concerned about what name it holds. You have gotten off very lucky so far. Nobody has killed you. The reason you are still alive is that nobody knew what you are up to. Now you have invited a group of savages to join you in your endeavor and opened the can for all the world to see. It was a bad move and it could get you killed."

"I have been very discreet and frankly, I hadn't heard from you in months. I thought you took the money and ran."

"You don't get it, do you? If I had taken the money, I would have left your corpse behind. I don't leave witnesses. Haven't you learned that?"

"But you have. The Troy brothers saw you, I assume. I know Henry Cuthbert saw you."

"Those are not witnesses, they are employers. They have as much to lose by fingering me as I do. You are a witness. We are speaking together because you are on the inside and I am on the outside. You feed me the information and I pull the deal. Our last operation was a resounding success, yes?"

"Yes, except I thought…"

"You thought I deserted you. You thought that I was a man with no honor. I can see you still have much to learn about those around you. When honor is present, trust follows. I can see your trust is not easily bought, nor should it be."

"Speaking of bought…"

"Your part is in your little apartment in Orange. If you can call it that. It's not very secure."

"You broke in my room?"

"Yes. I needed to provide you with your cut. You have some impressive weapons in that room but it is not very secure. A good dead bolt lock on the door would help. I practically walked in."

"Thanks for the advice."

"Think nothing of it."

The water stopped running in the shower and they could hear the girl moving around in the bathroom. The hair dryer whirred up.

"So, what is our next target?"

"I need to assess how much damage you've done by talking to this Saxon creature. We may need to back off entirely. You may have little regard for your life but I prize mine highly. I will get back with you. Remember, if you can get information that nobody knows you have, that makes the best target. If they can't trace it to you they will blame someone else."

"I'll see what I can get."

"What about this woman? Is she going to compromise us?"

"No, I don't think so. I've known her a very long time now." Terry didn't mention that she had been his first, the woman that had completed his transformation to manhood after his first kill.

"You know, this Saxon is no match for the Troy brothers."

"I know."

"Then you also know that even if we put him in power he won't be able to hold it." MacMaster was punctuating his comments with his cigar.

"Yes, I know. I think they call it mutually assured destruction."

"You had best have a plan for stepping out of the way when the 'mutually assured destruction' starts flying. I've seen many men caught in a vortex they created only to have it suck them in."

"Noted. I was thinking we could leave the country at that point. I will have done everything I set out to do by then."

It was on the news the next morning. Henry Cuthbert was a fugitive from justice, wanted in connection with a triple homicide. The fact that the third victim was a dog did not matter. "Buttons" was a registered constable who had been killed in the line of duty. Every officer in New South Wales was looking for Henry.

"Jerry, please I have nowhere else to go."

"Go back to your gangster friends. They were always more family to you than I."

"No, Jerry its not true. Remember when you had that crop failure a few years back and you needed a new tractor at the same time. Who came up with that John Deere? And the hose for the irrigation system, who brought that in?"

"Oh, aye. You did me some favors over the years but it won't take long before they're on to ye. Bloody hell, Henry, you shot three constables. What on earth were ye thinking?"

"They were setting me up. There was nothing in the trunk. I never carry anything in the trunk. They towed my car a week ago. I know they put something in the trunk then, or they had a key made. I had nothing in the trunk. I never do."

"Get the car in the barn. Then come inside, Beth has a stew on and we'll get you some new clothes. You'll be wanting some iodine on those cuts, too."

The next day Jerry was digging a big hole with his back hoe. Henry's car went into the hole and the dirt was plowed over it. The cabin was not so much a summer getaway; it was more of a hunting lodge type of structure. The amenities were Spartan, as it was not designed for the long term. Nor was it on the beaten path. Of course, Jerry's sons knew where it was but his wife could probably not have found it right away.

Henry was temporarily hidden from the world.

It did not take the Provincial Police long to show up on Jerry Cuthbert's doorstep, looking for Henry. Jerry told them his brother and he had limited contact since Henry had moved to Sydney, that he had not seen him and that they would do better to look in the city. The neighbors were interviewed as well but the distances between people here precluded anyone having seen anything. Henry's car was nothing special, nothing to cause notice anywhere there were roads.

Senior Sergeant Randolph Black had not ruined his career in that he had not been drummed out of the service of the state. He could never look forward to a promotion, however. Senior Sergeant was the best he could expect in his life and while it was not a bad position, it did not carry the perks of an inspector's position. It was the spot where the rank changed from chevrons to pips, the equivalent of an enlisted man's highest ranking. Once surpassing that, the perks and the pay were much better.

"Didn't you tell the officers what they would be dealing with?"

"This was not the team that was supposed to do it and they were not supposed to do it during the day. The night shift was instructed to do the deed that night but the instructions were not public. The day crew weren't rookies, either. They were seasoned officers with years on the street. Cuthbert got the jump on them. I can't be sure how he knew but we have the footage of what he did. He shot both men and the dog. Not before the dog took a bite out of him and we know he was shot as well. He never showed up at a hospital, but he left some blood at the scene."

"That's hardly a bloody consolation then is it, Sergeant? I think it would be in your best interest to remember that if word of your little operation gets out, I might be forced to retire, but you will be incarcerated with the very same men you have been arresting your entire career. I think that would be sufficient motivation for you to find and silence this man." Superintendent Barlow had a reputation for being cool under fire. He seldom showed his fangs in his advancing years. The Sergeant noticed that this Saturday, it was not just that he was not invited to have a drink, there was no bottle in evidence at all.

"Yes Sir. We have checked out his regular spots, the places he does business, he hasn't been there. His regular associates haven't seen him. We checked out his brother's farm, no luck. His face has been on the telly. I would have expected someone to have recognized him by now and given us a call. We have advertised a reward and gotten the usual jokers calling in but nothing of substance. I would think some clerk in a petrol station would pick him up somewhere."

"What's next?"

"Well, I think we need to expand our search. He's on the run or he went to ground. On the run we'll get someone eyeballing him getting petrol or a quick bite. If he's hiding in the city somebody is supplying him and we have everybody on alert."

"It's not enough. I want the men who reported to him brought in. Anyone you think had any ties to him needs to be brought in and questioned. Squeeze their heads and see who sweats about it."

"Yes Sir. I'll get on it right away."

"You're damned right you will. If you fuck this up again there's gonna be hell to pay. And I want to know why the day crew took the initiative on this. Seasoned veterans my ass. I saw the footage. Both of them staring into the trunk like little boys with Cuthbert free to clobber them. Dismissed."

Sergeant Black was glad to leave the office and get back to the men who reported to him. Superintendent Barlow had looked like he was going to take a bite out of him if he made a move.

Black went to work on the list of Cuthbert's potential subordinates. The details on the list were from direct observation and surveillance. They had known of Henry's nefarious associations, but they had not yet made a move on him. They lacked good evidence previously. Now they had more than they needed and knew everybody to question.

When the operation began it was no long-term affair. The constables moved in like cowboys on a herd of cattle, rounding them into pens made for criminals.

When Henry had gone on the run, everybody who reported to him had been ordered to hold their post and continue as if nothing had happened. Some of them did. The more experienced men took a little dodge to the side to get out of the immediate spotlight. Terry Kingston left the city entirely. He could smell the operation before it was formed. He knew the moment was on hand. Before the Olympics they had rounded up a lot of men just to get them off the streets so there would be a smooth and memorable event. This was not such a benign operation. The men were being interrogated by teams for hours. Some of them talked but it was all about old infractions, stuff that had been done years ago. As hard as they squeezed, nobody knew where Henry Cuthbert had gone.

"Welcome back, Terry. We haven't seen you for quite a long time. Where have you been?"

"James, Billy, how have you been?"

258

"You know, not much happens out here in farm country to get our attention. I imagine your life has been much more interesting, living in the city."

"Oh, not really. Orange is no teeming metropolis, you know. I've just been taking care of the agency and laying low. It's good to get back to the farm."

As was his habit, Terry had left the Holden in Orange and taken the company van back to the farm. The two local constables had seen the van in the driveway and stopped in to talk for lack of anything better to do. Terry invited them in for a beer but they declined, since they were on duty. They left quickly after taking a couple of dozen eggs that Ginger insisted they accept.

Terry was quick to outline what had happened since they had been in touch and Ginger listened intently. He had not gotten a letter since they had last spoken and was concerned about his nephew's state of mind. Living a double life had tripped up more than one man and unbalanced more than one mind. He approved of the plan that Terry outlined for him, but it was laid out according to Terry's perspective and Ginger could not see the entire layout. He was too far removed from it.

Jerry Junior stopped by the next day for a chat and a beer. One beer let to another and soon enough Jerry Junior and Terry were potted. As is so often done when men drink together, plans were made. The two of them committed to hunting the following day. Terry wanted to hunt his uncle's land since he knew it so well, but Junior was quick to tell him of the rabbit problem that his father's land was prone to. The fox population had been taken care of but once the foxes were killed, the rabbits came back in force. The two of them decided that they would hunt the Cuthbert land instead. Junior told Terry about the American company he sold the fox tails to. They supplied fly fishermen with various furs and feathers so they could tie their own flies. Terry promised to bring him some in the morning.

The summer was waning and there would not be much good hunting left in a few short weeks. Rather than ruin the meat with a shotgun, the two hunters would go out with .22 rifles. Even though the objective was to destroy the rabbit population, neither of them could justify killing them without eating them and both men loved rabbit.

The morning came early and Terry was on hand with his rifle. He had forgotten the fox tails, however. Junior was a little slower this morning, but he was ready in short enough order. The dew was gone from the grass when they reached the woods, but it would not be hot for a few hours. Both men were accomplished hunters. Junior knew the land better, but Terry was quieter in the woods. Between them they bagged eight rabbits by noon and decided it was time for some food.

The gunshots were more like cap guns at the cabin, Henry could barely hear them. He had not hunted well while he was there, the city had dulled his edge a bit and while he had bagged some game, he had wasted more ammunition than he had used. He blamed the gun sights on his brother's rifle, but the truth was that he had never been a good hunter. He lacked the patience and that indescribable smoothness that allows some men to become one with the forest.

The rabbits were skinned and tossed in the pot. Beth was bustling about preparing lunch for the men. The rabbit would serve for dinner. She insisted that Terry stay, but he explained that he had some things to do and promised to return at dinner time.

Beth put up a good front and let things appear normal. Truthfully she was angry at her husband for allowing Henry to occupy the cottage. They had known he was a gangster all along. His gifts were always welcome, though suspect, and they had not seen him for years. They never spoke of each other, these brothers who had chosen different paths in life. It was as if they tried to forget each other.

Terry stopped back for dinner and, in an unusually gregarious moment, he began to regale them with humorous drinking stories. He felt good being among people he did not have to fear and mistrust; people he had known most of his life. He relaxed a bit and in relaxing realized how tense he had been.

Terry never saw Henry Cuthbert at Jerry's farm and did not know they were related. He never saw Henry that day either, but he was noted from the tree line. Henry saw him arrive and rubbed his eyes, not believing what he saw. With the typical lack of patience he could not wait there until Terry came back out, but he did come back later, saw that the van was gone and debated crossing the field to the house. Coming out of the woods made him feel exposed. What if someone pulled in while he was standing out there like a bloody wallaby? So he waited until after dark to make the trip. He was not certain that he had seen his former associate, Thompson Barber. It was a long way across the field. Jerry gave him a bit of stew that had been set aside for him and answered his questions. No, he was told, that was not Thompson Barber but Terry Kingston. They had known Terry for many years and he lived in Orange, not Sydney. Henry accepted the answer. He had no reason not to.

Being in the house after dark meant Henry was going to spend the night on the couch. The field could be traversed, but there was the trail to the cabin and he might not be able to find his way by flashlight.

Morning came and Henry had taken a long hot shower, grateful for the hot water. He was shaving with his brother's razor when he heard an engine pull in the driveway. The bathroom window looked out on the driveway so that when he pulled back the curtain, he saw Terry Kingston getting out of the company van with a bundle of fox tails. He had

261

forgotten to bring them by the day before and was dropping them off on his way back to Orange. This time there was no mistake. Henry was looking at the man he had known as Thompson Barber. The wheels began turning in Henry's head.

Evan McCormick suspected his new associate had something to do with the manhunt that was on for Henry Cuthbert. He was paying a lot of attention to the structure and makeup of the Sydney organization. To say he was fully committed is not totally accurate, for while he liked the idea of being the man in charge of the entire operation, he did not think it would work the way it had been described to him. He also had a healthy suspicion that the man he knew as Thompson Barber would double-cross him as easily and readily as he had turned on his current employers. Evan "Saxon" McCormick was already picking out Thompson Barber's gravesite.

The meeting was held in a motel room in Blackheath. Saxon and eight of his higher ranking men rode out and rented rooms. The proprietor was not happy about seeing the motorcycles because a different group had trashed the place badly a couple of years before. The manager insisted that the rooms be paid for with a credit card so he had some legal recourse if there was a repeat of prior events.

Terry Kingston got there just after the women arrived in a couple of vans. Self described biker bitches, they hung around with whatever bike club treated them right and they swapped clubs often. They had no loyalty and could be had by anybody. Their lack of moral standards had a certain appeal for the men.

Terry paid for his room with cash. He did not have the look of the bikies and the manager figured he was probably the only other lodger he would get while the gang was staying.

262

Saxon watched very closely while trying to be nonchalant. He arranged for Rita, a fine looking woman, to approach Terry with a bottle and a smile. Evan liked to test people to determine their moral compass and their proclivities. He was surprised that while Terry drank he did not drink much, and while he obviously enjoyed women's company, he was more interested in business. Most men Terry's age could not have turned Rita down and she really poured it on that day. She all but unzipped his pants.

After a few minutes, once they determined that they were not being watched, Terry and Evan went into a room together. Both men were armed this time. Evan was confident enough to allow Terry to keep his guns. This was not lost on Terry and as a gesture of faith he took off his jacket and his holsters and threw them on the bed. Evan did not follow suit.

"All right, Saxon, I must say I like your choice of meeting places."

"Yeah, I like the Blue Mountains."

"What I have will require precision and coordination. I do not have an exact schedule, but when I do it will be very time sensitive. If any of the elements show up late the plan doesn't work and we scrap it. That's for the future. For now, I have something easy and profitable. What we get is a tanker full of gasoline for your pumps. What we need is a woman you can trust, some GHB and a good driver. Your servo tanks hold how much?"

"30,000 liters."

"Damn big tanks."

"It used to be a truck stop. I had the diesel tanks pulled out and scrapped but kept the petrol tanks."

"All right. There is a regular run of gasoline from the Petroleo depot in Sydney. The driver's name is Wally. He is not the full quid but he is a man of habit. He pulls out of the depot for whatever run he is making and his first stop is the

Silver Spoon restaurant where he has breakfast. There is a motel next to the Silver Spoon…"

"I know the place."

"Good, then I won't need to explain that the trucks park behind the restaurant and you can't see them from the windows of the motel. What I propose is that we have a competent sheila grab this galah and drop him some GHB. He's out snoring and we nab his truck, pump your tanks full and then bring it back to him. He wakes up, don't know what happened and goes on his way. He won't say anything until they notice he's a few thousand liters short but he won't have anyone to blame."

"Is this every morning?"

"Five days a week. Sometimes he works Saturdays but he doesn't have the time to stop on Saturday. So it won't work on the weekend. Remember though, the woman must be good. She needs to allay his natural suspicion, dope him and get him to the motel without arousing his suspicion. The only way that's going to happen is if he's convinced it is his idea. And he's not too sharp."

"Well then, do you think Rita could do it?" Evan watched closely to see Terry's reaction. He did not trust men who were too easily swayed by a woman but he also detested poofs. He had killed homosexuals on general principles when he was young. He did not expect Terry to be such a man but the test was not over.

Terry deliberately wiped his hands on his blue jeans. "Yes, Rita could probably make a priest forget the love of God."

"Yet you blew her off to talk to me."

"This is business. Business always comes first. Women will always be there but opportunity does not always wait."

"Wait here." Evan McCormick walked out the door but he was not gone long. Terry heard a motorcycle fire up in the parking lot, a few seconds later it left. Evan returned and tossed Terry a liter of rum. Business was concluded and it was time to party. The door had barely closed behind him before a woman entered with a pair of plastic cups full of ice and a bottle of cola. She was not Rita. She locked the door behind her and proceeded to pour them both a drink.

Henry Cuthbert did not call Jimmy Cognac. Jimmy had not been in charge long enough and did not have the credibility Henry required. Henry called Abel Troy.

The receptionist claimed that Mr. Troy was out but she took a message as was usual. Abel Troy called Henry personally two minutes later.

"Henry, what have you done now? There is nothing I can do to save you. You know this, don't you?"

"Well, that's not quite right. You can provide me with passage to China and some funding for survival."

"Henry, this leaves me open to aiding and abetting a killer. Tell me what would cause me to take such a risk?"

"I know who your snake is. I know who has been doing all the damage."

"What are you referring to?"

"The man who hit the money van, the American. I know who is feeding him the information. Get me out of the country and provide me with some cash. I will tell you who he is and where you can find him if he runs. But I can't tell you till I get in the vicinity of Thailand or Burma. I will not take the chance of ending up strapped to a chair."

"Henry, we would never do such a thing to you."

"Bullshit. You've done it to better men than me and you'll do it to whomever you like for as long as you think it will advance your cause."

"Henry..."

"Don't give me that shit. I know what the story is. What I need to know is do we have a deal?"

"Of course. Whatever you want. You have been nothing but an asset to us. Where do you want to fly from?"

"Oh, no. You won't catch me with that old line. I need a passport to get out of the country. You will send it to a Post Office Box in Canberra. When I am out of the country you will learn who your spy is. Send the passport and enough cash. I'll contact you."

As Henry would have expected, the Canberra Post Office was watched carefully. The package that was sent was forwarded from there to a private company who forwarded it to a box in the Molong Post Office. One of Henry's nephews picked it up from there. Working with the Troy organization had inspired no trust in Henry Cuthbert but he had learned to cover his tracks.

"Well, that went off like clockwork. We got us a tank full of free petrol. That's worth a bit." Evan McCormick was smiling broadly.

"Glad I could help," Terry replied.

"Was your night good?"

"Most enjoyable."

"Glad she could help. She had some good things to say about you as well."

"Once again, glad I could help."

"What's next?"

"First one's free. I expect to get a bit of a return off the next."

"I think that's only fair."

"The next operation will take four men. You will need one in a Spartan Security uniform. One experienced checker and two fork truck drivers. I will need them on call within a moment's notice and I will call you with the details."

"Fair enough. I'm sure I can find the talent. They will be ready I will wait for your call but make sure you say nothing over the phone. If you do, that will destroy our agreement. If anyone else answers at my number, hang up. I don't trust the telephone."

"Righteous, mate. I'll tell you what, then, no matter where I tell you to meet me, it'll be Cardigans. You know the place?"

"I don't like it." Evan was not the sort of clientele that frequented Cardigans.

"No worries. You name the spot."

"The Camshaft Grill next to the raceway."

"That does it then. Look, I've been gone a few more days than I should. I've got to get back. I know they miss me."

Saxon smiled for the first time Terry had ever seen, then his face went flat again. It still looked like a sign. Terry checked out of the motel and headed back toward Sydney. Much of the way there he had a motorcycle escort.

Jimmy Cognac was hot under the collar. He wanted to know where Terry had been and what he had been doing. Terry was not supposed to disappear like that and leave Jimmy running the show when Henry Cuthbert was on the run. Nobody else had run off. Terry closed one eye and looked at Jimmy out of the other while he slowly fished out a cigarette and lit it. They were sitting in the office space of a warehouse that dealt in legitimate items.

"Jimmy, what happened?" Terry's voice sounded like he was addressing a child.

"What happened, that idiot cocksucka shot two cops, on film no less. Then he leaves his driver's license and registration in the cop car. What a fuckin' idiot. I'd kill him myself if I could."

"Tell me where he is, I'll kill him."

"Oh, no. I'm not gonna have two of you on the run. I may be angry but I'm not stupid."

"I tell you I'll kill him. That means I will kill him." Terry spoke slowly pronouncing every word carefully.

"No you won't. Not without the word."

"You said you'd kill him if you could. I can and will if you say."

"Forget you. You go back to work and do what you do. We'll take care of Mr. Fuckall Henry Cuthbert."

"Whatever you say." Terry briefly considered killing Jimmy on the spot. He would need to kill the security guards if he did and that would be distasteful to him. Since it was a legitimate warehouse, the security guards were underpaid wannabes with a high school education and no prospects. He decided to work it a different way.

Jimmy Cognac didn't know what to say. He was used to people groveling or lying or pleading. He was not used to a man who calmly sat smoking a cigarette and discussing murder. It was not that it was an unusual thing for him to have done, but Terry said it so out of hand that he could have been discussing a fish dinner. Frustrated, Jimmy dismissed Terry and went back to brooding about his situation and how he should never have left Brisbane.

It was plain why Cognac was so frustrated. He was getting pressure from above to increase his control over his given area, but events were against him. Henry was the branching point and Jimmy was really nothing but a buffer between the real power and the enforcers. So the Adam and Abel were untouchable and Henry was unreachable. Jimmy Cognac was left to run an organization he was completely unfamiliar with, staffed by people he had never met. These people were taking advantage of the situation and not supporting the structure. Some of the lower level were going rogue and some were simply disappearing. This had been happening for some time now, even before Henry left. A weakness was detected in management, fueled by the unresolved attacks. Once Henry went on the run, desertions escalated from fear and avarice. The skein was unraveling exponentially faster.

As the authority and influence of the primary network decreased, every other group in this eclectic society began to take a bite of the pie. Nobody wanted war and nobody was ready for it. Nobody with plans of staying in Sydney, that is.

Gordon MacMaster had no plans for staying in Sydney. He did not even stay the night on the rare moments he stepped foot in the city. Gordon's plans were of a different nature.

Since infiltrating the Oriental underworld was not an option, Gordon picked his target from their ranks. They were as secretive as any crime syndicate but it was not difficult to determine who had been making money without a high paying job. The young men were very fond of souped-up Japanese cars and the ones with the fastest and fanciest cars were also men without legitimate employment. They held road racing events on back roads outside the city, always changing the locations. The events were never advertised and it was seldom announced before hand where they would be racing. This kept the police in the dark and there were seldom crowds of onlookers. If one wanted to participate, one needed to follow the racers to their destination.

The car Gordon was driving was fast but by no means in the same league as the street racers. He could follow them but he could not race. The car had been stolen from a Russian loan shark that night, while he was having dinner and drinks in an exclusive club frequented by his associates.

The target was a Cambodian enforcer. He was a flamboyant character with many friends and he had won the race that night, taking home a substantial pile of cash. His name was Chip Long Tim and he had many friends and admirers. The man was very good with his hands and feet and was often used as muscle by the Chinese.

Chip was a gambler and had headed toward the casino with his winnings when he had an accident. His sporty little import was no match for the Ford that hit him. It spun him around and caused extensive damage to the rear end of his Mitsubishi. He was forced to get out the passenger side since the driver's door would not open after the collision. The accident had not been his fault, and with the typically brash attitude of youth, he was determined to take some revenge on the man who had caused it. He could not have known that he was attacking a former Scots Dragoon; he only saw a large man he assumed would be slow and contrite. He could not see his opponent's face as the headlights of the Ford were behind him.

Gordon MacMaster was neither slow nor apologetic. As Chip Long Tim ran toward him, the Scotsman's huge freckled fists, encased in brass knuckles, met him in mid stride. Chip was not used to being hit. Most of his opponents were afraid of him or too slow to initiate contact. There was no time to be surprised, however. He had never seen brass knuckles used before, they were too old-school for the modern times and Chip favored oriental weapons or guns. The brass knuckles opened up his face and split his skull. The Cambodian dropped like a slaughtered cow and was relieved of his winnings.

MacMaster could not have cared less if the man lived or died, as long as the correct evidence was left on the scene. The car belonged to a Russian, the half-full bottle of Vodka in the front seat was a Russian import and there was a pack of Russian cigarettes on the dashboard. He left both cars there and walked a quarter mile away to where there was another, less identifiable, vehicle. His victim survived but he would never race again. The encounter left him with an uncontrollable random tic down the left side of his body. His face was scarred, but not horribly so.

White men have forever been baffled by what they first called inscrutable, yellow devils. The Oriental religions and philosophies are often less violent and their gods less terrible and vengeful than the European patriarch. This would lead

270

foreigners to believe that Easterners were pacifists, and while some were, most were simply patient. They were willing to learn and had already accepted that a certain amount of control could be given up for a certain amount time to increase the lot of the whole. When aroused the Oriental could be a terrible adversary.

Among the Chinatown community in Sydney, there was an eclectic mix of cultures and many of them looked down on the others. The Vietnamese and Cambodians were separate from the Thai and none of them identified with the Filipinos. The Chinese and Japanese had a long-standing hatred of each other and the Koreans stood separate from every one else. The assault on the popular young Cambodian man was not enough in and of itself to unite the cultures, but it was enough to ignite open discussion about the Russians.

Terry Kingston was counseling Evan McCormick on the proper moment to strike. He was learning a great deal about strategy from his new Scots mentor and trying to put it in effect. The city had grown naturally, without any real urban planning at its inception so many of its boundaries were geographically determined. This made it easy to turn one community against another because they did not share an open and porous border.

It had taken a long time for Gordon to earn Terry's trust, though there had always been respect. Their arrangement had almost dissolved when Terry had brought in the outside elements but Gordon stuck with it for a while once Terry outlined the plan. The Scot would have gone for a more direct action, a targeted surgical strike rather than the chaos inducing crossfire that the Aussie was generating, but he had to admit that it would most probably be effective.

The second assault victim did not survive. He was a loan shark in the heart of the growing Russian sector. He was a particularly brutal man and this gained him fear and respect. His attacker did not respect him. He was killed with a sai, the edgeless dagger used in martial arts training. The weapon was left in the Russian's chest. There was no love lost when this man died since he had few friends but there was a message read from the choice of weapon. The Asians would not bow down to the Russians. The second attack was not enough to ignite a war since much of the community was relieved to be rid of the loan shark

The Russians in question were not all of pure Soviet descent; many of them were Ukrainian, Slovakian, or Romanian. Despite the long history of occupation and subjugation, these ethnic groups clustered together in one area. Much of this was due to the similarity of the languages.

It is physically impossible to tell a South Eastern Russian from a North Eastern Chinaman. They share the same genetic background and would have coexisted peacefully. The Western Russians, on the other hand were much more aggressive in their outlook. They had lived through the Soviet Union's demise and now they wanted to get some of what they had been denied.

Gordon MacMaster's third attack took out one of the main figures in the Oriental network, who, accompanied by his bodyguard, was visiting one of his many lady friends. Both men were shot as they approached the car. The street was busy but no one else was shot and none of the witnesses saw who had shot them. The police determined it was a sniper who hit them from three blocks away and took them both out within seconds. On the roof the shots had come from, was a pack of Russian cigarettes. There was no doubt now, this was to mean war.

The Eastern contingent did not come swarming out of their neighborhood waving swords like some kind of kung fu movie. They drove out in sleek, fast cars and carried semi-automatic weapons. They hit the Russians quickly and with precision, causing very little collateral damage. The Russians hit them back in the middle of the night with gasoline bombs.

The Molotov cocktails burned homes and businesses indiscriminately. The Sydney Fire Department lost two men that night and the constables went to work in the morning. With or without reasonable justification they rounded up every Russian, Ukrainian and Romanian they could find that was not on his way to work. The Chinese took the opportunity to rob and loot the stores operated by the Russians. This cycle only lasted a couple of days since the pool of recruits for each side was limited. In a couple of days, they counted the dead and went into mourning. They had each suffered badly and their operations were ripe for the picking.

Evan McCormick and his Dark Knights moved in. There was some difficulty keeping the rowdy bikies focused on the job at hand, but eventually the real leaders and organizers proved themselves. Evan may not have been a great strategist, but he was able to recognize genius in someone else's strategy.

Chapter Fifteen
The Play

"Chief Inspector Slaughter, what have you brought me on this bloody race war?"

"Superintendent Barlow, as near as I can tell we have this Chip Long Tim, second generation Cambodian. He was put in the hospital by Sergei Karskeroff. Karskeroff ran into him on the road and then beat him unconscious with something, probably brass knuckles. We have Karskeroff in custody but he denies any knowledge of the incident. He claims he was in the Beluga having dinner when his car was stolen. He did report it stolen, but not until about half an hour after they found this Tim character leaking his brains on the roadside. We should be able to get a statement from him in a couple of days, but given his condition it may not be reliable. He's no longer in a coma but the doctors are talking about brain damage.

"That was the first problem. It looks as though Tim's friends retaliated, killing one of the Russians with one of those funny three pointed knives they use in the movies. He had no wallet, neither did Tim. I think they were lifted but I don't think robbery was the primary motive.

"The Russians won't talk to us any more than the wogs. We spin our wheels trying to get anything out of them."

"So you have nothing?" Barlow looked like he was about to rise from his chair like a dragon of old and smite the Chief Inspector with liquid fire.

"Well, not exactly. The long range killing of Kim Tang and his bodyguard was done with a .223. This was in retaliation for their killing the Russian. We haven't gotten the ballistics reports back yet but I'm willing to bet it's the same gun that killed the two wise guys on the docks a few weeks back."

"What evidence do you have?"

"Long range assassin's shots. Amateurs don't even try shots like that. Both were done with the same caliber weapon. Two men in each hit, two shots, two kills. Professional. Small bore weapon, only professionals can even make the shot, one, two. Dead before they hit the floor."

"So he's a Russian?" the Superintendent asked, his eyes boring through his subordinate's skull, trying to draw out the knowledge.

"I don't think so, Sir. I think he is someone playing both sides against the middle. The evidence was a little too pat. An empty box of Russian cigarettes on the roof where the sniper was indicates a sloppy amateur. This killer is no amateur. The box was placed there for us to find; to point the Chinamen in the wrong direction. It did, too.

"The Chinamen went on a rampage and killed a half a dozen Russians that we know of. The Russians burned half of Chinatown in revenge. Then the Dark Knights moved in and took over. They restored order as if they were the fucking Gestapo."

"The bikies? You're shinin' me on now."

"No, Sir. They came in as if they knew it was going to happen and were just waiting for the lead to stop flying so they could take over."

"It's a fuckin' bikie then?" Barlow's expression was incredulous.

"That's what it looks like but we don't really know what they're up to. It looks like they set up both sides and then rode in to take over. I can't believe they got away with it."

"This is not the kind of thing I would have expected out of them. They're mostly a bunch of degenerate idiots. Drunks and fuckalls can't plan an operation like this. Hmm. Who were the first men killed? Not the Chinamen, before that."

"Wise guys. The ones on the dock worked for the mob is what it looks like." Chief Inspector Slaughter had put a lot of thought into his theories. He knew they sounded a bit far-fetched but he also stood behind them. He didn't want to debate the points because they were just theories but was afraid the Superintendent would reject them out of hand.

"This thing has been going on for a year and a half or so, maybe longer." Superintendent Barlow was unexpectedly taking the Inspector's side. "The attacks began with assaults on the shipping, north of the city."

"I thought we closed that case. Didn't they decide Lee Pierce was behind that?" Slaughter was not beyond a little reverse psychology. He discovered that his thoughts were not far from Barlow's.

"Lee Pierce was a bully and a wife beater. He sold guns to anyone who wanted them, but he didn't do the truck killings. Yes, the evidence all pointed to him but it was bullshit. Why would a man with a cache of new firearms use an old rifle, with obsolete ammunition, and then leave it in his trailer? The answer is, he wouldn't and didn't. He was set up the same way the Russians were set up. The same way that mob cash van was set up, down in, what was it, Hill Top? Yeah, Hill Top. Same way, same man or team of men. This is what the problem is, but this is also where the solution is going to lie. Our professional is starting to get greedy and is looking to take a big slice of the fat Sydney pie for himself. Find out who is new in the Dark Knights. Within the last couple of years. That's going to be our man. Use Senior Sergeant Black. I coordinate with him on Saturdays from time to time. He seems amenable to proper suggestion, but be discreet.

"Sergeant Black, a drink?"
"Only if you insist, Superintendent."
"Oh, but I do."

276

"Yes, Sir."

Barlow poured two tall glasses of scotch and they both savored the flavor before getting down to business.

"I've got what seems to be as complete a list of the bikies, the uh… Dark Knights. The recent recruits, last few years, are a miserable lot of bottom feeders. If you put the lot of them in a train station, they couldn't find the pisser. There isn't one of them with the brains god gave a 'roo. It's not that they're not dangerous, though. Lately, the Knights are picking up men who've crossed the line."

"What line?"

"Well, Sir, the line between bollux and brains."

Theodore Barlow chuckled and took a sip. "Yes, there is a fine line between bollux and brains."

"Indeed, sir. But these men have crossed it deeply. Brains are not their claim to fame."

"What about their upper… their leadership."

"Evan McCormick is their president. He has been for a long time. He's a sharp man but without the real ambition required to pull off the jobs we've seen lately. They hold elections from time to time and the ranks move about a bit, but they haven't brought in anyone new that we know of. I agree that they are acting with outside direction, but we cannot determine precisely who it is."

"Maybe we need to backtrack. Think about this. The man who set up Lee Pierce used his wife for the job. If we can get his wife to tell us who she was working with we have our brains."

"That case is closed, Sir. If we bring her in it will need to be for something else. Or we can interview her away from the usual channels."

"Set her up. Drop a bag or a gun in her trunk and bring her in to regional. I want to be there when she is questioned. No cameras, no lawyers."

"Yes, Sir. When do you want it done?"

"Next Saturday. Work me up a file on her first, I want it Wednesday morning."

"Yes, Sir, I'll start that today and get in touch with the boys in Orange."

The two men made small talk and drank their Scotch for a while.

"I can understand why you would think that, Mr. Troy, but the bottom line is that he is in there under a false name. He lied about where he was born and everything about his past." Henry was calling from out of the country. He had managed to escape and was making good on the promise for information.

"Henry, why would this man do this? What possible motivation would the son of a farmer from Molong have for attacking our business and killing our men?"

"He is not the son of a farmer. He is his nephew. His father was killed 15 or 16 years ago. Both his parents, I think, and this man took him in. Check it out, Terry Kingston. I'll tell you now, this is the man you've wanted by the cods all this time. Thompson Barber's the name..."

"Yes. I was introduced to Mr. Barber," Adam Troy said.

"He's been tearing into you all the while, getting set up with good jobs. As I said, Terry Kingston is his real name. I stake my life on it."

"We will look into it, Mr. Cuthbert. I hope you are enjoying Borneo."

"Dreadful place full of diseases that real white men don't know nothin' about."

"The best place to hide in the world is where nobody wants to go to look for you. Lay in for a while and we'll find a position within the transport industry for you."

"Thank you, Sir. I'll be available."

278

The connection was cut and Henry Cuthbert sighed deeply. He was not in Borneo, he was in the Philippines. He was having anything that was sent to his address in Borneo forwarded to an accountant who deposited the checks for a small fee and covered his tracks. He knew the game and would never attempt to work with the Troys again. There was nothing but a pine box for him in that direction.

Adam Troy looked pensive for a moment and picked up the receiver again. He spoke for only a moment and hung up. Then he called Abel. Abel agreed that despite the dearth of manpower they were currently experiencing, it was a proper move to have this Thompson Barber brought in. If Henry Cuthbert was right, it would stop the vigilante crusade against them. They acknowledged that Henry Cuthbert might well be lying about the whole thing in an attempt to divert attention from his own stupidity and thereby save his own skin. They also agreed that Henry knew too much about the organization and would need to be killed. He would be drawn back into the fold with promises of a position in the transport of southeast Asian heroin and killed quietly. No drawn out torture for him, he had not been traitorous just stupid, and there was no sense in bringing him back to Sydney for it. Kill him quietly and sink him in the ocean.

Then the conversation turned from Henry to Thompson Barber again. Adam had already put out the word to have him brought in. Once he was in their custody, he would never leave alive but they also agreed that there might be some investigation in order. They thought that it was a good idea to verify what Henry had told them.

Jimmy Cognac had been unhappy with Thompson Barber for a short while. Tommy tended to disappear from time to time without telling anyone where he was going and he was always vague about his excursions upon return. Jimmy was happy to get the news that Tommy was to be brought in for "questions." Very few men ever survived

279

when there were questions of that sort. The only disappointment was that he was required to wait a couple of days. That order was given at the last second. Tommy was to be watched closely in the interim, however.

Hercules always set out to making a ruckus when someone pulled in the driveway. Strangers were best advised not to exit their vehicle until he had been given the command. The BMW filled with men in suits would not have looked out of place in Los Angeles or Miami, but it stuck out like a cat at a trout farm in Ginger Kingston's driveway. And Hercules did not like it.

Ginger did not get much company and never had. It was unusual enough to get one of the neighbors stopping in, let alone some fancy suits. Ginger had a scope trained on them from the moment they pulled in the drive, but they did not exit the car and they did not display any weapons. They sat patiently in the car. Finally, Ginger decided they must have some business with him other than simply asking for directions.

It got the men's attention when Hercules took off running for the pasture. It was even more attention getting when a large, balding, red headed man tapped on the back window with a shotgun. Even if they were armed to the teeth, that shotgun had the entire interior of the vehicle covered. If it were loaded with slugs, there was a chance one of them might survive, maybe even two, but there was no telling what sort of load it held.

The driver's window slid down and the man behind the wheel smiled as easily as one might expect. He made his greeting and asked if Terry Kingston was available. Ginger replied that there was no Terry Kingston there. Then he asked what business they had with him. The man told him that there had been an accident and that they were from an insurance company. They were there to assess the damage.

That shut Ginger's response down to zero. He did not want to shoot these four men in the driveway of his own home. He felt sure that with a five round clip filled with buckshot, and one in the chamber, he could kill all four of them. He also knew they were not insurance investigators and that they were probably armed. Terry was in big trouble. It was obvious that something had happened and he was on the run.

Once it was plain that they were going to get nothing out of Ginger, the men in the BMW left. This was one of the few times in his life that Ginger found himself wanting a telephone badly. The nearest phone was some way off. Ginger debated calling Terry for only a minute and then he stuffed a .45 caliber Smith and Wesson revolver under his arm and a .32 in his waist band. The shotgun was in the truck with him as he exited his driveway. The men had driven off toward Orange, Ginger went the other way, toward Molong.

Wednesday morning the report was delivered to Theodore Barlow's desk before he arrived in the morning. It was just one of a number of reports that he was reviewing that day, so it took him a while to get to it. When he did, he scanned it carefully.

Linda Pierce was using her maiden name, Pettigrew. She had just begun using that name a couple of months before and had not officially changed it back so there was some confusion in the file but it was not insurmountable. She had begun using her maiden name again when she had accepted employment at the Kingston Agency.

Superintendent Barlow had only recently begun wearing reading glasses and often left them in his desk drawer. As he ran across the name of the Kingston Agency, he opened the drawer and put them on thinking there was some sort of error on his part. The glasses brought the words into sharper focus and confirmed that Linda Pierce, under the name Linda Pettigrew was employed as a secretary.

She was employed by the insurance agency owned by Terry Kingston.

When Superintendent Barlow thought of Terry Kingston, he saw a frightened and confused eight year old who had just witnessed the murder of his mother. He could not help thinking, at the time, that the boy was emotionally disturbed beyond reason by the event and that he would need some sort of therapy for the rest of his life. That had been a long time ago.

It had been a long time since Theodore had thought of Terry Kingston, but time had not dulled his memory of the event. He remembered driving out to Molong to visit Terry's only living relative though he could not remember the man's name, he distinctly remembered the man. He pushed the intercom button and summoned his secretary into the office. It took her a while to find the file he was interested in, but once he had it, he was sure of what he was seeing.

Any good investigator will tell you there is little coincidence in the real world. Theodore Barlow did not believe in coincidences of this magnitude. He had already intended to set Linda up and to apply pressure to her but this changed things.

"Sergeant Black, you are coming in to work today," He said when the man had answered his phone.

"Uh, I'm sorry, Superintendent, I… uh, I'm not scheduled to work today. I just got home from the night shift an, uh, an hour or so ago." Senior Sergeant Randolph Black had obviously been sleeping.

"I did not ask you if you were reporting to work or when. I told you that you were reporting and I meant now."

"Yes, Sir. May I have a moment to get a shower and a shave?"

"Of course. I expect you to be presentable. When you see me you will have an undercover car already assigned to you. It will be filled and ready to go. You will be ready to drive."

"Yes, Sir. I will be there in short order. Might I ask where we are headed?"

"We are going to Orange."

Terry Kingston had not been answering his phone for two days. He didn't have the kind of cell phone that displayed the number of the incoming call. If the message a caller left was important he would call back, otherwise he could not be reached. The call from Ginger was urgent, but by the time Terry had listened to the message, the phone booth it was made from was empty. The call from Linda Pettigrew did not have the same urgency of tone but it was, in fact, more telling.

Both messages told Terry that there were men in suits looking for him and they were disguising their true business. They were not looking for Thompson Barber, obviously, they were looking for Terry Kingston.

Since he could not call Ginger, he called Linda at the agency and asked who it was that came inquiring about him and where they had said to contact them. This was most telling. They did not leave an address or professional reference; they had merely left a telephone number. They had not claimed affiliation with a business, they had not identified themselves as policemen, and they were not customers. Two of the men had come into the office, but Linda had also seen two more in the back seat as they drove off.

The later message was every bit as disturbing.

Senior Sergeant Randolph Black wasted no time in getting to the station. He took the bare minimum of time getting himself presentable, and after checking out the undercover car and pulling it into the front parking lot, he joined Superintendent Barlow. The two of them drove directly out of town with Randolph saying nothing until they were outside the city limits.

"I assume, Sir, we're paying a visit to the widow Pierce?"

"Your assumption is correct, but for her to be a widow, they would have needed to be married at the time of her husband's demise."

"Fair enough, the ex-Mrs. Pierce. The question is, what makes her important enough today to get the Superintendent of the whole province to speak with her personally?"

"It's not so much that she is important, it is that she knows somebody I knew once. Remember, Sergeant, the same way assumptions will trip you up, coincidences, true coincidences are rare. What are the odds that Linda Pierce gets a job working for someone I knew 15 years ago?"

"Oh, I don't know. That's a long time, and Orange is not that large a town."

Linda's next message told of a pair of policemen, plainclothes officers, who were asking to speak to Terry about an accident in Sydney. Linda included the information that there was no policy number given and no claims had been filed out of Sydney for weeks. Linda knew cops, after all she had married one. She was certain that these were genuine. They had left a business card. Terry took down the information over the phone while his mouth hung open in shock. "Superintendent Theodore Barlow" must be an extremely old man by now. He was not young when he was an inspector.

It may have been completely innocent, but Terry doubted that. For Theodore Barlow to visit his business in Orange the same day as four mob figures could not be a coincidence. Something had happened.

284

"Understand me. This Terry Kingston has been seen in that immediate area within weeks of now. Regardless what the farmer said, Terry Kingston is there or has been there recently. I need you to go back to that farm after dark and find out where he is now. Use whatever means necessary and do not leave a witness. That is correct."

Adam Troy hung up the phone with one eye on the meter they used to check for wire taps. He turned to his brother and after a sip of brandy, Abel asked him to explain what it was that he had discovered.

"All right, this begins quite a long time ago. I don't think you ever met the Viper, did you?" Adam's question was rhetorical. "Well he was quite good at what he did, and performed some useful functions for us. Of course, you remember Randy Arganmajc?"

"What do the two have to do with each other?"

"Arganmajc contracted the Viper to kill Felix Ribbaldi after Felix went south on us. Well, the Viper killed Felix for us and then for some reason it appears that Randy contracted two other men to kill the Viper. They accomplished this task. One of these men was a sociopath who kept the Viper's wife bound in his cellar until he slipped up and she actually killed him. She beat him to death with a piece from his stove top. The other man was Bradley, I know you remember him. Well, he went back and eliminated her from the picture."

"Bradley died recently, didn't he?"

"Six or seven years ago."

"So where does this all go?"

"The Viper's real name was George Kingston."

"Kingston?"

"Yes. The elimination of the woman was witnessed by two. Bradley was supposed to have taken care of these two, years ago. He told me he was going to do it and I never questioned as to whether he had or not. After all, there was no evidence linking them to us… Except Bradley."

"And he's dead?"

"Murdered. In his own home. He was retired. Hadn't taken a job in years."

"And you think the man who witnessed her contract killed him?"

"Yes, or the boy. I mentioned there were two witnesses. One of them was the Viper's son."

"Aaahh. This was Terry then?"

"Precisely. Terry Kingston, and if Henry is to be believed, he has been working within our organization for some time now as Thompson Barber. That is what I get for not following up on things. I trusted that Bradley would take care of the situation, and I think he did not. He let it slide until it jumped up and bit him. It has been biting us ever since."

Hercules did not bark at cars that did not pull in the driveway. If they were simply cruising past, they were ignored. This one was obviously coming in, and it had its lights off. The barking stopped abruptly. The shot was muffled but the dog's yelp was unmistakable. Hercules had just performed his last labor.

The four men approached the farm house with care. Looking down the barrel of a shotgun is a sobering position and none of them wanted to see if the man was ready to use it. Their prey had been described to them as a tall blond man. They were also told not to hesitate if they recognized anyone at the site. The Kingston farm was enemy territory and everybody there could be considered an enemy.

The farmhouse was quiet and the lights were off. The old pickup truck was parked in the driveway and the hood was cold. It looked as though they would catch the residents in their beds. The men slipped inside quietly and moments

286

later began blasting away. When the BMW left the Kingston farm, the yellow corona of the burning farmhouse was visible through the back windshield.

"Oh, Terry." Linda's voice sounded like she was about to burst into tears. "I just got a call from the police in Molong. I don't know how to say this. Your uncle was in the house last night when it burned to the ground. They want you to come to the morgue and identify his body. Dear God, I'm so sorry. I'm sure this has something to do with me. I'm leaving work and going back to the farm. I'm scared."

Terry started shaking and hyperventilating. Despite Linda's assertion, he knew it had to do, not with her, but with him. He had been in the shower when she called and by the time he called her back, she had left the office. She did not carry a cell phone with her.

Gordon MacMaster did have a cell phone and was closer to Molong than Terry. The directions were easy to follow and the address was described with the familiarity of a man who lived there. Terry needed to know if the farm house was indeed burned. Terry's tone told the tale; gone was the cockiness and confidence he had exuded from the first. It was replaced by fear and guilt.

The farm house was an old, dry wooden structure and undoubtedly went up quickly, but he thought that it may have been an accident never crossed Terry's mind. He knew with a certainty that if it had burned, the fire had been set and Ginger's death was due to his nephew's activities. He physically staggered and sat, naked, on the floor of the hotel room. His long, drawn out revenge had been an exercise in hubris and the gods were beginning to take their own revenge.

The fact that Terry was in a hotel and not his own apartment was not coincidence either. He had noticed that he was under surveillance. He assumed, as any mob figure would assume, that the police were monitoring his activities so he gave his observers the slip and was spending time alone. He had not, in his confidence, realized that the men performing the clumsy surveillance were the same ne'er-do-wells he had been consorting with. He had learned to never answer the phone when he was on the run and thanked God for the answering service.

The next message that was left was Linda again. She sounded as upset as she had before or more so. "Terry, I was followed home from work. There are men watching the farm. I don't know who they are, but I'm very frightened."

Terry called back immediately. "Linda, do not leave the farm. Load your guns and keep your eyes open. Warn your family that there are some very bad men and they are looking for me. I cannot join you right now."

"Terry, where are you? I need to know where you are." Something in Linda's tone told him that the men she referred to were closer than she had said.

"I'm at that old fleabag motel in Molong, but I can be there in a couple of hours. I'll call you back."

"Ok. I'll be here at the farm."

Terry hung up wondering how he was going to do that since he had no available vehicle.

The next message was from Jimmy Cognac. Jimmy had been calling regularly, using a variety of devices to make Terry think everything was all right. He acted concerned one time and angry the next. He told of jobs that Terry was missing and obligations he needed to fulfill. Terry did not return the calls.

When Gordon MacMaster called it was to tell Terry that the farm house had indeed burned. The story was in the newspaper in Orange. One man's body was found and it was assumed to be that of Ginger Kingston. The fire was listed as being of suspicious origin. This call was returned.

288

"Glasgow?"

"Tarrytown."

"It's all turned to a huge shitstorm. They killed Uncle Ginger. I think somebody is in Linda's house, trying to get me to go there. The fucking Superintendent for New South Wales showed up at the office looking for me in particular. Somebody is watching my apartment in Sydney; I thought it was the cops but I'm not so sure now. It was fun while it lasted, but the game is at an end now. I'm afraid I'm a dead man walking." Terry's voice was shaking with the impact of it all.

"Calm down. We cannot take care of business in a professional manner if we are overwhelmed with emotion. Call your friend the bikie, and call in a favor. I have the address of the farm. If the bikies show up at the farm and take Linda out of danger, we can be sure it is not they who initiated this. Leave the men watching the apartment alone. It ties up their resources. I assume you are not there?"

"No, I'm…"

"I don't care where you are and I don't need to know. There is nothing we can do for the dead, we can only hope to salvage the living and get out of the country alive."

"My whole life just blew up in my face, Glasgow. I no longer care if I live or die. I'm not important. My life is not important. I don't know how they found out about all this, but they have and now I intend to do what I should have done in the beginning. Instead of playing around, I should have just gone in and killed the sons-of-bitches and been done with it."

"Calm down. We can do everything you need to do, but we must have clear heads to do so. Do not do anything rash. Call in your favor from the Dark Knights. I'll be watching for them."

289

Three hours later, a stream of growling motorcycles poured through Orange and headed up the road to the Pettigrew farm.

The sheer number of riders precluded any question that they were going to have their way. They rode up the driveway and surrounded the front of the house. They were armed in a variety of ways, but there was no effort made to disguise the fact.

A man in a business suit came out of the house, onto the porch and calmly told the mob that they were on private property, and if they knew what was best for them, they would be leaving in short order. They did no such thing.

One particularly brutal looking individual with a disfiguring scar across his nose pulled a sawed-off shotgun from a custom leather sheath on his bike and strode up the steps. He stuck the double barrel right in the stranger's face and grinned, exposing his rotten teeth.

The man in the business suit did not move a muscle. He was as cool a customer as you could get, but he also recognized an untenable position. There was nothing he could physically do against this crowd, but he also knew better than to back down too quickly. A show of cowardice would have them abusing him like a stripper in a cell block.

One short, thin, gothic-looking woman in tight fitting black leathers dismounted and strode up the steps like a cat. Very few women rode with any of the gangs unless it was on the back of a man's bike, but this club had a number of women riding. This woman did not have the physical stature needed to hold her own in a fight against the mountains of testosterone-pumping flesh around her, but there was something about her that set her apart. She stalked past the man on the porch without looking at him and entered the house as if she was in charge.

Inside there were two more men in business suits and two men in overalls. There was a professional-looking

290

woman in the downstairs bedroom, looking very anxious. The men in suits had their hands on their pistols, inside their jackets but one look through the window was enough to convince them they wouldn't get far.

"Give me your cell phones, boys." The woman's voice sounded like chocolate syrup. "Or do I need to call my friends in?"

The men decided that discretion was the better part of honor and handed over their devices.

"Now, I need your guns too." The woman was smiling.

The two men looked at each other and then out the door at the men who were beginning to fill up the porch. Once again their decision was on the side of self preservation through acquiescence. They handed over their pistols. The woman in the bedroom came to the doorway, but did not know what to make of the proceedings. She had never ridden on two wheels.

Two mountainous bikies entered the doorway and stood on each side of it.

"Hang on boys, I wouldn't want you to get hurt," the leather clad woman purred. She slunk up to the men one at a time and ran her hands all over their bodies, slowly, sensuously, looking for hidden weapons. She found a .380 in an ankle holster on one and a straight razor on the other. She took delight in the straight razor and smiled demonically as she cut the off the man's necktie.

"Oooh, nice and sharp," she purred as she closed the razor and slipped it in next to one breast. Then she turned and said, "Linda, you're riding with me," and stalked back out the door.

Two miles down the road Gordon MacMaster pulled over to the side as he saw the line of bikes coming the other way. He noted that two women were riding together in a protected position at the front of the group. The gang all

291

wore the colors of the Valkierie Motorcycle Club. He did not personally care if Linda lived or died, there was no percentage in it for him, but Terry cared.

Up the road, there were still motorcycles in the Pettigrew driveway. Gordon did not care what happened there as long as nobody knew the trap had been sprung. He could not risk having anyone see him who might recognize him. The fact was that now action had been initiated, it must be followed through.

Terry was still feeling quite emotional. He knew that a professional never made it personal. He also knew that he had been exposed. He could not show his face in any of the usual places. To take action now would be tantamount to suicide. His only reasonable course of action was to leave the country. If he wanted to complete the mission he had set for himself, he needed to distance himself from the affair and slip back in later. His thoughts whirled in his head like the chatter of a crowd. Individual reason was forced out as one train of thought was overwhelmed by another. The guilt of having been responsible for Ginger's death burned. The required cold-as-steel attitude was melted away by the red hot fires of rage and shame. He wanted a drink but did not want to leave the hotel and feared to allow himself to get drunk. He did push-ups and sit-ups until he was sweating from every pore. Then, even though he had already showered, he drew himself a hot bath and sat in it breathing deeply and trying to meditate. The hot water helped relax him, but he could still not clear his head.

The phone rang and he waited a minute then checked the message. Linda had been removed from the clutches of three wise guys. It did not look as though they had contacted anyone else. Evan owed the Valkieries a favor now, and by extension Terry owed Evan a favor. Terry promised to come through and Evan promised to protect Linda for a few days.

292

Gordon called. He was in Terry's room in Orange. Terry had still not installed the dead bolt he should have. When they spoke, the two made plans to meet the following day. MacMaster loaded the arms into the back of the Land Rover that night, cursing himself for getting in this deep. Everything he knew told him to turn and walk away. The profit margin had disappeared when Terry made it personal. He didn't need to pad his reputation, he was already well respected in his field, and he did not need an apprentice. It had always been his policy that friends would get you killed in this line of work. The fewer who knew who you were and what you did, the less likelihood of someone squealing. So he repeatedly asked himself what he was doing and what was in it for him. The risks far outweighed the rewards, especially when the fact that Terry was an emotional amateur was factored into the equation. He was torn. He did not do charity work, nor did he decommission men frivolously. There was always an angle to be played, and it usually involved cash. Honor was a factor but seldom a deciding one. It was honorable to always complete your mission. It was honorable to never target women or children. If an employer attempted to stiff you for the money, it was honorable to leave his head on a post in the town square. But, jobs were not initiated for the sake of honor or moral indignation. That turned one from an honorable assassin into a mad dog serial killer. At least that was Gordon's feeling at that stage of his life. He felt that many men acted tough for no better reason that to convince the world at large that they were not homosexual.

He almost headed for the airport when he thought of an angle.

Terry knew he was wanted for questioning. He did not know what the questions were. He also knew he was needed to identify his uncle's burned body if he could. The only reason he did not go to the morgue was he didn't want to be taken into custody. What he did not know was the extent of the interconnectedness of all electronic data. He did not know that when a man bought a pound of butter, the dairy league knew that butter had been sold before it left the store, and if it was paid for by a credit card, they knew who bought it. The loopholes would be closed before long, but shortly after the turn of the century, the computer revolution was flooding the advertising and manufacturing sectors with unbelievable amounts of free data. The point here is that it was becoming more and more difficult by the day to disappear.

Terry had taken the hotel room as a safe place to meet and plan, but he had gotten stuck in there by the knowledge that his cover was blown. Young and brash he had almost thrown caution to the winds and gone down to the warehouse on Elizabeth Street to decommission everyone in the place. He had thought better of it since they were lower-level thugs and goons without the pull or the time to order things done. He knew he wanted to eliminate Jimmy Cognac, but Jimmy was not settled into a routine that could be predicted. He might be in a place for two days and then not return there for weeks. Jimmy was also sharp and observant. He had no problem sanctioning somebody's decommission on the basis of suspicion. Of course, the Troy brothers were the real target.

Once his head had cleared a little, Kingston picked up the phone. "Mr. Glasgow?"

"Ah, Mr. Tarrytown. I was just thinking about you."

"I hope that's a good thing. Look, I have an idea. It's certainly not a novel idea, but with Uncle Ginger gone, I have no need to stay. I have a business. I can sell the business for a tidy profit or I can milk the parent company for a lump of cash."

"We need to discuss this further. Take no such action and allow me to tell you why. The company you so aptly described as "parent" has one reason for being and that is to make money. If it allows an affiliate agency to rob it, then they pave the way for anarchy. If you milk them for a lump of cash they will be willing to spend 10 times that lump of cash to find and prosecute you. There will be no shallow, unmarked grave. It will be a full-blown media circus whereby your picture is broadcast all over the world. It will be 'look at this fool who thought he could pull one off on the Helping Hands.' Even if they never catch you, your face will be published and you will be worthless to me and a pariah for anyone in my line of work." Gordon had rattled the speech off as if it were a long practiced soliloquy on Broadway. He needed a deep breath when he was done.

"Well the truth is that the money was going for a good cause. I need a partner if I am to begin an endeavor the scope of which I have in mind. Partners of that caliber cost a lump of cash. I am willing to pay that lump of cash for the services of such a professional contractor." Terry's speech patterns were improving some. His written style had been first and his spoken language skills had followed.

"That we must speak of later. We may find it to be unnecessary. I will join you in the morning. Get some sleep."

With the morning came the grinning Gordon MacMaster with a bag of breakfast, some coffee and a collection of guns in the back of the Land Rover. After breakfast they sat smoking and talking.

"Are you absolutely sure you wish to pursue a life that will leave you with no home and no family? You'll have no friends for long and may need to eliminate them when you leave. Are you sure you care for that? And I want to know why." Gordon got deadly serious very suddenly, throwing a wet blanket over the camaraderie of the morning.

Terry caught the sudden change of attitude and adjusted his manner accordingly. "Mr. Glasgow, I have no more family since Uncle Ginger died... was killed. I have no friends and never really have. While some people will be happy spending every day on the farm with the sheep shit and the cackling chickens, I want more. I want to see the world and experience life."

"Become a truck driver. You'll see the world that way."

"I have driven a truck, remember, I saw nothing but the miles of blacktop before me. I never saw the country, just the road."

"True. Well then, what did you have in mind?"

"I can commission my solicitor to sell my business. The profit from said sale would be sufficient to retain your services for a few days, yes?"

"Yes."

"Then I will work on that. I have some other small resources I will need to access. That will only take a day or two. I will get a forward from the solicitor, enough to pay you a retainer. Then we can get to work."

"You still haven't told me the details."

"It's a matter of self preservation now and I can't perform the surveillance I could before. They know my face now and yours as well. I played the game as far as I could go and now I need to end it."

"Obviously, but have you given thought as to how deep you need to go? There may be men you have never met who would take it personally if you decommissioned their superiors. On the other hand, they may thank you for it as they cut you down. How well do you trust the bikies? If you put this Evan McCormick into power, how long will he let you live? Are there enough of them to storm the castle, so to speak? I'm only asking these questions because I wish to leave the country upright and breathing." Gordon watched Terry very closely. He had a nagging fear that Terry had lost something when Ginger had died, something inside. It could be caution, it could be the will to survive, but he had seen men who had lost this preserving instinct before. Raving berserkers seldom lived long.

"I'm thinking the best way to take out men like these is to turn their own force against them. It works so nicely when properly done, but we don't have time. Yes, we did have some small desertions over the past couple of years but nothing on the magnitude of a full-scale revolution. Now there is no time for the subtlety and subterfuge that would require. We will need to hit them from afar in a way that they do not expect or see coming. We need to block them off from support and eliminate them quickly, together before they know they are under attack."

That was the sort of answer Gordon MacMaster wanted to hear from his young associate. Too many men would be leading with their chin at this point and get their bells rung in the first round, so to speak. Terry had not only retained his spark but was keeping his head.

Any criminal underworld is a many-headed hydra and even when the heads are turned against each other, two will eventually sprout for every one that dies. It can be made to hide, it can be made to temporarily shrink, but it cannot be killed. The best that can be hoped for is a temporary lull in activities while a restructuring and regrouping is accomplished. Gordon was pleased to find that Terry had come to terms with that and had no illusions about being some medieval Galahad assaulting the towers of injustice. Terry assured his senior that had lost those illusions when he became part of what he assaulted. Later that day, MacMaster went out and got Terry a nondescript Toyota with tinted windows to assist in their endeavors.

Chapter Sixteen
No Cover

"Oy, I see you're back."

Billy's voice was not unexpected, Terry had seen him pull in, but it still sent shivers down his spine. He stood stock still with his hands at his sides. His revolvers were in their holsters under his arms as usual and he had them covered with a vest that did little to conceal their presence.

Billy continued, "What's with the Japanese car? Where's the Monaro?"

"It sucked a valve into the head. I wrung it out a bit too high on a back road, lost the retainer and dropped the valve into the piston. I couldn't get parts for it right away. A valve I can get, but a new piston's not so easy. Computer says there isn't one in the bloody country and I need to wait for a shipment from America. You know what they would have charged me to ship it on a plane?"

Terry was standing in front of the charred remains of his deceased uncle's farmhouse calmly discussing the price of air freight. That might have struck some men as being unusual, but Billy had known him a long time.

"So, you coming down to the morgue to identify the body?"

"Aye. I suppose there's no getting around it?"

At that minute, James pulled in the driveway in his personal car and Terry knew that there was only two choices. He could go with them or he could decommission both of them. He had known both of them most of his life and did not like the idea of shooting them for more than that reason. It was terribly bad policy to shoot the police and they had no doubt radioed in their location. He was wanted for questioning at this point but not for capital murder. If he had thought for a second that he would be identified and cornered on the farm, he wouldn't have come here, especially

298

during the day. The location was remote enough that he thought he could slip in and out again.

"The chickens have not been fed in two days and the sheep are still in the pasture. I can smell the barn from here, so I need to get out a shovel and take care of that as well. Can you give me some time before you haul me in?"

"Jerry Junior will be coming by when he is done with his own chores. He sends his condolences, by the way. We cannot let you go. We are under orders to retain you for questioning and to get you to identify your uncle's body."

"Oh, aye. Is it him? I mean you've known him your whole life, you could have identified him."

"Terry, the rules are that the next of kin must do that and... well, I couldn't bear to look at him and, you know, the morgue is in Orange so it's well out of our way."

James had remained silent since exiting his car, but inserted himself into the conversation with "it might be best if you handed over those revolvers."

There was no doubt that this had been coming. They all knew the rules and the only reason the constables had come on so soft is that they had known Terry a long time. For his part, Terry was uncomfortable with letting anyone take his guns; he was also uncomfortable with getting in the back of the highway cruiser. James headed toward Molong while Billy drove Terry toward Orange. Terry had not been given enough time to access the underground bunker and retrieve the cash hidden there. That had been his primary objective, not to overlook the fact that he would have filled the trunk of his new car with ammunition.

"Superintendent? We have him sir, Terry Kingston turned up at the family farm and was taken into custody by the constables from Molong. He is currently at the station in Orange. He identified his uncle's body."

"His uncle's body? What's that all about?"

"His uncle died when his farmhouse burned. The fire department couldn't do anything for the house."

"Could it have been Terry? He's probably the beneficiary of the insurance policy."

"The neighbors say he was around a while back, but that he hasn't been on the farm for a couple of weeks. I don't think the officers from Molong consider this much of a possibility either. He is all they've got, though. We had questions last time we went to Orange and there's a boat load more now."

"All right, Sergeant. You and I will be going out immediately. It's going to be a long day."

"I could have him transported here."

"No, Sergeant, I have a feeling the real story is out there. Have Linda Pierce brought in for questioning as well. Do not let the two of them talk, keep them separate. We've finally buttoned down a long running mystery. The problem will be to get the story out of them since we have no real evidence. We need to convince them we do and go from there."

"Do you want Linda brought here?"

"No. There. Orange. Have a car ready for when I get there. I'll call C.I. Slaughter and get a substitute sent in for you. You are driving me." Barlow hung up the phone. It was indeed going to be a long day as the sun was already going down.

"Hello, Terry. It's been a very long time."

"Aye. Last time I saw you, it was Inspector Barlow."

"And I thought I had gone as far as I could. I expected to retire, as an inspector."

"It seems fortune has smiled on us both."

"How so?"

"Well, you have become Superintendent and I have the fortune to know the superintendent personally. I must say we meet under remarkably similar circumstances as before. Are you sure you're not really the angel of death scouting for more souls?"

"No, I leave the souls to the priests. I only need the bodies."

"Well, I've identified Uncle Ginger for you, but that required no visit from the top. You have something on your mind that needs to be let out."

"Indeed I do. I need you to tell me about your secretary, Linda Pierce." The Superintendent's manner was grave. He was not greeting an old friend; he was investigating murders.

"Linda? My secretary? Her name is Pettigrew."

"Yes, Linda. What is your relationship with her?"

"She's a good secretary. I met her, I don't know... uh, a few months ago. We hit it off. I dated her a few times. She's older than me. I had some fun with her, but we were never meant to be together for long. When Gretta wanted to retire I thought Linda would be a good replacement. She's been working out well."

"I see. Tell me about her husband."

"She's not married. I've been to her house. I've met her family. She lives on a farm with her parents." Terry knew he had made a mistake in having any connection with Linda after they had set up her ex-husband, and he knew he needed to play it cool and ignorant now.

The superintendent bored in with questions about where he had been on this date and that date. Who had he been with, who had he spoken to, what he had done. Terry could do nothing but feign ignorance. He never knew where he had been or what he had done on those dates. It was much too long ago to remember.

Frustrated, Barlow left the interrogation room to talk to Linda but he found that she was not there. She had not been at work today nor had she come home. Her father had told the investigator that had been sent to pick her up, that she had left with a bikie gang and he did not know when she would be back. He didn't remember what the name on the jackets was. He said he couldn't read it properly. The investigator knew the Valkieries had gone through town two days earlier. That was the only gang that had been seen.

Sergeant Black and one of the locals were left in the room with Terry. They continued to grill him about his whereabouts on certain dates and he continued to tell them he could not remember. To give them anything would be suicide. He also came to the realization that he should have had a fabricated log book for his activities for every day of the last few years. Something like the truck drivers are expected to keep, only for everyday business activities. What he did have was his signature on a number of dated documents at the insurance agency. He would not pull them out unless pushed into a tight corner and they were of questionable value since they were dated in one handwriting and signed in another. He often signed documents days or weeks after they had been drafted, depending on his schedule.

"I think you should tell me what this is all about. I'm getting a little tired of all these questions I can't answer, and I have no idea what they pertain to. In fact, I would like very much to consult my solicitor." Terry had not spoken to his lawyer for quite some time but Mr. Streng had always been in the background at the agency. The attorney seldom took criminal cases any more, but in Terry's case there would be no question.

"You are entitled to a solicitor when we actually charge you with a crime," Sergeant Black retorted. "Until now we have been having a quiet conversation, there has been no charges filed against you."

"A quiet conversation in a sound-proof room where I am not allowed to smoke, where I am being filmed, where there is a one-way mirror that I am undoubtedly under observation from." Adopting a woman's voice, Terry finished with, "Well, thank you for the tea and crumpets, I must be getting back to my washing." The high-pitched quavering voice Terry adopted for the last statement made Superintendent Barlow laugh out loud on the far side of the observation mirror.

"He certainly is a cool customer. Especially considering that he just identified the charred remains of his dead uncle. His last remaining relative. This is the sort of man to plan the set up of Lee Pierce. He's also correct. We have nothing to hold him on. I had hoped he would slip and let something out, but I don't think that will happen." Barlow rose from his chair and went back through the door into the room. "Mr. Kingston, are you aware that your secretary is consorting with outlaw motorcycle gangs and is probably planning to rob your agency blind?"

"That's why we have an accountant and a solicitor to keep an eye on each other. A system of checks and balances."

"And who keeps their eye on you?"

"Nobody needs to. I do nothing wrong. I may have one too many from time to time and I do like to boff the ladies, but there's nothing wrong in that, is there?"

"You should be more careful with whom you consort. You might find yourself in dire straights otherwise."

"I'll take that under consideration. Now, if there's nothing more, it has been an incredibly long day and I would like very much to get a shower and go to bed."

Billy drove back to Molong in silence. He was not privy to the questions asked in Orange, but he assumed they were regarding Terry's whereabouts for the last couple of days. He assumed it was about the fire. His shift had been over for hours and he was more than ready to go home to his wife. He and Terry parted on friendly terms with no love lost.

The young Kingston stood, facing the blackened remains, waiting for something. He didn't know what it was he was waiting for. He more felt than heard the old generator kick on underground. If he had not known it was there, or if the wind had been blowing, he would not have felt or recognized the tremor. The barns had escaped the flames, though it completely destroyed the house. There was no power to the lights in the barn and there was no flashlight in the Toyota, so Terry fired it up and turned on the headlights. Inside the barn, the concrete block was exposed. That seemed odd, but the hoist was not attached to the lifting ring. He ran the cable out and hoisted the block. Of course, Terry had a key for the security door.

"That took balls, if you'll pardon the expression, Constable."

"Of course, Sergeant Black." Senior Constable First Class O'Reilly emphasized the word 'sergeant' in response to being called Constable. She was considered a first class officer and she did indeed have what it takes to enter difficult situations.

"A lot of men would think twice about walking into the Valkieries' clubhouse in or out of uniform."

"I was there looking for someone in particular who was not a club member. If she were a club member, I would not have gone there. Anyway, I took Tank with me. I didn't get anywhere as it was. They gave me nothing. I didn't see anyone fitting the description and I had to ignore a lot of what I did see. That's a sordid bunch, there."

"You don't suppose they did away with her, do you?"

"Sergeant, they may have done anything with her. It is out of character for a farm girl and secretary of an insurance agency to suddenly up and run off with a bunch of bisexual bikies. It doesn't fit, unless she took a sudden liking to women. Women in black leather."

Sergeant Black had a sudden intuition, fed by the expression on her face, that perhaps Senior Constable First Class O'Reilly had taken a sudden liking to women in black leather, but he held his tongue.

"They could have started pimping her out, but that is not what they do as far as anyone can tell" O'Reilly continued. "They may have used her up and eaten her alive for all I could tell. The men in Orange kept a sharp eye on them in and out of town. They saw a woman in business attire riding with one of the gang, but did not see who it was. I'm convinced it was this Linda Pettigrew, but I can't say where she went."

"Very well, Constable O'Reilly, I'll make sure the Superintendent knows of your invaluable assistance." The truth was he was desperate to prove how valuable he could be. Black knew the Superintendent had only a few years at the best and would be replaced with someone who had no knowledge of him or love for him. If he were to make a mark, he needed to move soon, while his star was still on the horizon. At this juncture that meant finding Linda and bringing her to talk to Barlow. But he had no clue where to look. Finally he concluded that his best chance of finding Linda lay with observing Terry Kingston. Terry was the key to it all.

"Did ye bring me a cigar, mate?"

Terry jumped out of his skin. Before he knew it he had a .38 out and cocked.

"Oh, oh, oh. Terry, you wouldn't shoot your old uncle would you?"

"Ginger, for the love of God. You scared me right out of my trousers."

"Only two kinds of men coming through that door, friends and enemies and I don't have many friends."

"So you hide under a blanket and scare the life out of one of the few you do have?"

"Precisely."

"Shit, how did you expect to get out of here? How did you close the slab behind you?"

"House jack and a bit of timber. This is a bloody good place to hide."

"For a while." Terry did not look entirely convinced.

"You have fresh air, bottled water, food. I wouldn't want to stay down here long but a couple of days is no strain."

"You're dead, you know. I identified your dead body at the morgue." Terry lit a cigarette.

"I'll thank you to address me as Horace in the future. I needed a change anyway."

Terry grinned. "Uncle Horace. Sounds like some child-boffing pervert from a wizard book."

"Have a care young man. This old pervert might boff your ears for you."

Terry spread his arms and hugged his uncle in an unprecedented rush of emotion. Ginger thumped him on the back and asked if there was a chance of getting out quietly and if Terry had any cigars.

There was no doubt about the Helping Hands cutting Terry a check for the disastrous fire and the death of his uncle. There was actually a substantial life insurance policy that both Kingstons had forgotten about. It was paid automatically and in perpetuity by Mr. Streng, Esquire, in Terry's name. Mr. Streng made a small percentage for representing the interested parties, and a much larger commission for selling the Kingston Agency that was snapped up within days of going on the market. It should have sold for more, but time was of the essence.

Ginger could not be convinced to leave the area with a pile of cash. He had not raised and trained his nephew in the clandestine arts just to be shoved under the bed when the action started. He was already dead in the eyes of the law and the bastards had burned his home, so he felt he had a legitimate grudge.

When Ginger heard that the three men who had survived the assault on his farm had been kidnapped from the Pettigrew farm, and were locked in the back of a panel truck behind the Dark Knight's clubhouse, he was all for eliminating them. Terry thought they might be more useful alive. Ginger agreed that one might be useful, left alive, but three were unnecessary. Terry argued that there was no percentage in killing them without some sort of return on investment. Ginger accused Terry of becoming greedy and Terry said he was just being practical. It turned out to be a dead issue since a couple of days in the back of the truck without water had killed all three of them from dehydration. The bodies disappeared without fanfare or funeral.

Evan was taking care of Linda in a house outside the city. She shared the house with another woman and there were assigned guards all night and all day. They were not professional, walk-the-perimeter kind of guards but they would not allow any harm to come to their charge.

Ginger Kingston and Gordon MacMaster got along in fine order after a few minutes of uneasiness. They recognized a kindred spirit in each other and neither of them were supposed to be there. They spent a day smoking cigars and drinking rum while Terry was coordinating with the Dark Knights. Neither Evan McCormick nor Gordon MacMaster wanted to meet the other and this made for a difficult arrangement. Evan spared no breath in reminding Terry that he already owed him a favor. The corpses of the wise guys served as a strong marker against Terry's credit. Terry was quick to point out that he was working toward handing control of the city's underworld over to the club's president. Evan was chosen as successor to the Troy brothers. He would be the next ruler of the underground empire.

Evan was not convinced. He had not seen enough positive progress against the main target. The targets chosen had been fringe targets or competition. It was true that the Dark Knights now had control of both the Russian and Chinatown areas, but Evan was also realistic about his ability to hold said control. The Asians were already trying to work around their new suppliers and creating new pathways for their products. Too proud, individual and independent, they would be good for some short-term customers, but to try to control them for the long run would result in a great deal of blood shed.

Terry had not been on the inside for a couple of days and would never be in again. This meant that he was not privy to the information he needed to plan further coups against the criminal network. It was all or nothing now. There was no more standing on the sidelines and sniping easy targets. The spigot was closed and to access the flow, it needed to be chopped off.

Jimmy Cognac was the first target needing a fast decommission. Most of the men under him needed direction from a superior. They were not leaders; they were very dangerous men, but they needed direction. The one problem with killing Jimmy was finding him. Jimmy had lived in the world of corruption and betrayal his whole life and was nobody's fool. He had no long lasting habits, no pattern of associates or locations that he favored. He did visit the Kings Cross section about once a week but changed houses almost every time, preferring the anonymity of prostitutes. He had no permanent position, no legitimate business that was a running concern and required monitoring. He showed up at warehouses when and where he felt like and kept a low profile as far as clubs and pubs were concerned.

308

Terry could send Jimmy Cognac a message to meet him somewhere but Jimmy would show up with an army of wise guys and might not even be there in person. Jimmy would never consent to a meeting with any of the motorcycle gangs, either, unless he picked the location and secured it. Gordon was supposed to be gone from Australia and he intended to maintain this subterfuge until the end. And Ginger was dead.

Terry finally admitted that he did not know where to proceed from there. If he had done it earlier, when he was an unknown quantity, when he was an unrecognizable hick farmer, he might have gotten away with it. He had been around too long now. His face was too well known by too many people.

Gordon and Ginger were half in the bag and Gordon was talking about things he did not usually discuss, things he had done in the past. It had been a long time since he had consorted with men that had done what he did for a living, even if it had been a long time ago. They were so engaged with their own conversation that they actually alienated Terry. They were too drunk to conceive of a good plan anyway.

The next day over breakfast they looked at the situation again.

"Why do we need to eliminate Jimmy Cognac, anyway?" MacMaster wanted to know.

"Well, he's next in line for the uh... position," Terry said.

"No, not really. The way the thing is set up, no one is in line for the position. Whoever is listed on the wills of these two men, the Troys, that is who is in line. Remember, as despicable as they are, most of their business is legitimate. They have reinvested the dirty money over the years and built themselves a clean organization."

"It's not that part of the business that we're attacking. I mean we haven't attacked it. Cognac represents the other side of the road. You bring up an interesting point, though.

I wonder who is actually going to benefit from this. Neither of the brothers has a wife or any children. Blast! If I hadn't sold the agency I could probably figure it out."

"It's not public record, is it?" Ginger asked.

"No," said Terry. "Not till after the will has been executed."

"Who executes the will?" Ginger asked.

"The lawyers do that. Why?

"If we know who their heir is, it gives us leverage."

"What sort of leverage? What? Are we going to kidnap whoever is on the document? That makes the whole thing much more complicated than it needs to be, Uncle. It was that sort of complication that almost cost you your life. I was ready to shoot the bastards through the window of the limo."

"Yes, but think of all you would not have learned, had you done that." Ginger was examining his half-burned, unlit cigar as he spoke.

"But you would still have a home and I would not be on the run."

"I told you this life is not for those seeking stability. You must be ready to make the move in a heartbeat. No ties."

"My father managed a family and a business while living this life."

"Your father tried to have both sides and it killed him." Ginger's voice was harsh and his visage became very cold. "Now, let's figure out how we finish this up and get out of here."

Terry's nostrils flared at his uncle's coarse treatment of what was still a tender subject but he kept his tongue. He knew Ginger was right, recent events had proven it. The life of an assassin was an anathema to stability and the thought that the two could coexist was the height of self-delusion.

310

The young man had not known how much he was going to miss having a home to go back to from time to time.

Gordon MacMaster watched this interaction very closely as he was making a show of eating his eggs and toast. The slightest friction can cause hesitation or heat that cannot be justified in a combat situation. He saw that Terry's father had become a sore point but also wondered who the father had been. His name would have meant nothing to him, since he had never worked the Australian continent before, but it was becoming clear that there was more to this family than he knew and that there were secrets that they were very good at keeping. In all the time they had been together, and all the drinking they had done, Terry had never told him about his father having been in the business. That sort of self-control was an admirable trait. It increased the respect Gordon felt for his potential protégé. He knew it was not important in the short run, but his curiosity was piqued. Gordon MacMaster simply had to know who the father had been and what he had done.

One thing Gordon had discovered, and was to remain relatively certain of, was that drug addicts, gangsters, wise guys and bikies were seldom found in the library. He had used libraries as meeting places on a number of occasions in the past and was, in fact, a very well read individual. The internet was becoming a huge source of information on current events, but much of the older news was never scanned in and was only available on microfilm.

Leaving Terry and Ginger in the hotel room under the guise of "reconnoitering," Gordon visited one of the larger local branches of the library. He researched the Kingston name and found out about the murder of Marcia, the disappearance of George and the shooting of Ginger Kingston in the hospital in Goulburn. There was no link between the family and any assassinations that may or may not have been perpetrated. If George Kingston had been a killer for hire he covered it very well. The reason for Terry's personal vendetta was uncovered, however.

Gordon MacMaster ruminated on the methods and patience that Terry Kingston had displayed. He had not gone hog wild and started blasting away at everything, even before the Scotsman had begun to coach him. He had displayed some style, though not much, and some skill, certainly. More than that, he had displayed the commitment to the long-term objective necessary of a professional, and he had been able to swallow his feelings and act as one of the men he was trying to destroy. MacMaster decided then that there was sufficient justification for his long-term association, rather than just a fast pile of cash. To this point he could not decide if he should disappear at the end of the job or not. He had never wanted an apprentice because of the inherent risks involved. He had known many competent men in his life but did not know of one he would have consorted with after the job was done. Until this point, regardless of what he said, Gordon had been unsure of whether or not he was going to eliminate the young Australian at some point in the future. Now he knew.

"Do you mean to tell us that four men could do nothing about a farm boy and his sheila? That all four men just disappeared?" Abel Troy was not his usual erudite self. It seemed as though he was becoming slightly unraveled.

"Mr. Troy, Sir, as far as I can determine, the three men who survived the encounter at the Kingston Farm were kidnapped by bikies at the Pettigrew Farm."

"Preposterous."

"It may seem so, Sir, but nevertheless, true. When they went into the house looking for this Terry Kingston, they opened fire on a man and caused an explosion. That explosion took one of them down and burned the house and anyone in it. They called to tell me about that. Then they

312

went to the Pettigrew farm, thinking he would go there if they manipulated the woman. That blew up in their faces as well, so to speak and nobody has heard from them since."

"What gang?"

"Valkieries."

"Do we know where they are?"

"Yes."

"Hit them. Hit them hard and fast. Kill everyone there and if this son-of-a-bitch is there with them, bring me his head."

"Are you sure you want to commit the manpower necessary to…"

"You stupid little worm! Did I ask your feedback on this? Did I tell you to question my judgment? Did I give you a fucking order? I'm not giving you permission to hide under a rock. Get onto the fucking job and bring me this little cock suckers head on a fucking plate." Abel Troy was becoming unhinged at this point. Spittle was flying from his mouth as he screamed. A dispassionate observer might have labeled him as having gone over the edge.

Jimmy Cognac headed for the door with a stream of invective pouring after him. He thought it was a bad idea to go to war, especially now, but he had been given no choice. He began gathering the troops oblivious to the fact that he was being observed as he did so. He knew he was making a mistake, he could feel it, but he dared not go against orders. He had worked for the Troys for a long time and had never seen either of them lose their composure before.

"Mr. Troy, Adam, I need to talk to you."

"Jimmy, what is it now?"

"Adam, I've worked for you for a long time and in all that time I have never refused to do anything for you. Sir, do you trust my judgment?"

"It has proven to be sound on some occasions."

"Then, please, do not allow this action to go on."

"What action?"

"The assault on the Valkierie clubhouse in hopes of finding Terry Kingston there."

"What are you talking about? Who authorized that?"

"Your brother, Abel."

"Oh, no. Stand down. I repeat, stand down. I need to examine this in depth before we go expending manpower on what could be nothing more than a snipe hunt."

"Thank you, Sir. You have no idea how relieved I am. If they had the slightest hint we were coming, we would never have left."

"Why?"

"The Valkieries' clubhouse is the old Airie Hotel set into the end wall of a box canyon. One way in, covered on both sides from above. Passage is narrow enough to block with a car and we're ducks in a barrel. We'd never see the far side of that scrap."

"Where are you?"

"Warehouse on Irving. I didn't want to bring this to you, but it's the very worst thing we could do. I know the two of you back each other up on all things but this was so far over the edge that I…"

"Don't be alarmed. I will talk with Abel about it and determine if his motivation was sufficient for the risk involved."

"Thank you again, Sir. If we are to do this it will require planning and coordination of a sort I do not have the capacity for without maps and photos. We cannot go into that canyon without a way out." As Jimmy Cognac hung up he heard the first of the sirens approaching. He stepped out on the floor of the warehouse and addressed the crowd, telling them to stay where they were, that they were not going on an excursion after all and to remain calm. The sirens stopped right outside the personnel door.

314

A few miles off, Adam was on the telephone with his brother. Abel had calmed down after his little flare up and they spoke civilly to each other. Their conversations had been a bit strained of late since Abel was a strong advocate of paramilitary tactics and Adam much preferred a surgical strike. The Troy brothers had ruled the city for a long time after their initial takeover without a serious challenge from any sector and had expanded operations quickly. Their methods were dissimilar, but they balanced each other well.

"Abel, I regret that I was forced to halt immediate operations as a result of a tactical diagnosis."

"Whatever do you mean, brother? I simply called for the extermination of a very annoying little scorpion. He has taken up with the Valkierie Motorcycle Club and I took the logical step in calling for the extermination of them all."

"But, Abel, I think if we examine the circumstances, we may discover that there is more to the arrangement than we imagined. The choice of locations, for instance. Most of the bikie clubs use kind of a stockyard layout, you know like a bunkhouse for ranch hands, with the stockade fence. This club house is an old resort hotel set in the back wall of a cul-de-sac canyon. It's a trap. I will not allow men to so much as enter that canyon. Let me spread a little butter and in a couple of days we'll know everything we need to know without the bloodshed. This Terry Kingston is better than we gave him credit for, but he is not better than us. Remember, divided we fall. Are you with me?"

"Of course. I admit, I got a little hot. One of our best men is dead and three others are missing, ostensibly kidnapped by the Valkieries. It upset me momentarily and I over-reacted. Thank you for your attention to logic. I will call off the assault."

"I already have, but thank you for your acquiescence. I will initiate the information gathering program and keep you in the loop. It would be best to watch the bulk of this gang, just to determine where they frequent and what they do. I will use discretion, as bikies are often speed heads and it makes them jumpy."

"This man has not shown up at his Sydney apartment. He also rents a room in Orange but he has not been there either. He is with the degenerates. He has not only assaulted us, but he has betrayed us, and I will not stop turning Heaven and Earth to find him until I hear his screams of agony. And to think, we had him in the basement once." Adam could not see that Abel's eyes were shining with a kind of madness as he spoke.

Gordon MacMaster was just about to pack up the microfilm he was scrolling through when a headline caught his eye. It was from the day in question, the day George Kingston had been murdered on his yacht. There had been another killing, in the town of Greenwell Point and a related shooting that had left a man critically injured. It did not immediately make sense, there was no evident connection between the two events, but that sort of coincidence was rare. MacMaster decided to dig a little deeper.

According to the newspaper, Albert Cohen a prominent jeweler who resided in Greenwell Point, but did not do business there, was shot through the spine, hospitalizing him in intensive care. The unfortunate incident happened as three or four men attempted to rob him at gun point. To his credit, one of the men never made it out of the neighborhood as the citizen blew his guts out with a .44 Magnum.

"Have you ever heard of Albert Cohen?" Gordon asked Terry when he had returned to the hotel room.

Terry replied in the negative but Ginger started shuffling his feet and looking at the floor. He obviously had something to say but it was not going to come out by itself.

316

"Ginger, are you having a hard time finding a way to say what you need to say?"

"Ah, I'm just putting together the words. Why do you ask about Albert?"

"I was doing some research and ran across his name."

"Albert and I never got along, even before. Something in our make-up led us to despise each other, even though we're kin."

"Kin?"

"Aye. Albert is my half brother on my mother's side."

"You mean I have another uncle?" Terry was leaning over with his palms planted on the table. His face was getting red and almost looked swollen.

"Aye. Albert Cohen was the first born son of my dear mother. She had a fling with a man when she was still too young and gave birth to Albert. From what I understand they had told Albert his mother had died in childbirth when they took him into the closed little world of Jewish money and diamonds. He and George got together in their early twenties and formed some sort of relationship. I only met him once and saw no reason to meet him again. We were raised under different circumstances. Me and him, we would never have got along. It was immediately apparent."

"Is there any reason you can think of, why he would have wanted your brother dead?"

"Oh, we got the killers. They're both planted in the ground years since."

"That's not what I asked. I asked if there was a reason Albert Cohen wanted George Kingston dead."

"No, I don't think so."

"The news, that means probably the police as well were convinced it was a robbery. Cohen never recovered from his coma and his obituary is printed a week later. This article was printed in between however." Gordon unfolded a sheet of paper from his pocket and smoothed it out on the table. It read "Man with Suspected Ties to the Sydney Mafia Hospitalized During Robbery."

Terry snorted, "Mafia. There is no fucking mafia in Australia."

Ginger ignored his nephew and read the article word for word. When he was done he said, "I had no idea he lived in Greenwell Point or I would have made the connection. I find it unlikely that he would pay to have George killed. It looks more like George interrupted something he was not supposed to see and his poor timing cost him his life."

"I thought he was killed for doing the Felix Ribbaldi job," Terry said.

"I think it may have had something to do with it," Ginger said thoughtfully. "Look here. Third paragraph down. 'Mr. Cohen has reputed ties to the Ribbaldi crime family and was reported as being on the list of suspects for a money laundering scheme.' In case you wonder what that means, it means Ribbaldi ratted out his boss and Cohen was about to do the same. That's why he's been planted. They probably thought George was going to do the same."

"Would he have done that?"

"No. I'm sure that was not where he was going. I still don't know why he was there, in Greenwell, but that's not important. It was his relationship with Albert that got him killed. I know it now. I told him he was no good, something about him smelled bad. But that's not here."

"If you look at it," Gordon said slowly but with authority. "George may have killed Albert and been killed for it."

"I'm thinking no," Ginger countered. "He was killed later that day. It takes time to set up this sort of thing. He was killed right after he left town and he was killed by professionals who did not know why the man had been targeted. That means he was a hired hit, not a knee-jerk killing. Someone knew where he was and where he was going. Terry, what can you tell me about that day, Mate?"

"My memories are all chaos. I can't remember anything clear and what I think I do remember came to me in dreams. You know I was all fucked up by it. I can't say if what I remember is real or a dream. I think we left town in a hurry and I know we were chased by a speed boat but the Agamemnon was sunk well to the south so I may be wrong."

"I'm thinking they sailed the boat south and then sank it. You probably were chased out of Greenwell and George was killed there." Gordon spoke softly, aware that he was treading on tender old wounds.

"You know what? All this old rubbish is nothing now. All it means is I have another score to settle with those steaming piles of shit. I'm tired of playing, I want them dead." Terry was starting to get flushed again and a steely resolve flowed from between his clenched teeth.

Chapter Seventeen
Assault

"Superintendent Barlow, you are not going to believe this. I think it may fit well with the series of events you are interested in."

"Well, I don't have all day, Inspector, what is it."

"We got an anonymous tip that there was a body in the dumpster behind this old warehouse on Irving Street. When the constables got to Irving Street, we find half an army in the warehouse, dressed to kill and outfitted for the same."

"Speak plainly Inspector Slaughter. I know you fancy yourself a poet but I am not a literary critic. Why was the army in the warehouse?"

"Sir, the men in the warehouse were all dressed in suits. They were not the army. They were gangsters and they were all heavily armed. The weapons ran the full slide from brand new and legal to old pieces from before the license laws. Some of them were stolen pieces but the guns are not the real issue." Chief Inspector Slaughter paused for effect.

"I assume you are going to tell me the real issue some time before I retire?"

"Yes, Sir. The call said there was a body in the dumpster and there was."

"A dead body in the dumpster behind the warehouse on Irving Street where there was an army of gangsters armed to the teeth. Is that the issue?" Barlow was looking quizzically at his subordinate with one eyebrow arched.

"Yes, Sir. I thought you might like to know because this sort of set up interests you." Slaughter was sounding a bit deflated now.

"And you think this is a set up?" Though it was obvious, Barlow saw that he was embarrassing the Chief Inspector and needed to give him a little more string.

Slaughter liked to crow and it seemed best to let him make a little noise.

"It has to be," Slaughter continued. "An anonymous tip that there is a body in a dumpster? The tip comes when there is a large group of individuals of questionable moral character? Armed as if they were going to war I might add. It was a set up. Unless I miss my guess, this is in preparation for something else."

"What?"

"I don't know, yet. There is nobody left in town that can possibly be a serious threat to organized crime. Since the Chinese and Russians went at each other, it's been quiet."

"What about the gang that muscled there way in there, in the vacuum that the gang war left?"

"Unpredictable at best. It's almost impossible to get an informer into the inner circles of these gangs and they don't let the recruits, the younger members or the locos know what is going on."

"Any word on that woman?"

"No, Sir. Ms. Pettigrew has not surfaced. We have been trying to watch the Valkierie clubhouse, but it's in a location that can't be monitored very well. The old Aerie Hotel. They just picked this one up a couple of months ago and it looks like they chose it for tactical advantage."

"So where are the gangsters being held?"

"We had to split them up because of the number of them. They wouldn't fit in the local, so some of them went to the downtown jail and some to other locals. Oh, I thought you might like to know that Jimmy Cognac was among those in the warehouse."

"And they were taken into custody without incident?"

"It was actually Jimmy Cognac that prevented bloodshed. I was not on the scene but the report reads that the constables were heavily outnumbered and outgunned. If

Jimmy had not kept his head we might be looking at dead officers."

"Interesting. Bring Mr. Cognac to see me. We obviously have a similar interest." When Chief inspector Slaughter had retired from the room, Barlow called the morgue and left instructions to bump the autopsy on the dumpster gangster, as he had been christened, to high priority.

Superintendent Barlow had an hour to wait before Cognac was delivered to him. In that time, he reviewed the recording of the anonymous call. He looked up the location of the warehouse and did a little research on its owners, but did not go deep enough to discover the connection to the Troy brothers.

"Mr. Cognac, please have a seat."

Jimmy was rubbing his wrists where the cuffs had been and was looking around him. He was alone with Barlow in the sumptuous office of the Superintendent of Police for the entire Province of New South Wales. Evidently the Superintendent was not worried about assassination, or at least not worried about Jimmy Cognac.

"I have some cognac, but I'm afraid it's not very good. I prefer scotch myself."

"Cognac will be fine, no ice." Jimmy said suspiciously. His name had doomed him to drinking cognac his entire life, not that he saw that as a bad thing.

Barlow made a show of pouring his guest a drink and then poured a scotch for himself. He thought it unlikely that the long time mob boss would loosen up, especially while in custody but there was always that possibility. After all, they were both civilized men.

Cognac drank sparingly as they exchanged small talk. He was no brash young man to be fooled into thinking he was anything but a criminal under arrest and being interrogated.

322

"Why do you suppose I've invited you into my office this evening?"

"I suppose, that you've gotten sick of talking to ivory tower suck-ups and you need some real conversation. You could have gone to a pub."

"I could have but I doubt I would have such an interesting subject in a pub."

"So we're not here to talk about rugby."

"No, I thought maybe you'd like to explain the corpse we found in the dumpster behind the warehouse you were in this afternoon."

"I dunno. I never saw it before. None of us put it there. We were on our way out for a hunting party." Cognac was clearly not worried about the situation.

"And what was it you were planning to kill with all that firepower?"

"Rabbits."

Barlow had to reign himself in. He was starting to get angry and that would not do. "I believe we have a mutual enemy. I can only turn my back on the situation for so long before it comes back on me. Eventually the situation must be dealt with."

"You hate rabbits too?"

"Mr. Cognac, we can work together or we can butt heads all day. I am giving you the opportunity to work with the finest police department on the continent. I am trying to help you eliminate a threat before it eliminates you and all the men you are working with."

"That hardly sounds like rabbits."

"You know what I'm talking about. I am offering to assist you in keeping yourself alive. There have been too many killings of late and though they have all been somewhat marginal members of society, they make the news. I have ignored the problem long enough and I feel it biting on my heels."

"You'll have to release me, and my men."

"Perhaps, in good time. I need to know what you know about whoever is attacking your concerns. You can work with me or we can attempt to achieve the same goal in a parallel fashion and perhaps we will both fail."

"Perhaps we'll talk about it more when you have released us from custody. I try not to negotiate from a position of weakness and you have me at a disadvantage. Release us and set up a meeting. We'll talk."

"And what will we discuss?"

"Rabbits."

"I wouldn't call Terry Kingston a rabbit." Theodore watched his captive's face closely and saw what he expected. Cognac hesitated before he replied. His manner was still smooth but it was the first hesitation of the conversation.

"Who?" came out too weak and too late.

"I think you know what I'm talking about."

"Try looking at Thompson Barber. Maybe you have something in your files on him.

Superintendent Barlow called the constable back in to escort Jimmy Cognac back to jail. He had not expected cooperation from the seasoned veteran of the streets, but he had gotten what he wanted. He knew for sure they were after the same man. They were just short on physical evidence linking him to any of his operations and Linda had not surfaced. Barlow was tempted to say it was a mob problem and he had no business protecting the mob. Terry Kingston disturbed business as usual, however. He was no longer the frightened little child they had fished out of the ocean. He caused major disturbances and the Superintendent did not like major disturbances.

Barlow poured himself another scotch and wondered who was playing who. The body in the dumpster had no holes in it. He was a wise guy with a criminal record but he had not been shot, stabbed or beaten to death. The real cause of death would have to wait for the coroner but the fact remained that there were no holes in the body. Nobody noticed when a gangster disappeared, except his family, and it was very rare for the bodies to ever surface. Turf wars were one thing but this was no invasion. It was another set up. Somebody had known the men were gathering there and had planted the body to implicate them. Terry Kingston was learning. He was becoming smoother, but he was also in the crosshairs of both the coppers and the mob. What did he hope to gain? Had the years of grief turned him mad?

Barlow called for any files on Thompson Barber and then ordered some dinner. He called his wife to tell her he was working late and called Senior Sergeant Randolph Black. Sergeant Black would never get the promotion to Inspector he desired, but was more than willing to do whatever was necessary. He would seek that elusive promotion for years.

Adam Troy sat in his sumptuous home on Unwin Street, in the Earlwood area of Sydney, and contemplated the situation that confronted him. First there had been a lot of money invested in the phantom businesses, but that money had been recouped and reinvested, primarily in legitimate businesses. Second there was a growing resentment within the population toward the gangsters. Third, his brother who had been so professional and so removed from emotional involvement in his younger years, was becoming less stable.

The Troy Brothers were financially set for life. That was beyond question. The wave of anger against organized crime was in part due to the actions of the vigilante who had caused so much trouble and death recently. The real problem was the media, which had romanticized the lifestyle for years, and was now turning against the mob. As goes the news, so goes the populous.

Adam Troy loved his brother as much as such a man could love anyone. Neither of the pair had much feeling for women and they had no children. All either of them had for a personal relationship was the other. Abel Troy had been a genius when it came to setting up the system that allowed the two of them to eventually take over the entire Australian black market. Adam had been more on the recruiting end of the business at first but his role had diminished greatly once there was a hierarchy in place. But, Adam feared his brother was no longer objective. He saw the actions against the organization as assaults against himself. He was starting to see himself as a general, commanding an army. The 'soldiers' were not military men however, they were just wise guys. They were effective at getting restaurant managers to cough up some cash every month. They could break a few jaws with brass knuckles and they could kill when they were asked to, but they were not an assault group. They could not be sent into a situation like they were the Los Angeles SWAT team. And that is exactly what Abel thought he could do.

The Mossad agents could and would react as a military team if required to do so. The guards hired to protect Adam at the Unwin Street mansion were that sort of professional, trained as a team. The gangsters were not capable of that level of coordination and precision. And now they were in custody, arrested for the second time because of a set up. And the man they were searching for, the real thorn in their sides, had become a ghost.

Abel Troy sat in his modern apartment on Castlereagh Street, with its high ceilings and its 360 degree view of the city and the bay, chewing on his dilemma. His brother had countermanded his order to attack the Valkierie clubhouse. Adam had never tried to take command like that before. Decisions were mutual but Abel had always had the last word on tactical maneuvers.

A glass of brandy had not calmed Abel's fears. He knew his brother was losing that undefined thing that gave the two of them the ability to wrest the helm from its

326

previous, fragmented leaders and consolidate the whole country under their flag. Abel feared his brother was veering from their mutually accepted path at the worst possible time. They were in more danger at this junction than they had been at any point previously. The vigilante, who had infiltrated their ranks, had disappeared. He, who had caused so much damage to the organization, was sequestered with a bunch of bikies in a mountain rat hole.

Who did Adam think he was, countermanding his brother's orders before they had even conferred about it? Abel Troy was the master of all he surveyed, the conquering hero striding the land like a giant and crushing those who opposed him beneath his heel.

Abel called for the helicopter to be prepped and fired up. He had requested that all calls be held so he was annoyed when the phone rang. He was about to reprimand his secretary when she told him that it would be best if he took this call. The connection was to the Superintendent of the New South Wales Regional Police.

"Ah, Superintendent Barlow, I was hoping we could get in touch with each other." Abel's voice echoed cheer and dripped sincerity, a polar opposite of his real feelings.

"Mr. Troy…"

"Please, call me Abel."

"Mr. Troy, I have been involved with your activities for most of my career and I have the greatest of respect for your abilities. If you were any less talented than you are I would have ended your career by now."

"I don't know what you're talking about. I'm a simple businessman…"

"Let us not play the game today. I called to tell you that we finally have the witness we need to end your dominance of the Sydney organization."

"Please, Mr. Barlow, if there was any truth to what you are saying you would have arrested me by now. You call me up at home, in the evening and tell me some fairy story of a witness against me for something I'm certain I never did? I don't know what you are playing at but I assure you it will not work. I am a businessman and nothing else." Abel Troy hung up the phone and it rang again, almost immediately. He was even more upset at his secretary this time but she insisted that he could not afford to miss the call. It was the law firm of Elroy, O'Toole and Sneed, their primary legal advisors. The news was of the entire warehouse full of men being detained on weapons and suspicion of capital murder charges. A creeping suspicion and fear began to grow in Abel's mind. His entire street-level army was temporarily detained, including Jimmy Cognac. None of that army had personal testimony that could damage his brother or himself except Jimmy.

The whirring of the chopper blades, as the machine came to life on the roof, interrupted his train of thought.

Evan McCormick's call brought a grin to Terry's face. He could not remember the last time he had smiled. The whole situation had dragged on much too long and become much too involved. In the process, what had started as enjoyable had turned deadly serious.

"Yeah, mate, the whole stupid lot of them, dragged off to the block house."

"Then it's time. Are you ready to become what you were born to be? Are you ready to lead?" Terry was counting on this drive in his associate's make up to hold the scheme together.

"The men are in place."

"I asked if you were ready. If you're not on the job the plan will crumble."

"Aye. I'm on the bloody job."

"Good. The dragon has been tied down, it's time to cut off its head... uh heads."

328

"Just give the call."

"Very soon. Once again, we want both of them together when we bring it down. Timing is critical. If there's only one in there, the one left alive will be killing every bikie in the city. To start with.

"I got the message, mate. It will happen as we planned. Is the diversion set?"

"Yes. Once again, the timing is critical."

"No worries, mate." Evan McCormick had lots to worry about but his outward demeanor was calm as any good leader should be.

The telephone call to Abel was the mere planting of the seed. Theodore Barlow knew that the Sydney Police Department had its share of corruption and that the conference between himself and Jimmy Cognac was not going to remain a secret for long. The Superintendent saw a chink in the armor and was preparing to home in on it. Jimmy was kept incommunicado; he would be getting no visitors, he would be making no phone calls. He would not talk to the police but in this case it was not predicated on what he said, but what Abel Troy thought he might have said. It was all a shell game. Barlow called for an undercover car to take him to the residence of Adam Troy. He planted the seed, now he would try to nurture it.

The police reacted predictably to the report that the Valkieries had gone hog wild in a downtown casino. The security was overwhelmed by the number of angry, drunken bikies and there would be shootings if the constables didn't present themselves soon. Every on-duty officer for miles was pressed into service to protect the casino.

As soon as the neighborhood was clear of constables, the Dark Knights went into action. While they had been clear about the Valkieries being unarmed for the operation, the Knights were far from it. Dynamite and Molotov

Cocktails sailed over the walls of the Unwin Street compound. It sounded like a full blown military assault.

Inside the compound, Adam Troy had just sat down with the Superintendent of the Police. He was hoping there could be an amicable arrangement negotiated between them. Theodore Barlow had always rebuffed overtures of friendship and cooperation in the past but there was always a chance.

The conversation had not progressed past the preliminary small talk when the sound of the helicopter landing on the pad in the yard intruded. The rotors had not stopped spinning when the first of the explosions was heard. The quick thinking pilot fired them right back up again.

Adam's first thought was that the helicopter had exploded. Then as the explosions continued, he realized he was under attack. Gunfire began punctuating the sound of the dynamite as the guards returned fire against the attack. Adam's next thought was to run into the basement but he knew he could not chance the Superintendent seeing the torture room. That would destroy any chance of an amicable relationship.

Two of the three ex-Mossad agents whirled into the room with drawn pistols.

"Mr. Troy, we must get you out of here right now. Your brother has returned to the helicopter and we suggest you do the same. You and your guest should fly out of here right now and leave the professionals to disperse the rabble assaulting your home."

Adam Troy knew a reasonable suggestion when he heard one. He and Superintendent Barlow allowed themselves to be herded to the helicopter and jumped on board. Abel was already back in the passenger bay along with the third of the Israelis.

The assault had turned into a gun fight as people took cover from the opposing fire. The occasional shell ricocheted off the body of the helicopter as it rose from its pad. From

330

inside, the passengers got a good look at the situation. Some of the combatants from both sides were down. Big holes had been blown in the lawn but the dynamite had more of a psychological effect. Fires were raging from the Molotov Cocktails but they were confined to the bushes and outbuildings. The main house did not seem to be in danger.

Terry Kingston had been working toward this for years. At first, without help, he would have achieved his objective but would probably have died in doing so. Some of the Dark Knights were down in the street, a couple of them were not moving. Terry had no time to weigh the trade off, the helicopter was rising from the smoke.

The surface-to-air missile was one of the ballistic innovations dictated by the helicopter warfare first used extensively in the Vietnam War. Their accuracy depended on being heat seekers. Terry had never fired one before, but they seemed simple enough. As the helicopter rose above the battle, it rose right into Terry's sights. There were five men inside, including the pilot. That almost ensured that both men were inside the machine. It was too hard to tell with all the smoke but there was no time for second thought and no time for verifying the target.

Terry pulled the trigger and the rocket shooshed from the shoulder held tube. He knew in his mind that this was one of the finest moments of his short life. This was the final step, the culmination of his revenge. Then he saw his mistake.

The rocket was a heat seeker and the fires that had been started in the yard were hotter than the engine. The SAM's exhaust drew a smoke line out from the launcher, directly toward the rising chopper, and then it arced downward into the flames. The resulting concussion was impressive and dramatic, but it had missed its target and the helicopter was quickly out of range of the next rocket. It was not out of range for the Barrett.

Gordon MacMaster squeezed the trigger smoothly and the armor piercing incendiary round blew a hole through the clear canopy. MacMaster had wanted to hit the fuel tank, but missed. While a regular round might not ignite the tank, an incendiary round was guaranteed to. The fuel tank was spared, but the pilot was not. The .50 caliber round took him through the side of the chest and out through the other side of the canopy. The stench of burning flesh filled the enclosure. The pilot did not have enough time to feel the pain. He stared stupidly at his chest for a moment and then slumped forward.

The Israeli guard reacted with precision and speed. He was not an experienced helicopter pilot but he was knowledgeable enough to grab the stick from the dead man's hand and slowly guide it to a stop on a lawn. When the canopy had been punctured, the sound of the rotors filled the interior. Adam had started screaming like a child. Abel had begun yelling instructions and Barlow had begun cursing and yelling that they needed to land. Smoke was still rising from the corpse of the pilot, gagging the guard and blinding him. It was almost pure luck that the vehicle could be landed at all.

The cockpit door was thrown open and the four men piled out and ran for the house. The door to the domicile was open and they rushed inside. Inside the house, a woman was yelling at them. She was screaming that they had to leave, that this was her house and that she would call the police. When she reached for the telephone, the Israeli guard shot her through the face with a 9-mm pistol.

Theodore Barlow could not believe the situation he had found himself in. He had gone to the house to foment suspicion and discord and had been caught in a catastrophic crossfire. He was a clear and level-headed man, but he was also an agent of the law. When the guard shot the woman, he

332

reacted as any good cop would have and shot the man repeatedly. He almost signed his death warrant in so doing. Abel Troy turned and pulled his own pistol from inside his jacket. The .45 thundered and the round blew a hole in the door jamb next to Barlow's head. Theodore dove as best he could into the next room. He was not a young man any more but fear and adrenaline absorbed the pain of age and allowed him to move like an athlete.

Ginger Kingston had taken a relatively safe position on the far side of Wolli Creek. Wolli Creek bordered the Troy Estate on the south and there was a stand of trees on the far side that made for good cover when the bullets started flying. His position left him closer to the chopper when it landed than anyone else. He was already moving toward it before it touched down.

"What the fuck are you doing?" screamed Adam Troy. "That's the bloody super of the coppers. You can't shoot him."

"Shut up. Can't you see what's gong on? Find some bloody keys and let's move. There's got to be an auto here."

Adam dumped out the woman's purse and found a set of keys. He tossed them to Abel who charged out the side door and into the garage. The electric garage door was just beginning to open when the first of the rounds pounded through it. Abel dove to the floor and Adam jumped back into the house. Ginger Kingston was in the driveway with his Thompson machine gun. The automobile within was devastated by the hail of lead, destroying that escape.

As the door rose, Ginger could not see Abel Troy lying on the garage floor. He did see the flash of the .45 in the dim interior, however and he felt the bite of the bullet as it cut a furrow through his calf. He screamed like a madman and emptied the drum as he fell to the side.

Adam was screaming like a child again and covering his ears. He had completely lost control finally. Abel grabbed

333

him by the collar of his shirt and shook him, screaming that they needed to move or they were dead. The bedroom door opened and Abel fired twice in that direction. The door closed again.

Abel started moving, dragging Adam behind him. Adam was still screaming. They were headed back toward the chopper. The engine was still running and the rotors were still spinning but both men with any expertise were dead. It would be a hell of a gamble.

Abel was hauling the corpse of the pilot out of the cockpit when he saw the motorcycle coming down the street. The powerfully-built blond man riding the bike was pulling a revolver from the inside of his vest. Abel grabbed Adam and spun him around between himself and the new threat. The .45 blasted twice and then clicked. The rider went down, but not before blowing a large hole in Adam Troy's head.

"Sorry, Brother," was all Abel said as his brother's corpse slipped to the grass. Then he was in the cockpit and speeding up the engine. He had never flown the helicopter before, but he had seen it done enough times that he had a good idea what all the controls were. The bird began to rise as Gordon MacMaster drove the van over the bridge. He squealed to a stop, hauled the sniper rifle from the back and braced it against the lip of the open window. Again, he wanted the fuel tank but did not have a shot at it so he went for the pilot. The huge burning round hit Abel Troy in the elbow and blew his forearm off his body. The hand was still gripping the stick, still controlling the helicopter, but Abel was no longer in control of the hand. The machine canted wildly to the side and caught a power line. There was a blinding flash as the transformer exploded. The helicopter tilted wildly and the tips of the rotors began plowing up the ground.

Theodore Barlow was watching from the window of the bedroom. His pistol was in his hand but his target was

334

not clear. Before he had a clear shot, the helicopter leaned over and began chopping its way across the lawn at him. He felt exactly like a toad as the lawn mower passes over it. The chopper did not stop at the house, it sliced into it, exploding the wood around it, destroying the structure and sending the debris flying about. It chopped through the living room and the kitchen where it tore the stove from its mooring and wrenched the gas line from the floor. The pilot lights were out but the arc created as the wires were severed provided enough spark to ignite the gas. A column of fire shot upward and a now ruptured fuel tank stood right in its way. The explosion was legendary. Burning fuel splattered all around. It was a scene from Ragnarok.

Barlow had jumped under the bed when he saw the chopper blades gouging their way across the lawn. It would not have saved him from the blades but it did save him from the detonation. The mattress was his shield against the explosion but the concussion of it knocked him momentarily senseless. When he regained consciousness, Terry Kingston was pulling him from the wreckage of the building.

The sirens were wailing as the police and fire departments raced to the scenes on either side of Wolli Creek. They gave Barlow courage and resolve. He stood and stumbled as he was being pulled across what was left of the lawn. He threw his hand underneath Terry's vest and pulled out a .38 revolver.

Terry was momentarily stunned as he saw the business end of his own pistol. "Ted," he said, "this is a bad idea."

"I'm sorry, Terry, I know what you have been up to. I can't let you go. You're under arrest."

"No, Inspector Barlow, I'm not. You'll need to shoot me and I don't think you have the stupidity to do that. Look behind me, at the open window of that van."

The barrel of the .50 caliber sniper rifle was protruding from the window and it was pointing directly at him.

Superintendent Barlow did not move, nor did he drop his aim.

"I might be able to convince the man holding that rifle to spare you if you drop the gun. If not, he will blow you in half with it."

Theodore Barlow was caught in a Mexican standoff. All he needed to do was wait until the rapidly approaching sirens reached him, but he knew he did not have that much time. The other fuel tank finally erupted in a delayed reaction and burning fuel and wood once again shot all over the neighborhood. A large piece of window frame caught Barlow in the back of the head and he went down again.

Chapter Eighteen
Exiled

Ramni Mirza Ali Gupta could not be called Doctor because he had lost his license to practice medicine. He had been too free with the prescriptions and had become too fond of pharmaceuticals himself. These days he was more likely to be seen in a bottle of gin. The law required that any doctor who treated a bullet wound report it to the police but Ramni was not a doctor any more, so the Dark Knights retained his services for days like today.

Once the helicopter had lifted from the mansion there was no more need for an assault. It was unfortunate that the operation had not gone as planned, but once the helicopter cleared the creek, the bikies packed up their casualties and moved off. The guards honored the white flag but had no idea what was going on. They had never had to defend the grounds against anything more pressing than a Girl Scout troop. The Knights were gone before the fire department and police arrived and they were not identified since they had not worn their colors.

Ramni still had connections within the medical community and could get pain killers and local anesthetics in limited supply. The prescriptions were written to fictitious workers at a small video store and insured under those names. Ramni's sister owned the video store and the paychecks went into a fund for her sons' education. He no longer dispensed the drugs the way he once had but they were still there when absolutely necessary.

Some of the men were beyond repair when the arrived at the compound. They had taken too much lead. Some were in need of a still drink and a cigarette. Others required surgery and Ramni Gupta provided this. The conditions were not sterile, but they were clean. The instruments were sterilized with bleach and gin. The ex-doctor was assisted by his former nurse, who was still quite in love with him, and his sister whom he had trained. The Dark Knights and some of the other bike clubs in Sydney paid very well for keeping the news of their wounds out of official channels.

The bullet that had struck Ginger's leg had missed the bone. In fact, it had just cut a channel in the flesh of his calf. It was bleeding a great deal and very painful but was by no means life threatening.

Terry pulled the van into the compound with his uncle in the passenger seat and a damaged motorcycle in the back of the van. Gordon MacMaster was nowhere to be seen.

Evan McCormick strode up to Terry as he exited the van and laughed explosively. The police radio scanner had told the tale of the exploding helicopter, it also told the tale of an all points bulletin for Terry Kingston AKA Thompson Barber. "Tommy, lets have a drink and you can tell me all about it," Evan roared.

"I've got to get my uhh, this man taken care of. He was instrumental in taking down the chopper but he took one in the leg and I need the doc."

"Boys, we got one more. Get this man in the trailer so the doc can have a look at him. You can find me in the bar. I've been there all day. Drinks are on the house today. It's my birthday." The bikies almost forgot to move Ginger into the trailer where Ramni was stitching up the wounded. The prospect of free drinks was a powerful lure. It was not long before the men in the bar looked as though they really had been drinking there all day.

Caution dictated that Terry not get too drunk for his own good. A drink or two would be fine but any more than that and his judgment would be impaired. He could not help but notice that Evan was trying to get him drunk. He excused himself and went back through the back door to check on Uncle Ginger. Ramni Mirza Ali Gupta had not reached Ginger yet and it looked as though it might take

338

some time. A combination of pain killers and alcohol had sedated most of the injured bikies. A leather-bound bikie with a full beard who had been a medic in the UN forces at Sarejevo was cleaning their wounds and evaluating the level of threat. Ginger was near the bottom of the list.

Terry stood around for a moment and realized he could do nothing productive. When he got back to the bar, he was surprised to see Gordon MacMaster sitting in a corner with a beer in front of him. It simultaneously made him nervous and relieved. It leaped to his mind that the Troy's had retained Gordon for a job, but once the job was over, it was no impediment to his being hired to kill them. Terry sat at the bar and stuck to beer. Evan was pushing the hard liquor from behind the bar but Terry had second thoughts. The whole situation was becoming tense. Questions passed through his mind: why was Gordon in the bar? Why was Evan trying to get him drunk? Why was Evan not drinking, himself?

If Ginger had not been in the trailer, in the back, Terry would have headed out. As it was, he left the stool at the bar and put his back to the wall at a table across the room from Gordon MacMaster. Evan continued dispensing the spirits but was imbibing in none himself. Terry smelled something wrong. It was nothing he could be sure of, nothing that stuck out glaringly but he was sure he smelled it. He stood with his beer half finished and stepped through the back again to check on progress.

The unlicensed surgeon was making his way through the room. It looked as though the ones who had arrived alive would stay alive. When Terry entered, his uncle stood and hobbled toward him. "We gotta go, now," Ginger said.

Terry was full of questions and almost sat the elder Kingston back down, but instead he helped him down the steps of the trailer. When they got a few feet from the trailer, Ginger hissed in his ear. "They tried to give me a shot. They got men in there in serious condition and they had no shots for them but they tried to give me a shot. I barely kept them from sticking me."

The door opened behind them and the ex-medic filled it. "Oy mate, you can't leave 'til we get that leg stitched up. That man's likely to bleed to death from that. Get your stupid backside back in here."

Terry ignored the demand and kept walking toward the van. They stopped to readjust his hold on his uncle, glanced back and saw the medic pulling a gun from his waistband and following them. Ginger reached under Terry's vest and as they turned, he jabbed the medic in the guts with a stun gun. Fortunately the man's finger was not on the trigger or it would have tightened up and gone off. The crackling of the weapon sounded like a TIG welder in the distance. It was a minute later when the shot went off.

The tavern full of drunken patrons emptied itself through the back door to see the white van moving slowly across the dirt compound toward the gate. Evan McCormick had no more patience for the game and pulled his pistol. "Shoot the traitors." He exclaimed. They just killed Mickey." Indeed, Mickey was lying unconscious outside the trailer's doorway. The bikies had been drinking a lot of hard liquor and could not have hit anything smaller than the van at that range, but something that large was difficult to miss. The barrage that resulted left nothing in doubt. They knew they had killed whoever was in the van and Evan moved to confirm that as it coasted to a stop against the compound wall.

When the shooting began, it drowned out all other noises. Nobody paid any attention to the sound of motorcycles here as a rule, they were firing and riding all day every day. These two should have been noticed, however. When everybody else was watching Evan, opening the doors of the van, these two motorcycles charged out of the repair

340

barn, around the back side of the meeting house, and directly for the steps behind the bar. The drunks turned too late to see them coming and scattered as the bikes charged up the steps and through the back door. It was not a straight run through the bar to the street, but it was straight enough for a motorcycle as long as the bike wasn't raked too long.

Terry and Ginger burst through the front of the bar, not through the narrow door, but through the window. The confiscated leathers kept them from being sliced up by the glass and the helmets protected their eyes.

As he went through the window, Terry saw Gordon MacMaster with a rocket launcher pointed right at him but the weapon did not track to follow him; it spit its load of death into the tavern door, demolishing the building from the inside, out. It also prevented the Dark Knights from reaching their motorcycles on the front side of the wreckage.

The Land Rover was running and dirt flew from the tires as MacMaster followed the Kingstons down the road.

"How did you know?"

"What?"

Terry spit into the campfire and asked, "How did you know we would make it out of there alive?"

"I didn't. All I knew was that if anyone could have made it out, it would have been you. I was only there for back up. If they hadn't let me drink in the bar, I would have been waiting outside anyway. When the gunfire started I expected you had breathed your last. If I'd been holding a gun instead of a rocket launcher I might have shot you myself with those helmets on."

"You knew they were going to try to kill us, though?"

"No," Gordon said slowly. "I didn't know that. In fact I didn't even suspect it."

Terry was not convinced but he had no other friends at this point. The mob wanted him dead, the bikies wanted him

341

dead and the police just wanted him. "Well, I've just about bollixed this all up," he said.

"Look, mate," Ginger began. "You're still on this side of the grass so there's still a chance but I'm afraid there's no going back."

Terry could not help but look at the crude job he had done sewing up his uncle's leg. "No, there's no going back," he replied, softly.

"Quit pissing and moaning," Gordon growled. "You got what you wanted and now maybe you didn't want it? It's true you can't go back. Not for 10 or 20 years. It doesn't matter who is in charge, the constables or the jackasses, they'll want you dead."

"You knew that was going to happen too, didn't you?" Terry opined.

"I've seen it happen before. There is so little honor today."

Terry heard echoes of his father and his uncle in the statement and it touched him. "I'll tell you what, Gordon MacMaster, I have pledged to be honorable and I pledge it again. Like the Samurai, an honorable assassin."

MacMaster just laughed.

Epilogue

Mr. Streng had been Terry's solicitor his entire life. He was sorry to hear that the Viper's son would need to leave the country but was willing to facilitate whatever needed to be done. Large amounts of cash can be difficult to explain, though it can be shipped a variety of ways. Mr. Streng accepted the rocket box full of cash that Terry had accumulated, promising to invest and steward the money according to his best efforts.

Linda Pettigrew was still under guard but this could not be maintained in perpetuity. The groups that protected her soon wanted information she did not have. The matron of the house lent her a car to go to the grocery store. She was careful in what she said but Linda got the idea that returning to the house was a bad idea so she headed south and took up residence in a small town outside Melbourne. Within a year she was married to the local chief of police.

Evan "Saxon" McCormick survived the explosion at the compound. He moved quickly to consolidate his hold on the underworld network the Troys had left in place. He was ruthless and decisive, but there were too many interests, in a delicately balanced web that disintegrated once the heads of power were killed. Evan was not enough of a builder to regain what had been in place and he learned how valuable a man like Terry Kingston would have been. He deeply regretted their falling out and tried, in vain, to reestablish contact with him. The underworld operations quickly became fragmented as each disparate concern began to slide further from what had been a central power. Some of the gangsters were willing to work for him, but Evan found that many were angry over the death of their leaders, and others simply did not have any respect for bikies. Since the gangsters were not going to get legitimate jobs, they all tried to take a slice of the pie for themselves and the streets ran red with the blood of rival factions vying for control in the wake of the power shift.

Superintendent Theodore Barlow was flabbergasted. He had been inches from the perpetrator of so much death and destruction, and he had been forced to let him go. He was certain that there would be a time when he once again looked into the eyes of the child that had been pulled from the ocean, and he longed for that time until his death. Most men would have retired from service before this time and certainly in the turbulent wake but not Barlow. Theodore was destined to die in the service of his country and while he was alive, he made it his first priority to capture the man who had pulled him from the burning building; the man who had danced through the shadowed world of corruption, carving a place for himself where he could attack from within. Theodore Barlow saw Terry Kingston as a cancer and he was to be removed from the body of Australia. Theodore Barlow never again saw Terry Kingston.

7550347R0

Made in the USA
Charleston, SC
16 March 2011